MASQUERADE

To Jason Foxe, the dangerously attractive American who offered to help her, she was Nicca Montcalm, the lovely and shy French student.

To Baron Willy von Walenberg, the elegant nobleman who gave her refuge, she was Hilde Hoffmann, the spinsterish nurse/companion to his aging mother.

To Detective Inspector Leo Trumpf, who relentlessly pursued her, she was Veronica Kent, the elusive foreigner with a mysterious motive for murder.

But only Veronica knew, that for all her daring duplicity, she was taking a desperate gamble, in which one false move could cause the fragile boundary between trust and betrayal to come crashing down. . .

STRANGER in Vienna

STRANGER in Vienna

Harriet LaBarre

POPULAR LIBRARY

An Imprint of Warner Books, Inc.

A Warner Communications Company

POPULAR LIBRARY EDITION

Copyright © 1986 by Harriet La Barre

Popular Library® is a registered trademark of Warner Books, Inc.

Cover photograph by Bill Charles/Magic Image

Popular Library books are published by
Warner Books, Inc.
666 Fifth Avenue
New York, N.Y. 10103

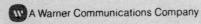 A Warner Communications Company

Printed in the United States of America

First Printing: February, 1986

10 9 8 7 6 5 4 3 2 1

Prologue

Done it herself! ... destroyed her life, ruined it, or she wouldn't be here, deep in these woods outside Vienna, scrabbling in the dirt, burying the blood-spattered clothing. A dozen hours ago, she had been a confident American girl in a yellow dress, a square-faced gold watch on one wrist, booking into the Vienna Hilton. Now, whimpering with fear and exhaustion, pounding down dirt and scattering twigs so the ground would look undisturbed, she could hear a rustle in the bushes; she knew it was the brutal-faced young man in the leather vest that revealed his muscular arms. He had sat down beside her not twenty minutes before in the coffee shop near the Mödling woods; he had slouched close to her on the stool, staring, whispering insinuatingly; Rudi, his name was. He had delivered the unwanted information in lower class Viennese dialect. Whispering, licking his lips suggestively, he had let the back of his hand brush her thigh; she had smelled his sexual heat.

"Ahhhh ... !" The bushes parted and sprang closed. It was he.

"Been waiting for me, Schatzerl?" He moved toward her, grinning, breathing quickly. There was spittle in the corners of his mouth.

1

Chapter 1

"Yes, *Gnädige Frau*—excuse me, *Gnädiges Fräulein*. Room eight sixty-five. It overlooks the Stadtpark."

The desk clerk at the Hilton fingered his tie, then caressed his balding head, bowing over the register. His smile was respectful, but he was alert with secret pleasure. Gambling was his joy. He'd wager a thousand schillings this American girl had beautiful legs. Certain physical characteristics went with certain others—yes, a thousand schillings. He was a student of women. This American, Miss Veronica Kent, was perhaps five feet five, with polished brown hair cut just below her earlobes and brushed back from her brow. She wore a long-sleeved, yellow wool dress, hardly rumpled from the plane trip. Yes, certain physical characteristics: a slender neck, and that kind of triangular face with full lips—those narrow hands and slender wrists. *Two* thousand, he'd go two thousand schillings on the legs.

"My luggage . . . if you don't mind."

No trace of impatience in her voice, she was looking straight at him. Blue eyes, almost violent, rimmed with short black lashes. An astonishing effect.

"Pardon me, Fräulein Kent!" He snapped his fingers for a porter.

She turned from the desk. Outside, the September evening had turned rose-tinged purple. It was eight o'clock. Within, brass and lights glittered, mirrors reflected jewels. Guests were picking up theater tickets at the concierge's window, or waiting for dinner partners in deep soft chairs, or crossing the luxurious carpet, laughing and chatting. Piano music came from somewhere, she could not distinguish where . . . perhaps the Klimt Bar across the lobby. The bustle created a thrilling promise of expectancy.

Evening pleasures.

But not for me. She viewed the scene with an indulgent eye. She had other fish to fry. For herself, she would have a delicious, forever-lasting shower—if not forever, at least for twenty minutes—then an omelet and a croissant and a pot of tea, in her room. After that she'd snuggle into bed and plan for tomorrow. *Here I am in Vienna.* Incredible. Here to do a job on which her whole future depended: rags to riches; stale bread to caviar. And she would deliver. That was as inevitable as her next breath.

"Fräulein Kent!" The desk clerk.

She glanced back. He was holding out her tinted eyeglasses. She's left them on the counter.

"Thank you." Glasses in hand, she turned to follow the porter—and collided violently with a solid body. Her head jerked back, and pain shot up through her neck. "Oh!"

A man's hands seized her arms, steadying her. *"Entschuldigen Sie, bitte!"* A deep, concerned voice. *"Sind Sie in Ordnung?"* Dazed, she shook her hair back from her eyes. "My fault." Disoriented, she spoke in English; then, realizing, she added in German, "I was in a hurry."

"I don't know anyone who isn't." He spoke in English, with an Austrian accent; an amused voice. His hands now released her arms. "Haste is endemic, isn't it? In . . ." He paused, waiting.

"New York." She was still dizzy. The man's face took focus. A handsome man, silver gray hair, gray eyes. He wore a dark suit, and around his neck a white cashmere scarf, one end thrown cavalierly back over a shoulder. Romantically handsome. Perhaps an actor? Molnár plays, the gaiety of Vienna in the early 1900s . . . ladies in drifting chiffon and lovely, dramatic hats . . . Strauss waltzes, violins, whipped cream, and roses, whipped—

"You're sure you're all right?"

"Yes. Honestly."

Leaving him, going toward the elevators, she was sure he was looking at her.

Delicious, the hot shower beating strongly on her naked body. She tipped up her face, closed her eyes, and poured the scented turquoise bath oil, courtesy of the hotel, down between her breasts.

Fifteen minutes later, wrapped in a big bath towel, wet hair slicked back, she padded barefoot into the bedroom. Her bags were still unpacked. Well, let that wait. The omelet too. First, Frau Tröger.

At the bedside table, she called the number Sarah Hamilton had given her before she'd left New York.

Frau Tröger herself answered. Bertha Tröger, aged sixty-five, Vienna-born, had been Sarah Hamilton's secretary before she'd retired to her beloved homeland two years ago. Veronica had never met her.

"Ach! I have been waiting!" Bertha Tröger sounded solid as a harvesting machine. *"Ja,* I have Mrs. Hamilton's letter. I do my best. . . . Already I have a list! Three places!"

Frau Tröger's "places" would be inexpensive *pensionen* not far from the Theater Collection of the Austrian National Library or from the Burg Theater Collection. But for the first week, Veronica would stay at the Hilton, get acclimated. "Expensive!—but I can deduct it," Sarah Hamilton had said, "—even room service and the telephone. It can be a business deduction like what I'm paying you."

Sarah Hamilton, sixty-eight, soft-bodied and rosy-faced, wrote internationally renowned books on theater history. She was the James Michener of theater history, the Barbara Tuchman of the stage. She had written on Japanese, French, Chinese, and English theater. She was currently finishing a book on Thai theater.

Sarah Hamilton was married to wispy little Ellery Hamilton, who did something mysterious and brilliant in computer design. Ellery's name often appeared in business and computer publications, in which he was referred to as a genius. Besides being a genius, Ellery Hamilton was a vegetarian. He believed goats' milk was superior to cows' milk so the Hamiltons kept goats. Their house stood on two acres in Redding, Connecticut, and fortunately, the neighbors did not complain about the goats; instead, they bragged about the Hamiltons. People who came for Sarah Hamilton's autograph held their breath as long as possible, then took short breaths, and finally, back on the tarred road, they breathed deeply, saying "Phew!"

If Sarah Hamilton had not come to the Theater Research Department at Lincoln Center one rainy day and found Veronica Kent behind the research desk frustratedly biting her fingernails, Veronica would not now be in Vienna.

Sarah Hamilton knew nothing about Veronica's past, and cared little about it. What interested her was Veronica Kent's remarkable facility for finding undiscovered material—"Like a magician fanning out a handful of aces," Sarah Hamilton had put it. She had first hired Veronica to do part-time research, at Lincoln Center, on Viennese actors who had performed in the United States. She had discovered that Veronica spoke passable German. Veronica's German was the result of a two-year love affair with a Swiss ski instructor she had met in the Laurentians and with whom she had spent a summer in Zurich. She did not confide this to Sarah Hamilton.

For reasons that were equally obscure to Sarah Hamilton, Veronica spoke fluent French, although, as Sarah had remarked, it was French with an odd pronunciation. Veronica had seen no reason to enlighten Sarah Hamilton about that, either.

Their conversations were never personal anyway. Their sole topic was Sarah's work. Veronica was receiving sixteen thousand dollars, plus expenses, for the Austrian research. That was approximately three times what she would have earned at Lincoln Center, and Sarah had given her a four-thousand-dollar advance. Already Veronica felt rich. But the sixteen thousand was only a start: it was the minnow landed before the big fish—a fact that made Veronica's excitement almost insupportable. Sarah Hamilton had plans for her. But, as wispy little Ellery Hamilton had, humorously but factually, warned his wife in Veronica's presence, Veronica Kent was "a wild card." She had yet to prove herself.

A wild card? A pity that Ellery Hamilton couldn't run the wild card through a computer and have "BRILLIANT RESEARCHER" and "SURE BET" flash on the screen. *Wild card?* True enough, she took risks, she was daring . . . but was that a failing? Wasn't it better than being a coward? Yes!

Her success in Vienna would determine her stake in Sarah Hamilton's three future books: It would earn her a contract to research them; and, despite the anguished outcry of Sarah Hamilton's literary agent, she would receive a share of their royalties and subsidiary rights. Four percent. Four percent of the stream of gold that poured into Sarah Hamilton's coffers! With pencil and paper she had calculated the income of the Hamilton book on Chinese theater. The figures had dizzied her. If she succeeded in Vienna, she would have a future of sable-lined trenchcoats, lobster dripping with butter, a pied-à-terre in New York—a career in which she traveled the world, exploring theater history. At age twelve, gawking at a production of *Hamlet*, in one fell swoop, like Newton's apple falling to the ground, she had lost her heart to theater . . . or rather to its unknown artists and artisans, those creators of incredible pageants, from the early Greek to Kabuki, from Balinese pantomime to Stratford productions—and now to Viennese. An absorbing interest. Like Sarah Hamilton's. And to be paid for it! Actually to be paid!

"Frühstück at nine o'clock tomorrow morning, *ja?"* Bertha Tröger was saying. "I come to the Hilton?"

"Fine."

They would breakfast downstairs in the Café am Park, then Frau Tröger would take her to inspect the pensions. "A *quiet* pension, for your work. *Ruhig!*—not a noisy neighborhood with parties, shops, too many children."

"Yes . . . yes. *Auf Wiedersehen, auf Wiedersehen."*

She hung up, collapsed back onto the bed, gazing at the ceiling. She should call room service; but she wasn't hungry. Jet lag. She'd leave a call for 7:00 A.M. and go to bed right now; she wouldn't even unpack.

She yawned, then frowned. Tired as she was, her muscles were drum tight. She was exasperatingly wide awake, tense with excitement, anticipation. *My new life.* Once, when she'd been a child, on the night before her birthday party, she had been too excited to sleep. At midnight she had climbed out of bed and dressed in her party dress. Then, sitting bolt upright in a chair, she had counted the minutes to next day's thrilling party. That was how she felt now. *My new life. Thank you, Sarah Hamilton, thank—*

A knock on the door.

Surprised, she sat up. "Just a minute."

Her robe was still packed so she snugged the bath towel tightly across her breasts and opened the door. A boy in the hotel uniform stood before her, holding a florist's box, long, white, shiny.

"Guten Abend, Gnädiges Fräulein. Blumen." Bowing, he came in and placed the box on the foyer table beneath the mirror.

She tipped him, glad she had changed fifty dollars' worth of travelers' checks at Schwechat Airport. *"Aber . . . "* She hesitated, *"Ich habe kein . . . kein . . . "* The word eluded her; she gestured toward the flowers.

"A vase?" the boy said. "Right away, *Gnädiges Fräulein."*

When he had gone, she untied the satin ribbon and lifted the lid. Nestled in waxy green tissue were roses— deep red, rich, velvety, magnificent. She leaned forward, closed her eyes, and took an enormous breath: "Ummmmm!"

But who? She didn't know anyone in Vienna except Bertha Tröger; and she didn't really know her either. She withdrew the little white envelope, damp with the dewiness of the roses. She slid out the card.

I will wait for you in the Klimt Bar . . . hoping ferociously that you will come. The note was unsigned.

Ferociously. The word sent a tingle down her spine. The handwriting was masculine, strong and spare. No flourishes. No open-end "significant" three dots that so often signified nothing.

But that word: *ferociously.*

She was frowning down at the card when the boy returned with the vase. *"Danke schon."* She took it from him. "The flowers—from the flower shop in the hotel, are they?"

The boy nodded. *"Gewiss!* The best in Vienna! . . . But he gave them to me himself at the elevator and told me to take them up."

"He? You mean the florist?"

The boy barely refrained from rolling his eyes to the ceiling. He said, painstakingly: "No, *Gnädiges Fräulein.* Not the florist. A gentleman. A gentleman in the lobby."

"Thank you." She'd be damned if she'd ask him another question. Besides, now she knew: the man she had collided with in the lobby. Romantic Vienna in a white scarf, Schnitzler and Molnár, violins and roses. She knew he had watched her follow her luggage to the elevator. Obviously he had found some clever or expensive way to learn her room number from the desk clerk.

But anyway—she closed the door behind the boy—she was going to bed.

She tucked the towel more tightly around her breasts. In the bathroom she filled the vase and arranged the roses, then carried them out to the dresser. Velvety red glowing against green leaves. Careful of thorns, she broke off a rose. She wandered to one of the French windows, pushed it open, and stood gazing out at the Stadtpark, absent-mindedly twirling the rose between her fingers.

Lights, like fireflies, glimmered among the trees, casting minute pools of yellow radiance on walks that curved and meandered in the park; rows of lights, like diamonds, sparkling on the Kursalon terraces, the restaurant and café. She could even hear, faintly, the music of the Kursalon orchestra: out there at the Kursalon in the park they were dancing, sipping wine, dining. They were having a good time. She felt like a child again: at eight, she'd had to go to bed on summer nights when it was still light out and other kids her age were still playing run-sheep-run. It hadn't been fair.

She twirled the rose faster. She *should* go to bed. She touched her hair—it was still soaking wet from the shower—and the word *ferociously* slid through her mind, making her uneasy.

But . . . the man hadn't looked ferocious. He was probably using the word playfully, to intrigue her—and intrigue her it had. It was like a deliciously scary word in a fairy tale. "The lion snarled ferociously." No. "The *cowardly* lion snarled ferociously," not anything truly dangerous. She shivered, then laughed.

I will wait for you in the Klimt Bar.

She turned abruptly from the window. She was not going to bed.

She walked across the glittering lobby, enjoying the cool feel of her silk dress swishing against her legs. She wore sheer ivory-colored stockings and high-heeled shoes. She had pinned a red rose to her waist.

Just inside the Klimt Bar, she stopped and looked around, touching the ends of her hair, which was still damp. She felt a thrill of expectancy. She was wonderfully awake, alert. She would spend an hour with this Viennese male charmer, only an hour, have a glass of wine. She had promised herself that. It was now exactly nine o'clock. At ten, she would be back in her room, absolutely, and in bed—after a perfect introduction to romantic Vienna.

The Klimt Bar was subtly lighted, elegant, uncrowded; a pianist played softly at an ebony baby grand. A few people chatted quietly at tables. Two lone men sat at the bar. One was fleshy and porcine-looking, the other dark-browed, dark-haired, and young.

No one else.

Where was he? She hesitated, uncertain; people were glancing at her. Had she come so late that he'd gone away, disappointed? Or should she wait? Well . . . but not in the bar.

In the lobby she chose a chair from which she could watch the entrance to the Klimt. She sat there for twenty minutes, glancing often at her watch and biting off her lipstick. At nine-twenty, she abruptly got up and glanced again into the Klimt in case she had somehow missed him. But no; he was not there. Well, that was that. She hoped he had, at least, fallen downstairs and broken a shoulder, been trapped in an elevator perhaps, or suffered a violent attack of gastritis.

Go to bed, she told herself. *Go upstairs, throw the red rose in the wastebasket, take off the gold-and-green silk dress, cream the makeup off your face.*

But that was impossible now. She was keyed up for a touch of magic, a Viennese evening, she was wide awake, perfumed, her eyelashes touched with mascara, mouth reddened. She had been promised something that had not been delivered. It has been tantalizingly held out, then snatched away.

Something. She had to have *something,* or she'd never be able to sleep. A walk perhaps. A half-hour in the enchantment of the purple evening; a walk would relax her. The Stadtpark was across from the hotel, its walks lighted, festive. Minutes away.

Without bothering to leave her key at the desk, she left the hotel.

In the Klimt Bar, the dark-haired young man checked his watch. Nine-fifteen. So she wasn't coming. He had been sitting there at the bar ever since he'd sent the boy up with the roses.

He knew she must have received them because as he'd come from the florist he had glimpsed her at the desk: blond, plump, not-quite-pretty Miss Wicks, picking up her mail and key. He had even heard the desk clerk's *"Guten Abend, Fräulein Wicks."* So it was clear she had received those hellishly expensive roses. That meant she was still angry at him. Or, more likely, sick with shame and guilt. She had probably torn up his note.

He was sorry. Sorry for Miss Hortense Wicks, not for himself. It was tough on a woman, a one-night affair, ending up in bed with a man she'd met only hours before. Forget it!—what a woman told herself about emancipation. They still had guilt bred into their bones—even a snobbish, so-called emancipated American fashion editor like Hortense Wicks. In bed, after their passionate lovemaking, she had begun to talk sentimentally of their love, fancying some undying romance. He had sensed her need to deny that she had gone to bed with him, a stranger, strictly out of sexual passion. All she knew was that he was an American sociologist, in Vienna on a grant from a Texas foundation. When he had gently—and foolishly—implied as much, Hortense Wicks had burst into tears. She had sobbed wretchedly as he'd dressed and left.

Her guilty misery had bothered him all day. He couldn't let it end on that note. He would send her roses, beautiful red roses, take her to dinner; he would throw out a sociological theory or two, to mitigate her guilt and comfort her; they would part friends.

He recognized, of course, that Miss Wick's tears had been partly due to champagne. The champagne party celebrating the fashion crew's final shooting had landed them in bed together. The crew had wrapped up their Vienna shooting in the Brunners' pension, a narrow, elegant yellow house on Langegasse. Jason was staying at the Brunners' on the recommendation of a fellow sociologist, a Viennese professor on the faculty of the nearby University of Vienna. The house was so given over to Herr Adalbert Brunner's passion for Art Nouveau, which in Vienna was known as *jugendstil*, that every sofa, vase, and chair had sinuous contours. Even the hall mirror was framed in sylphlike naiads painted on glass. The Brunner pension was consequently in demand by magazines— European, American, even Japanese—seeking Art Nouveau backgrounds. Such shootings brought the Brunners extra income. At Herr Adalbert Brunner's request, Jason had allowed his room to be used for an American magazine's fashion photography. Here in Jason's room, where the furniture had rounded edges so marvelously Art Nouveau that whatever Jason placed on a table inevitably slid quietly to the floor, here he had met Miss Hortense Wicks. Here Miss Wicks had posed her hired Viennese models in multicolored satin nightgowns, in drooping, boneless, Art Nouveau poses, their heads bent like rain-heavy lilies on slender stems. As for Hortense Wicks herself . . .

In the Klimt Bar, Jason signaled the bartender, "Check, please."

As for Hortense Wicks, she had insisted so eagerly on Jason joining the champagne celebration that was to take place an hour later—"You've been *so* kind, letting us use your room, interrupting your work! You *must* come," her mouth pouting a little, eyelashes fluttering—that Jason, his work already disrupted by the shooting, had thought, *Why not?* The celebration had been held in the green- house on the Brunners' roof. The greenhouse was Adal- bert Brunner's botanical kingdom. Here his passion for the lush had carried him away. Exotic flowers bloomed purple, golden yellow, and deep red amid shiny, dark green leaves. Fernlike palm trees feathered out of terra- cotta pots; and dwarf trees drooped, heavy with oranges, plums, and peaches. And here Hortense Wicks had posed the last Viennese model, nearly naked in a diaphanous lime green negligee, among glowing purple pinks and the deep green foliage. The crew had cheered and the models had joined in. The champagne corks had started popping.

Now in the Klimt Bar, waiting for the check, Jason had a momentary impulse to call Hortense Wicks's room to make sure she had received the roses. After all, how could she have resisted the appeal of those magnificent blooms, so deeply, velvety red?

In fact, a girl had just appeared at the entrance to the Klimt and was looking around, a dark-haired girl in a gold-and-green silk dress and high heels. The light left her face in shadow but fell across her shoulders, and he could see that she wore a red rose at her waist. *You see?* he told himself. *You see? Red roses. Irresistible.* But Miss Wicks had obviously resisted. No, he wouldn't call.

"Danke schon." The bartender gave him the check.

Paying, Jason frowned down at the polished mahog- any. An old Austrian proverb was rising out of memory, nagging at him. Roses, roses. Something about roses. That Viennese saying, like a dark cello note . . . . s . . . *Red* roses. Ah, he had it! *Zwei Anlässe für   Rosen: Liebe und Tod.* Yes, that was it: "Two occasions for red roses: Love and Death."

When he looked up again, the girl in the gold-and-green dress was gone.

A perceptible chill in the September air—definitely sweater weather. She shivered. Her silk dress had only fluttery little cap sleeves. She walked faster to warm her blood.

The path she entered was graveled and charmingly lighted, the beams turning the leaves overhead emerald green and casting yellow pools on the flower beds and lawns. She passed strolling couples, and girls and boys in jeans and T-shirts, sweaters rolled up and tied around their waists. Young children, out with their parents, walked sedately. At a turn in the path was a spotlighted statue of Johann Strauss playing the violin—she had seen postcards of it.

And here was the lake, black water reflecting lights, and the path skirting it leading to the glittering, neobaroque Kursalon. The tiered terraces were crowded, couples waltzed on the dance floor; in a brightly lit little pavilion the conductor, in white tie and tails, led the orchestra, wielding his baton like a wind-up toy. It was a fairy tale, unreal as a stage set, recreated gaiety of the Hapsburg era.

She walked up the path. Incredible to think that in the 1940s Vienna had been in ruins, bombed, rubble everywhere. First the Nazi Anschluss, then the Russians. She hugged her chilly arms, rubbing them. She hadn't even been born then. She was twenty-four now, born in 1962.

Chilly. The waltz ended, dancers returned to their tables, and white-jacketed waiters rushed around, bearing trays of pastry high in the air, refilling glasses.

She was suddenly dying for a glass of wine and a slab of luscious chocolate cake with raspberry filling . . . thick, soft, mochalike chocolate on top, maybe even a dab of

whipped cream—*Schlag,* the Viennese called it . . . or
was it *Schlagobers?*—and a glass of red wine. Ah, how
she'd sleep after that. And she had schillings in her little
evening purse.

She stood, hesitating, near the dance floor, looking up
at the terraces. Every table was taken; moreover, she saw
no women seated alone.

"Gnädiges Fräulein?"

An elderly waiter, skinny as a twig, with a drooping
black bow tie, was at her elbow. "One person? . . . The
gentleman"—and he jerked his head toward a table on
the first tier—"Herr von Reitz has offered to accommodate, kindly to accommodate." The waiter waved her
toward the table and rushed off.

Herr von Reitz.

Later she was to recall her conversation with Herr von
Reitz, over and over, agonizingly, searching for a clue (a
word? a phrase? a revealing inflection in his voice?) to
justify the unjustifiable. Backward and forward she
would go, an ant trapped in a maze.

When she approached the table, Herr von Reitz came
to his feet so astonishingly like a jack-in-the-box, that she
smiled involuntarily. He was a cherubic-looking man,
pink-cheeked, corpulent, balding, probably in his mid-
fifties.

"Guten Abend, Gnädiges Fräulein."

He bowed. His eyes, blue-gray, twinkled behind rimless glasses, but there was a shrewd look in them. He
wore a dark suit and a pink shirt. He had the well-fed,
sleek-skinned look that resulted from good nutrition and
affluence. His hands were plump and professionally
manicured.

"I knew you for a foreigner immediately," he told her
when they had exchanged names. His tone held a touch

of rebuke. "A Viennese woman of your class would have known the social, ah . . . impropriety of coming to the Kursalon alone at night. The . . . ah, hazards." A squeaky voice. He enunciated each German syllable meticulously. He ordered Veronica's chocolate cake *"mit Schlagobers"* from the skinny waiter with the drooping bow tie.

"Red wine?" He frowned away the idea. Veronica must share his champagne. "Champagne is the only wine to drink. As for hard liquor and beer . . ." He made a repugnant face, screwing up his mouth, which was very small and pale.

"Thank you for rescuing me."

He waved away her thanks. "Other cultures, other mores." The superiority of Viennese culture was implicit in his tone, and that tone was faintly prissy.

But he was an engaging conversationalist and a skillful questioner. By the time Veronica's chocolate cake arrived, he knew a surprising amount about her project for Sarah Hamilton, and she noticed that his shrewd eyes, behind the rimless glasses, judged everything. When the skinny waiter set the cake before her, he studied the moist, dark confection with its great glob of whipped cream, then he gave his verdict: *"Schön!"*

"Danke schon, Herr von Reitz." The waiter flashed a smile. He had a gold tooth.

Herr von Reitz was a lawyer. "Like my father and generations before him," he told Veronica, "beginning with Ludwig von Reitz. But they were not in corporation law, as I am. They principally represented playwrights of the Burg Theater . . . and actors, the famous ones of the time. That would have begun . . . let's see . . . ah! when Franz Josef had just become Emperor."

She held her fork suspended, about to take a mouthful of cake. She stared at Herr von Reitz. His voice might be as squeaky as an unoiled hinge, but his words were gold nuggets. She put down the fork. Her heart was thudding, her mouth dry. She wet her lips.

Cautiously, go cautiously!

"I suppose their documents, records—you'd have, oh—briefs? Transcripts of cases that . . . that your great-grandfather, Ludwig von Reitz—"

"Great-*great*-grandfather," Herr von Reitz corrected. He pursed his small mouth. *"Natürlich,* documents! The von Reitzes do not scatter their family history to the four winds. Also, remarkable old photographs. Original sketches of scenes in pen and ink for projected plays. Litigation over others. A Raimund drama, never produced, written just before Raimund committed suicide." Nodding to himself, he continued, "Some original plays in holograph, in payment. A few unfinished dramas, even into the 1900s."

His twinkly, shrewd eyes looked sharply through the rimless glasses at Veronica's plate. "You don't care for the cake?"

"Oh, yes! Delicious." She forced down a bite. "Has . . . has any of this collection ever been seen?"

"Ach! The Austrian National Library nags me, begs me! They'd like it for that Theater Collection of theirs—the one Joseph Gregor started in 1922. But"—he turned out his plump hands—"family possessions! I have not even lent them. I keep them in my office safe. I am a true, sentimental Viennese; they are precious. . . . What can I do?"

"So . . . " She could hardly breathe. "This material goes back to? . . ."

"The Backhendlzeit era. You know it?"

She nodded; her fork trembled against the plate. The 1830s, the Backhendlzeit period: the fried-chicken era. It was called that, Backhendlzeit, because chicken fried in breadcrumbs was the dish the ordinary people could afford for special occasions during those hard times. "The fried-chicken era."

"I see you have already been at work for your Frau Hamilton! Yes, the time of Nestroy's greatest success as a playwright, beginning with a comedy.

"Nestroy and Ludwig von Reitz had been law students together, jurisprudence, they were friends. That was before Nestroy abandoned law for the theater. Then— ach, Nestroy—then Nestroy ran into such terrible troubles . . . quarrels, finances, politics. Scandals! The good Ludwig took charge of everything for him."

Nestroy!

If she could only get her hands on— *The dark spirit of disillusion*, the Viennese of that Hapsburg era had called him—Johann Nestroy, wildly funny, while relentlessly exposing the snobbery and greed, the other vices and human weaknesses of his fellow Viennese. Nestroy certainly had not ground out the usual, stale drama of the Viennese theater!

"Shreyvogel. Even before, it was Shreyvogel." Twinkle, twinkle, behind the rimless glasses. "You know of Schreyvogel?"

She hardly dared breathe. Schreyvogel, poor wretched genius, artistic director of the Burg Theater! Schreyvogel, who had created the first repertory theater in Austria, the brilliant, sad man who had produced dramas by Schiller, Goethe, Lessing, Kleist; who had translated Corneille, Racine, Molière. Shakespeare.

"It was said he died of cholera." Herr von Reitz's rimless glasses glittered at her. "Others claim it was heartbreak."

She sat with bated breath. What did Herr von Reitz's family documents reveal? Schreyvogel, alas, had stumbled over an intrigue in Franz Josef's court. He had been dismissed at once from the Burg Theater. Two months later, in 1832, he had died.

Heartbreak or cholera? Or suicide . . . or murder?

She waited, gazing across the table at Herr von Reitz, but patience had never been her virtue:

"Nobody can possibly know which!"

On the cherubic face, a smile. "Ludwig was still a young man; Schreyvogel was sixty-four when he died of—" His smile widened: bland, flat, concealing. "But they had met through Nestroy and become friends. Some chemistry of personality drew them together. They corresponded. There exists a bundle of letters: Schreyvogel's plans, hopes, French translations—also, . . . how he innocently discovered the intrigue at court. All. *All!* Ludwig was with Schreyvogel two days before he—before he died."

The rest she heard through a numb haze; greedy for the bundle of letters, her mind was whirling with schemes, hopes, amazement. She smiled and smiled, never taking her eyes from her corpulent host as he talked on about his antecedents, telling her how Ludwig's son, Franz, had carried on the von Reitz law firm in the 1870s, then of his son, Friedrich.

She managed to swallow the cake in her dry mouth by sipping champagne. "Yes," she said, and "Yes," gazing so intensely into the cherubic face that she became aware of a habitual nervous twitch to the prim mouth in that well-fed pinkness. The law firm's association with the theater had dwindled in his grandfather's time; in his father's time it had become almost nonexistent.

"Up to about 1937, a few theater connections. In 1938, as you probably know"—a slight cocking of his head made his glasses again glitter—"the Nazis."

"Yes. I've done some research." In 1938, Jews prominent in the theater had been rounded up and arrested by the Nazis. Herman Roebbling, manager of the Burg Theater, the Austrian National Theater, had been dismissed and replaced by Mirko Yelusitch, a well-known anti-Semite. The manager of the Josefstadt Theater was also dismissed. So was the manager of the Deutsches Volkstheater. The stage manager of the Josefstadt Theater was replaced by an Aryan. That had been in March 1938.

"Yes," she said. "The Anschluss. By April, all Jewish members of theaters were dismissed."

Herr von Reitz shrugged his shoulders, shrugged off the Anschluss. "Naturally, the von Reitz firm could no longer—" He gave a little laugh. "It was inadvisable to be associated with theater people's problems, unjust as the dismissals may have been. The . . . ah, *circumstances* did not offer an opportunity for litigation!"

She experienced a feeling of distaste, of outrage; but she had to agree: What could they have done? Nothing.

She also had to get her hands on that precious von Reitz material. *Don't rush it*, she warned herself. *Patience!*

She swallowed some cake, widening her eyes prettily at Herr von Reitz. Then she begged for his advice on good Viennese shops and restaurants. In anguished impatience, she learned that Frau Sophie von Reitz preferred Horwath on Kärntnerstrasse for jewelry, but also liked Hügler. The two von Reitz daughters, both married, bought their sports and ski clothes at Resi Hammerer's. "Resi Hammerer, you know? She was a ski champion, she won a bronze medal for Austria, now she designs clothes; boots, shoes, gloves." But Frau von Reitz shopped at Admüller's in the fashionable little boutiques in the four-hundred-year-old palace of Count Esterházy. Frau von Reitz always shopped an entire day in Vienna, since the von Reitz villa was in Klosterneuburg, an hour's drive from the city. "Really?" Veronica murmured. She wet a finger and dabbed at crumbs of cake.

"So you like chocolate cake? You must go to the Gerstner's, they cater to the Vienna Opera. Sit upstairs, it is quieter. Order the cake with hazelnuts and chocolate cream. It has shaved chocolate on top."

Torture! Had he forgotten about Nestroy and Schreyvogel?

But she was aware of the shrewd glint in the man's eye, despite the half-smile on his prim mouth. He must realize how desperately she wanted that material. But if he wouldn't release it to the Austrian National Library, why to her?

She could . . . she could make herself a whore, try to seduce him, go to bed with him—would that work? But she was joking. He was too puritanical, too straitlaced; or perhaps he preferred lush blondes. Besides, in some inexplicable way, this corpulent, well-fed man repelled her physically. His prim mouth and plump, manicured hands made her flesh shrink, made something block up her throat. She had never understood how prostitutes could do it.

" . . . buy my shirts at Striberny's."

The hell with diplomacy! He would or he wouldn't! She leaned forward and said earnestly, "Herr von Reitz, excuse me. I would not presume to ask to borrow your family documents, but if you would allow me to look at them, just study them for a few hours—a few hours only—I—"

"Ach! Ach!" Herr von Reitz raised both hands chest-high, palms outward. He chuckled. "That is possible! If they could be of help to a serious researcher, a special, formidable project . . . why not?"

Stunned, she stared at him—at the twinkling eyes, the

palms upraised like a Hindu Brahmin's, the little smile playing around his mouth.

She said weakly, "Thank you." Then, realization and delight flooded her. She sat up straight. "Oh, thank you! Tomorrow morning . . . Is that possible? Could I see them then?" She'd cancel her appointment with Frau Tröger; her search for a suitable pension could wait. Herr von Reitz's cache was within her grasp! She saw herself poring over yellowed letters, handwritten manuscripts; she would bring her tape recorder, read aloud into it. Later, she would transcribe the information. Oh, miraculous world! She saw herself on the long-distance telephone to Sarah Hamilton. She—

"Ach!" Herr von Reitz's face screwed up in a rueful smile. "What impatience! Unfortunately, tonight I leave for Hamburg. A late flight. That is why I stayed in town for dinner; that is why I now sit at the Kursalon listening to Strauss waltzes and"—he lifted his champagne glass—"drinking champagne with a charming American." Although seated, he made a stiff half-bow.

Damn! She clasped her hands together tightly, disappointed. Frustration! Curse it, *curse* it that he was going to Hamburg!

"When do you get back?"

Herr von Reitz shrugged. "Maybe three days in Hamburg with my client. Then to Geneva—I have a case in court. Geneva perhaps a week . . . or weeks. Depending." He shrugged again. "But don't worry, Fräulein Kent! I shall not forget you!" His eyes twinkled.

But he would forget her, he *would*. Rotten, rotten luck. She was a canny researcher, an expert; she had been through this before. The possessor of valued material would become sympathetic, be thawed by friendliness or softened by alcohol, a good dinner. But, given time to ruminate, there was often a change of heart, and the door was slammed in her face. *Don't give him time!* She licked dry lips.

"Credentials," she said. "If you will come with me to the Hilton, I can furnish you with credentials. I am asking only to borrow"—she hesitated, selecting swiftly; it was always better psychology, she had learned, to define a segment—"to borrow the Nestroy material alone. Only the Nestroy! If I could borrow it tonight, keep it just until you return . . ."

Audacious, she knew she was being audacious, but it was worth a try. Why would he agree? Why should he? But he *might*.

She leaned forward a fraction and tried to meet Herr von Reitz's eyes so that he would see in her own blue eyes faith, honesty, integrity, and a dozen other remarkable virtues that would sway him in her favor.

But Herr von Reitz was gazing down at the dance floor, watching couples swooping and swaying to a Strauss waltz. His face had darkened with anger. "Look! Look there!" Outrage thickened his squeaky voice. "Those two women dancing together! At a family party, little girls dancing together, in the bosom of the family, all right! But two adult women clasped in each other's arms! On the Kursalon dance floor! Ugh!" He hissed out a furious breath. "That pair! I have seen them dancing here before. . . . Look how the dark one caresses the other woman's neck! With people like that, love is a crime that demands an accomplice. Disgusting . . . *Nicht wahr?"*

She bit her lips, trying to quell her impatience. Would he let her borrow the Nestroy?

Then, sensing a stillness in him as he kept his eyes on the two women dancing, she knew that he was waiting for some reaction from her. Something . . .

But what?

She could not take her eyes from his prim, pale mouth,

his darkened face, his averted gaze. His corpulent body was a block of ice, congealed away from her. Waiting. Was he probing to discover whether she shared his concepts of Sodom and Gomorrah? If she espoused his moral view of sin and the sexes, would *that* make her enough of a white-winged angel to be entrusted with his precious documents?

She dug her fingernails into her palms to stifle a surge of rebellion so strong that her body stiffened. *No,* she shouted inside her head: *No! I will not ally myself with your moral condemnation!* To capitulate, to agree, was only a different way of being a whore, and she suddenly wanted to spit out, No. It is *you* I now find disgusting!

But . . . What a coup—those documents! She ached for them. Even to Ellery Hamilton they would prove her research abilities. She would triumph; the contract and royalties would be hers . . . Already she felt soft, rich sable nestled under her chin.

Despising herself, she said, "Yes. I, too, find it quite . . . quite revolting." *Whore,* she thought: *You whore* . . . and felt her face flush with shame.

Herr von Reitz brought his gaze back to her. He smiled. He made the stiff, sitting-down bow again.

"*Gnädiges Fräulein,* your credentials are not necessary. You have my trust." He looked at his watch. "There is still time. You shall have the Nestroy."

Chapter 2

Herr von Reitz's office was on the Opernring. The taxi swept up the brilliantly lit boulevard past the Schwarzenberg Palace, where spotlights played on fountains, statues, and splendid baroque façades. A hundred yards beyond was the office building: it housed branches of many international corporations. Herr von Reitz unlocked the glass entrance doors.

The law offices were on the sixth floor, modern, glass and steel, immaculate. Herr von Reitz led the way, trotting on elegantly-clad feet through the outer rooms and unlocking the door to a private office. Biedermeier furnishings, oil paintings in gilt frames adorning expensively-paneled walls. All portraits, all of men with the same bulging, stone-blue eyes as Herr von Reitz's. Which of these bewhiskered patriarchs was Ludwig? If only she had a flash camera! Never mind, she'd manage photographs later, somehow—if not from Herr von Reitz, then possibly from archives. Photographs out of musty law books.

What else for her? She looked around. Heavy chairs, a carved oak desk, a plump couch. Figurines of birds perched everywhere: on bookcases, tables, even in a row on the massive desk.

"Objets d'art." Herr von Reitz picked up a painted bronze parrot from the desk. It was about eight inches tall. "I collect them. Handmade. Three artists, whose names are not divulged, made several of these—they come only from Popp and Kretchmer, across from the Air France office, near the Opera. Every few months I look in. And there are other sources." He indicated a bronze owl on a quartz base. "A beauty! Nine inches. That one cost me a fortune. I keep this office locked."

The files—she couldn't wait to get her hands on the documents.

Herr von Reitz caught her restless glance. *"Sofort!* Immediately!" And he trotted through a door behind the desk, closing it after him.

Left alone, Veronica hugged herself, thrilled. She had been in Vienna only . . . what? Barely six hours! And look! She had shown courage, audacity, the Greek *hubris*. The Greeks feared hubris; in Greek it meant insolence. But in English it often connoted self-confidence, audacity, daring. And . . . yes, a touch of arrogance. The Greeks feared it because they thought the Gods might hurl a thunderbolt from the heavens, striking them dead for their godlike presumption.

But *she* would not be struck dead. She could almost feel the pen in her hand, so sure was she that she would sign contracts with Sarah Hamilton. She would travel on the Concorde and her royalties would multiply like rabbits. Rich, she might even start a theater that children would love: Japanese No plays, pantomimes with tinkling music from India. . . .

She raised her arms straight up in the air and, taking a deep breath, stretched, a great, marvelous stretch. Lowering her arms, she rolled her head around to loosen her neck muscles. It had been a strain. Now she felt wonderful. Proud of herself. And why not?

"Fräulein Kent!"

She whirled. Herr von Reitz stood in the doorway. He was in his shirt sleeves and suspenders, his round belly protruding. His pink face was flushed red, his glasses were gone, and his bulging blue eyes were wide. "Fräulein Kent! I am not well." One plump hand fumbled its way to his chest. "Diabetes. I am a diabetic, I am having a . . . what we call a reaction." He took a few stumbling steps into the room, coming toward her. His feet dug heavily into the rug. "You will have to help me!"

She looked at him, alarmed. "A doctor . . . Can I telephone for a doctor? What is it? Do you have pills?"

"No, no!" He was closer now; she could see sweat on his nose. He held something in his hand. A syringe. "I am squeamish; I cannot give myself the insulin shot. My wife usually does it for me. Please." He held up the syringe.

She stared at the needle. She had always had a terror of hypodermics, they frightened her. She was no more capable of giving Herr von Reitz his insulin shot than he was.

"I don't know how! I can't do it!"

"I will show you." He was close now, very close, his breath on her. He held up the syringe, and she could see little hairs glinting between his knuckles; he held the syringe between his first and second finger, thumb on the plunger.

"No . . . please! I can't!" She shrank back and looked from the plunger into Herr von Reitz's bulging, stone blue eyes. His eyes, something about his eyes . . . they looked so strange. And there was a loose, wet look to his prim mouth that was no longer prim, as though some inner elastic that held it tight had broken. It was the diabetic shock, of course. It must be that. *It had to be that*. But she suddenly had the terrible, the macabre, the insane idea that it was not himself that he wanted to inject, but *her*.

"Help me!" He jerked her arm toward him, the syringe in his other hand.

"No!" In terror, with a reflex she could not control, she flung her arm upward against his, sending the syringe flying up over the desk.

His eyes bulged. "Bitch! American bitch!" He lunged at her. His hands grasped her upper arms so painfully that a wave of nausea struck her. He pulled her against his body, his furious eyes glaring into hers. His face was distorted, his lips drawn back.

He will kill me, she thought wildly.

She lost her head completely then. With the strength of fear, she yanked her arms free and her hands scrabbled along the desk behind her. One hand closed on something heavy and warm—something that could save her life. Twisting her body, she swung it toward Herr von Reitz, swinging the object hard. It caught him on the side of the head.

He stood still, a petrified figure, a corpulent body made of stone with bulging stone eyes. Then he sagged, fell back to a sitting position, put out a hand on the rug, slipped to the side, and collapsed onto his back. Blood gushed from his nose and mouth.

"No . . . God!" Her voice was a horrified whisper. Panting, trembling, she shrank back against the desk, staring in disbelief, in shock. *"No!"* She was going to

faint; she fought for control. The bronze parrot lay on the floor where it had tumbled.

"Herr von Reitz!" She pushed herself from the desk and fell to her knees beside him. "Herr von Reitz . . . Oh, *please!*" In pity and fright, she shook his shoulder. "Herr von Reitz!" *Wake up, be all right, be alive.* His face was gray, his mouth slack . . . and the blood, the blood! "Wait!" she begged frantically. She got quickly to her feet. The phone! There on the desk! She almost fell on it. It took an agonizing minute to reach emergency, to hear the questioning voice.

She opened her mouth to answer—but at that moment she saw Herr von Reitz move. Instantly, she thought: *insulin shock!* It had to be, she knew she hadn't struck him that hard. Insulin shock! She must save him! She must give him the injection—quickly, *quickly!* He could die. By the time emergency sent help or the police arrived, it would be too late.

Don't let it be too late!

"Never mind!" She dropped the phone. The syringe— she must find the syringe and give him the injection. She would force herself to do it.

She flew to Herr von Reitz's side and knelt down. "Hold on!" she encouraged him frantically. "You'll be all right! Hold on, I'll give you the injection right away!" But even as her words of encouragement died away, she realized, with a terrible sinking feeling, that Herr von Reitz had not moved at all; she had only wished, *needed* him to have moved—in her hysteria needed to prove to herself that he was still alive. Kneeling there, staring at his bloody face, the blood coagulating, she could only think: Too late, too late.

A wave of nausea washed over her; she closed her eyes, fighting it, the world was swaying. . . . Then she became aware of a voice squawking from somewhere. She opened her eyes. The telephone. The receiver was dangling over the edge of the desk. As she looked at it, the voice ceased. She could not rise, did not have the strength to get to the desk and hang up the phone. It was as if she were trying to barricade herself away, to lock a door against a terrible truth.

Her gaze fell on the painted bronze parrot. The murder weapon, she thought with horror.

"I didn't mean to hurt you!" She whirled around to Herr von Reitz's body, flinging out her arms. "I didn't!" She wailed her protest aloud, accusingly, as though it were his fault. She had a crazy, irrational impulse to sink down and shake him back to life.

"It wasn't me!" she protested wildly. Surely, *surely* he had died of insulin shock, not of the blow she had dealt him . . . surely the medical report would prove that! Or would it? And hadn't she deprived him of the chemical that could have saved his life? She, the paranoid Fräulein Kent, had become hysterical, like a child having nightmares after watching too many horror films. So, in terror, she had denied von Reitz help, and he had been the victim of her irrational fears, her insane fears. In either case, it was her fault.

She could go to prison. Prison! It would destroy her hopes, her very life. She thought of her beautiful new career, that promising future with Sarah Hamilton, so tantalizingly within her grasp yet now lost to her. Lost . . . lost . . . If the blow she had struck had not killed Herr von Reitz, if he had died of insulin shock, she *might* not go to prison. But if the blow *had* killed him? She moaned. Whatever he had died of, she could be found guilty. Did Austria have a death penalty?

Nevertheless . . .

With dragging feet, she went to the desk and picked up the phone. She had a moral, an ethical— She must call

the police. She was perspiring, even her hands were wet,
the phone slippery in them. Yet, she shivered: She was
seeing herself in a coarse prison gown in a cell. . . .
Would there be rats in the prison? Prison . . . maybe
forever. *Don't! Don't call the police! You can't help Herr
von Reitz. You will only destroy your own life too. Run.
Run away.*

The phone, slippery in her hand, clattered to the desk.
She picked it up as though it were on fire and dropped it
into the cradle. In a panic, she snatched her evening
purse from the desk. *Run!* She must run away. Then
abruptly she dropped her evening purse, grasped the skirt
of her silk dress, yanked it up to the phone, and frantically wiped away her fingerprints. That was what they
did in movies. She had to save herself. If it came to a
murder investigation, the police must not be able to trace
her. Her heart was beating so hard that she felt as if she
were suffocating.

She was halfway through the outer office when she
remembered: the bronze parrot! Her fingerprints were on
it.

At that moment, she almost gave up; she could not
bear to go back into that office with its gilt-framed
portraits and see Herr von Reitz's body crumpled so
pitifully on the rug. But she had to.

She forced herself to return to the room, knelt by the
bronze parrot, and rubbed at it with the skirt of her dress.
At the door again, she could not help casting a last glance
back at Herr von Reitz. Blood had dried on his face,
giving him a crusty mustache. A black line of dried blood
led from one corner of his mouth to his ear.

She fled.

Outside on the Opernring, she was disoriented. Which
way? The glittering lights and the evening theater and
café crowds were a blur; she blinked away tears. Heart

pounding, she dared not signal one of the taxis speeding by on the broad boulevard, mingling with limousines, cars that resembled gleaming bugs, motor scooters. She began to walk, numbly placing one foot in front of the other; then almost immediately she saw that she was going in the right direction to get back to her hotel. In a few minutes she had passed the Schwarzenberg Café on the Kärntnerring; the crowded, outdoor terrace looked so festive, so enviably carefree. Now she had only to walk the Schubertring and the Parkring alongside the Stadtpark.

Already she could see the hotel looming across the park, lights glimmering over the trees. She kept it in sight along the Parkring; then she turned right and found herself on Weiskirchen Strasse . . . and there, farther up on the right, was the Hilton, like a savior.

She quickened her step. It had been a ten-minute walk from the Opernring, but it had seemed a laborious and long journey.

She reached the hotel. The entrance was brightly lit, a sanctuary. She almost ran toward it; in a moment she would be safe.

"*Guten Abend, Gnädiges Fräulein.*" A man, walking past, bowed slightly. He smiled. A flash of gold tooth.

The skinny waiter with the bow tie.

In her room, she stripped to her panties, flinging her clothes aside, and wrapped herself in her fleecy robe. Then she sat, leaning against the headboard of the bed, pillows jammed behind her.

She could not stop shivering. The waiter had recognized her! He knew Herr von Reitz, had called him by name. Tomorrow morning, Herr von Reitz's body would be found. His shocking murder would be in the papers.

The waiter would go to the police. The police would come to the hotel. The waiter would identify her.

She whimpered and drew her robe closer around her shoulders. Lost—she was lost. She had made a terrible mistake: She had put a noose around her neck by running away. *The murderer fled.*

If only she had telephoned the police!

No. . . . Except for the freakish accident of running into the waiter outside the Hilton, she would have been safe. She had wiped the office telephone clean of fingerprints, the bronze parrot too.

In desperation she cast about for loopholes. It had been at least eleven-thirty when the waiter had seen her entering the Hilton. If only . . . if only she could get around that one unalterable fact.

In despair, she gazed straight ahead. She finally realized that she was gazing at the dresser on which she had dropped her little evening bag. It held her evening comb and compact and the monogrammed silver lipstick case she had given herself for her last birthday. Did they let you use lipstick in prison? . . .

The lipstick case! What if she told the police that after the chocolate cake and champagne at the Kursalon, she had bidden good night to the kindly, good-humored Herr von Reitz and returned to the Hilton? . . . *"Yes,* Inspector," she could say, "I am, after all, a serious researcher here in Vienna on a major project, not a pleasure-seeking tourist." Then she would have arrived back at the Hilton by ten-thirty and . . .

"And, Herr Inspector, I had undressed and was about to go to bed when I missed my monogrammed silver lipstick case." She had a bad habit—("admittedly a bad habit, Inspector!")—of taking her key out of her purse while still on the street; she would add that she thought that was when she must have lost the lipstick case. She had dressed again and gone out to look for it; she had searched up and down the street, so difficult in the dark, and had almost given up when she found it—"so lucky to have done so." It had rolled into some shrubbery a half-block from the hotel.

And on the way back to the hotel, she had encountered the waiter. "Yes, Inspector, that would have been about eleven-thirty," as the waiter had undoubtedly said.

Who could contradict her tale? In the busy lobby, no one was likely to have noticed her going in and out; and the elevators were self-service. "You're welcome, Inspector. If there is anything I can do? That's quite all right, no intrusion; please don't hesitate to call on me. . . . I'd certainly be glad. . . . "

Sick at heart, shivering weakly, she sank farther back against the headboard and tried to think of tomorrow morning and her appointment with Frau Tröger. "*Guten Morgen, Frau Tröger,*" she would say pleasantly; and she and Frau Tröger would breakfast on croissants and jam at the Café am Park. She would force herself to swallow, force her hands not to tremble. Then she and Frau Tröger would go to inspect the pensions.

But, shivering, she saw before her a cherubic pink face, now gray. *So you like chocolate cake? You must go to Gerstner's, they cater to the Vienna Opera.* That sprawled body had been a twinkling-eyed little Viennese who, beyond the social affability of champagne and cake, had been generously willing to help her.

The cake with hazelnuts has shaved chocolate on top.

Her lips quivered, tears rolled down her cheeks; she could not stop weeping.

Her face was still wet with tears when a half-hour later she fell asleep against the headboard.

* * *

When she woke, she was on her side, facing the chair where she had flung her clothes.

Her eyes opened on the sun-splashed clothes, but it was a whole minute before her mind registered what she saw there. Not her slip, or the crumpled green and gold silk dress dappled with sunlight because she had not drawn the curtains—but the shoes. The shoes beside the chair.

Her high-heeled shoes. Those pale green satin shoes were grimed with black splotches. Drowsing, she gazed, mind drifting . . . red and green make brown; blue and yellow make green; red and white make pink. What makes blue? Red and green make . . . blood.

She closed her eyes in denial, begging some nameless power for respite. But the insides of her eyelids were red, and against them she saw what had haunted her sleep: a cherubic face with eyes that sometimes twinkled, sometimes glared; stone-blue eyes that shot baleful glances, malicious stone-blue eyes and a prim mouth gone grotesquely loose; and a pink face of an odd color, so gray . . . gray and red make—

The shoes! Her eyes flew open. Wide awake, she leaped from the bed and snatched up her shoes. Rusty-black blood. Blood might also be on her stockings!

She found the stockings under her slip. Tiny blood spots. And the police would, politely but firmly, search her room, a matter of formality.

In the heart of the city, bells rang. To her, a sound of doom. She looked at her watch. Seven o'clock. Panic flooded her. Time! She needed time before Frau Tröger arrived—time to get rid of these things. She dared not throw them away in the hotel. Burn them? Impossible, unless she set the hotel on fire; beside, the shoes probably wouldn't burn.

Despair melted her bones. Quit. Give up. Give up!

No. If she gave up, she was finished. But if she had

time, some possibility of escape might materialize, something that would save her.

She held the shoes. A garbage can . . . she would stuff the blood-splattered things in a garbage can on some street or alley. Risky. But she had no choice.

She dressed frantically, yanking her tan sweater and skirt from a suitcase; tan would be inconspicuous. She shoved the blood-spotted evidence into a plastic laundry bag she took from the bathroom shelf, then dropped the bag into her kidskin shoulder bag—her blessedly big, drawstring bag. Hurry, hurry! Be back before Frau Tröger—

At the door she gave the room a final backward glance. Her gaze fell on the green and gold dress. She shuddered; she never wanted to see it again. She ran back, snatched it up, and stuffed it into her shoulder bag. She'd destroy that too. Hurry!

Money! She'd better take money; who knew what eventuality . . . She snatched up her evening purse and dumped the schillings from it into her shoulder bag, too much in a hurry to transfer the money to her wallet. Now, go! *Go!*

Outside the hotel, luggage was piled, guests were arriving, leaving. The doorman beckoned taxis, porters were at work, and the air smelled fresh, smelled of the green park across the way.

She walked quickly to the left and made a right turn onto a broad street; then she realized it was too broad a street for subterfuge. She felt conspicuous, like a criminal under a battery of lights. Which way?

She walked quickly, head down, and at the first corner made a turn. At the next corner she turned again. Before her was a big paved square filled with people and lined with tour buses. Bus drivers stood chatting, while uniformed tour guides, both men and women, some with clipboards and megaphones, walked around or stood at the bus doors.

Autobusbahnhof Landstrasse, read a sign on the terminal building. Languages mingled: French, Italian, German, English, Japanese.

The terminal building! Holding her shoulder bag close, she looked past the buses lined up like elephants. A trash can in the terminal building! Garbage trucks must arrive frequently. She visualized broken souvenirs, apple cores, a stale pastry, empty cigarette packs, candy wrappers, and the blood-spattered evidence of her crime swiftly being compacted into a mass, then shredded, chopped, compressed. Unidentifiable. She hoped.

She started toward the terminal.

And stopped short.

The waiter, the waiter with the gold tooth! He was walking ahead of her toward the terminal building. She recognized his skinny figure, the shape of his head. Good God, did the man never sleep?

She shrank back. The waiter had stopped. He lit a cigarette, then tipped up his head, smoking. He put his hands in his pockets, looked around, a man at leisure on this fresh morning. He exhaled smoke and surveyed the crowds. In horror, she saw by his stance that he was about to turn; he would see her, he was only three feet away—

The heat of the bus behind her. She turned quickly. The bus door was open; she fled up the steps and hurried down the aisle, her shoulder bag bumping along the already-seated tourists. She sank into a seat, her heart thudding. She felt like the murderer in *Night Must Fall,* the man who carried a head around in a box. *But I am not that, I am not!*

The bus door hissed closed and the bus began to move.

"Buon giorno a tutti! Sono Signorina Cassola." A

stout young woman in a navy-blue uniform was standing beside the bus driver, talking into a microphone. *"Tale gita della duranta di mezzo giornati vi mostrera i magnifici dintorni di Vienna, come pure notevoli . . ."*

She put up a hand to shield her face from Signorina Cassola and looked out the window. The waiter from the Kursalon had turned; cigarette smoke was blowing in a stream from one corner of his mouth.

Only it was not the waiter. It was another man entirely, with a squarish face and thick neck. Her fear had betrayed her.

". . . il castello Liechenstein. Visiterete inoltre il lago sotterraneo . . ." Across the aisle two children, a boy and girl both in white stockings, bounced on the seat and chatted in Italian. This group must be from Italy, the bus chartered especially for them. *". . . si andra a Mayerling, ex padiglione di caccia e dove si suicidó il principe ereditario Rodolfo . . ."*

Mayerling. A Vienna Woods tour, probably like the four-hour tour she had planned to take next week: a tour that went to the Seegrotte, the subterranean lake, and to Mayerling, the former hunting lodge where in 1889 Crown Prince Rudolph had committed suicide with his young mistress, though some said it had been a hushed-up murder. Death in the Vienna Woods.

She drew in a breath; she put a hand on her shoulder bag. She knew now that she was going to bury the blood-spattered things.

But . . .

Frau Tröger! It ws now eight-thirty. In another half-hour that worthy woman would be telephoning Veronica's room from the Hilton lobby. Disaster loomed, an insurmountable mountain. Helplessly she gazed at the back of the green plush seat before her.

"*Primo di tutto, il nostro giro ci porta alla grotta sotterranea di Mödling, quindici chilometri da Vienna.*"

She strained to understand. Mödling. *Quindici chilometri*—fifteen kilometers. *Primo di tutto*, that meant "first" in Italian. Thank God!—at least their first stop was only a few kilometers away, at Mödling. A half-hour? Longer? A *grotta sotterranea*—subterranean grotto. At Mödling, near the Mödling woods. Convulsively, she clutched her shoulder bag. At Mödling, the others would troop off to the grotto; she herself would get her bearings, then slip into the woods. Afterward . . . afterward, at the Seegrotte, a bus, a taxi, *something* to speed her to Vienna. She'd be back at the Hilton in an hour—late, an hour late. What could she tell Frau Tröger? What, *what*: A blank wall. Then, stubbornly: I will think of something, some excuse: *dear Frau Tröger* . . . Yes? *Oh, dear Frau Tröger! Forgive me! I woke up at seven, it was such a dewy-fresh morning— this lovely city, your Vienna, it seduced me. I went out exploring, I got lost, lost in* . . . in Saint Stephen's cathedral? No, no good, maybe Saint Stephen's wasn't open so early. Something else. *Something.* Too late to try to telephone Frau Tröger, she would have left; and in any case, how could she explain phoning from Mödling?

Something. She would smother Frau Bertha Tröger with apologies. And with a remarkably plausible excuse.

So she sat, stubborn, fearful, one hand twitching spasmodically on her shoulder bag, the green plush before her, the outskirts of Vienna slipping past. She would think of something.

She had to.

Chapter 3

"Bitte." The policeman stood politely aside.

Jason Foxe preceded him into the foyer, then the hotel room itself—beautiful, spacious, done in Art Nouveau. Besides the policeman, there were three people in the room.

A short, fat man with beetling brows stood between the windows and a desk. A woman, very stout, gray-haired, sat upright on an upholstered chair, nervously twisting her hands. She wore a too-heavy tweed suit and one of those mannish fedoras so popular with Austrian women. A boy of about eight, wearing glasses, sat on a straight-backed chair with his legs wound around the rungs. He was munching something from a paper bag. He smiled at Jason Foxe. He was the only one who did.

The room had a look of orderly disorder: a woman's clothes were in piles on the bed; books and notebooks were stacked on the desk; miscellaneous makeup was laid out on the dresser. As Jason entered, a lipstick in a silver

41

case rolled off the dresser onto the rug. He picked it up and put it back.

"Herr Foxe? Jason Foxe?" The man with the beetling brows shambled toward him. He wore a brown suit that hung loosely on him, heavy as he was. "Inspector Leo Trumpf," he introduced himself.

"Yes. What's the problem?" The police had arrived at his pension while he was going over Professor Schindler's papers. Would he accompany them, *bitte*. He had done so with a definite increase of adrenaline but a greater increase of curiosity. He had not even demanded an explanation. Besides his omnivorous curiosity, he had a taste for the inexplicable, an addiction to puzzles. Moreover, he was alert to the possibility of a sociological aspect, something he could utilize in the future. The police had made some idiotic mistake, but he was not the one to stop at its source a river of potentially interesting fish . . . he would at least exploit the situation, wring out what insights he could. So here he was, eyebrows raised in inquiry.

It was twelve noon.

"So." The inspector had melancholy brown eyes and a steady, probing gaze. "Your friend, Miss Veronica Kent, appears to be missing. Her associate, Frau Tröger"— he indicated the stout woman in the fedora—"is worried. She—"

"Never!" burst out Frau Tröger, voice shaking. "A researcher that Sarah Hamilton trusted—*Never* would she not keep an appointment! *Nie!* And it is already noon!" She flung out despairing hands to the inspector.

"Disappeared! Like that woman last week from the Europa! The same circumstances, the very same! Luggage not even unpacked! And the poor woman still missing!"

Inspector Trumpf made soothing, gravelly noises in his throat. His melancholy brown eyes gazed sadly at Jason.

"So. Frau Tröger arrived at the Hilton for a nine o'clock breakfast with Miss Kent. Miss Kent's room did not answer the telephone." By ten-thirty, he continued, a near-hysterical Frau Tröger had prevailed on the Hilton management to open Miss Kent's room with a passkey. The room had proved to be empty. Miss Kent's luggage had not even been unpacked. The bed had not been slept in.

"The obvious conclusion is that Miss Kent went out last evening—and never returned."

"Well?" The inspector waited, brown eyes steady on Jason.

"Well?" He was mystified. What was the inspector getting at? What had it to do with him? This Miss Kent had undoubtedly gone out on a date, had danced, had drunk too much wine; at this moment she was probably in the bed of a newly-met lover. It happened all the time, in Paris, Amsterdam, San Francisco, Zurich, Berlin—you name it. Frantic relatives and associates like this Frau Tröger were always hysterically reporting young women missing. Ordinarily the police waited a good forty-eight hours, knowing that ninety-eight times out of a hundred the "missing" young lady would turn up, to the embarrassment of all involved.

Ergo, Detective-Inspector Trumpf was here only because the Vienna criminal investigation department must be investigating a possible connection between this Miss Kent's disappearance and that of the woman missing from the Hotel Europa.

But his puzzlement still remained: What had any of this to do with him . . . intriguing as it was? He wished he had brought along a tape-recorder.

"So, Herr Foxe. Please to recount your movements last

night with your . . . ah, friend, Miss Kent. What time you met in the Klimt Bar, where you went, exactly where you parted, at what time, and, ah . . . under what circumstances."

"What have you done with her!" Frau Tröger was wringing her hands, her breast heaving beneath the tweed.

Jason looked from Frau Tröger's frightened, accusing face to Inspector Trumpf; he felt a flicker of uneasiness. He frowned. Don't play around, he told himself, this is serious. An ugly thing may have happened to the girl. He sighed. "I'm sorry . . . I can't help you."

"You can't—"

"I don't know any Miss Kent. There's some mistake."

Frau Tröger let out a long wail. "Impossible! Inspector! That's—"

The inspector held up a hand; it stopped Frau Tröger short. She made a strangled sound and subsided. The inspector's melancholy gaze rested on the wall behind Jason's head, as though words were printed on it. He said carefully, "Yesterday evening, a half-hour after Veronica Kent registered at the hotel, you sent her a dozen roses."

"No! Absolutely not! I sent her nothing. I told you—I don't know any Miss Kent."

The inspector continued, inflexibly, "Last night, at eight-fifteen, you bought a dozen roses from the florist in the hotel. You charged them to your credit card. You also sent a plant to—" he referred to a notebook—"to Herr Adalbert Brunner, Langegassestrasse. That is how we traced you.

"So. A half-hour after Miss Kent arrived, you sent her those roses. That would be about eight-thirty."

The inspector lumbered to the desk and picked up a card. He read aloud, *"I will wait for you in the Klimt Bar, hoping ferociously that you will come."*

A silence.

"Around nine o'clock," the inspector went on, eyes on Jason, "one of the maids passing in the corridor saw Miss Kent leave her room. She even remembers that Miss Kent greeted her with a *'Guten Abend,'* and that she wore a green silk dress with gold threads."

The inspector sighed; he said forbearingly: "Now, please, Herr Foxe."

He was getting it, he was beginning to get it. Oh, Christ, he'd—It should have been funny, but it wasn't. He looked from the inspector holding the card to the roses. "What's this room number?"

"Room eight sixty-five."

"That's it, then! There's your mistake!" He felt triumphant, relieved. "I sent roses to a Miss Hortense Wicks. Room five eighty-six, not eight sixty-five. Someone must have—" He stopped abruptly. Not someone. Himself. In a flash he knew it without knowing it clearly: He hadn't wanted to see poor Hortense Wicks at all. So much for his loused-up Sir Galahad intentions. "I must have accidentally—I must have written the wrong room number. A Freudian slip." He wasn't doing himself any good there, either: The word *Freudian* was hardly popular in Vienna.

"I see. But you did *not* spend the evening with Miss Wicks . . . since she never received your note?"

"No."

"Then . . . with whom?" The inspector's voice was soft.

Jason responded, uncomfortably, walls closing in, "I worked. At my pension. That is, at the Brunners'. On Langegasse. Near the university."

"Ah."

The inspector obviously thought he was lying; that possibly even the Brunners would lie for him, give him an alibi. Against what? Kidnapping? Murder? The missing Miss Kent?

Mysteriously missing . . .

"Herr Foxe, we would appreciate your not leaving Vienna. For the present." Polite, but clearly a command. He was under suspicion. He thought wryly: I could save myself considerable trouble by finding this girl. He glanced at Frau Tröger. She sat hunched over, gazing at some terrible, imagined scene. No help there.

He approached the bed. On a pile of underclothes was the skimpiest bra he had ever seen, a slithery handful of silk jersey. So, Miss Kent was hardly curvaceous.

Another pile: practical-looking clothes—woolen skirts and sweaters, plain shirts and jerseys. A pair of corduroy jeans lay beside the utilitarian clothes; from the jeans, he judged her to be about five feet four, five feet five.

A couple of belts, one patent leather, one suede, both short. So she had a narrow waist. Hats? No hats . . . but a worn-looking French beret, navy. That was her style, was it? A French-type chic?

He turned to the inspector. "Who is she? What's she doing in Vienna?" At a startling thought, he looked at the bespectacled little boy who was now eating a marshmallow from the paper bag: "Is that her son?"

"That is *my* son, Josef," Inspector Trumpf said. "Pepi!—we call him Pepi—Pepi, that's enough marshmallows!"

The boy gave his father a teasing look and popped the rest of the marshmallow into his mouth, but obediently rolled the top of the bag closed. The inspector licked his lips and sighed. Then he concisely revealed the little the police had learned from Frau Tröger.

Listening, Jason wandered to the desk.

He stood looking down at the notebooks and the half-dozen books. The volume on top was entitled

Hundertfünfzig Jahre Theater an der Wein, by Anton Bauer. He picked it up and looked at the book beneath. *Die Alt-Wiener Volkskomödie,* by Otto Rommel. So the girl knew German well enough to read it knowledgeably.

The notebooks were the same as the mustard-colored ones he himself used: pocket-sized, loose-leaf notebooks, five by eight. He flipped one open and read:

"That bastard Metternich's censorship of the drama! Born 1773, probably tyrannized his own mother from the age of three, setting spies on her." A line skipped, then: "Raimund, the actor and playwright born seventeen years after Metternich; committed suicide in 1836 from fear of dying insane ... Odd the prevalence of suicide among those gifted. Think about this, but *don't go overboard.* Facts first, theories second! No matter how tempting."

There followed notes: "Work: Buy three felt-tipped pens, red, green, blue. Tipping: Tip washroom attendants about three schillings. Taxi drivers get ten percent of the meter reading." The next line read: "Personal: Buy mascara." The final note read: "A dangerous byproduct of Schnitzler's romantic plays those erotic tangles, with Viennese ladies weeping into their pastry and coffee at Konditorei: the self-inflicted tragedy of stuffing oneself to death on pastries!"

He couldn't help grinning. Then he grew serious. He studied the handwriting. In his teens, he had been fascinated by handwriting; he'd read books on handwriting analysis, had analyzed his friends' and enemies' personalities from their handwriting. This girl. Strong upward strokes, round *D*s and *B*s. More curvaceous than the bra. Dashing. Took risks. Poetic, courageous, humorous. He looked closely at the strokes. Unexpectedly restrained, veering off, losing heart. In and out of the shadows she went. Curious.

He turned to Frau Tröger. "This Miss Kent—what does she look like?"

Frau Tröger looked up from her imagined horrors. "I never met her! We were to have breakfasted and then looked at *pensionen*. Lunch at Zum Hochstrahlbrunnen. Then my niece, she works for the Fremdenverkehrssband für Wien—the tourist office—she had arranged a tour for Fräulein Kent, the Inner City. Sarah Hamilton wrote that Miss Kent was to get an eye-bird's view of Vienna; Mrs. Hamilton was always for the eye-bird's view. She used to say: 'Orientation saves time.' " Frau Tröger made a high, keening sound. "Ach! Ach! Mrs. Hamilton!"

Surprisingly, Inspector Trumpf handed Jason a passport. "This is a likeness."

The photograph was the usual, unflattering shot, made somewhat better by being in color at the extra cost. The subject had wavy brown hair worn off her brow and behind her small ears, but the raised government seal had been stamped carelessly across her face, blurring the features. It had missed the eyes, though. Light-colored eyes, the blue of shallow water on white sand, with a darker ring around the iris. They seemed framed by short, black lashes. Yes, the eyes. Lovely. Once seen, hardly forgotten.

He handed back the passport. He became abruptly aware that the melancholy-eyed inspector was watching him intently.

"So . . . you have never seen that young lady?"

"Never."

He looked over at the roses in the vase, still so velvety, so magnificent, so deeply red, almost magenta. Almost as a mental exercise, he counted them. Then counted again.

Eleven roses.

But he had sent a dozen! Had the florist? . . . No. Not the florist. That twelfth rose. He had seen it; he had seen it last night on a girl in a gold and green dress, at her waist as she stood expectantly in the entrance to the Klimt Bar.

Five minutes later Jason left the hotel. He was tangled in a net, suspected of some possibly hideous crime, involved in the disappearance of Veronica Kent. Two years ago, he had graphed a sociological profile of crime in a dozen cities, among them Hong Kong, New York, Boston, Marseilles, Rome, and Vienna. Vienna's statistics were astonishing. Compared to Boston's many homicides a day, Vienna had a mere twenty-five a year. But when they happened, they were equally horrendous, involving rape, kidnapping, and drugs. He shuddered, thinking of what might have happened to Veronica Kent.

Walking, he turned the corner onto the Parkring and glanced back. A nondescript car was idling along behind him. Police? Might the police, armed with a search warrant, have already searched his room at the Brunners' on Langegasse? Had they tumbled his possessions about, looking for traces of blood or hair, a girl's torn underclothing, a bit of fingernail—evidence for their forensic department to analyze?

He cursed suddenly and hailed a taxi. Those precious papers of that little Viennese professor! All Schindler's work on Oscar Lewis and the Mexican sociological-anthropological works—he'd left them on his desk, and Schindler hadn't numbered those dozens of insertions. If the police had messed up the papers in their search, it would take hours to clean up their Humpty-Dumpty mess. Damn it! He shouldn't have been tempted to help the little professor in the first place.

In the taxi, he glanced back as they sped along the Ring and up toward Langegasse. He'd been right; the nondescript car was there as though pulled along by a string.

Rudi. He stood, the bushes still quivering behind him. She could not believe it was going to happen to her here in the Mödling woods, the threatened assault that had made her conscientiously keep her door locked in New York and her mental antennae alert on dark streets. All those news reports: GIRL RAPED AND STRANGLED IN MANHATTAN APARTMENT; WOMAN JOG-GER'S BODY FOUND IN CENTRAL PARK; SEV-ENTEEN-YEAR-OLD QUEENS CHEERLEADER'S BODY FLOATING IN—

"A girl goes into the woods, she wants to be followed, eh?" Rudi was grinning. His hands were big and dirty, his thumbs hooked into the pockets of tight black jeans, his fingers dancing on his thighs.

"Kissed me off in the coffee shop, did you? Like I'm nothing!" His voice was hating her. The dancing fingers danced closer to his crotch. "I've got something for you." His eyes gleamed mean and resentful in his fleshy, hand-some, brutal face.

Don't let the bear smell your fear and he will not attack. Don't let the snake sense your terror. Look the snarling dog in the eye and he will cower.

Reason with him.

She could not open her mouth.

She thought hysterically: I'll tell him I'm passionate for him, we'll form a liaison, Rudi and I, we'll have a love affair. *Schatzerln:* Sweethearts! *Am I going crazy?* She thought she was going to be sick.

"Against the tree, the tree!" He was upon her, he had her by the shoulders, his fingers like claws digging deeply into her flesh. He was backing her over the ground; she stumbled backward.

"That skinny tree! I'll nail you against that tree, I'll nail you right *onto* the tree!" He laughed resentfully, his face vicious, he was in a fury.

Play along, she told herself frantically. Go limp, laugh, flatter him. Above all, smile, be pliant. For pity's sake, *flirt!*

He put his dirty hand on her breast.

She screamed and raised her fist, to find it caught in midair, jammed down, and wrenched agonizingly behind her back. This time her scream was one of pain.

"Up against the tree!" He thrust her roughly back, gasping, laughing. She felt the tree trunk along her spine; the man's body pressed against hers; his left arm went around her, his right hand worked to open his pants. He was breathing in little grunts; his unshaven chin dug like fire into her forehead, scraping it raw as he shifted to lean down. Still fumbling at his pants, he bit her neck. She yanked her head aside, sobbing now.

A voice from somewhere crashed over them—Jove, hurling thunderbolts:

"Beast! Beast!"

Something dark flashed past her eyes. The man screamed and released her. "Ahhh!" He grabbed his shoulder and went down on one knee, shoulders hunched, face turned up, agonized, eyes squeezed shut, lips drawn back from his teeth.

"Franz! Be careful!" A woman's voice.

"Nonsense, Liebling! The beast!"

Veronica sagged against the tree, seeing them through a haze of shock: a fierce-looking old man with a thatch of white hair and a hooked nose, and behind him a woman. The man was tall and strong looking. He stood an arm's length from the moaning Rudi, holding a heavy walking stick, ready to strike again if the bear, the snake, the snarling dog was not sufficiently crippled.

"Fräulein . . . you are all right?"

Yes, shaky but all right. Crime, struck down by a walking stick. It faded behind her, eclipsed—became something read in a book, a newspaper. It happened to other women, not to her. She managed a whispered "Yes."

"Come around him."

She obeyed, edging warily around the fallen man. He seemed a species of animal, unfamiliar, but intrinsically loathsome. He was now on both knees, swaying from side to side, cursing and whimpering that his shoulder was broken. Minutes ago, he had intended to be her rapist, perhaps her murderer. It was difficult to take it all in.

"Leder. Leather. Animal skins, dressed for use," the fierce old man was saying, looking contemptuously at the leather-vested Rudi, "—to be worn. But put it on a despicable back, and that semihuman reverts to being an animal." He shifted the walking stick as if tempted to, again, bring it down on the cursing Rudi. "Can a woman no longer take a stroll to breathe fresh, sweet air without—Schwein! *Schwein!* You should be prosecuted!" He turned his head abruptly to Veronica. "Fräulein?"

She froze. It was so wildly awful, so ludicrous yet macabre; she felt hysteria, like a bird flapping its wings at her, beating at her. If she refused, what excuse could she give? The white-thatched man, tall, erect, expectant, was waiting. She looked away, looked down, looked at the fallen Rudi. In utter revulsion, she gave a great, involuntary shudder. "No!" she cried out, "No!"

"Understandable." The elderly man's voice was crisp, not disapproving.

They left the man Rudi there on his knees among the leaves and twigs. Walking safely with her rescuers, heading back to Mödling where the tour buses were parked, she felt like a false innocent. *Murderer! Murderer!*

"Franz Mahler," the elderly man introduced himself. "And my wife, Marianne." Politely, he waited.

She cast quickly about for a credible tale. "Miss Gaylord," she introduced herself, "Sarah Gaylord. I'm staying at the ... the Imperial. On Kärntnerring, near the Opera." She remembered that Sarah Hamilton had mentioned the Imperial as Vienna's most elegant and expensive hotel; she did not mean to impress the Mahlers, masquerade as a millionairess, but the Imperial was the only hotel she could think of, besides the Hilton.

She found it incredible that she could think at all. She stumbled wearily along, pulling her tan sweater low around her hips, a nervous gesture. She was wearing lightweight, sling-backed shoes, and her feet kept twisting on the uneven ground. But at least her shoulder bag was mercifully lightened of its incriminating burden.

"Ah? And this beautiful September morning you could not resist a tour to our Vienna Woods!" That was Frau Mahler. She had soft brown eyes and she wore her brown hair in a bun; she looked to be in her forties. She wore a loose, french-blue coat, soft, expensive-looking.

"Yes, a tour." How could she make plausible her walk in the woods? Her mind scurried this way, that way. "Yes, one of those tours, but the boat ride, the Seegrotte ... you see, I'm claustrophobic." How quickly the lie came! It shamed her. "So instead I thought I'd take a little stroll until the others returned." She kept her eyes down. "I stopped for a cup of coffee first, at that little place next to the Seegrotte." That was true, a cup of coffee to steady her nerves, get her bearings.

"That leather-vested Schwein! I saw him speak to you at the coffeeshop," Franz Mahler said.

"Oh?" It gave her a shiver to realize how much strangers saw, witnessed. "I hardly thanked you." She pulled at her sweater, tense with anxiety—hopelessly late now!

Frau Tröger must already have returned to her suburban home, vexed at the time-wasting American who broke appointments and didn't even leave word. Meantime, Herr von Reitz's body, the police ... Out of this shambles, what could she rescue?

Frau Mahler tripped. Her husband gave a little cry and grasped her arm. "Liebling!" Frau Mahler's coat swung back, revealing her figure. She was pregnant. A good six months' pregnant.

His wife's near fall unleashed Herr Mahler's tongue. "We try to be so careful, Miss Gaylord! You see, a pregnancy at Marianne's age! She is almost forty-three!"

"Ah, such a worrier!" Frau Mahler smiled at Veronica. "Every day, he insists on a little trip for fresh air."

The Mahlers were Viennese, city people, jewelers. They spoke a cultured German, smiling frequently at each other, Herr Mahler's guiding hand always under his wife's elbow. Her first pregnancy, Frau Mahler confided to Veronica in a soft voice; she had had no children by her previous marriage. It was her heart's desire to have a child, and Herr Mahler's. "I confess, I am relieved, Fräulein Gaylord," broke in Herr Mahler, "that you do not wish to prosecute that Schwein. My Marianne in the witness box, in her condition, having to swear to that violence in the woods!"

"Yes ... well ..." They were emerging from the woods. Across the road was the entrance to the Seegrotte, and there were parked cars and tour buses nearby. "I must find a taxi, return to Vienna. Perhaps I can telephone. ..."

"No, no!" Frau Mahler put a gentle hand on Veronica's arm. "Enough country air for today! Yes, Franz? We will take you back to Vienna with us."

The Mahlers' car was a silver-gray Mercedes. In the back seat, as it moved off, the feeling of motion, of going forward, was like an escape . . . an escape until she could begin to think again. Right now, all she saw was a simple, brilliant picture: the man, Rudi, on his knees, whimpering, looking down at the very spot where she had been scattering twigs to make the earth look undisturbed.

From Mödling, the road ran straight into Vienna. "Did you know that Beethoven composed the *Missa Solemnis* in Mödling?" Herr Mahler, driving, asked. "But I will never again identify the town only with Beethoven's music." He sighed; then said comfortingly, "It is only a few kilometers now to Vienna, Miss Gaylord. We'll have you back at the Imperial in half an hour. Less."

A quiver of alarm. The Imperial was too far from her own hotel, and there was still a chance— If she could only think . . . "No, please! If you would drop me at . . . at Dr. Karl Lueger Platz." That little square near the Hilton, wasn't it? Three minutes away? "There's a shop, I . . . if you don't mind." Lying to the Mahlers pained her, as though she were destroying something precious between the Mahlers and herself. Each falsehood seemed to be a sharp knife turned upon herself: the wounds were all hers.

They did not question her. They dropped her at Dr. Karl Lueger Platz. The sunlight had thinned, the Platz looked dismal; a few teenagers stood smoking near the statue's pedestal, a handful of others were buying lunches of bauernwurst and sauerkraut from a nearby stall; the air smelled of stale coffee and sauerkraut. Herr Mahler pressed a scribbled address into her hand. "If you need us, Miss Gaylord." Frau Mahler reached from the car and drew Veronica's head close to hers and kissed her warmly on the cheek. "You'll be all right," she whispered.

The Mercedes gone, Veronica stood still in the Platz, tethered by doubt and fear. It began to drizzle. Still she

stood, rooted, envisioning the man Rudi on his knees—
Rudi who had devoured her with resentful, hate-filled
eyes. By this time, Herr von Reitz's body had been found;
the gold-toothed waiter had reported the "girl from the
Hilton" to the police. No matter how plausible her explanation about her lost silver lipstick case, her picture
would surely appear in newspapers and on TV. *Rudi.* He
would recognize her as the girl in the woods. What sweet
revenge! And maybe a rich reward from the von Reitz
family besides. Again she saw Rudi on his knees looking
down at the carefully scattered twigs. If he did not find
the buried bloody evidence, the police would. They would
search the woods.

She knew then that she had been building a glass
edifice of hope: a fragile edifice of nonsensical hope. Now,
soundlessly, it had shattered; she stood amid the shards.

The drizzle grew heavier. The teenagers straggled off.
She sank down on the pedestal. Roses! All because of the
red roses. The drizzle became a gray curtain. A gust of
wind sent a crumpled coffee container against her leg.
One hand rested on a dank paving stone. She felt bruised
and dirty, her wrenched arm ached, and the bite on her
neck began to throb. She was getting wet through; her
sweater sagged. She shivered. Five minutes away was the
warm, luxurious hotel: music playing, people lunching,
crystal and china and silver, pink napkins. She thought of
rich carpets, soft pillows—of clean, fresh, dry clothes.

Where could she run? Hide? How could she save
herself? She rummaged in her shoulder bag, only half-
aware of what she was looking for. Yes, her lipstick . . . as
though reddening her lips would give her courage,
strength, mask her inner pulsations of alarm. Bravado,
that was what she needed—bravado. A good name for a
lipstick.

But her lipstick was not there, she must have left it at

the hotel. The lack of it was somehow too much to bear. She began to cry. Yet, sitting there, swamped and miserable and hopeless, she thought suddenly, absurdly, with that quirky, desperate humor that used to exasperate her French-Canadian aunt: If I at least had a lipstick! . . .

Chapter 4

In earlier years, Detective-Inspector Leo Trumpf was always afraid he'd be found out, that his superiors would realize he'd been merely lucky and his brilliant solving of a case was only a fluke. He used to awaken in a cold sweat of fear. But over the years, as his reputation grew, and even before he became a senior detective, he had come to know that he largely made his own luck.

He did it by fitting negligently odd pieces together—bits of information, well-grounded knowledge, and even fancies—until they formed something that nagged and tantalized him from the edge of his peripheral vision. They merged into something like a string, floating and swinging in a breeze, just on the periphery. At a climactic stage of realization, he would turn and seize that string.

He was still as astonished as his chief and his assistant, Detective Staral, when he grasped that dangling, tenuous thread and pulled it in. He had a sense of unease only while the thread dangled; his triumph was breaking through, grasping it, and solidifying the case.

So he played with the fancies and knowledge he had about the missing girl with blue eyes ringed with black, Veronica Kent.

He sat at his desk in the Criminal Investigation Department in the Rossauerkaserne. In Franz Josef's time, this chilly old stone building had been the imperial soldiers' barracks. Now it was one of Vienna's main police stations. Ordinarily, the Veronica Kent disappearance would have been handled by the Missing Persons Department. But because of the possible connection between Fraulein Kent's disappearance and that of the young married woman from the Hotel Europa, the matter had been assigned to Detective-Inspector Trumpf.

It was now four o'clock in the afternoon. Outside, it was drizzling. Trumpf's still-wet raincoat hung on the coat rack, his umbrella dripped in the pan. At the Hilton, room 865 had been carefully investigated. Miss Kent's luggage was at the Rossauerkaserne for further examination. Frau Tröger had wailed off home on the Schnellbahn.

And—irony of ironies!—not five minutes ago his interoffice phone had buzzed and he had learned that the woman who had disappeared from the Europa had turned up and was now enfolded in her husband's arms. That woman, it turned out, had a history of such disappearances, a fact the husband had unfortunately not . . . and so on. Inspector Trumpf, doodling, listened. So the Europa disappearance was in no way related to the Hilton affair.

In any event, Veronica Kent's disappearance had inadvertently become, as the Americans called it, his baby. Not that he was averse to that. Just the opposite, in fact. Something indefinably peculiar about this case whetted his appetite. He felt alert, honed to a keener edge; it was a feeling that exhilarated him, reminded him of his younger days. Not, he thought to himself, that he was now so old—just a little overweight.

In the last several hours, he had amassed certain information concerning this Affair of the Roses, as he had come to think of it. *Miss Hortense Wicks.* Miss Wicks, a softig blonde, Nebraska-born, aged twenty-nine. Miss Wicks was indeed a guest at the Hilton, Room 586, as Herr Jason Foxe had stated. Miss Wicks, in a startlingly noisy yellow blouse—taffeta, it was called, and she kept nervously ruffling the high collar, making it even noisier—Miss Wicks had stated flutingly that Jason Foxe was hardly an acquaintance; she had met Mr. Foxe only once. That had been at the Brunners' pension, during a shooting for *Sophisticate. Sophisticate* was the name of Miss Wicks's fashion publication.

Nor could Miss Wicks imagine, hazel eyes widening— anxious but rather pretty eyes that distracted attention from her somewhat thin lips—why, yes *why*, therefore, Mr. Jason Foxe might possibly have sent her roses. "He had no *reason....* " Miss Wicks's light, flutelike voice, at this point rose, to a higher pitch. To the inspector's eye, this curvaceous young woman was in affrighted retreat from any connection with Jason Foxe. A girl had disappeared! *It might have been me!* Was that it? ... Was that what shone fearfully from Miss Wicks's widened eyes?

In any case, Herr Foxe was under surveillance. Jason Foxe: sociologist, in Vienna on a six-month grant from the Texas Foundation for the Humanities. The effect of World War Two on the Viennese psyche, young adult population of the 1980s. Psyche? Good luck, Herr Foxe. On leave from a college in Brunswick, Maine, U.S.A. Bowdoin. The inspector clipped the dossier on Foxe to a pile of papers on his desk and marked it with a red pencil. He sat there, thinking. He was distinctly aware of the name, Jason Foxe, just inside his peripheral vision. He would keep it there.

Meantime, contact with the United States had furnished a dossier on Veronica Kent. An ex-roommate, located in Boston; Lincoln Center Library; Sarah Hamilton, the famous theater historian; and a dozen other sources had delivered, thanks partly to the magic of computers.

The information was a faceted diamond: many facets, each with its own surface, each facing away from the others. So: Veronica Kent. Born Boston, 1962. Only child of psychiatrist father, social worker mother. Both parents slain in burglary of their Chestnut Hill home when she was nine. Brought up by aunt and uncle in Quebec, the aunt a housewife, the uncle an accountant; a respectable, middle-class household. French background. Catholic faith. Attended Convent school, though of Protestant faith. At sixteen, entered McGill University in Montreal. Two years later, at eighteen, returned to Boston. Boston University on scholarships, augmented by Saturday and evening tutoring jobs. Majored in European literature and languages.

The inspector sat back. What languages? Did she speak German? He returned to the notes.

In 1981, aged nineteen, married fellow college student. Marriage annulled after six months. Immediately afterward, moved to New York. Various research jobs: European history, literature. Copy editing for two publishers. Poetry prize of five hundred dollars awarded by Chaucer Society. Lincoln Center Library, theater research department, until April. No political history. No memberships in organizations—literary, feminist, or any other.

Inspector Trumpf looked up, reflecting. A woman who

preferred to run her own show entirely, not—he glanced down at the note—marriage annulled—that she ran it with unalloyed success. What might her sexual proclivities be? Irregular? Attracted to other women? Had she gone out last night in search of an irregular sexual connection? Or a regular one? That fellow student she had married, had the marriage foundered on his sexual—what did they call it these days?—orientation?

He straightened the papers and slipped them into the folder.

So. Veronica Kent had now been missing for exactly twenty hours. At two P.M., the inspector had released photos of her passport picture to the media. The girl's face would already be on television; and what with radio news breaks and late newspaper editions, the phone would start ringing with tips, leads—some false, but among the dross perhaps a real clue.

The inspector sat back, picked up a pencil, and sat tapping it, frowning. He was fancying again. He fancied it was odd that the police blotter for those twenty hours showed such a flatly uneventful day: shoplifting at Gerngross' department store, a dope raid at a student hangout, some heads cracked in a roughhouse at a Heuringen ... piddling crimes. Why couldn't young men drink less wine and eat more cold cuts in between? Nothing much else: a quarrel over a taxi in front of Eve's, the striptease nightclub; a Belgian businessman had blacked an Arab diplomat's son's eye.

Trumpf tapped ... and tapped. He had a nagging notion that something was lacking. "It usually comes in pairs!" he suddenly said aloud. "A related incident." It was true: Invariably when he was faced with Crime X, simultaneously, or at least within twenty-four hours, there was a report of another crime, Crime Y, that drew his attention. But . . . again he scanned the day's listing. Nothing.

"Papa?" Pepi came in, sneakers soaked, hair wet. His poplin jacket was buttoned unevenly. "Hi, Papa."

"How was it at the Radstadium? The soccer?"

"Rained out." Pepi sat down. He had a new paper bag. Even across the room it smelled of chocolate. Pepi squirmed his hard little behind back into a chair. The Rudolf Steiner School was carrying out a special project and Pepi had been one of twenty children chosen to participate. It would not start until the third week of October, weeks away, but Pepi was certainly making the most of this distinction, especially now that his mother was away. Klara, poor Klara! Klara was at her parents' in Villach, her mother had a broken hip. So the inspector was temporarily father and mother.

Detective-Inspector Trumpf's children by his first marriage were grown up; at forty-six, he had fathered this child by his second wife. Klara, his Klara, was sturdy, loving, with a heart bigger than a Volkswagen. He, Trumpf, had much to be thankful for. And nothing to complain about . . . except his weight. Another thirty pounds off, and he'd be, in Dr. Albrecht's words, "like a brand-new BMW." That little dizzy spell two months ago had been a timely warning. Since then, he brought his own lunch to the office: scraped carrots, celery sticks, a tomato, a plastic container of cut-up cabbage-and-apple. Few calories, plenty of roughage. Munching carrot sticks, he had to keep reminding himself that the coronary heart disease rate of the Bantus in Africa, who lived on a diet with only ten percent fat, was practically zero. Out of autopsies performed on twenty-two Europeans and forty-two Bantus, all of whom had died suddenly for any reason whatsoever, only one Bantu had atherosclerosis. But all of the Europeans—how many might have

been Viennese, Inspector Trumpf shuddered to think—
had had extensive damage.

"What do we do next?" Pepi was looking at him
expectantly. Next to chocolate, he loved police
investigations.

The intercom buzzed.

"Bitte?"

A phone call, reported Sergeant Redlich at the desk; a
possible lead on the Fräulein Kent case. The inspector
took the call: an excited Italian woman, Signora Cassola.
Signora Cassola was a tour guide, this morning she had
taken a group of Italian optometrists and their families
on a special four-hour trip to the Vienna Woods. Two
children on the bus had insisted to their parents that the
girl they had just seen on television, the missing Signorina Kent, had been on the bus. The children were positive! The parents had telephoned Signora Cassola. It was
impossible that the girl had been on the bus without her
noticing, but the children both swore it was the girl. They
said that she had gotten off at the Seegrotto, but after the
subterranean boat trip, she had not gotten back on the
bus.

"Wearing?" asked the inspector.

A tan sweater and skirt. But the children were positive!
The very same girl on television! "It could be the Ameri-
can girl . . . *Magari!*" Signora Cassola finished. *Magari.*
God willing.

Near Mödling . . . The inspector hung up. The woods.
Rabid dogs had been reported in the woods in that area.
Newspapers had advised people to carry a stout walking
stick with a pointed metal tip when walking there. The
young woman might have been attacked by a dog, or
dogs.

Inspector Trumpf ordered the woods searched. Then
he hunched bearishly over the desk, brooding. He was not

sanguine. A girl in a tan sweater and skirt. That had to be a different girl. Veronica Kent had been kidnapped or murdered or she was wandering somewhere with a mind blank as a sheet of paper. If the former, they would find her body; if the latter, they would find her in dirty, torn green silk. Green silk. According to the maid at the Hilton, Miss Kent had been wearing a green silk dress with a gold sheen when she'd left the hotel the night before. She had not returned to the Hilton at all.

Where then, during the night or early morning—a supposition only, mind you!—could she have found a tan skirt and sweater? Unless—

"Papa? *Now* where?"

Inspector Trumpf looked at his son. "Down the corridor. To look for something among the American woman's effects."

"Look for what?"

"If I find it, I'll let you know." Murky, it was all so murky, not getting clearer but more opaque. But wasn't it always that way? The British expression, "The plot thickens," was applicable: a lot of murkiness, a dense thicket. The denser it became, the more he had to work with.

He smiled. All to the good.

A torment, worse than a hair shirt. Inside the cheap, transparent red plastic raincoat, her damp woolen sweater steamed her body. Her skin itched intolerably. Rivulets of sweat slid down the sides of her neck. Her hair was wet, her shoes sodden.

She walked woodenly on. The drizzle had turned to rain, then it had lightened to a heavy, warm mist. But she had to suffer the raincoat snapped closed right to her neck; it hid her tan skirt and sweater. She had paid eight hundred shillings for the raincoat, buying it in a plastic

envelope at a stationery-store counter near Dr. Karl
Lueger Platz, fumbling out the required schillings, think-
ing drearily: What will I do when my schillings are gone?
She must hoard the few she had left.

Ungergasse, she was walking on a street called Ungergasse, outside the Ring, somewhere east, her gaze forag-
ing among nondescript shops, hunting, hunting; she felt
like a mangy cat. At the bottom of her shoulder bag, she
had found her tinted glasses and had put them on to hide
her eyes—at least that much of a disguise.

There! Across the street was a narrow shop, the sign
above reading Noch Einmal. Once Again. A secondhand
shop. The gods—evil gods?—were with her. She splashed
across the street.

Inside, an acrid, musty smell; clothes jammed on iron
pipe racks; scrawled prices on gray cardboard above each
rack. Bins of shoes, bins of children's clothes, remnants of
material, a grimy glass case displaying cheap-looking
jewelry. An anemic young man in red satin stretch jeans,
with strings of glass beads around his neck, was perched
on a stool near a counter, chatting and laughing on the
telephone.

"Guten Tag." Her voice came out a hoarse whisper.

The young man glanced at her with inquiring eyebrows, then made a grimace of annoyance and waved her
toward the racks. She approached the rack with the
cheapest prices. Behind the racks was a cubicle with a
faded chintz curtain.

Fumbling through the clothes on the rack, she could
hear the young man squealing with laughter on the
phone.

Martha Krieger Schratt refused to have a maid, even
for one day a week. Busyness was all. The old apartment
on Langegasse near the university was huge. It was on

the second floor, above the ground floor and the mezzanine. There was no elevator.

The apartment had high ceilings, and was shabbily elegant. Off the square entrance foyer were the *Herrenzimmer,* which had been her father's old study; the living room; the dining room; and the kitchen. A door led to the long hall. Off this hall were the bedrooms, the water closet, and a bathroom with a tub on a marble base. There were three bedrooms in all: the master bedroom; the *Kinderzimmer,* which was a children's room; and the maid's room. The narrow little maid's room was still unrented. The *Herrenzimmer* was occupied by an elderly Czech woman from Prague. She was visiting her daughter, who lived near the Votivekirche. It was a leisurely visit, six weeks, with five more weeks to go. A wispy, elderly accountant at Gerngross' department store on Mariahilfer had the *Kinderzimmer.* Martha Schratt had kept the master bedroom for herself, though she might have slept in the living room on the old Biedermeier couch. Sometimes she considered doing that, but she could not resist keeping the master bedroom; it was her one luxury.

It was not simply for the money that Martha Schratt took in roomers. She needed people to "do for," as she thought of it. Busyness was a frenzy with her. She shopped, cleaned, baked, cooked, vacuumed. She stripped the beds, she did the laundry, she washed the walls. She did not want one minute to herself, not one instant to reflect on the past. The horrors were long over. The Compensation of Victims of the Nazi Regime had returned the Krieger apartment to her, the widowed Frau Krieger Schratt, in 1951. It was her *Wahlrecht*—her "right"—to live there; but she did not own the apartment, she paid rent.

She was now sixty-six, a strong woman with capable-looking hands and a square face with a broad, pure-looking brow. She wore sensible clothes and sturdy, laced shoes on feet that had broadened with age. At night, taking off her shoes, she often paused and giggled girlishly. How incredible that as a young woman she had had delicate little feet adored by Stefan Schratt! Her husband's first pencil sketches of her, naked, had elongated her lovely feet and slim hands, her long neck. Later he had painted her slender young body and pretty face all in cubes or like colored mosaics: breasts like egg crates, knees like boxed stationery.

But the paintings had caused excitement. Collectors had paid thousands for a Stefan Schratt; gallery owners had courted him, his work had brought him fame and money. It also had made Stefan Schratt feel strong and invincible, and that had been unwise. In the end, it had not been enough that he was a famous painter and a Schratt of irreproachably "pure" Aryan lineage. Fame had betrayed him into feeling clothed in armor, into seeing himself as his own man and Martha's knight against the dragon. He had fought the dragon, fiercely, cleverly. And for her, he had won. But even after he had hidden her safely away in Merano, he'd continued to fight the dragon, raging against it, subverting it in Vienna's coffeehouses, with his brilliant, underground satirical cartoons. Until too late. His defiance had finally brought him death.

So she shopped and cooked and cleaned and ironed.

Martha was setting the dining room table for supper— two places, one for herself and one for the elderly accountant she invited to dinner every year on his birthday—when the doorbell rang.

She went through the kitchen to answer it, stopping to turn down the flame under the *Tafelspitz*. The kitchen was filled with the delicious smell of the beef and greens simmering on the stove. A little crackling sound came from the potatoes roasting in the oven; supper would be ready soon. It was almost six o'clock. She took off her apron and went into the foyer, smoothing her dress.

She opened the door to a young woman. She knew immediately by the newspaper clutched in the young woman's hand and folded to the *Wohnungsmarkt,* that she was answering the ad for a roomer.

"Guten Abend, Fräulein . . . Kommen Sie herein."

"Danke schön."

Yes, the young woman explained, standing in the foyer, she had come about the room. Her voice was low and weary. She wore an ill-fitting navy suit and brown shoes and stockings. Her pale face was made paler by violet-tinted glasses, and the fact that she wore no lipstick. Her hair was concealed by a cheap, paisley scarf. A brown shoulder bag hung half-hidden behind one arm that hung straight down, weighted with a worn-looking Air France airlines bag. She looked exhausted.

A French girl, from Rouen. A student. She had arrived an hour ago at Schwechat. She had picked up the *Kurier* and seen Frau Schratt's ad for a room near the university. "Nicole Montcalm," she introduced herself, her voice almost dying away from fatigue. And no wonder, thought Martha Schratt. A Rouen-Paris-Vienna flight, after all. Air travel was dehydrating; the girl's lips looked dry. She spoke German well, but halted occasionally, searching for a word.

Martha Schratt led the way down the hall. She had a special feeling for the tired, the wounded, the courageous. She thought she sensed all three in this young French student: why, she didn't know. Two things, however, she was sure of. First, this French girl had very little money; that was obvious from her worn clothes and the old flight bag. Second, the girl was a taker of risks. The average foreign student who came to the University of Vienna made living arrangements months in advance, at a dormitory or elsewhere. A few careless ones, with money, stayed at the Hotel de France, that big old warren on the Shottenring, near the Votivekirche, until they found satisfactory living quarters. And how expensive the Hotel de France was these days! What with inflation, schillings melted overnight. Schillings! Martha Schratt knew all about schillings, right down to the rising cost of the special Hungarian flour so good for making strudel. Her pension from the Compensation of Victims didn't go far under inflation. But she prided herself on being a good manager. With cinnamon, a little sugar, and stale bread, it was amazing how far an apple could go. She felt a stirring of sympathy for this French girl.

In the maid's room, the girl barely glanced at the narrow bed, the fat, bowlegged bureau, the tourist posters of Italy and Holland that brightened the walls.

"Thirteen hundred schillings a month, is that correct, Frau Schratt? With use of the bath?" The girl stood near the bed, her flight bag dragging down one shoulder.

Martha Schratt hesitated. The ad in the *Kurier* had said thirteen hundred. But she had an unreasoning temptation to let this French girl have it for twelve hundred . . . or even eleven. Inflation gnawed at these university students. But she was too soft-hearted! She must be stern with herself. "Yes, thirteen hundred. Three hundred schillings payable in advance for the first week."

"It will do." The girl lowered the flight bag onto the bed.

"If you wish, you can also have breakfast included. One hundred and twenty schillings a week. With a boiled egg."

Something happened to the French girl's jaw: an odd

quiver, then a tightening. She looked away. "Just the room."

"Whatever you wish. You are welcome, Fräulein Montcalm, welcome to this house. The closet is there, the light switch—"

"Thank you." The French girl did not appear to be listening. She was carefully counting the money from her wallet. "Three hundred schillings." Her hand, a narrow hand, hovered over her wallet; then abruptly she withdrew more money. "Breakfast too . . . after all."

"Excellent."

Frau Schratt tucked the money into her apron pocket. She went to the window to adjust the blind; it was raining again, rivulets ran down the glass. "Your baggage?"

Silence behind her. Then the French girl's voice, so fatigued it trembled. "My baggage . . . yes. In Rouen. My . . . my mother will send it when I write and give her the address."

"You can even telephone your mother from here, if you wish. The telephone call can go on your bill." She finished straightening the blind. She turned, pleased.

"Now! Everything is arranged! You will be happy here." She smiled warmly at the girl. "I know it!" She herself was happy—no more advertising in the *Kurier*, no more running to answer the doorbell when she was busy with the supper, the ironing, the cleaning.

"I will make out a receipt, Fräulein Montcalm. Four hundred and twenty schillings in advance for room and breakfast . . . your passport, please."

The French girl was not smiling back at her. She simply stood motionless, she had gone even paler. How exhausted she must be! But then Fräulein Montcalm roused herself.

"My passport." She sat down on the bed and opened her drawstring shoulder bag and began to rummage in it, head bent. "It is here, somewhere." She rummaged further, then sat still. "No, that's right! I put it in the side pocket of my flight bag." She twisted around to the flight bag on the bed and slipped her hand into the side pocket; then she withdrew it, empty. "How stupid of me! I took it out of my flight bag and put it in the suitcase. I had a little suitcase, a few clothes until I could send to Rouen for my things. The suitcase . . . I left it in a locker at Schwechat."

"Ah! That's all right, then! You can go to the airport and get it." Martha Schratt drew a relieved breath; for a moment she had felt uneasy. At that instant, a smell from the kitchen made her nostrils twitch. She cocked her head, taking experimental little breaths. The potatoes? In a minute they would be burning.

She withdrew the four hundred and twenty schillings from her apron pocket. "You had better keep the deposit until you return with the passport." She held out the schillings. Any minute, the potatoes!

The girl on the bed made no move to take back her money. Instead, she turned her head and looked toward the window. Gusts of rain spattered against the pane, which rattled under a sudden, heavy spate.

"Tomorrow . . . Would tomorrow morning be all right?" The girl's voice had thinned with fatigue. She sat slumped on the bed; the rain beat on the window, the room had darkened. Martha Schratt's heart sank. She couldn't let the girl stay overnight without a passport, it would be breaking the law. The regulation was strict, she had to register every guest's passport immediately with the police. Hotels, inns, pensions—all establishments were subject to the regulation. She could be fined, lose her license. . . . God knew what! She dared not risk it.

Heavy with disappointment, Martha delayed answering. She turned on the shaded lamp on the bureau. A rosy

light lit the darkened little room. It shone on the girl's
pale face, framed in the paisley scarf. Such a cheap scarf,
pathetically cheap! And that shabby flight bag! Martha
Schratt was suddenly filled with resentment and anger.
So many rules! Rules to break the heart! And the potatoes, the potatoes!

She stuffed the schillings back into her pocket. "All
right, tomorrow. But immediately after breakfast you
must go to Schwechat for your passport." She hurried
toward the door. "Breakfast is at eight o'clock, you come
to the dining room, you can have tea or coffee, also a
Kaisersemmel, very fresh, I bake the rolls myself. Butter,
marmalade, and honey. A boiled egg." And at the door:
"Guten Abend."

Hurrying down the hall to the kitchen, she thought:
Maybe two eggs. Herr Herbst, the accountant in the
Kinderzimmer, took breakfast, but not the Czech
woman. Herr Herbst was one egg. Still, he wouldn't
know that the French girl was not paying for two eggs, so
he wouldn't complain that she was favoring the French
girl. She sighed and shook her head, shamefaced at her
weakness. Her feeling for strays would sooner or later get
her into trouble. She felt guilty and worried about the
passport, but she also felt defiant and happy with herself:
Stefan Schratt would have approved.

Veronica locked the door behind Frau Schratt and
turned to the flight bag on the nubby pink bedspread. She
zipped it open, thinking numbly: *Let me not think now
about the passport . . . I must live each minute that I
still have.* She felt she could taste death in her mouth.
Herr von Reitz's? Hers?

She took the damp sweater and skirt from the flight
bag and spread each in a drawer of the bureau to dry—
safer than the closet. Then she took out the plastic rain-

coat; it was creased. She straightened it as best she could and hung it in the closet. Finally she pulled off the paisley head scarf.

Next, she drew out a cellophane-covered child's paper-doll set, complete with blunt, cut-out scissors and crayons. The cellophane was cracked and dusty. Six schillings at Noch Einmal, regular scissors would have cost fifteen. She broke open the cellophane covering, she took off the glasses with their violet lenses, and stood looking at herself in the mirror above the squat bureau, thinking, not seeing herself. Then she went to the closet, took out the plastic raincoat, and spread it over the embroidered linen runner on the top of the bureau.

Leaning well forward over the raincoat, she began to cut her hair. A tantalizing smell of onions, herbs, and meat seeped under the door. Her stomach quivered with hunger, juices ran in her mouth. She was hungry, so hungry. Tears of self-pity blurred her vision. But she would have to wait until breakfast, she did not have to count her schillings to know that: she knew exactly how many she had left.

She blinked away the tears and stopped hacking at her hair with the blunt scissors. Too late! In the mirror she saw the crude, ragged cut, her hair slashed to halfway up her ears; she had given herself torn-looking bangs, besides. Ugly, so ugly. She pressed a bent forefinger to her lips to stop their quivering. No fairy godmother was going to materialize with a magic wand to undo that haircut. Just as no fairy godmother would make Herr von Reitz's blood run again in his veins, or touch his sprawled body with a magic wand and make him spring instantly to life.

Dead. She stood with bent head, but frowning: Something stubborn in her, something fiercely arbitrary, kept rejecting the scenario as she knew it. It militated against her giving up. If only she could hear the news on radio or TV—glimpse an evening paper! PROMINENT LAW-YER MURDERED, AMERICAN WOMAN SOUGHT. She told herself that reports of Herr von Reitz's death would be revealing; they would cast a startling light on that terrible evening, would solve an equation. From them she could learn something important that would determine her actions. But she must wait until morning for news, she dared not leave this safe little room tonight. Meantime, she would have to figure out something about the passport. Lies, more lies.

Head aching, she put the blunt scissors aside. Then she began carefully to wrap the scraps of hair in the plastic raincoat.

Chapter 5

Ellery Hamilton. Like a bald little gnome! He is the only man I've ever seen who ruffles the hair he no longer has! He just reaches up a hand, absent-mindedly, and makes that ruffling-his-hair motion when in perplexity over something he is working on. And he hasn't any hair! That tickles me.

Jason Foxe raised his head from the mustard-colored notebook, grinning. He had been reading Veronica Kent's notebook for the last hour. Notes for his own work lay on the Art Nouveau desk beside his portable electric typewriter. Professor Schindler's pages of insertions and the professor's sociological article itself lay neatly piled beside them, luckily untouched by the Vienna police. They had not searched his room at Brunners'.

Sarah says Ellery likes to create a bad first impression on meeting people, so that later if he does something halfway decent, people will say in surprise, "Why! He's really a wonderful fellow after all!" Whereas if he makes a good first impression, and then does something not so perfect, people will say, "And I thought he was a really swell guy!" Then something crossed out, indecipherable, followed by: *Sarah and Ellery. When I am with them in Connecticut, when I see them together, it almost makes me believe in love, though I know better!*

The notebook had been begun ten months before. The left-hand pages were a personal diary, comments, reflections; the right-hand pages were research notes. The last page contained the mixed notes on Metternich and mascara. It was dated two days before. Jason guessed that Veronica Kent had written that on the plane to Vienna.

He had found the notebook in his jacket pocket on returning from the Hilton. He must have automatically put it there; the notebook, mustard-colored, was so like his own. It amused him to contemplate Inspector Trumpf's chagrin when he realized the notebook was missing.

He chewed his underlip. Oddly romantic, this girl; funny too, sometimes poignant. And why did she no longer believe in love? He tried to picture her laughing, frowning—her face in motion, not like it was in the flat passport picture. But doing so was like looking at shadows on a wall in flickering candlelight; it was no guide to reality. What would her voice be like? Not that it mattered. What mattered was here, here in her notebook. This was she, Veronica. "Veronica," he said aloud. Was she safe? Was she alive? From the notebook, she sounded like a survivor. He hoped to God she was.

He picked up the phone and called the Rossauerkaserne, only to learn that Inspector Trumpf was not there and they could give him no further news concerning Miss Kent's disappearance.

He slid the notebook into the desk drawer and stood at the window frowning, staring out at Langegasse. She could be out there in that lashing rain, alive but injured. He was determined to find her, to help her—but how? His knowledge of Vienna was only a teenager's knowledge . . . and consequently dated. When he'd been eighteen, in 1973, he had been an exchange student in Vienna, but what good was it now, that student year when he had embraced Vienna like a lover? In those golden days, he had argued fervently in coffeehouses about life and philosophy; he had drunk new wine at a dozen Heurigers in Grinzing and Sievering and Nussdorf and had ridden home drunk on the streetcar, squinting so as not to see double. He had experimentally smoked pot with some visiting Dutch jazz musicians behind a dance bar on Graben; he had tried unsuccessfully to get into the Casino on Kärntnerstrasse though he was under age. He had gone rock climbing on the Höhewand, and he had formed one of those strange, blood-brother friendships with another boy, Florian Königsmark. Wandering, lost, in the zoological section of the Naturhistoriches Museum, Jason had come upon the tanned, athletic-looking Florian seated on a folding campstool, sketching birds. He had also, at eighteen, made love for the first time. The girl, a sophisticated nineteen, was an art student who sometimes posed nude for art classes. Her sexual knowledge had been dazzling. Jason had believed her capable of adding a chapter to the *Kama Sutra*.

Sex; something sexual invariably played a part in a woman's disappearance, but in the case of Veronica Kent, he shied from thinking about what part.

At least he could give her notebook back to Inspector Trumpf. It might contain a clue that Trumpf's professional eye could detect. First, though, he would Xerox every page; he could not wholly let the notebook go.

Strange. He had wanted to find the girl only to protect himself from Inspector Trumpf's suspicions. Now he was determined to find her for another reason. She was no longer a nebulous figure: She was Veronica.

In an apartment on Gumpendorferstrasse in the fifth district, Detective-Inspector Leo Trumpf brooded into the bathroom mirror while he shaved.

It was six o'clock Wednesday morning. At eight, he would again go through Veronica Kent's luggage at the Rossauerkaserne. Yesterday, he had not found what he was looking for. He felt he was gliding like an owl through the dark, guided by his senses; he knew he would reach a secure perch. But until he found that unknown thing, he was not sure what it was he was looking for. Or—a fleeting thought stopped the razor in his hand— had he found it and not recognized it? That was the kind of blindness he feared: to look at something that glared significantly back at him and not to see it. But today he felt optimistic.

He rinsed the razor and began to clip his mustache with cuticle scissors, knowing that in three hours it would again look straggly. That was his fate. No matter how he curried his mustache, shaved, tanned his skin under the sun lamp, and dressed in fresh-pressed clothes, by noon his façade would fall apart. His clothes would melt into shapelessness, his heavy face would sweat, his beard would poke bluely through his chin, and he would almost feel his tan fading.

Pepi was the opposite; Pepi was like Klara. His wife and son could wrestle pigs in mud and come out spotless. But at least he had lost seventeen pounds. Klara still affectionately called him *Knöderl*—dumpling. A fine thing: to be named Leo—lion—and be called *Knöderl!*

Ferociously . . . This Jason Foxe, his note with those red roses: hoping *ferociously*. The word implied savagery, danger, a lion's fangs. Which girl had Jason Foxe really sent the roses to? If to Hortense Wicks, as he claimed, in what kind of sadistic sexual activities had the pair indulged? What did *ferociously* imply? Miss Wicks would be in Austria a week or two longer—fashion shootings in Klagenfurt and Portschach on the Worthersee, also in Velden. He would question her further, subtly, tactfully.

But if Jason Foxe had sent the roses to Veronica Kent? Might he have forced some dangerously lascivious activity on the girl? An activity that could have been responsible for her disappearance?

He stood, frowning. Jason Foxe. Dark, curly hair cut like a cap. The man's eyes had looked almost black in his tanned face—an ugly, strong face, with flat cheeks . . . yet certainly attractive to women, that type of face. And Foxe's mouth: a curly, sensual mouth. The man was a good height too, at least six feet. And lean. Lean as an exercise instructor.

Trumpf went into the bedroom and dressed. He would pay a visit to Jason Foxe. This tenuous, dangling thread that was Jason Foxe, reeled in, might—who knew?—lead him to Veronica Kent.

"Breakfast, Papa. I boiled the eggs." Pepi was in the doorway, dressed, hair slicked down, eager to get going.

"*Ja,* I'm coming." And another thing: the girl's missing notebook. "The man took it . . . Herr Foxe," Pepi had told him yesterday at the Rossauerkaserne, "he put it in his pocket."

Yes, a visit to Jason Foxe.

She came into the dining room, the shabby room bright with sunlight. Frau Schratt and a thin, elderly man with a fringe of gray-white hair were sitting at the dining room table eating breakfast; the man was reading aloud from a newspaper. *"Guten Morgen! Guten Morgen,*

Fräulein Montcalm!" Frau Schratt was getting up. "I'll get your breakfast." She introduced the elderly man: Herr Herbst, also a guest at the pension. Herr Herbst, in a mouse-gray business suit, gave her a shy smile and a polite *Guten Morgen.* He wore thick-lensed glasses. His skin was pale, his nose reddish. "Herr Herbst was reading me the news," Frau Schratt said. She went off to the kitchen.

Herr Herbst put a hesitant hand on the coffeepot. "Would you like me to pour your coffee, Fräulein Montcalm?"

"Thank you." She was grateful, her hand might have shaken. The coffee smelled fragrant, fresh ground. Herr Herbst poured carefully. A scattering of crumbs lay on the table near his plate; the tablecloth looked so clean, so freshly ironed that she felt she could almost smell the warmth of the iron.

She bent her head over the coffee cup, breathing in the fragrance, feeling she might faint with hunger before her first sip. Steam rose up and fogged her tinted glasses; the dining room became a violet blur.

"Ach, here I am again!" Frau Schratt, smiling, came from the kitchen bearing a tray; she set down a basket of rolls wrapped in a napkin, then put before Veronica an egg cup containing one egg, and a saucer with still another egg. She sat down to her own half-finished breakfast. She picked up a pack of Gauloises from beside her plate and shook out a cigarette. "You don't mind?" When Veronica shook her head, she struck a kitchen match, lit the cigarette, and inhaled down to her toes.

Herr Herbst picked up the newspaper and continued his interrupted reading of items to Frau Schratt. He read well, in a tenor voice; projecting, enunciating meticulously, and clearly enjoying what appeared to be a regular morning performance. Listening, tense, devouring the hot, boiled eggs and Kaisersemmel roll with heroic restraint, Veronica waited in anguish: The *murder!* The *murder!* But no. Herr Herbst's voice read coverage of international news, political scandals, an upset in the Börse, the Philharmonic's new program . . . had he already read about the murder before she'd entered the dining room? Her hand shook and her cup clattered down as she turned to glance at the television set on the sideboard.

Frau Schratt noticed her glance. *"Genug, Herr Herbst!* We'll see some of the morning news in pictures." She got up and turned on the set.

Immediately, the passport picture materialized on the screen. But the newscaster was saying bewildering things: "This American girl might have been kidnapped. Foul play is suspected. The police are dragging the Danube Canal, the Vienna River. A search is being conducted in the woods of the Hauptallee in the Prater, where young couples, at night, are sometimes robbed and beaten. Amnesia is also a possibility. . . . " A young woman had been seen wandering on a highway toward Krems.

But nothing about Herr von Reitz. The newscaster was talking, talking. " . . . a single police lead. An American sociologist, Jason Foxe, reportedly sent the girl roses and a note only hours before she disappeared. According to Herr Foxe, the roses were meant for another American woman. Police will not divulge the contents of the note. The police are not holding Herr Foxe. However, a further investigation into the Affair of the Roses is being conducted."

"Herrgott!" Frau Schratt lit another cigarette. "The Affair of the Roses! Like in a book."

"Bitte, pass me the sugar," Herr Herbst said to Veronica.

She handed him the sugar bowl. He stirred sugar into a fresh cup of coffee. A few minutes later, his breakfast finished, he left the table. Frau Schratt accompanied him to the front hall.

Left alone, she put her elbows on the table and sank her head in her hands. At any minute they would find Herr Reitz's body, then the innocent "kidnapped" girl would be exposed as a murderer. Now, Frau Schratt would return to the dining room. There was her step. *Get ready*.

She lifted her head and moved her lips, soundlessly rehearsing the passport story she had concocted during the sleepless night. Such a hopeless lie. A mere eggshell! It would shatter instantly under Frau Schratt's discerning gaze, and when it shattered, then what? What was that phrase? *From pillar to post*.

Martha Schratt closed the front door behind Herr Herbst. If she hadn't accompanied him, he would have forgotten his umbrella in the hall rack, even though he had just read aloud the day's forecast for rain. When winter came, she would have to remind him to wear his thick woolen scarf for protection from the raw weather. But she didn't mind; little Herr Herbst needed looking after, and her hands weren't so full that she couldn't pay heed to her tenants, *nicht wahr?*

She came back into the dining room. The French girl turned her head so alertly that Martha Schratt was reminded of an alarmed forest creature . . . and reminded of something else: herself in Merano, over the border in Italy, disguised as a servant girl for the Ziegler family. One day when she was gathering radishes in the Zieglers' vegetable garden, two booted Nazis had tramped past the gate and turned to stare at her. That had happened a week after the invasion of Italy. A dozen soldiers had been billeted in the villa next door. Fear had turned her faint. The next day, the Zieglers, bless them, had hidden her in the mountains with their former housekeeper.

"Frau Schratt! I must confess something to you." The French girl pushed at her violet-tinted glasses.

"Yes?" She was not surprised, only disappointed. She sat down heavily. She noticed that the girl had a pinched look. She wore the same navy skirt as last night, but instead of the shabby jacket, she had on a very faded pink shirt—and such a jagged haircut! Maybe that was the style for students in Rouen, but it made her look like a ragamuffin. And she was almost as thin as those pale-faced Viennese kids who took dope and went around on spindly, pipestem legs. "Yes?"

"You have read about the student riots in Paris? Well, we had them in Rouen too! We were only trying to get recognition. But the police, tear gas . . . In Rouen we wanted a *peaceful* demonstration, but the *flics—they* started it."

Martha Schratt folded her big-wristed hands on the table, listening. Broken heads, arrests, boy and girl students in prison. True enough, student riots at the Sorbonne, and in Lille and Rouen—she'd heard, she kept up, she read the news in the *Neue Krönen Zeitung*, she saw, on TV, bottles thrown, tear gas, police wagons.

"With us," the girl went on, "it happened in July, I was arrested for kicking— I had already matriculated at the university here in Vienna, my mother was frightened, she had insisted. Anyway I was arrested, and I could have lost the whole year! What was I to do? Please! It will all be cleared up. The authorities think I am still in Rouen, but I borrowed a friend's passport and managed to get here. My friend risked— She lent it to me. At Schwechat yesterday I mailed it back to her. I had promised her! I was supposed to receive my passport from my mother in Rouen—it was promised to us by the police; they only took it temporarily—but it did not arrive!"

Martha Schratt looked down at her folded hands; she matched her thumbs. She was too embarrassed to look at the French girl. It was all lies. She wasn't born yesterday! Would the French police really take troublemaking students' passports while they held them under arrest? For sure, they wouldn't! For sure. Not likely, not likely at all. Still . . . it *might* have happened. It was just preposterous enough to be true. With the French and that government of theirs that changed political leadership once a week like dictatorships in South America, who knew?

" . . . so my passport will arrive! Not today, maybe, and perhaps not even tomorrow. But I cannot go to the police—you can see that, can't you, Frau Schratt?—or to the French Consulate."

"Yes, I can see that." She felt an almost humorous admiration for this French girl in the violet-tinted eyeglasses and the ragged haircut. Last night, the girl had fooled her with lies. Suppose this too was an ingenious lie?

But the girl was certainly in some kind of trouble. Political? Romantic? Certainly nothing criminal! Martha Schratt prided herself on being astute about people, so she could tell that much, she certainly hoped so. She had that much discernment!

Well . . . suppose it was a bouquet of lies, and she let the girl stay? In a week, Mademoiselle Montcalm would have a different excuse if the passport did not arrive. But there was the bare possibility that this time the girl was telling the truth.

Martha Schratt knew she dared not take a chance. Nevertheless . . .

"A pity about student riots! All right, Fräulein Mont-

calm, I will wait—but a week only." She began to clear
the table, shy and embarrassed by the girl's grateful
thanks, refusing her offer to help. "No, no one is allowed.
The housework is my job."

When the girl had left the dining room, she switched
off the TV and carried the loaded tray to the kitchen. If
any question arose, she would say the girl was her niece,
visiting from France. Her French niece. She smiled rue-
fully. So now she had a French "niece" who was in
trouble.

In Strohmayer's Service Garage near the Votivekirche,
he sat on a chair balanced against the wall, chewing a
toothpick and reading the boss's morning *Neue Krönen
Zeitung.*

"Jessas! Herrgott!" He brought the chair legs down
with a bang. That bitch! It was that bitch! The bitch from
the woods! *Herrgott!* The same one, for sure. Her picture
was staring at him from the front page.

Missing. He felt a shiver of fear followed by an inner
cry of denial, as though already the police were grilling
him at the Rossauerkaserne. *"Jessas Na!"* It hadn't been
him! If she was missing, it was that Moseslike old man
and his wife. They'd done something with her, had her
tied up in a cellar, whipping her—some fancy sex thing.
They had gotten excited by seeing him with her, what
they were doing up against the tree. They had stolen her
from him, the rotten perverts.

He read the news item feverishly. No reward, not one
verdamnte schilling. So why should he stick his neck out
for the bitch? Let her bleed somewhere. Those cops with
their computers. Tap, tap-tap. Letters appearing like
magic on a screen, and they'd be asking him about the
fire at the wine tavern in Grinzing. That bastard tavern

owner wouldn't let him park his motorcycle under the trees, so he had deserved it.

He got up and went to the garage door. The Honda was parked near the gas pumps. It was red and black, polished, the chrome gleaming. Magnificent. When he rode it, he was a king among the jacks on the road, sweeping past cars, swerving, swooping, the wind at his throat. The saddlebags were new, real leather. But he felt differently about the inside of the motorcycle, the workings of the motor, the precision—he had a different love for it. Working with motors, he felt skillful, happy, calm. If only . . .

Two years he'd been here at Josef Strohmayer's, servicing cars, pumping gas, wearing the brown overall with *Strohmayer's Reparatur* embroidered in red on the back. If he could only get his hands on some money! If, if, if! It was always *if*. But *if* he could, he'd open his own place, he'd specialize in motorcycles. Chewing a toothpick, he brooded.

A car horn blasted. An open Volkswagen had stopped at the pump, three girls were in it, all pretty, all in those loose sweaters. He almost bared his teeth in anger. Bitches! He had taken this job with Strohmayer's partly because it was near the university, in an area full of girl students in show-off tight jeans that accented their rounded behinds, and in those loose sweaters without brassieres underneath. Hans had said the new ones would be easy to get, especially the foreign ones, especially if you caught them early, before they'd made any friends. "Like newborn kittens," Hans had said, "eyes not open yet." Bitches! It was Hans Strohmayer's fault. He'd met Hans though the motorcycle club, Hans's father had needed someone to pump gas at the *reparatur werkstatt,* off Langegasse, near the university. Hans had said it would be like a dessert table, full of whipped cream and cakes. He'd liked that: a whole tableful. He liked to snake his hand up the back of a girl's head and twist, so that her eyes slanted back, and her mouth opened. Then he'd go to work on her—except that these university girls snubbed him in his brown overall with that red embroidery on the back. *Guten Morgen, Guten Abend, Grüss Gott,* Go to Hell. If he'd been the boss, if he'd been Strohmayer with a string of Strohmayer gas stations behind him, it would have been different. If, if, if! As it was, he still scrabbled around the Heurigers and wine taverns for girls. Sometimes he felt like a bird hopping after crumbs.

The car horn blasted again. *Jessas!* He'd fix those girls, he'd teach them to snub him. That girl in the Mödling woods, he thought, walking toward the Volkswagen, sexy enough to make a man hungry for it . . . which of course the *Neue Krönen* hadn't mentioned. And . . .

A random thought struck him, slowing him. Why was she in the woods anyway in high-heeled shoes without any backs to them, just a little strap? Who goes walking in the woods in shoes like that? Yet there she was near that skinny elm, just bending over and brushing dirt and leaves around with a stick, as though she had nothing else to do. Unless . . . unless she had been waiting for him to follow her from the coffee shop. Though from the way she went at him with her fingernails, he guessed not.

Near the elm. Peculiar. It was something to think about.

Approaching the Volkswagen, he put a hand on the car door, an inch away from where the girl driving rested her arm. *"Guten Morgen."* He stared hard into the girl's face, then down at her breasts. He said politely, yet somehow suggestively, "How can I . . . serve you?" and watched with satisfaction as the girl colored with embarrassment. That would humble her, rub a little dirt into her skin; then when he took her money it would stir him sexually. He repeated the ostensibly polite question, first licking his lower lip, then running his tongue slowly over it. *"Womit kann ich dem Fräulein . . . dienen?"*

Chapter 6

The moist jungle of Adalbert Brunner's rooftop greenhouse was already at ninety degrees from the morning sun, though it was hardly eight o'clock. The humid air smelled pungently of earth, the foliage so high and dense that Jason Foxe tried one narrow path, then another, without seeing Herr Brunner. Then, just beyond a towering plant with oval, white-veined leaves, he heard a soft, absent-minded humming as of a swarm of bees. He turned a corner and there on his knees, looking like an enormous brown beetle, was Adalbert Brunner, trowel in hand, blissfully humming away. He was patting dirt around a plant in a red earthenware pot, a plant with a single brilliant vermilion flower so erotically constructed as to make Jason's lips twist in involuntary amusement.

"Herr Brunner?"

The brown beetle looked up. He wore a cotton hat with a green celluloid brim, khaki pants, and a brown T-shirt that advertised Nissan cars. He was certainly not the correctly dressed Herr Adalbert Brunner of the immaculate little office downstairs with its gleaming files, computer, and polished toylike intercom through which Herr Brunner issued orders to the maids. Down in that office, Herr Brunner played like a child, played at a game called "running a pension" —in his case, obviously a profitable game. Up here in the greenhouse, he happily played botanist, creating his lush green universe. His wife Anna, quick, cheerful, and plump, left everything to him. She went her own way on a happy circuit of shopping trips, visits to the hairdresser, and gossip sessions on the telephone and over tea in pastry shops. There was also a married Brunner daughter, a chick not too long out of the protective Brunner barnyard, and needing the benefit of Frau Brunner's considerable marital knowledge.

"Guten Morgen, Herr Foxe." Adalbert Brunner tipped his head back so he could look squarely up at Foxe from under the green celluloid of the canvas hat. He had bright hazel eyes and a neatly trimmed, sand-colored beard. He looked shrewdly at Jason.

"Yes, to your unspoken inquiry, Herr Foxe. Yes, I read this morning's *Kurier*. I am abreast of the news, from politics to the kidnapping of young women."

Jason nodded. "So then, I won't embarrass you further with my presence, Herr Brunner. I'm sorry about all this. I'll pay my bill this morning. I can be packed by noon and move into a hotel." In fact, he had already begun to pack. "I've appreciated—"

"Bitte, Herr Foxe!" Adalbert Brunner sat back on his heels. "Despite your sensational reputation in the *Kurier*, I picture you as better at drinking champagne with Miss Hortense Wicks, and then . . . h'm. Red roses, eh? Miss Wicks, certainly. Oh, certainly! But not, certainly *not*, the sinister woods of, say the Prater, with a murderous heart and strangling hands." Herr Brunner shook his

head; he stroked his sandy beard. "I see no reason for you to leave the Brunner pension, Herr Foxe. I am no fool. I have no fears that—"

"But your other guests! It could drive them—"

"Puhh! Exactly the opposite, Herr Foxe! My other guests are visitors to Vienna on business or vacation. Do you know why many people choose pensions over hotels, Herr Foxe? Not always the cost, not that! Pensions are not always cheaper. You know that the Brunner pension certainly is not. But visitors love the coziness of a pension like mine. They enjoy the friendliness. Most of all, Herr Foxe, they want conversation. That's the real attraction of my pension. Conversation! They want to exchange ideas at the breakfast table, to boast, to form little friendships, to gossip. You see? My dear Herr Foxe, you are providing an extra service: a possible murderer at the breakfast table! Think what tales they can take back to Budapest, Lyons, Prague, Leipzig! 'He sat right next to me, he handed me the sugar—I can tell you, Clarissa, my flesh crawled!' 'I passed him in the upstairs hall, my sleeve brushed his, I thought: "I have touched a murderer! Horrible. That poor American girl!" '

"Your problem, Herr Foxe, will be to *escape* my guests' attentions. Drive them away? You will only wish it!" Herr Brunner gave a snort of laughter. He stood up, trowel in hand, fondly surveying his astonishingly erotic plant.

"By the way, Herr Foxe, I have you to thank for this new plant. You remember, on the evening that the American girl disappeared, besides sending your dozen red roses to Miss Hortense Wicks, you also sent me a plant. I presume it was to thank me for having the bigger desk moved into your room, and the two extra lamps, so that you'd be able to work better, yes?" And at Jason's nod, "Yes . . . Well, Herr Foxe, my tastes in the botanical are not identical to yours. I exchanged the plant you sent me, admirable as it was. I got this one instead. This beauty." Herr Brunner unwound a green plastic hose from a drum. "Look at this nozzle, a spray like a lady's perfume spritzer!" He turned on the water and a misty spray descended on the new plant. Clearly, the subject of Jason Foxe's leaving the pension was closed.

"Well, then . . ." Downstairs, he would unpack the few things he had already put in a suitcase. Later this morning he had a meeting with Professor Schindler at the university; and there was his own work to get on with.

"You're pleased with the Porsche?" Adalbert Brunner had turned off the spray. He was regarding Jason. The sun shining through the green celluloid brim cast a green shadow over his distinguished-looking face and beard. He looked like a green emissary from another planet.

"I have you to thank again, Herr Brunner." The little rented Porsche convertible, smelling of new leather—that, too, was Herr Brunner's doing. The Porsche came from an enterprising new car agency that Brunner had recommended; the rental price was lower than those of the company's competitors. Jason had begun to think of Adalbert Brunner from a sociological viewpoint, as a *helper* personality. The man disseminated helpful information the way wasps, bees, and other insects pollinated, from plant to plant, flower to flower.

"Good!" Adalbert Brunner looked pleased. "And now, about your shirts: She only does mine, she has done my shirts for years—and beautifully. Only mine . . . but occasionally, as a favor, when I ask for a friend—We've been neighbors here on Langegasse since I was born—neighbors except for the time of the Nazis." Adalbert Brunner no longer looked pleased; his lips twisted and he muttered something under his breath. "After the war, she got reparations money from the Austrian government, and she takes roomers. She needs money, but it is not for the money that she washes and irons my shirts. It is for something else."

Herr Brunner's hazel eyes focused dreamily on the past. "Before the war, when she was a young woman, she washed and ironed her husband's shirts. Can you believe, Herr Foxe, a woman who misses that? . . . The ironing in the kitchen, the peace of it, ironing shirts, standing in the kitchen ironing the shirts of someone you love?" There was sadness in Adalbert Brunner's voice. Then he blinked and looked around at the lush foliage of the greenhouse. "Sometimes she helps me here with the pruning and planting. She loves the greenhouse, growing things. During the war, she was hidden in the mountains above Merano. They ate from their garden; but even so, she tells me, they grew flowers. You have the address?"

"Yes, you gave it to me yesterday." He would stop there and drop off his shirts on the way to his meeting with Schindler.

Herr Brunner repeated the Langegasse address anyway, and the woman's name: Frau Martha Krieger Schratt.

In her room, Veronica took the shabby Air France bag from the closet. This dirty flight bag was now a friend. The inspiration to pretend to be a foreign student from France had come to her when she'd seen the bag in a pile of battered luggage at that secondhand place, Noch Einmal.

And this pension, Frau Schratt's, on Langegasse . . . Yesterday, already wearing the worn navy suit, she had stood in a doorway out of the rain, searching among the newspaper ads for the cheapest pension. Dazed and exhausted as she was, she had known enough to choose this one because the ad had said it was near the university; she could logically pretend to be a student. There was a cheaper pension advertised as well, but it was in another part of the city; so she had chosen Schratt's.

She put the Air France bag on the bed and drew out the three books from Noch Einmal. They were cheap and well thumbed. She had bought what the secondhand place had had. Ironically, one of the books even had a worn brown paper jacket with the University of Vienna seal on it. She looked at the titles. Political science! All of them. A subject she knew nothing about. But what difference did the subject make? The books were heavy too; thick and heavy. Well, as far as Frau Martha Krieger Schratt would know, she was a French student from Rouen studying political science at the University of Vienna.

She slung her jumbo bag over her shoulder, but she carried the heavy books in her arms, the one with the University seal on top. About to leave the room, she glanced into the mirror. Pale face, no lipstick, so pinched, so *ugly*, and with that ragged haircut. But what did any of that matter? All that mattered was that she must somehow rescue herself. Incredible, strange, but she did not, *could not* feel she had committed a ... a murder. It was not that she was refusing to admit to a terrible crime: there was an *X*, an unknown factor that had operated in that office on the Opernring—something strange that she had sensed but could not put her finger on. But she must! She must! Otherwise ... She shivered. There was something she must start searching for, and find. Quickly.

But she did not know what it was.

She turned finally, helplessly, from the mirror, pushed the violet-tinted glasses higher on her nose, pulled down the back of her shabby navy blue jacket, and left the room. She carefully locked the door behind her. In the hall, she thrust the key deep into her shoulder bag.

Wearily, she started down the hall.

Nearing the foyer, she heard voices: Frau Schratt's and a man's. Herr Herbst? But the accountant had left twenty minutes ago, directly after breakfast.

She came into the square foyer. Frau Schratt, her back to Veronica, was standing next to the baroque console table with the marble top; a sizable bundle in a blue pillowcase rested on the table. Frau Schratt was talking with a tall, dark-haired young man. "Today is ... let's see, Wednesday. Is Monday morning all right? Early?"

"Fine." Past Frau Schratt's shoulder, the man glanced at her. *"Guten Morgen."* He had a baritone voice. He wore a V-necked gray sweater over an open-throated white shirt, and he was tanned and somehow conveyed an easy sense of well-being. His dark hair, thick and curly, was close cropped, his face arresting, dark-browed, and flat-cheeked, with a jutting mouth. It was a face that would draw glances. "Fine," he repeated; he was still looking at her.

"Guten Morgen." She wanted to slip past, but she'd have to go around Frau Schratt and the man stood squarely in the doorway. Besides, Frau Schratt had turned and was already introducing them. Herr Foxe. *Foxe!* There must be dozens of people in Vienna named Foxe; it didn't have to be this one! But she must have paled. Frau Schratt had noticed.

"Herr Foxe comes recommended by a friend, a neighbor I have known for forty years ... a gentleman whose judgment I trust."

So it *was* that Foxe, the suspect. And Frau Schratt knew it, she had heard the same radio broadcast. Frau Schratt knew and she didn't care, didn't fear.

"Monday, then ..." Jason Foxe was thanking Frau Schratt. He opened the front door and waited for Fräu-

lein Montcalm to precede him. She had no choice. They
left together, Frau Schratt closing the door after them.
Walking down the stairs, Jason Foxe behind her, she kept
a steadying hand on the iron balustrade; it was orna-
mented on the underside, with small iron roses that her
fingertips bumpily negotiated. Yet if she did not hold on
she knew her trembling legs might give way. On the
mezzanine floor, Foxe's voice at her shoulder, polite,
incurious; "So you're a student, Fräulein Montcalm?"

She shifted the heavy books. "Yes, at the university."
With sudden anxiety, she realized that when they
reached the street, she would not know in which direction
the university lay. If this Jason Foxe did know, and she
started off in the wrong direction, he would notice. Her
tiniest mistake could somehow ... do what? Wasn't it
such infinitesimal errors that gave fugitives away?

Outside on the street, in front of the gloomy old rococo
apartment building stood a gleaming little Porsche convertible, the top down. "Glad to give you a lift," Jason
Foxe said. "I'm on my way to the university myself."

She had no alternative, she dared not even hesitate ...
yet she hesitated. She stood there, clutching the heavy
books. Jason Foxe was eying her burden. "You need a
mule for a load like that. The day will come when
students will press a button and class material will pop up
on a screen in your own study." But now, as she stood
there, he was looking at her more closely; she could
almost feel his dark gaze taking in her faded pink blouse
and the miserably-fitting, old navy suit, the run-down
shoes and brown stockings. All of her seemed to fall
under his scrutiny: the ragged haircut, even the curve of
her jaw. Then he shrugged.

"I assure you, Mademoiselle Montcalm, I am innocent. I did not kidnap the American girl and gruesomely

do away with her. It is perhaps ten blocks to the university, no more. You'll be safe with me."

Now he was studying her face; she did not know where to look. He went on, the baritone shading to the ironic: "I can even go by way of Trautsohngasse and past Parliament, the very seat of Austrian rectitude . . . or perhaps you would prefer by way of Josefstaderstrasse and almost into the very arms of the august Town Hall? *Not* of course on the park side, with its shady trees that cast dark shadows—certainly not!—but on the west, the innocently flat, open-to-the-sky Franz Schmidt Platz." He was laughing at her! It was unmistakable. "But I won't pressure you, Fräulein Montcalm."

Helpless, scenting danger, she stood there. Any contact with this suspected man, Jason Foxe, could be dangerous. The police must be watching him. Yet there *he* stood, watching *her*. She glanced down the street, hoping for a clue as to which way the university lay. Bicyclists were going past in both directions—boys, girls, a couple of young women in tailored suits and sensible shoes, their purses in their bicycles' wire baskets; even an executive with a briefcase, pedaling. None of the young bicyclists had books strapped to their carriers, nor did anyone walking along the street carry books. It was a fifty-fifty chance she would start down the street in the wrong direction. Dare she risk it?

She gave up. "Thank you."

Jason Foxe opened the car door and she got in.

It was the kind of crisp, clear Viennese morning that Austrian poets wrote nostalgically about, a challenging morning that lured schoolchildren into playing hookey and office workers to noontime assignations. The city was still green and green-smelling in early September; trimly clipped yew hedges bordered parks and park paths. Linden trees were thick with leaves.

The new leather that upholstered the Porsche smelled headily of luxury, the seats were soft and butter-colored; the car was dappled with sun and shade as it traveled up Langegasse. But within blocks, they came to a traffic jam; they slowed, stopped. Word filtered back that there was a collision at the corner of Floriangasse.

So they sat there in the sunlight for the next ten minutes, during which Herr Foxe, glancing down at Fräulein Montcalm's books, expressed surprise and curiosity at her field of interest. He looked at her with careless inquiry. Fräulein Montcalm's only response was to slide her hands so nervously up and down the strap of her shoulder bag that Herr Foxe lifted an eyebrow and immediately turned the subject to himself. Fräulein Montcalm learned that Herr Foxe was in Vienna on a six-month grant from a Texas Foundation and that he taught sociology at Bowdoin College in Maine. "Longfellow's college," he explained. "An American poet—the Longfellow of *Hiawatha*, an Indian poem. Also the author of *Evangeline*, a narrative poem about the French Huguenots who migrated to Canada . . . but likely not well known in France." No, Fräulein Montcalm murmured, not well known, "at least not in Rouen."

Herr Foxe went on to say that he had lived in this neighborhood, on Piaristengasse the year he was an exchange student in Vienna. He and a roommate had shared a room in a turn-of-the-century building—plaster cupids and garlands on the ceiling, crocheted antimacassars on their two heavy old Biedermeier chairs, two iron bedsteads. It had been like living in the *fin-de-siècle* period. "We used to blink when we came out into the streets and saw 1970s' cars."

In response to this information, Fräulein Nicca Mont-

calm stretched her neck up and craned her head to the
side to see what was happening up ahead. Something
was. A policeman with a whistle in his mouth was ener-
getically beckoning traffic; cars moved, picked up speed.
Within minutes the Porsche passed Franz Schmidt Platz
with its flat, sun-smitten greenery.

"I'll let you off on Universitatsstrasse because"—
Fräulein Montcalm was conscious of Herr Foxe's quick
sidewise look—"I'm going to park in the underground
parking garage next to the Votivekirche—that labyrin-
thine underground, that shadowy subterranean garage
where lurk hidden . . . who knows what?"

Definitely, he was definitely laughing at her again. She
turned her head and looked at him, at his flat-cheeked yet
attractive face. Around the jutting mouth hovered the
ghost of a smile. A solid sense of himself, oddly reassur-
ing, rose from his lean frame. He bore the burden of
police suspicion well, because, of course, he was certain
of his own innocence.

She wished she could lift that burden from her own
mind, but she could not.

"So it's the Universitatsstrasse?" her suspected kid-
napper-murderer was asking again.

"If you don't mind."

In the barracks-like Rossauerkaserne, in a room two
floors down from his office, Inspector Trumpf looked at
the long steel table laden with boxes of clothing. He
frowned at the effort to nail down how he felt—then
suddenly he had it: tenacious. That was it: tenacious.
Because here he was again, drawn back to Veronica
Kent's effects . . . like an elephant on tiptoe, examining
them. He could almost feel his sensitive elephant trunk,
with its tiny, miraculously sensitive hairs swaying over
the clothes. He was going to sniff out a lead to this

vanished girl, he knew it. There would be something . . . a torn scrap of paper with a house address . . . the address of a nightclub . . . a scrawled telephone number. Once, four years ago, in a disappearance, he had found the address of a shoemaker's shop; and when the shoemaker opened the door, the police had pushed in to find, in a locked room at the back, a horror which—He shook his head. He looked around.

"Pepi, shove that box over here." It was a cardboard carton, property of the Vienna Police Department. It held the only effects of Veronica Kent that Trumpf had not yet examined. He had gone through the rest of the girl's possessions meticulously. He had even run his fingertips carefully into the toes of the black saddle shoes, the sheepskin-lined bedroom slippers, the inside of a pair of well-used ski boots. He had turned out the pockets of jackets, sweaters, and a poplin jacket. He had looked inside the pockets of a soft, reddish fake-fur coat that he could have sworn at first was real fox; it had a satin lining and was feather-soft, the kind of coat Klara would love. Maybe he should get her one like it for Christmas? Klara's beaver could still be her good coat. He picked up the carton, put it on the table, and tugged open the flaps.

"Inspector?" It was Staral in the doorway. "The chief . . . it's a quarter past . . . he's waiting."

Trumpf looked at his new wristwatch with the expandable steel band and the extra little calculator buttons. It told the day, date, time; it was water resistant and a stopwatch besides. Also, it had an alarm for which he'd set to chime on the hour so he wouldn't be late for his meeting with Fuhrmann. But the verdammte watch hadn't chimed. Or maybe he'd set it wrong. He'd have another look at the instructions, that tiny print on the tissue-thin instruction sheet . . . if he hadn't thrown it away.

"I'm coming." At the door he glanced back regretfully. That carton . . . He hated to stop now, hated to wait; there had to be something, it was in there—in that carton. With his elephant trunk delicately searching he would sniff it out. He knew it.

The coffeehouse on Dorothergasse had a narrow, modest entrance. Veronica paused. Her arms ached from carrying the heavy books. She felt she had been carrying them halfway around the world, though it was only an hour since Jason Foxe had let her out of the Porsche on Universitatsstrasse. She had walked and walked, aimlessly, trying to look as though she had a purposeful destination. At least the violet-tinted glasses hid the dark smudges under her eyes, and the hunted-animal look that might make people take a second glance at her. The brown shoes were too wide for her narrow feet; she had laced them tightly, but the heels rubbed painfully. She could feel blisters coming. She was trembling.

Hawelka, the sign over the coffeehouse said. It could be a refuge while Frau Schratt thought she was at university classes. She turned in.

One square room, a jumble of round small tables and comfortable chairs. There was a banquette of worn red plush and an old mahogany antlered hatrack. The walls, partly paneled in dark wood, were thick with paintings and posters. An elderly waiter was busy at an old stove behind a counter; a few customers sat drinking coffee and reading. The room was quiet except for the rustling of magazine and newspaper pages turning. Peace; a haven.

She found a seat. The waiter came from the stove, he had a gentle face and wore a white apron. *"Guten Morgen."*

She almost replied in German, then caught herself and answered in French. Immediately she apologized, switched to German, and ordered coffee. *Keep in mind that you are a French student*, she warned herself fiercely. *It is your disguise.*

Minutes later, as she sat over her coffee, the waiter gently nudged her shoulder. *"Bitte,"* and he laid a copy of *L'Express* and a copy of *Marie-Clair* on the table. *"Wir haben alles:* France Soir, Elle—*alles!"* Smiling, he indicated the newspaper rack and a table of magazines.

"Danke schon." She trembled, on the edge of tears at his gentleness.

On the wall a big, hexagon-shaped clock ticked away the morning. She took tiny sips of coffee and pretended to be immersed in *Marie-Claire*. The few customers who came in greeted the waiter by name, and she realized this was Herr Hawelka himself. At eleven o'clock, he busied himself with baking an apricot cake. The delicious smell of the Marillenkuchen baking in the stove was torture. Breakfast this morning at Frau Schratt's had been her only food since Monday. Now it was Wednesday.

The terrible thing was being in limbo: Nothing out there in Vienna was happening to guide her; she was floating on a tide that went neither in nor out. On Graben, before turning in to Dorotherngasse, she had passed a radio-television ship. Outside a radio had been playing, she had stopped to listen. But the local news bulletin was again about the American girl's disappearance: A respected business man, a Herr Franze Mahler, jeweler, had reported meeting a Miss Gaylord in the Mödling woods. Miss Gaylord resembled astonishingly the passport picture of Veronica Kent. She had been wearing a tan skirt and sweater, she had blue eyes and shiny brown hair that swung as she walked. Herr Mahler and his wife had driven the young woman back to Vienna; she had said she was staying at the Imperial. But according to the police, no Miss Gaylord was registered at the Imperial. Dead end.

On the radio, the newscaster had announced, "With me now is Herr Leon Kraus, amateur criminologist. Herr Kraus's popular "Liebe Leute" program is heard over this station every Friday evening at seven o'clock." A pause, then: "Herr Kraus."

"Guten Morgen, meine lieben Leute!" An oil-smooth voice with a lilting innuendo. "Since when does Vienna's criminal investigation department move with such elephantine slowness? Or with such arbitrary blindness! While a young woman's body may lie weighted with stones at the bottom of the Danube, or savaged and buried in the Vienna Woods, *where is the Foxe*? The Foxe of 'ferocious' lusts? Perhaps at this minute he sits smugly in his *Stammcafé*, his favorite café, over an Einspänner . . . or does he sip, at ease, a *Mélange mit Schlag*? Why *meine lieben Leute*, does the criminal investigation department not cage the Foxe? What has happened to *Öffentliche Sicherheit? Where is Public Security? Meine lieben Leute*, I leave you to ponder that frightening question!"

On Hawelka's wall, the hexagon-shaped clock struck. Eleven-fifteen.

The badgered Foxe. But he needn't worry: any instant now, the gold-toothed waiter would recognize the passport picture, and the trail would lead to Herr von Reitz. She suddenly had a repellent picture of the police questioning a plump, bloody, recumbent Herr von Reitz who, though dead, pursed a small, bloodless mouth before each studied reply as to how Veronica Kent had killed him.

Involuntarily, she moaned.

"Bitte?" Herr Hawelka was bending over her, gentle face anxious.

She covered her confusion. *"Ja, danke—Noch einen*

Kleinen Braunen, bitte." It was the cheapest coffee, fifteen schillings, and it had a dash of milk. She would add plenty of sugar.

The hexagonal clock struck again. Eleven-thirty of a timeless time, time that drooped like Dali's bent watch. She felt time stretching like elastic, time shrinking her into a tiny waiting figure, she could see time booming her into a giant at the end of a telescopic lense. She felt dizzy. Hunger? She was suddenly terrified that she might faint. Blood to the head, that was it; it had been in her Girl Scout manual. She dropped her teaspoon on the floor. She bent down to pick it up, pretending to grope beneath the table for the spoon, giving herself time for the blood to rush to her head. *Do not faint.*

"Bitte gnädiges Fraülein, ein Kaffeelöffel."

She came up slowly. She took the clean spoon. *"Danke, Herr Hawelka. Die Rechnung, bitte."*

She paid the bill. Then, still sitting, she at last let the thought lurking in the back of her mind take hard shape. The strange yet possible deduction took possession of her: *I only imagine Herr von Reitz is dead. I did not kill him. He is alive and going about his law business in another city, in Hamburg. The bronze parrot—I only injured him with the bronze parrot. I mistook—in my hysterical state—jet lag, the champagne, the syringe, I thought—*

It could be that! It was possible! That was why the media was not reporting the terrible murder: *There had been no murder!* She was hiding *for no reason.* All this torture was self-torture. It was based on her own crazy—

Of course! Hungry, wretched, terrified, *for no reason.* Was it possible? Yes. She looked at the clock. Eleven-thirty-five.

She had to make sure. She got up.

She knew where she was going—to that law office on the Opernring.

* * *

The French girl, Nicca Montcalm ... that slender figure walking along the Opernring, wasn't that Frau
Schratt's roomer? That was Vienna for you! Barely two
hours before, he'd dropped her off on Universitatsstrasse,
and now, as he drove along the Opernring in the Porsche,
there she was again. He slowed the car. He couldn't resist
the idea of offering her a lift twice in two hours. It would
certainly startle her. His lips twitched. He drew the
convertible to the curb and sounded the horn. "Fräulein
Montcalm!"

She did not seem to hear, she kept on walking, not
turning her head.

"Fräulein Montcalm!" Didn't the girl know her own
name? "It's Foxe! Jason *Foxe!*"

At that, she stopped dead. She turned a startled face.
It was Nicca Montcalm, all right: those lilac-colored
glasses that covered half her face, that chopped-off hair
that made her look like some little pickpocket out of
Oliver Twist. And that faded pink blouse. The girl puzzled him. Why, for instance, would a girl from Rouen
come to study in Vienna instead of going to Paris? Did
the University of Vienna have a better department of
political science than the Sorbonne? He'd bet not—not
by a long shot!

"Fräulein Montcalm! Can I give you a lift? Consider
me your chauffeur!" He was early for his appointment
with Florian Königsmark on Zaunergasse, outside the
Ring; besides, if the girl was walking, wherever she was
going, it wouldn't be far.

Instead of coming to the car, she stood immovable.
"Vielen Dank, Herr Foxe ... but no. I have errands
in ... in this vicinity." She was standing as though her
feet had grown roots, she was never going to move, people
walking in both directions flowed around her, she was an
island.

"Right . . . Auf Wiedersehen." He took off.

In the rear-view mirror, he saw her still rooted, motionless; he had the idea she would not take a step until he was out of sight. Why not? Wary because he was The Foxe, suspected of some unspeakable violence? That made sense. She had been edgy in the car; but she was no fearful neurotic about men, not this girl. There was something . . . well, *mutig*—courageous—about her, something in the curve of her delicate jaw that suggested she could handle sexual advances pretty adroitly.

He turned the corner. She was now out of sight. Sexual advances, yes, she probably had plenty. In spite of the faded blouse and the ragged haircut and her paleness, she was a girl you couldn't help looking at. It was more than her figure, more than the shape of her face, the way her hair grew at her temples—no, he could not define it. Chemical appeal. He wondered what her eyes behind those glasses were like. . . .

But of course, he himself was indifferent to Fräulein Montcalm. He was indifferent to every woman he saw. His heart lay Xeroxed on the desk in his room at Brunners', in a sheaf of papers. His emotions were so focused on what might have befallen Veronica Kent that every hour he telephoned the Rossauerkaserne for news. And always, generally from Detective Staral, Inspector Trumpf's assistant, he got the same stock answer: No further news. That stone wall led him to intolerable imaginings: he nightmared her into the hands of—What? Sadists, sodomists, perverts crazed with drugs?

A siren sounded. Coming toward him in the opposite direction was a cavalcade of stretch limousines. As the glistening cars slid smoothly past, he glimpsed dark-faced, turbaned Arabs. The oil-rich Arabs were meeting in Vienna to decide the price of crude. What if a lustful

Arab eye had turned itself on Veronica Kent? Nothing
was beyond imagining.

But he would deliver the mustard-colored notebook to
Inspector Trumpf—at least that! And right now! He
made a sudden U turn and headed north. At the Rossauerkaserne he found the inspector busy at his desk,
alone except for Pepi reading near the dusty window. He
gave the notebook to the inspector, apologizing. "I work
so much with these same notebooks, that I automatically—" He stopped. The inspector would believe him, or
not. "Anyway, there it is. I suppose you missed it."

The inspector was studying him from beneath those
eyebrows that looked like overused toothbrushes, bristles
all awry. "Sit down, Herr Foxe . . . yes, there, fine. Yes,
Herr Foxe, I missed the notebook. So, Herr Foxe, you
took the notebook, ah . . . *innocently?*"

His jaw tightened. "As a babe in arms."

"I see. And now, Herr Foxe, now you are returning the
notebook. Exactly. *Intact,* of course . . . Herr Foxe?"

"Intact." Bitter realization swept him: Trumpf suspected that he had stolen the notebook, stolen it to rip out
incriminating pages, notes Veronica Kent might have
made about him. Christ! Forget about offering to help in
the search for Veronica Kent. The inspector would
assume his offer was a trick, a Jason Foxe trick to
monitor the criminal investigation, to protect himself.

He rose to go, but the inspector held up a hand. *"Bitte,
Herr Foxe."* He sat back down. The inspector fidgeted
with a pencil, frowning; his heavy face was reddening.
Foxe realized in amazement that the inspector was
blushing.

The inspector cleared his throat; he coughed. "Pepi,
bitte, get me a fresh thermos of water, let it run very
cold."

The boy gone, the inspector dropped the pencil and looked squarely at Foxe.

"Ferociously," he brought out. "An extraordinary word in a note with roses to a young lady ... *nicht wahr?*" His eyes bored into Foxe's. "Extraordinary ... *Hab'ich nicht recht?*"

"Ferociously?"

What the hell? ... But the inspector's reddened face enlightened him: he was suspected of some sort of stomach-turning savagery, unknown and frightening. And his looks contributed, he knew how they impressed people: His face was too dramatic, too lean and dark with the flat cheeks that made the sensuous mouth stand out. It was a face to associate with dark passions—a hell of a face for a serious sociologist ... but there it was.

"An inside joke, Inspector." The humor was peculiarly American, would Trumpf understand? He tried to explain: Ferociously had been a key word, a joke word, among Hortense Wicks's fashion staff. It had sprung into being at Adalbert Brunner's pension when the American photographer had instructed the Austrian model to look "ferociously" into the camera; but the girl could not comprehend why, though she was posing in a white satin gown whose bodice was embroidered with black sequin cats. "Ferociously!" the photographer had kept shouting, exasperated. "The camera is a big mouse, Fräulein! A big mouse! So, a fantasy! *Bitte, Fräulein!* Ferociously!" And the photographer had made fierce, clawing gestures. "Ah, *ferociously.*" Light dawned on the model's face. Ferociously had instantly become the crew's joke word: changing outfits in a hurry had become changing ferociously, sandwiches brought in from Zum Weissen Schwan were more ferociously thick with ham than from Zur Traube; Miss Wicks's assistant was ferociously in need of more borrowed jewelry for the shooting.

"They were working hard, Inspector. It lightened the tension. Instant humor." No response. "A buzz word, Inspector, it made the crew laugh and relax." How could he explain buzz word? The sociologist stirred in him. "A buzz word—"

The inspector held up a hand. "I understand."

Jason Foxe doubted it. Even the inspector's rumpled brown suit seemed to spell disbelief. "You do?" he said dryly.

The inspector said heavily: "*Sicherlich* . . . certainly! I see that you are only telling me what you affirmed at the Hilton, that you sent the roses to Miss Hortense Wicks, fashion editor . . . not to Miss Kent."

He was on his feet, tightlipped. "Check with the fashion outfit, they're still in Vienna. The model is Austrian, Viennese. Simple enough."

"*Natürlich.*" The inspector was equally short; but his mind seemed suddenly occupied elsewhere. "But even if true, that doesn't rule out—" He stopped. "Never mind, Herr Foxe. *Guten Morgen.*"

So where had he gotten?

Leaving the Rossauerkaserne, he slammed a fist into his palm: Forget Jason Foxe, Inspector. For Christ's sake, get on with the search! *Find Veronica Kent.*

Chapter 7

"So let me quote George Bernard Shaw," Jason Foxe said, "on love."

He stood behind Florian, who was sketching in the back room of the Königsmark Gallery—Florian's gallery—which specialized in bird paintings. He had arrived late, not that, with Florian, it made any difference. Parking the car a few minutes before, he had wondered idly if Nicca Montcalm had finished her errands on the Opernring. It was just past noon.

"So?" Florian kept on drawing.

Florian Königsmark sat on a high, specially constructed stool. It had a heavily padded swivel seat, half-arms, and no back. Ballbearing wheels allowed Florian to grasp the drawing board, push off, and sail himself across the room. He did not have to use his crippled leg at all.

Florian was big and blond, with a powerful upper body, and a broad, freckled face marked with pain. His gray eyes seemed always awash with distant vistas, even when he was politely dealing with an admiring public of naturalists, zoologists, artists, collectors, and tourists. He was twenty-nine, four months older than Jason Foxe. But he looked forty. Pain depleted his energy, and strong, labial lines from his nose to the corners of his mouth gave him a cynical look. It was a false impression. He was humorous and, as he himself was aware, only faintly, wryly bitter. He walked with a cane, leaning heavily on it. His BMW had special controls and a handicapped sticker in the windshield. He hated the sticker.

Twelve years ago, when Jason had come upon Florian sketching in the zoological wing of the Naturhistoriches Museum, Florian, then eighteen, had had two good legs. At sixteen, he was already a junior ski-jumping champion in the Tyrol. His interest in birds was an amateur's pleasure. Florian's true passion was skiing. At nineteen, he competed in the Olympics. At twenty, he married Lisl Haberstadt, who was as passionate and competitive a skier as Florian. She was a handsome, laughing girl with sturdy legs and a hearty appetite for skiing, food, and sex. Early in the marriage, Florian had written Jason, "We make love, we eat, we ski. That is our life. What philistines we are! I find little time now to read or sketch. We have a television set, even in the kitchen. Lisl insisted. Now we don't miss any of the competitions, even while making supper."

Six months after the marriage, the catastrophe: at a Tyrol competition, a gust of wind threw Florian off balance while he was forty feet in the air. When he landed— a single, terrible scream. For almost a year afterward, he lay in bed, sunk in depression, watching ski competitions on TV. The skiers he watched were former friends and acquaintances. But good-hearted as they were, they had no time for him. He was no longer part of their life. Lying in bed, he pretended not to overhear Lisl's whispered telephone conversations, giggling, sexually inviting. "I act the duped fool when she appears in the bedroom door," he had written Jason, "and says she is meeting a friend to go to the movies. She has already had two affairs that I know of. Now it is with Theodor. This weekend they are at Innsbruck for the competition—and sharing a bed. Well, she is human. I am still in a cast. But even when the cast goes, I won't be sexually adequate, at least not for Lisl. Perhaps I never was." Then, three months later, another letter: "Lisl is gone. I sent her away, we will be divorced. We parted friends. She could not help it that she hated being 'tied to a cripple' as I once heard her whisper on the phone. She sat on the bed and we both cried a little and drank a bottle of chilled Gumpoldskirchner. I even made her laugh! She is so relieved, poor girl! She was too loyal to leave me on her own—or not brave enough. Who knows?" A month after Lisl's departure, he had begun to sketch again.

Florian now lived with his parents and younger brother in Vienna's nineteenth district, an elegant district near Grinzing. The Königsmark family was rich, through rented lands. They were also Viennese blue bloods, cousins to Baron Willy von Walenberg and his mother, the old Baronin, who lived in Schloss Walenberg, a thirteenth-century castle in Styria, south of Vienna. Several times, Jason had driven with Florian to Schloss Walenberg to photograph birds in the castle's woodlands. Skinny little Baron Willy, now in his fifties, had eagerly wined and dined the pair of them. Now Baron Willy basked in the reflected glory of his cousin Florian's reputation. Florian's forthcoming book, *Birds of Austria*, was his second volume. It was half text, half Florian's remarkable drawings that were largely watercolor, but sometimes combined watercolor, crayon, pencil, pastel, and even oil. Advance copies of the book had been widely praised; comparisons with Audubon had been drawn. Baron Willy had ordered fifty autographed copies to distribute to his friends.

"Love?" Florian drew back, narrowing his eyes critically at his sketch. "Assuming Shaw knew anything about love, which I doubt. I know his works by heart. And who could figure out those love equations in his private life! But, anyway—*Bitte*. Proceed."

"Well, Shaw wrote: 'Who has ever wanted to sleep with the Venus de Milo? Ninety-nine hundredths of the sentiments in the world, including the maddest infatuations, are asexual. . . . ' "

Florian put down the brush; he raised his arms high in the air, stretching cramped muscles. "Lunch time. I hope you're hungry. I ordered from Rosslacher's." He swiveled the chair to face Jason *"The maddest infatuations.* So you're in love with a girl you've never met? . . . The girl from the notebook?"

"Apparently."

Florian gave a bark of a laugh. "If you were to meet that particular girl, your love would cease to be asexual. I assure you! That passport picture, I saw it on color television, the girl's eyes alone—"

The door buzzer interrupted him; it was the boy from Rosslacher's. Jason went through to the gallery, took in the lunch, paid the boy, and straightened the Closed: 11:30 to 2:30 sign. He locked the door and returned to the workroom. Florian had propelled himself to a table against the wall and set out silver, china, and linen napkins. Classical music poured from a radio on a shelf. "All the comforts of a Konzertcafé, *nicht wahr*?" He took the lunch from Foxe and set it out: cold trout with cucumber sauce, dark bread, cheese and apples. From a small refrigerator he selected a bottle of Reisling. *"Also, setz' dich."* And when Jason had pulled up a chair:

"They are closer to finding her?"

Jason shook his head. "Tibet is closer. . . . The reports are that the girl in the tan sweater and skirt in the Mödling woods couldn't have been Veronica Kent; the difference in clothing is too inexplicable. Also, the police scoured the Mödling woods and found nothing. The Mahlers' lead has been discounted."

"So the telescope is again trained on the Foxe?"

"Right . . . with the help of that bastard radio criminologist, Kraus. All to entertain his *lieben Leute*. He screams about the Foxe Affair of the Roses. The 'Foxe Affair' was even in the crossword puzzle in yesterday's *Kurier*. Next they'll have T-shirts with 'Catch the Foxe.' "

Florian poured the pale Reisling. "They have no other leads. You're the only fox in sight, so the media bays like dogs on your trail. A social commentator—an American, I believe—once said, 'News is what people think they read in the newspapers.' "

Jason raised his wineglass. "To Herr Leon Kraus then, Master of the Hounds, bugle—"

The concerto on the radio abruptly broke off. *"Sondernachrichten!"* came a commentator's excited voice, "Newsbreak! Herr Otto von Reitz murdered! The body of well-known lawyer, Otto von Reitz was found at noon today by employees in the von Reitz offices on the Opernring."

The commentator's voice machine-gunned the news: Herr von Reitz's body . . . private office . . . dead apparently two, three days . . . "Death appears to have been inflicted by a blow on the head." A heavy bronze ornament in the shape of a parrot had been found near the body.

"Poor bastard." Florian muttered, eyes awash with distant vistas.

The newsbreak continued: "Herr Alfred Kleiner, manager of the law office, states that the von Reitz staff was under the impression that Herr von Reitz was away on business in Geneva and Hamburg." A pause, a rustle of paper; then more information: Herr Kleiner had further stated that office personnel had not entered Herr von Reitz's private office when he was out of town. They assumed it was locked, since he always kept it locked when he was away. Herr von Reitz was very particular about his personal effects being tampered with, and there were valuable family portraits on the walls. Only an increasingly persistent odor, stated Herr Kleiner, finally led him to try the door. He had found it unlocked.

"Thank God I've got a strong stomach," Florian said, wryly. "Nothing like a little stomach-turning news with the trout."

"Who is this 'well-known' Herr von Reitz?"

"Von Reitz? Rich. A prominent, powerful family. Big corporation lawyer. His wife is the sister of a former ambassador, Gustav Bulheim. Bulheim is still a diplomatic bigwig, he now heads a government department, finance. Magazines aimed at the upper social strata always show the von Reitzes at their villa in Klosterneuburg—Sophie von Reitz, the wife, with her dogs; the garden, tennis courts, the usual. Sophie's brother, Bulheim, is honorable, starched stiff with honor—fierce too. He'll see that the criminal investigation department gets to the bottom of this killing. And—" he held up the crystal glass of wine and twirled it—"the murderer will get what von Reitz got. With an extra thumbscrew or two."

"A lethal world." Jason Foxe helped himself to a wedge of cheese. "Taste its joys while you can."

* * *

The von Reitz murder.

Inspector Leo Trumpf was a romantic. Three things intrigued him: Desire, death, and one's destiny. These three, like interweaving themes in a musical composition, propelled him in his investigations.

And now, this von Reitz murder: He had a strong feeling that this killing contained all three of his themes, though as yet only one was apparent: Death.

But another—unexpected, incredible—was surfacing. It set the inspector pacing his office, exultant. He was pleased with himself—no, delighted! That other thing, seemingly so unrelated to Herr von Reitz's murder! He smiled with satisfaction; his hand strayed to the bulge in the pocket of his brown jacket. A surge of exhilaration filled him. His stubborn, investigative persistence was now married to his peripheral vision and what surprising fruit they had borne!

Impatient, he glanced at his watch. Eight-twenty. At eight-thirty, he was due in the chief's office, their Thursday morning meeting. He was exhausted, his eyes grainy. Until midnight he had been in the forensic laboratory where Herr von Reitz's body was undergoing an autopsy. The results of the tissue sample would wind up the forensic examination; the medical examiner would have a full report for him by Friday night or early Saturday.

So. He patted the bulge in his pocket.

He entered the chief's office. In a moment he would have the pleasure of doing a Hercule Poirot. He had left Pepi in his own office down the hall, Pepi's face still puffy with sleep. Pepi had almost made him late, getting blueberry stains on his T-shirt at breakfast. They had not been able to find him another clean shirt. They had finally taken a soiled but cleaner-looking T-shirt from the hamper. Tonight, Inspector Trumpf would put everything in the washing machine. Meanwhile . . .

"Coffee?" The chief took one look at Trumpf, then swiveled around to his coffee machine and filled a plastic cup. "Black, no sugar." He handed it over. "So." The chief riffled through a half-dozen documents on his desk. "Under which shells are the various peas? You want to start with? ... "

"The von Reitz murder. An extraordinary—"

The intercom buzzed. The chief picked up the phone. "Yes?" Listening, he frowned, then raised his eyebrows forbearingly at the inspector. He sighed. "Send them in." He put down the phone. "*Verdammt!* Herr Gustav Bulheim, greatly agitated, and his confidential secretary ... Impossible! *Impossible* to get a day's work done with unannounced visitors! And I was hoping for a weekend holiday. But ... Gustav Bulheim! Under the circumstances I can hardly ... It is enough to make one a philosopher."

Two men entered. The inspector recognized Gustav Bulheim immediately, he had seen countless photographs of him in magazines and newspapers: Bulheim coming down the ramps of planes or the granite steps of public buildings, in the company of foreign dignitaries. With him was a slight, balding man in his thirties.

"*Entshuldigen Sie*, this precipitous visit!" apologized Herr Bulheim. "I come straight from my brother-in-law's in Klosterneuburg; all night I have been ..." He shook his head, spreading his hands. He introduced Herr Strobl, his confidential secretary. Herr Strobl dipped his head. He wore thick glasses and had yellowish skin.

Gustav Bulheim looked like an intelligent bulldog. His face was dark and horizontally creased, his brown eyes bulged slightly, and his thin, dark hair was polished flat to his broad skull. He was short, muscular, and skillfully tailored. He was a boxer, a fencer, and a gourmet, as well as a government official. Political opponents had found there was not an ounce of fat on his brain. He was tough, resilient, shrewd, but he was innately kind, a fact he kept well hidden. He was a widower, with a married daughter living in Paris. He had only one weakness: He was disproportionately vain when it came to the Bulheim family name. In his own opinion, he was merely proud of his antecedents. The Bulheims were descended from a landed, noble family in the Hungarian county of Torontal. Most of the Bulheims had performed remarkably well as vice consuls or consuls in the Austro-Hungarian consular service. A great-grandfather had been legation counselor in Warsaw in the time of Franz Josef. So why not be proud?

Now Herr Bulheim's bulldog face was drawn, the skin under his eyes sagged. He had not slept since he had received the news of his brother-in-law's murder. A telephone call from Herr Strobl had interrupted him at lunch at the Sacher with the Minister of Finance. He had raced immediately to the von Reitz villa in Klosterneuburg to be with his sister. Sophie von Reitz, his only sister, was a year younger. Their mother had died at an early age, and they had grown up on the family estate, best friends and playmates. At the villa in Klosterneuburg he had found Sophie alternately weeping and laughing hysterically, then in a frenzy, tearing at her hair. She had drunk half a bottle of Scotch before he had arrived. She had hurled the half-empty bottle at a group of newsmen, including the excessively persistent amateur criminologist, Leon Kraus, of *Meine Lieben Leute*. The bottle had smashed one of the French doors leading to the garden. The interlopers had given up and left when Sophie had locked herself in the study. Hearing her brother's voice, she had unlocked the door and fallen, weeping, into his arms. Her two daughters were vacationing in Italy with their families and could not be reached, so Gustav Bulheim had stayed up all night talking to his sister, trying to comfort her. Sometimes she had just stared at him, her eyes tragic in her swollen face, then she'd burst out laughing—that strange, hysterical laughter. Herr Bulheim had not been used to seeing such unleashed emotionalism in his sister, not since childhood. It had worn him out. The horizontal creases in his face curved downward. Inspector Trumpf felt sympathetic.

Seated in the chief's office, Herr Bulheim now offered the criminal investigation department whatever powerful assistance was at his disposal. As he did so, his hands were clenched as though he already had the murderer by the throat.

"*Danke schon*," the chief responded, and added that the von Reitz case was progressing: the forensic department had completed its investigations of the private office and had sealed the room, the autopsy was in progress. "Aside from that"—he looked inquiringly at Inspector Trumpf—"I believe, Inspector, you have some pertinent information you wish to? . . ."

Inspector Trumpf frowned at the chief. Gustav Bulheim was the victim's relative, an interested party. It was hardly criminal procedure—

"Inspector." The chief was smiling. "In light of Herr Bulheim's distinguished diplomatic career—and my certainty that we can depend on Herr Bulheim's discretion?" He smiled at the ex-diplomat, who said immediately, "And the discretion of my confidential secretary, Herr Strobl, I assure you, Inspector." His bulging bulldog eyes on Trumpf, he waited. Well, so be it. The inspector plunged.

"An unexpected aspect has come to light: A relationship appears to exist between the death of Herr von Reitz and the Foxe Affair. That is—"

"The Foxe Affair?" Incredulity brought Gustav

Bulheim bolt upright. "*Herrgott!* Foxe involved? The American? You mean, *he*—"

"*Bitte, Herr Bulheim!*" The chief held up an admonishing hand, a long pale hand that was as long and pale as his clever face. "*Bitte!* Step by baby step . . . one must avoid leaps in the dark."

Herr Bulheim's face was flushed with anger; for a moment it appeared he could not be stopped. His emotional reaction was so violent that the chief gave Trumpf their familiar, almost imperceptible signal, a flutter of his pale eyelids. It meant: Let him speak. Let the anguished person pour it out, let him wring out the bottle. "Life is too short," the chief had once said to Trump, "to be in a hurry."

But Gustav Bulheim, bulldog jaw working, got control of himself. He sank back in the chair, his creased face gray with exhaustion. "*Meine Herren, entschuldigen Sie, bitte.* You are questioning Herr Foxe about my brother-in-law's death?"

Trumpf said patiently, "It is not *Herr* Foxe, but the Foxe *Affair*, I wish to . . . An important avenue of investigation has opened up concerning Herr von Reitz's death. I will show you why." He tugged something from his jacket pocket. Persistent, he had been stubborn and persistent, and at last he had found among Veronica Kent's effects, what he had been looking for. It had taken a long time. He had found it at five o'clock yesterday evening in that last cardboard carton. Pepi, who was helping him, had actually found it. Pepi had held it up; and he, Inspector Trumpf, had recognized its significance.

Now he pulled from his pocket a clear plastic bag and took from it a small evening purse. The purse was brown satin, crushable, with an antique silver clasp. "Among Veronica Kent's effects were two evening purses, this one and another. But this one is of particular interest. That is because the lining is torn."

He paused; he looked from the chief to Gustav Bulheim, to Herr Strobl. " . . . And you know how it is with a torn lining." He smiled around at them. Then slowly, in the silence, he began to feel uncomfortable. Gustav Bulheim would never have a torn lining; neither would the chief. And it was absurd to think of torn linings in connection with the impeccably dressed Herr Strobl who was gazing at him expressionlessly through his thick glasses. Only he, Leo Trumpf, in shabby brown, knew about torn linings. Hercule Poirot would never have assumed— Trumpf sighed and cleared his throat:

"Caught under the lining was this." He held up a ten-schilling coin.

Again silence, mystified faces. Their puzzlement pleased him after his discomfort over the torn lining. "Now, Miss Kent arrived in Austria on Monday evening, her flight disembarking at six o'clock at Schwechat. A trace revealed that on arrival she changed American Express checks for Austrian money. Presumably, because it is natural, Miss Kent would have put the Austrian money in her wallet. *Richtig*?"

Three sets of eyes, watching, waiting.

"Yet we find this schilling in her evening bag. And we recollect—"

"That she went out for the evening and so would have put some schillings in the evening purse." It was Herr Strobl.

"*Danke, Herr Strobl.* More significantly, it means that Miss Kent *returned to the Hilton* that same evening— and left the purse. Then, for reasons we will conjecture in a moment, she *went out again*."

The chief was smiling at Trumpf, his familiar mouse-trap smile. Trumpf waited. "Why," demanded the chief, "can we not assume, Inspector, that the schilling in the evening purse was left from a previous visit to Austria—perhaps months ago even or earlier?"

"*Bitte*, the date on the schilling?" Herr Strobl again.

"*Danke, danke noch einmal, Herr Strobl.*" Trumpf was beginning to like Herr Strobl. A quick fellow. Herr Bulheim was lucky in his confidential secretary or he was a shrewd employer of personnel. "A brand-new schilling, Herr Strobl. Just issued."

Gustav Bulheim shifted in his chair. A black V formed between his brows. "What's all this got to do with my brother-in-law's murder?" He took out a morocco-covered cigar case, then put it back, unopened; his hands trembled with exhaustion. "*Entschuldigen Sie,*" he apologized. "Go on."

"I will postulate a simple scenario." Trumpf lifted a hand, extended a forefinger, and tapped it. "One: On Monday evening, Miss Kent received a dozen roses and a note. She dressed and went out to meet someone, presumably the sender of the roses, presumably to the Klimt Bar. But it was not Jason Foxe she met. I have learned, mostly through a 'buzz word'—later I will explain 'buzz word'—that Jason Foxe did indeed intend those red roses for Miss Wicks.

"But Miss Kent did meet someone. Where, we do not know. Whom? Let us call him Mr. *X*. Presumably, Miss Kent wore one of the roses, since Tuesday morning only eleven roses were in the vase; I myself counted them. The maid at the Hilton has since corroborated that Miss Kent wore a rose at her waist when she saw her in the corridor. So, wearing a red rose, Miss Kent met Mr. *X*.

"Two!" He tapped his middle finger: "The purse and schilling indicate that later in the evening Miss Kent returned to the hotel. In her room she changed from evening purse to wallet—no wallet has been found among

her effects. That implies that she also changed from
evening dress to daytime clothes, despite the fact that no
green evening dress was found among her belongings.

"Three: Miss Kent went out again; and has not been
seen since." Trumpf forgot about his fingers. He dropped
his hand. "The following information has not yet been
released by the criminal investigation department:
Approximately seventy to seventy-five hours after Miss
Kent left the hotel Monday evening"—he made a half-
turn toward Gustav Bulheim—"a dead rose was found
under your brother-in-law's body."

He paused. In the small silence, Gustav Bulheim
stared at him, then in disgust he made a repudiating
gesture, flinging out a hand. "Roses! There are roses and
roses! Vienna is full of roses!"

The chief was stroking his pale chin, smiling, looking
at Trumpf. "Continue, Inspector," he said softly. "So far,
supposition: From a ten-schilling coin you have constructed an edifice, a regular Eiffel Tower. Now you wish
to top it with a rose."

"Danke, Herr Doktor." From the flutter of the chief's
eyelids, Trumpf knew he was waiting for the inspector to
dazzle Herr Bulheim with the abilities of the criminal
investigation department.

Trumpf was willing to oblige. He hefted the satin purse
in his hands. *"Richtig, Herr Bulheim!* Hundreds of roses,
thousands, Vienna smothers in roses. But *because* there
was a rose, I placed this purse in the hands of the forensic
department. They have confirmed a minute, pinkish
smear as blood, human blood. One does not often find
blood on an evening bag, *nicht wahr?* . . . The blood is
Type O, Herr von Reitz's blood type. The serology tests
reveal that the smear is approximately seventy-two hours
old. Made at precisely the time your brother-in-law was
killed."

Herr Bulheim sat sunk in his chair, gazing at nothing. Herr Strobl said, "Then Mr. *X* was? . . ."

Trumpf hesitated. "These circumstances *indicate* but do not *prove* that Mr. *X* was Otto von Reitz." He addressed the chief. "As I reconstruct it, Miss Kent went with Otto von Reitz to his office. A crime was committed. Miss Kent returned to the hotel, changed her clothes, and fled. She was never abducted. She ran away."

The chief was murmuring, talking to himself half-aloud, as he sometimes did. Trumpf caught the murmured "*Yes . . . Gott verdammt.*" "Well then, Inspector." The chief blinked his pale eyes and looked at Trumpf, "Well then, Miss Kent. Have we any lead as to where? . . ." His look was expectant. It irritated Trumpf. Did the chief expect him to produce even more rabbits out of his hat? He was all out of rabbits.

"At the moment, nothing." That part was bitter. She could be hiding almost anywhere.

"So the girl in the Mödling woods, in the tan sweater and skirt? . . ."

Trumpf nodded. "Possibly. But until we have the medical examiner's report, we can only deduce that Veronica Kent was in von Reitz's office when he was killed and that she got blood on her purse. We have no evidence yet that *she* killed him. Despite the blow on the head, von Reitz could have died of other causes, even natural—"

"Of course she killed him!" Herr Bulheim was on his feet, bulldog jaw working, face mottled with rage. "She killed him with that damned parrot! That's why she ran away!"

"Herr Bulheim!" The chief's pale hand was lifted, it halted the outburst. "This is a job for the Criminal Investigation Department. We know our function, we have our procedures. We have allowed you a confidence. Now the media will besiege you. They will be a cloud of gnats around your head. However, Herr Bulheim, you will release no information to the media. It is premature. You will not breath a single word about what you have heard in this room. *Not one word.*

"You will not mention Veronica Kent. This department will decide precisely what information should be released. And exactly when. *Sie verstehen?"* A soft voice; steel in a velvet glove.

Recognizing the steel, Herr Bulheim compressed his bulldog jaw. He stood up and bowed stiffly, first to the chief, then to Inspector Trumpf. *"Ich verstehe."*

They were at breakfast. It was Friday morning. Herr Herbst was reading aloud the most recent news about the von Reitz murder. The shocking revelation of that murder had broken two days before. Herr Herbst, reading, would pause dramatically, glance up, then pounce on the next words. Martha Schratt kept shaking her head and exclaiming "Terrible! Terrible!" Nicca Montcalm was on her second boiled egg.

"Nothing new except that the ultraviolet light shows only von Reitz's blood." Herr Herbst regretfully folded the newspaper; it was time for him to be off to his job at Gerngross'.

"It is all von Reitz, von Reitz!" burst out Martha Schratt. "Last week, the news was about that poor American girl who disappeared. Now nobody cares anymore! She is forgotten. The public has fresher news: von Reitz. Real blood, a murder." She bit her lips and shook her head angrily at the deficiencies of humanity.

"Of course!" Herr Herbst said. "The public always wants hotter news, fresher blood."

Nicca Montcalm put down her coffee cup carefully, as though it were a bomb that might go off. *"Bitte,* may I borrow your paper, Herr Herbst?"

"Gewiss." He handed it over.

In her room, she devoured the scant news: There was the photograph she'd already seen on television—Otto von Reitz's covered body on the stretcher being carried by white-coated paramedics through the lobby of the Opernring building, just as she had seen it borne past her when wild hope had propelled her from Hawelka's to the Opernring building at noon. She scanned the column, looking for something specific in the newsprint. Ah, there! That puzzling bit that Herr Herbst had read aloud: a new quote from Kleiner, von Reitz's office manager, saying that Herr von Reitz had planned to go to Hamburg the next morning, taking a nine A.M. flight. "He often stayed overnight at the office when he had to catch an early plane; his home is an hour away, in Klosterneuburg, the other side of Vienna from the airport, and with the Air Terminal only five minutes from the Opernring office . . .

Odd . . . Had the *Kurier* got it wrong? Herr von Reitz had said he was leaving Vienna that same evening. What could he gain by a gratuitous lie? Unless . . . something sexual? Those women dancing together at the Kursalon, Herr von Reitz's face had been contorted with rage . . . and, yes, excitement. Leaning on an elbow, reading, puzzling, she became aware that she had unconsciously raised one hand and was moving her fingers, grasping at something invisible in the air.

She sat up and straightened the paper. Queer, so queer . . . Last evening she had again stood in the blue twilight on the path near the Kursalon; she had stood in shadow, watching the gold-toothed waiter, his skinny figure flying to and fro among the tables; she had assured herself that he still served patrons at the Kursalon. Then why, with all Vienna discussing Otto von Reitz's murder, had he not hurried to the police: *Ja, at the Kusalon, the missing American girl, drinking champagne with Herr von Reitz, that very night.* And why, when she had been missing in the first place, had he not informed the police he had seen her entering the Hilton late that night? Why?

"Herrgott!"

A drone of traffic outside the Rossauerkaserne; the five o'clock rush hour, Friday evening, cars heading out of Vienna for the weekend. In his office, the chief sat dumbfounded. Inspector Trumpf stood by, silent, with folded arms; his face was grim, perplexed.

"Herrgott!" The chief was staring down incredulously at the medical examiner's report that Inspector Trumpf had two minutes before laid on his desk. His long, pale face made a sudden grimace of revulsion. "Such insanity—such malevolence—to wreak further violence on the man's helpless body!"

Revulsion provoked by the startling medical report propelled the chief abruptly out of his chair and to the window. He stood with his back to Trumpf, muttering *"Herrgott! Herrgott!"*

Inspector Trumpf waited patiently. The chief finally sighed, turned, came back to his desk. He sat down and tapped his fingers on the medical report; hard, angry taps. "Vicious! What the devil do you make of it, Inspector? A psychopathic personality? Who kills the same victim *twice?*"

Trumpf knit his heavy brows. The medical examiner's report proved once again that you were flying blind until you had the laboratory's painstaking work, the final forensic findings—the medical examiner's report.

"In his thigh!" the chief exploded again. "Well, Inspector?"

"In his thigh," Trumpf repeated aloud, reflectively. Otto von Reitz had been killed by a lethal drug injection in his thigh. It was an injection strong enough to have killed three men . . . or four. The laboratory had detected the tiny needle puncture: It was in von Reitz's right thigh, just below the buttock. It had caused respiratory failure and death. The injury to von Reitz's head from the blow with the bronze parrot had revealed scant blood to the tissues, an amount insufficient to have caused death.

"Trumpf?"

The inspector brought himself back. "A psychopath? She could be . . . unless there were *three* people in that private office."

"*Three* people? Impossible! The time between the blow on von Reitz's head and the lethal injection was not more than . . . what? Fifteen minutes!"

"True." It was unfortunate that the seventy-two-hour time lag before von Reitz's body had been found made it impossible to tell which had come first, blow or injection. Trumpf said slowly: "You can hypothesize that if only two people were involved—Veronica Kent and Herr von Reitz—she struck him on the head first, then inexplicably killed him with the injection. I say *inexplicably*, because why, having struck him once, did she not continue and bludgeon him to death?

"Then, of course, there's an opposite hypothesis: She injected him somehow, then in a vicious, sadistic rage, struck him with the bronze parrot while he lay dying.

"With either scenario, she would wipe her fingerprints off the bronze parrot and take the lethal syringe with her. Our people did a thorough investigation of the office: combed, dusted, vacuumed—the works. No syringe was found."

The chief brooded. "Motive? So often these things

explode out of some orgiastic experience . . . like in the Frau Altdorfer case, sexual feasting releasing unexpected homicidal violence—an uncontrollable whirlwind, a tempest!" He tapped the medical examiner's report. "This American girl, this psychotic—*Herrgott!*—if she hadn't lost her head and disappeared from the hotel, she could have gotten away with it. Yes, certainly a psychopathic personality."

Trumpf could not refrain from adding: "Supposition, Herr Doktor. We are erecting an edifice, a regular . . . ah, Empire State Building of supposition of a psychopathic personality. The fact is, psychopathic or not, if Miss Kent is caught, she will most certainly be convicted."

The chief cast him a sidewise look. "Then get on with it. Inform the media of the facts of Herr Otto von Reitz's death, and say that Veronica Kent is now being sought for murder."

Back in his office, Inspector Trumpf gave Detective Staral instructions. Staral, looking stunned, jotted down all the details: Veronica Kent sought in murder of Otto von Reitz . . . Veronica Kent's evening purse discovered with its bloodstain . . . a lethal injection had killed Otto von Reitz. He even recorded the fact that the injection in von Reitz's thigh was a combination of heroin mixed with central nervous system depressants, and that the result was respiratory failure and death.

When Detective Staral had left, Trumpf sat doodling, thinking what a shock the news would be to amateur criminologist Kraus. Kraus was still screaming "Cage the Foxe!" on his "Liebe Leute" radio program. Kraus was a juvenile; he knew no more about criminal investigation than a child playing with blocks . . . no more than Pepi, sitting over there by the window reading one of his

American cowboy westerns in Spanish: *hombre* was now one of Pepi's favorite words.

Cage the Foxe. He himself had been pretty rough on Jason Foxe. He grimaced. A week ago, suspicious of Foxe, he'd promised himself to drop in on him at his pension on Langegasse. Now he'd drop in on Foxe and apologize.

Not an outright apology.

But he owed Jason Foxe a visit.

Chapter 8

On Saturday morning, Vienna exploded with the shocking news: Otto von Reitz's murderer discovered! The vanished American girl, Veronica Kent, was not a pitiful, kidnapped creature lying strangled at the bottom of a river or in the wooded outskirts of Vienna—she was a killer. She was more than a murderer, she was a psychopath who had done further malignant violence to Otto von Reitz's defenseless body.

Shudders of delicious horror shook the mirrored and mahogany-paneled walls of the coffeehouses. The right side of *Die Presse*'s front page, the "big news" position, featured the astounding revelation: Here again was the American girl's passport photo; here, too, the police photos of von Reitz's body on the oriental rug.

Bulldog-faced Herr Gustav Bulheim appeared on television, offering a reward of thirty thousand schillings for information leading to the capture of Veronica Kent. Bulheim unconsciously kept shooting his dazzling French cuffs, as though he might release a dagger from up his sleeve. A German psychiatrist briefly analyzed the female "murder personality," relating it to subconscious hatred of men. A bizarre murder in London's Soho was reported tied to the von Reitz killing; almost immediately it was reported to have no connection. An expert on poison, drugs, and forensic science was interviewed. A psychologist who had fortuitously just had a book published called *Predicting the Killer Personality* appeared and promised to be a consistently popular interviewee. His publisher seized the opportunity to advertise the book on the TV screen, even providing a telephone number for instant ordering.

At midweek, Otto von Reitz was buried fashionably in Klosterneuberg after a ceremony in the Stiftskirche, where polite, uniformed police directed the limousines. Crowds stood silently by while socialites from Berne, Milan, Hamburg, Lyons and Paris mingled with members of the Austrian diplomatic service and members of foreign legations who had come out of respect, obligation, or friendship for Gustav Bulheim. Special space in the Stiftskirche was set aside for the staff of the von Reitz law firm. Later at the cemetery, Gustav Bulheim had supported his black-veiled sister Sophie on an arm as steady as iron. His face, too, had seemed carved of iron, an iron bulldog. Sophie von Reitz had collapsed at the graveside, melting down against her brother's knees. The next day, Gustav Bulheim raised the reward for information leading to Veronica Kent's capture.

Meanwhile, on the radio, Leon Kraus was in his element. Veronica Kent, murderess! Kraus had made a complete turnabout, as though Jason Foxe had never existed. He was now in full cry after Veronica Kent, psychopathic killer. A whole new cornucopia of conjectures had spilled into his lap. And how beautifully the lurid death of the rich, well-known Viennese blended in with the Affair of the Roses! Here it all was. Here was brutal death. *"Meine lieben Leute,* truth is brutal, more brutal than fiction. . . ."

Jason wandered around Vienna soliloquizing, like Hamlet. He couldn't take it in—or he refused to. At dinner that first night with Florian at the Astoria, he had gazed at his beef roulade as if it had ants on it. "You may as well eat," Florian had said gently, "instead of just pushing the meat around. There's nothing under it but a design on the plate." Still, he could not eat. He left Florian early. He walked dazedly along the Kärntner-strasse, past the cafés, the casino, past the Vienna Opera house which was brilliantly lit, an enormous jewel. He saw none of it. Back at the Brunners' he went into the little Art Nouveau sitting room that Adalbert Brunner had set aside for his guests. The room was empty. He turned on the television news and sat staring at the screen with loathing, as though it were a poisonous snake that spewed forth deadly venom. He sat there for hours, sunk in a chair.

So black, so bitter, so ironical: Only a day ago—or was it a thousand years ago?—he had determined to hire some kind of superdetective to find Veronica Kent. A keen, imaginative, and doubtless expensive investigator. He'd intended to borrow money from Florian, if he had to. Telephone book in hand, he had been making out a list of investigative agencies, when he had heard the news on the radio.

Early Friday morning, six days after the shattering news, Jason Foxe rang Frau Martha Krieger Schratt's doorbell. After a minute the door opened and Frau Schratt, in a freshly starched apron, stood smiling at him.

"Come in, come in, Herr Foxe! Your shirts are ready since Wednesday. I suppose you forgot? How is my dear Herr Brunner? When I think of him as a little boy with skinned knees! And now with a beard!" Frau Schratt shook her head, smiling even more broadly. "Well! You can't go away without a cup of coffee. And one of my Kaisersemmel. I get up at five o'clock every morning to bake; it is not quite dawn, the peaceful time, only a few birds chirping outside and me in the kitchen, baking."

He followed Frau Schratt into the dining room. Nicca Montcalm and an elderly man were eating breakfast at a big round table with claw feet. The room had wainscoting in dark wood, and above it a fleur-de-lis design, once possibly red and gold, now faded. A heavy dark Biedermeier sideboard that would certainly take four men to lift stood against the wall. On it, atop a linen runner with lace edging, stood a television set and a filigreed dish of fruit so magnificent that it was most certainly wax.

The elderly man, introduced as Herr Herbst, was holding a newspaper. But as Jason sat down, he politely put it aside. Besides, it was time for him to leave. He bowed in an old-world, dignified way and departed.

The aroma of fresh-baked rolls and the delicious fragrance of coffee made Jason hungry for the first time in a week. He slathered butter onto the warm roll with its delicately crisp crust, took a luxurious bite.

"You like my baking?" Frau Schratt was filling his coffee cup. He nodded. "The best roll I've ever tasted." He turned to Nicca Montcalm, sitting across from him in a blouse that had once been white but now was yellowing. "Are Frau Schratt's rolls this delicious every morning, Nicca?"

"Exactly so, Herr Foxe."

"I envy you then." He sank his teeth into the roll. He couldn't get her to call him Jason. She was the most

formal girl he had ever encountered. Perhaps that was
the French way. Twice this week, on Langegasse, he'd
picked her up and given her a lift on his way to see
Professor Schindler. Now that he was no longer suspected of being a kidnapper or murderer, but was an
innocent, white-as-snow sociologist, she was more relaxed
with him. Nonetheless she still had him drop her at
Universitatsstrasse. And he'd noticed that when he let
her out of the car she stood on the street, the heavy books
in her arms, and watched the Porsche out of sight.

He took a final bite, devouring the roll, then drained
his coffee cup. "I'm on my way to the university . . . can I
give you a lift?"

She looked up. "Yes, thanks."

Downstairs, she got in the car while he put the package
of shirts in the trunk. The truth was, he had lied to
Fräulein Montcalm: He was not going to the university
this morning, he had no appointment with Schindler.
But, inexplicably, he wanted to give Nicca a lift. Was it
because he felt sorry for her? He had the disturbing
thought that she wasn't getting enough to eat. He had
noticed she didn't even own a wristwatch, not even a
cheap ring. He felt embarrassingly rich in his cashmere
sweater; and driving a Porsche, besides. Even though he
didn't own it.

If she hadn't sneezed she would never have discovered
it. But she did sneeze. It was a chilly morning and the
convertible top was down.

"Don't you have a sweater?" Jason Foxe glanced over
at her; then added hastily, "I'll put the top up."

"No, I'm all right. It's only a couple of blocks more."
A sweater, how she wished she owned a sweater! Perhaps
a soft, beautifully warm cashmere like Jason Foxe's. But
right now her nose was running, and she needed a hand-

kerchief or tissues. She didn't have any, she couldn't afford— She sniffed, then sneezed again.

"There are some tissues in the glove compartment."

"Thank you." Gratefully, she snapped open the glove compartment. Beneath a paperback book and a sheaf of papers held together with a rubber band, was the little packet of tissues. She drew out the packet, pulled a tissue free, and blew her nose.

"Keep them."

"No, but thanks." She hesitated, took an extra tissue and put the packet back on top of the pile of papers. . . . Those papers . . . Xeroxed . . . handwritten. The writing was familiar. She stared at it. It was some moments before she realized it was her own handwriting. She was looking at a Xerox of her notebook.

"You O.K. now?"

"Yes." She closed the glove compartment.

At Hawelka's she now no longer pretended to be immersed in issues of *Marie-Claire* and *Elle* for hair styles, cosmetic tips, new fashions in resort clothes, or recipes for glamorous candlelit suppers. Instead, she pored over Austrian magazines and Viennese newspapers. She devoured every printed word about the murder of von Reitz and every scrap about his life. There were magazine picture stories on the von Reitz family. Their villa and their vacation home in Montreux were illustrated. Their summer and winter activities, their charities, relatives, and antecedents were discussed. Here was a photograph of Otto von Reitz as a young man, leaning on a tennis racquet; there he was in a suit and vest with a watch chain, having just passed the bar and joined the family firm. Below was his wedding picture, his bride a dark-haired beauty with a pensively smiling face and a circlet of tiny white roses on her cloudy hair. To the right, they were dancing at the Opera Ball, he in tails and already plump, she still slender, in shimmering pink. Another article was accompanied by pictures of the two daughters as teenagers, wearing red coats and black velvet caps, in a horse show; and by a shot of one of those same daughters, now grown, married, and already divorced.

Endless labor. She made penciled notes, lists of the von Reitz friends and acquaintances. She also spent her dwindling schillings on magazines and newspapers that warranted later study in her room at Frau Schratt's. Here at Hawelka's she had the added difficulty of having to read through the violet-tinted glasses. Only when she was alone did she dare take them off.

Stubbornly she searched for a clue. *A lethal injection in his thigh.* Diabolical. *Who?* Who hated Herr von Reitz that much? The newspapers had said they were within minutes of each other, the blow on the head and the lethal injection. Someone else had been there, someone shadowy had . . . followed them? Lurked? *Who?* She had to find the answer. Otherwise—she shivered—*she* would pay the penalty. Yet under her fear was an enormous relief: What she had sensed after striking Herr von Reitz had been so! Her revulsion at hurting another person, no matter her own danger, had weakened her arm. Even as she had stuck out at him with the bronze parrot, she had held back. She had known it—in some far corner of her mind, *she had known.*

But now her money was running out, those schillings she hoarded like a miser, and she was so hungry, always hungry! Wherever she looked, she saw food, smelled mouth-watering aromas. Vienna was a city of delectable treats, like a gingerbread house in a fairy tale. In spite of the morning chill, it was an unprecedentedly warm September. The outdoor cafés that lined the streets were filled with patrons served by scurrying waiters. Everywhere she looked she glimpsed appetizing little salads of meat or fish, baskets of sweet rolls, luscious-looking pastry, heard the clink of china and silver; smelled the aroma of mocha, chocolate, coffee; saw forks cutting into strawberry tarts. She felt like a homeless orphan. Hunger gnawed at her stomach. Even the wax fruit in the filigreed dish on Frau Schratt's sideboard made her mouth water. She had bought a box of powdered milk and a plastic glass; at the bathroom sink down the hall at Schratt's, she filled the glass with water and then had a glass of milk in her room.

And yesterday! In the early afternoon, walking aimlessly but pretending to have a destination, near Josefstrasse she had passed one of the many Heise Wurstl stands. A couple of fresh-faced young boys in caps were handing over their schillings and turning away; they came in her direction, holding their sausages covered with mustard and nestled in thick slices of chewy bread. She had been unable to withstand the sight, she had drawn closer to the sausages sizzling on the grill, captured by the aroma, by the plump, browned sausages, even by the mustard pot. She had succumbed and bought a sausage. She'd been standing against a wall nearby, devouring it when she'd become aware of a disreputable-looking man in torn shoes wolfing down the same meal. Their eyes had met; it was as though they were aware of an affinity, each recognizing the other as a hungry skulker on the fringe of society. Overtaken by a feeling of fright, she had finished her sausage, gulping it down in one bite, and walked quickly away.

Now in Hawelka's, she put a hand to her cheek and ran her fingers under her cheekbone. Wasn't there a little hollow there now? Yes, she could feel it. And the days would be getting colder. She had no coat. She had only the tan woolen sweater hidden in the bureau drawer, and she could not wear that.

She looked down at the magazine. She had been holding it open at a picture story of the von Reitz family. On the right-hand page, Herr von Reitz and his wife, at their villa in Klosterneuberg, sat in white-painted rococo iron chairs on a sunlit lawn, a pair of golden spaniels at their feet. Herr von Reitz was reading; his wife Sophie had her dark head bent over a piece of needlework.

Staring at that picture of conjugal serenity, she had a sudden, almost shattering longing to turn to Herr Hawelka who was clearing the next table and make two requests: "*Bitte,* Herr Hawelka, I would like three pieces of apricot cake with a big cup of coffee with milk and whipped cream. And then, Herr Hawelka, please call the police and tell them you have found Veronica Kent."

Instead, she pressed her lips tightly, stubbornly, together. After a moment, still gazing down at the photograph, an absurd thought slid into her mind: That villa in Klosterneuburg, the von Reitz villa . . . could it yield a piece of the puzzle? If only she could find a way . . . But in her shabby clothes, in that rich neighborhood, she would be an object of suspicion. If only she had some money. . . .

"If they find her, they'll convict her." Jason Foxe was standing at the drawing board in Florian's workroom, jotting down the measurements for the publicity blowups of the reviews of Florian's previous book; he wanted them big like the sandwich-board reviews of plays that appeared outside theaters. Baron Willy von Walenberg was giving a press party for Florian's forthcoming *Birds of Austria*. The party would be at *Schloss* Walenberg, the von Walenberg castle in Styria. The thirteenth-century castle, south of Hartberg, was a perfect setting; at this time of year the forest and valleys and meadows that could be seen from the castle terraces would have that special, rich effulgence, a splendor peculiar to the Styrian countryside. And the air in that region now had a snap; it was already the hunting season.

"Damn it, she didn't kill him! Listen to this, Florian. In her notebook she said about Sarah Hamilton: *Sarah is very narcissistic, even more than I, and she is sixty-six. But she doesn't ever make a smiling face to hide her real face. I admire her for that.* Can you honestly believe a girl who wrote that could murder another human being? Never!"

"I believe," said Florian "that you are determined to believe what you want to believe about the girl."

"Ah," said Jason Foxe. He finished making his estimates. He would set up the blowups just inside the west terrace, the largest of the four main stone terraces of the castle. The flagged terrace was broad, kidney-shaped; on its balustrades, at intervals, were stone urns that the Baron's gardeners kept filled with freshly planted flowers. The wide curve of stone steps descended to the lawn. The party would be held on this terrace and on the lawn below.

It was to be given in ten days. Baron Willy had already had his calligrapher write the invitations from the list Florian had given him. The guests would include journalists, zoologists, members of the Austrian bird-watchers society, Florian's publisher and two editors, two representatives of the Smithsonian, a National Geographics editor, the curator of Vienna's Albertine Museum, and the curator of the Museum of Natural Science. There would also be press photographers and a few of Baron Willy's personal friends. In all, well over a hundred people. Danilo Lovchen, the manager of the von Walenberg estate, would be in charge. Danilo Lovchen was twenty-two. He was a Serb, a handsome, black-eyed Yugoslavian whom Baron Willy had adopted the previous year. The baron fondly referred to Lovchen as *"Mein Sohn,"* my son, but everyone knew Danilo Lovchen was also his lover.

"All set with this." Jason clipped his jottings together and stuck them to the drawing board with a pushpin. He had thrown himself furiously into helping Florian, acting as publicity release writer, errand boy, organizer, and secretary. Helping Königsmark was his lifeline; he found it impossible to concentrate on his own work. Alone at the Brunners' he would fall to reading the Xeroxed notebook; he had even taken to carrying the pages along with him in the car. He felt as though he were choking, he was desperate for air. Helping Florian released his anguish, and he intended to help Florian at Castle Walenberg as well.

He had also helped Nicca Montcalm find a job.

At least in a way, helped her.

It was three days after Nicca had sneezed that he spotted the ad. In the Porsche, he had wanted to pull his cashmere sweater over his head and force her arms into it—against her will, of course. It would have been against her will, for he knew she was stubborn, this Fräulein Montcalm. She was proud, she would not have allowed it; she would have been outraged. Possibly she would have wept; tears of anger, tears hidden behind those lilac-tinged glasses. No, he couldn't do that to her. Or . . . maybe not tears. Maybe she would have whacked him with one of those political science books for his insulting kindness. So there it was; she had needed soft, cozy warmth and he had been able to give her no more than a facial tissue.

He had gone out for an early morning walk in the

sparkling freshness that pervaded the city. Unidentifiable birds chirped and trilled in the linden trees. Waiters in long aprons were sweeping in front of the coffeehouses where sleepy-eyed people were already breakfasting and reading the papers before going to work. He had decided to join them. Over coffee and a crescent, he read the paper, even the Personals, which he studied with a sociologist's eye: the Personals revealed a lot about a society, the underbelly of a culture. Here were cries of loneliness, love, hope, here the eternal search for ultimate personal revelation. "Massage: A Holistic therapeutic approach— Discover yourself via Massage!" He read the Lost-and-Found ads "Lost: Yellow cockatiel with orange cheeks; answers to Lovey; will take bread from between your lips. Desperate for return." He moved on to Investment Opportunities, then Jobs.

Jobs. His eye fell on the ad . . . and lingered. "French tutor wanted." Why not a job for Nicca Montcalm? She certainly needed the money.

Twenty minutes later, newspaper under his arm, he rang Frau Martha Krieger Schratt's doorbell. He was impatiently drawing marks on the tablecloth with a fork, when Nicca arrived at the breakfast table. She was wearing the inevitable navy suit, and today that faded pink blouse. She must be sick of it, he was.

"Here is Herr Foxe, he's been asking for you," Frau Schratt said. She placed a roll beside Fräulein Montcalm's plate. "I'll get your eggs." She went off to the kitchen.

"Guten Morgen, Herr Foxe."

"Guten Morgen, Nicca." He noticed that her ragged hair needed cutting, it was falling into her eyes . . . or rather, it was edging over the lenses of those outsized glasses that hid her eyes. She had weak eyes, she had told him; they could not stand the light. Her face looked so

thin, almost gaunt. He noticed that she was beginning to eat her morning Kaisersemmel so scrupulously that not a crumb fell on the tablecloth. Gaunt or not, she still possessed that indefinable chemical attraction.

"Nicca, could this be for you?" He read the ad aloud: "French tutor wanted, three mornings a week. Hietzing area, eight hundred schillings a week." A phone number followed. "That is, if you have any mornings free." He hoped she had; or perhaps she could switch to a couple of afternoon classes.

"What?" She just kept looking at him. It was difficult to tell her expression because of the glasses, but these last few days he could have sworn that Nicca Montcalm had been surreptitiously studying him. He knew he looked terrible. He had been sleeping badly, and his usual zest had vanished. He was, he thought, suffering from an imaginary malady. A sort of romantic fever.

"Eight hundred schillings, three mornings a week."

A soft sigh. She put down the roll. "It is . . . where?"

"Hietzing. Fashionable, elegant. Mostly villas. You could call first, make an appointment."

"Oh." She turned her coffee cup this way and that, looking down at it, her face getting red. "In . . . in Hietzing?"

It occurred to him that she was mentally counting her schillings, maybe she was reluctant to spend money to take the U-Bahn to Hietzing to apply for a job she might not get. Abruptly, he felt impatient with her, a teacher with a reluctant student who has the goods but who is too emotionally entangled to deliver. He said forcefully:

"I'll take you. I have the morning free."

He was railroading her, but what the hell, she shouldn't hang back like a frightened rabbit—she should learn to take risks. He'd be getting her over her fears. Once she got in the water, she'd learn to swim.

"Well, then . . ."

"Fine."

He tore out the ad. Inexorably, he stood over her at the phone in the foyer while she called. He looked critically at her hair. Those ragged bangs would hardly impress a prospective employer. He borrowed Frau Schratt's good scissors. He'd clip Nicca Montcalm's bangs himself; she had only to sit still. Scissors in hand, he started to take off her tinted glasses so they wouldn't get in the way, but her hand quickly shot up and caught his.

"My eyes! The light hurts so, even for a moment!"

"I'm sorry." He was contrite. He cut carefully. Finished, he tipped up her chin and surveyed the result. Not the best job in the world—he was no hair stylist—but at least better. He blew on her forehead to get rid of stray hairs . . . a lovely forehead with a little blue vein pulsating near one temple. A proprietary interest in the girl's welfare swept over him; she was such a stray cat, hardly a survivor.

In the car, they stopped a few blocks away for gas, near the university, Jason's regular place, convenient— Strohmayer's Reparatur Werkstatte.

"Auffülen, bitte."

The usual fellow in a brown overall filled the tank. He was a compact young man with rust-brown hair and an insolent smirk. He had a handsome face, marred by mean-looking eyes. While the tank filled, he stood chewing a toothpick and staring at Foxe, then at the girl, then again at Foxe. Jason Foxe knew that look; it was a look he had encountered often since his face had appeared in the media. His flat-cheeked face with the dark eyes and the outthrust sensuous mouth was easy to recognize: he was the Foxe of the Foxe Affair. Curiosity, speculation . . . and from women, a sexy titillation. An elderly woman on the Kärntnerstrasse had brushed hard against him and then touched his wrist. His body had not been enough, she had needed his bare skin.

He paid and they drove off.

"Bitte," the girl said. They had gone hardly a half-dozen blocks. Her voice was faint. "I can't . . . I don't feel well. Please take me back."

He glanced at her. Her head lay back against the seat, her face turned up. She was dead white and perspiring. Sick, all right. Sick with fear. He drove steadily on. He said reasonably, "Look, don't fantasize something terrible, it's only a job! Suppose they *don't* hire you? They won't blindfold you and make you walk the plank. They won't do a Joan of Arc, burn you at the stake. They'll say 'No, thanks' . . . maybe because they've decided they want a male tutor, or somebody with an eye in the middle of his forehead, or they've already decided on someone else. So? If that happens, tomorrow morning's Kaiser-semmel will taste just as good." He made a right turn, heading for the Autobahn and Hietzing. He was a sociologist, not a psychologist, but he knew enough about emotional insecurity, to recognize its manifestations, didn't he? "Anyway, to win, you've got to take risks."

So he kept talking reassuringly, and by the time they were on the Autobahn, she was sitting up. She still looked shaky but her color was coming back. She took out a comb and fixed her hair, nervously combing it over and over; sometimes nodding and giving him a sidewise glance as he continued to philosophize reassuringly.

The villa in Hietzing was expensively enclosed by a low white stucco wall with a black, grilled iron gate.

"I'll wait." He reached over and slammed the car door when the girl got out. "There's something to read here." He snapped open the glove compartment, groped around, and took out the paperback a previous renter had left behind. He glanced at the cover. It was a murder mystery. He sighed. "This ought to keep me occupied. A good murder."

Nicca Montcalm gave a sudden, half-hysterical laugh. "Yes . . . I guess." She went up the walk and opened the gate.

When Nicca Montcalm came out, her face gave nothing away. In the car, as they started off, she thanked him.

"Thanks for what? You got the job or you took the rejection like a hero—heroine?"

"I got it."

Her pupils were twins, Fritz and Karoline Draxler, aged sixteen. Their father was a foreign trade consultant, their mother was in despair. Frau Draxler had nervously interviewed Mademoiselle Montcalm and had explained the horrendous problem. Without tutoring, the twins were doomed to fail their French exams, but the two previous tutors had left speedily and in tears, one muttering something about incorrigible, the other forgetting her exercise books and refusing to return for them. Frau Draxler had consequently raised the pay from six hundred schillings to eight hundred. She took Mademoiselle Montcalm upstairs to meet the twins "as though she were leading me into a lion's den." The twins were in their study listening to an eight-track rock tape. "The room smelled of pot. Karoline is overweight and worries about boys and her frizzy hair. Fritz is handsome and bites his fingernails. He worries that his father will kill him if he doesn't pass French, but he bluffs, saying he doesn't care." The twins had given Mademoiselle Montcalm dagger looks of enmity . . . until they'd realized that as their mother talked, Mademoiselle Montcalm had picked up the theme of the rock song and was softly whistling it. "I didn't know I was doing it, but after that they were puppy dogs, rolling over on their backs and wanting their

stomachs tickled." "The twins *like* you!" Frau Draxler
had exclaimed, dazed, when they had gone back downstairs, "and they don't like *anybody! Niemand!*
Nobody!" The poor woman had been so relieved that she
had given Mademoiselle Montcalm an advance of four
hundred schillings—probably to assure her return. "Four
hundred!" In the car, she laughed aloud.

It was the first time Jason Foxe heard Nicca Montcalm laugh.

Nicca Montcalm now took the U-Bahn regularly to the
Draxlers' in Hietzing three mornings a week: Wednesday, Friday, and Saturday. She wore a smart white
cotton shirt, and she had had her hair styled. It was short
and wavy, soft around her brow, and with a little point at
the nape. Her mouth was a brownish pink, courtesy of a
new lipstick, the shade currently popular in Vienna. She
was astonishingly pretty.

With her first earnings from the Draxlers, Nicca
bought necessities, scrupulously weighing each need
carefully. The haircut, expensive but vitally important.
The white cotton-polyester blouse. A raspberry-colored
sweater with a cowl neck: it was cheap but thick and
warm. Then the tan corduroy jeans. Wearing the jeans
and sweater, and carrying her books, she was the proto-
typical university student. Her prize purchase, though,
was the shoes: well-fitting, inexpensive navy-blue sad-
dleshoes. No more blisters! She wore the shoes out of the
store, carrying the old brown shoes in a bag; she pitched
the bag into the nearest trash receptacle on the street.
She had been too cautious to ask the shoe clerk to throw
them away. She had at first considered going to Noch
Einmal for some of her necessities. But then, with a
heart-lurch of fright, she had thought: What if that
anemic-looking young man in red satin stretch pants and

glass beads should recognize me, make a mental connection between that rainy night when Veronica Kent disappeared and—No, not Noch Einmal! In fact, no second-hand clothes at all, not ever. The thought of more used clothes against her body had suddenly made her skin crawl. She had experienced another moment of panic, had felt as though she were falling through space, plunging into an abyss. She must move more quickly. Now that she was not starving, taking action would be easier: she must push on, *push on*.

Yes, at least not starving now. Always hungry, but not starving. True, she still had to pull the nubby pink bedspread from the bed, roll it up, and push it against the bottom of the door to keep out the delicious smell of Frau Schratt's supper cooking, the savory smell that seeped under the door in the evening, making the juices run in her mouth, making her jaws ache. But now she had suppers of her own, more than just the milk powder and the occasional apple that she ate right down to the core, even the seeds, biting them between her teeth. Now in the flight bag on the closet shelf she kept oranges, a loaf of bread, biscuits, and two kinds of the cheese that came in a tube like toothpaste. As for lunch, on Wednesday and Friday after the morning's three-hour class with the twins, she lunched at the Draxlers' with the twins and their mother. And on Saturdays, when she came home from Hietzing, Frau Schratt always had "a little something" left over from her previous night's supper, perhaps soup and dumplings, just enough for a small portion for two—a nice noontime snack for herself and Fräulein Montcalm, but not enough to warrant payment from Fräulein Montcalm. Had Frau Schratt, Nicca wondered, noticed what a starving stray cat her French pensioner had begun to resemble? But no more.

She was still giving Frau Schratt excuses for the missing passport: an exasperating but near-comic mix-up in Rouen, Frau Schratt! The police had erroneously sent her passport to another girl, can you imagine! The other girl had returned it, the police had sent it to Nicca's mother, but she had never received it—those *flics* had misdirected it! But it would soon be in her mother's hands. She, Nicca, was sorry. It was altogether exasperating, like a snarled piece of knitting, but it would soon be unknotted, straightened out. Any day now, maybe even tomorrow, Frau Schratt, the passport would arrive. . . .

It made her ashamed that Frau Schratt listened so patiently, nodding, her head a little to one side, and did not press her. Occasionally, when their glances crossed while they were having the "little something" of soup and dumplings on Saturdays, Nicca fancied she saw a scrutinizing look in Frau Schratt's eyes.

Chapter 9

At twelve-thirty in the Draxler villa in Hietzing, Alma, the Draxlers' maid, in black uniform with white collar, stood at the foot of the curving staircase and shook the Tibetan temple bells that, in the Draxler household, served as the luncheon bell. That summons would take care of the twins and the French tutor, Fräulein Montcalm. Alma went through the living room and out through the tall doors and across the terrace. There she stopped, looked down the sloping lawn toward the little white vine-covered pavilion, and again shook the temple bells. Frau Draxler, in one of her decorating moods, had gone down to the pavilion to measure the wooden seats for next summer's seat cushions. The pavilion had been Frau Draxler's refuge all this past summer: she had had a telephone jack installed in it, and there, while enjoying the fragrance of flowers and grass, she talked on the phone with her friends. She tucked a cushiony ivory-colored plastic telephone rest between her ear and shoulder so that she could simultaneously chat and do her fingernails. Originally, she had fled to the pavilion to escape the thunder of Fritz's hard rock music. It was so peaceful out there, away from Karoline and Fritz and their overwhelming problems. Now, of course, since Fräulein Montcalm's arrival almost two weeks ago, the tumultuous raging sea of life-with-Fritz-and-Karoline had died to a gentle lapping of waves. The change was beneficial to Frau Draxler's nerves. Indeed, she had said to her husband Alfred, "I knew at once that Mademoiselle Montcalm was *exactly* the right person." Alfred Draxler, a foreign trade expert with a strong sense of personal dignity, responded that he'd be even more delighted if Karoline and Fritz would stop referring to him as "Freddy" . . . at least in his hearing. Not, he added grudgingly, that he, too, wasn't delighted by the effect Fräulein Montcalm had on the Draxler progeny: it was hardly credible, but he had actually overheard Fritz address Karoline *in French*.

Upstairs, at the musical sound of the Tibetan bells, Fräulein Montcalm turned off the cassette recorder, ending the haunting and not-quite-scatological Georges Brassens song-with-guitar. The Brassens would add plenty of colloquial French to the twins' vocabulary; and it included all the important tenses, besides French slang. On impulse, just before taking the U-Bahn to Hietzing for that first tutoring session, Veronica had parted with precious schillings to buy the Brassens. It wasn't new, it wasn't hard rock, but it was Brassens magic: the French singer's voice and songs had as much allure for many a listener, herself included, as the voices of the sirens had had for Ulysses. Karoline and Fritz Draxler had immediately fallen under the spell. She still brought cassettes to Hietzing, though not always Brassens. The cassettes had proved to be a master stroke.

But now, turning off the cassette recorder, she was not thinking of Karoline and Fritz's studies.

She was thinking of Karoline's motor scooter.

The motor scooter, a yellow Puch, was, right now, parked on its stand outside the covered passageway that led to the garage. Karoline and Fritz had each received a Puch from their parents months ago on their sixteenth birthday. Karoline's was yellow, Fritz's was dark blue. Fritz was possessive of his, and often took off on it, but Karoline was indifferent to hers.

The Puch. It had to be that; she'd try to borrow it from Karoline. Without identification she'd never be able to rent a motor scooter or a car. Not that she had the money, anyway. A taxi from the local train stop at Klosterneuburg wouldn't do either, not for the plan she had in mind.

No, her only possibility was the Puch. On a road map of Vienna and its outskirts, she had marked the best route from Hietzing to the von Reitz villa in Klosterneuburg. Hietzing, lying just beyond Schönbrunn Palace with its parks, vineyards, and hunting grounds, was in Vienna's Thirteenth District. Klosterneuburg, where the villas of the rich had more extensive grounds than those of Hietzing, was eleven kilometers north of Vienna. It lay below the Kahlenberg, the highest peak of the Wienerwald hills. Yet it was surprisingly close. Two days ago, on the Draxlers' terrace, looking down across the sloping garden and past the pavilion, she had seen in the distance among the hills and forested land, a medieval-looking tower. "An old fortress, now Leopoldsberg church." Fritz had identified it for her. "It's on that high spot, above Klosterneuburg." *Klosterneuburg* ... where she would pursue the mystery that kept her locked in a lilac-shaded world behind the tinted lenses she had come to abhor.

Fritz was whistling the Brassens in perfect pitch; he

was imitative as a monkey and had a true ear. "You'll leave this cassette too? O.K., Fräulein Montcalm? I've got the schillings right here." To Karoline who had reached to take the cassette from the machine, "Hands off! Hands off!" he yelled. "I'm going to play it again." He felt in his pocket for schillings. He was wearing his Astronauten-Look overall, poplin and nylon, and his handsome face actually looked cheerful and relaxed. He handed Fräulein Montcalm the schillings she had paid for the cassette. He didn't, this time, try to hide his bitten fingernails. He had stopped biting them a week ago. "How come?" Karoline, noticing, had asked him. Fritz had shrugged. "Who knows? Maybe now that Freddy has dropped the bullwhip about this French stuff—vive la France!" He had snapped a jaunty salute toward Fräulein Montcalm.

The Puch. This afternoon. The map was in her shoulder bag, which hung over the back of Karoline's desk chair. Surely Karoline would say yes, surely—

"Fräulein Montcalm?" Karoline had raised both hands to her frizzy mop of hair and was pulling at it, beseeching her: "Will you show me again, that way with the two little braids from in front, pinned back?"

"Yes . . . of course." She had several times deftly made the little braids for Karoline. She had sensed too, that it was not only her deftness that Karoline yearned for, it was for the touch of caring fingers on her unmanageable hair. "Come on, we'll do it in your room." There was time enough, it would be ten minutes before Alma's second and final temple-bells summons to lunch. They left Fritz standing over the cassette recorder on which the tape was swiftly winding back to the beginning.

In Karoline's room, large and messy and done over in white-enameled woodwork with sienna walls in Frau Draxler's latest redecoration of the villa, Karoline sat

contentedly at the dressing table while Fräulein Montcalm combed her hair and made the two little braids,
separating the hair from above Karoline's brow, and
finally drawing the braids to meet at the back of her
head, where she pinned them securely and added
Karoline's gold butterfly pin.

"There." Finished, Nicca looked with narrowed,
assessing eyes at the sixteen-year-old's reflection in the
mirror. The braids had snugged Karoline's frizzy hair
into a vaguely romantic shape, as though held by a
circlet. Karoline's brow, usually hidden by a messy
thicket of hair, emerged cleanly. It was a lovely brow.
But Karoline was one cygnet that was never going to turn
into a beautiful swan. Her features were too blunt, her
jaw unfortunate. Still, Karoline had something else,
something invaluable: a sense of style. It was in the
incubator stage, and needed encouraging, but it was
there. Right now Karoline was wearing jeans and a
baggy cotton shirt—good enough. But in her closet was
something new: a Kenzo outfit from Erika Eisenbaul's on
Graben. Karoline had pointed it out to Nicca in *Die
Presse*: loose black-and-beige trousers with a sash and
shirt. Perfect for Karoline, as the youngster had recognized immediately. "Come with me!" Karoline had
begged her, "Please! ... I don't want to go alone—and
not with my mother, *never*!" Unwisely, perhaps, she had
agreed. From Eisenbaul's, they had turned onto Kärntnerstrasse and had been irresistibly drawn into other
luxurious shops. For Nicca, the expensive clothing had
been a feast set before a starving person; a feast of which
she had been forbidden to partake. The opulent warmth,
the fragrance, the thick carpets; the bowing, correctly
tailored young male clerks; the saleswomen, themselves
so well dressed—the exquisite pain of it! How she would
love the feel of shifting silk against her bare shoulders,

silk sliding across her breasts and cool along her thighs.
At Admüller's, in the Esterházy palace, in one of the
boutique rooms decorated with one of the palace's original crystal chandeliers, she had been unable to resist
trying on a Givenchy mulberry silk: it was a kimonolike
evening dress belted with a twisted rope of gold silk. The
salesclerk, a woman in black wearing a long green neck-
lace, graciously seemed not to notice that this customer
was wearing a cheap suit and when she undressed, no bra
at all. Perhaps the saleswoman assumed she was one of
those young women who chose not to wear a brassiere,
being unaware that the one bra this customer owned had
been washed that morning and was drying over a chair in
the maid's room at Frau Schratt's pension. From Admüller's, they went on . . . and on. . . . At Braun's, in the
rococo fin-de-siecle building, Nicca ran a hand lightly
over a hand-embroidered, lemon-colored silk nightgown
and declared faintly that the color was a bit too lemony
for her. Karoline, beside her, happily clutching her
Eisenbaul box with the Kenzo outfit, for which she had
mortgaged her allowance for the next two months, enthusiastically agreed . . . probably not hearing a word.

On Saturday, in the Kenzo outfit, with the gold butterfly pinning back the little braids, and wearing makeup
Nicca had put on, using every trick she'd learned "in
Rouen," Karoline went with her brother to a club in
Grinzing. The twins went there every Saturday. From
one o'clock on, they and their friends danced to canned
disco music, drank beer and cokes, ate frankfurters and
pastry, and surreptitiously smoked pot. Karoline, overweight and with that unmanageable hair, had always
been accepted only because of Fritz. Fritz was one of the
triumvirate of popular boys. He was the handsomest, the
best dancer. He frowned darkly at inner, mysterious
thoughts; yet he could tell hilarious family anecdotes,

using his father, Freddy, as the butt. For these alone he
was the center of attention. Karoline was taken up by
girls who only wanted to get closer to Fritz—and, unhap-
pily, she knew it. But in the Kenzo outfit she attracted
one of Fritz's triumvirate, as though *this* Karoline had
been hatched from an egg. She had become a "new" girl
at the club. Fritz's friend had asked her to dance; that
night he had telephoned. Overnight, Karoline was magi-
cally transformed. She was no longer the Karoline who,
while gobbling a dessert of fried plums with chocolate
sauce, had announced defensively to Nicca that the
Emperor Franz Josef's beautiful, slender wife, Empress
Elizabeth, had been anorexic. "Absolutely! Disgusting
skin and bones. Ugh! She used to live for days on beef
juice and violet-flavored ices." Nicca knew it was true.
Her research into the theater history of Franz Josef's
time, and into the Emperor's liaison with the actress
Katharina Schratt—no relation to Frau Martha Krieger
Schratt!—had revealed as much. Violet-flavored ices,
yes, and sometimes rose, cinnamon, or chestnut-flavored.
Though presumably later in life the Empress, anorexic or
not, also drank milk. . . . At least, that slender Empress,
who found Vienna excruciatingly boring and who spent
years at a time away from the city, traveling, visiting
strange foreign lands, and riding to hounds in Ireland,
France, and England, had a pair of English cows that
accompanied her on her later travels. But that might
have been sheer eccentricity. The Vienna papers, after
the tragedy at Mayerling, had hinted that the Empress
was mad: that her son, Prince Rudolf, who had killed
himself and his seventeen-year-old lover, Marie von Vet-
sera, had inherited Elizabeth's family madness. It was
known, for instance, that when Franz Josef had asked
Elizabeth what she would like for Christmas, she had
asked for "a young royal tiger, or a locket, or a fully

equipped lunatic asylum." Well then, maybe she didn't drink milk—maybe she just liked cows. But Nicca knew one thing: Karoline Draxler would certainly forego dessert at the lunch table today.

The Tibetan temple bells sounded again from the bottom of the stairs. Frau Draxler, always the first to arrive for lunch, would already be waiting patiently downstairs in the hall, so that they could go together into the sunny sitting room where they would lunch informally at an English gate-legged table, served by Alma. The last time lunch had consisted of cold, thinly sliced lean veal with mustard sauce and asparagus, followed by a dessert. Nicca was already hungry. But. . . .

The Puch. She should ask Karoline now, get it over with. Besides, hadn't she just done her little braids again? And Karoline had a generous nature.

They left the bedroom and started down the stairs. "By the way," Nicca began, carelessly . . .

He stood at his window at Brunners', watching for a figure in corduroy jeans and a dark red sweater. She'd be coming out of that old stone apartment house down the street any minute now. He was primed for their usual hot debate over the morning's newspaper editorials and reviews. These occurred on the days she went to the university. There she was! He waited until she had passed the Brunner house; he always waited. Then he went downstairs and got into the Porsche.

"Save your tender little feet, Nicca?" He slid the car to a stop beside her.

She turned, smiling. "By all means, Herr Foxe." She got into the Porsche and dropped her weighty books on the seat. Tendrils of hair rested delicately on her brow; the pinkish-brown lipstick had been carefully applied. He noticed that her face was flushed. Excitement?

"Pick your subject." He always gave her first choice. Her choices puzzled him, for her knowledge lay in surprising fields. She was strong on the arts, particularly theater, but weak on politics. And since she was studying political science, her ignorance took him aback. She was bound to flunk.

"Oh, today I don't want . . ." She sounded alert, intense. "I didn't hear Herr Herbst read the paper; he wasn't at breakfast." She bit a fingernail. "Do you know anything about topiary?"

"Topiary? Ornamental gardening? Fantastic shapes? Cutting trees and shrubs to look like elephants or leopards? Or ducks?" He shook his head. "That's all I know, except why anybody would want to do it."

"Because it's an *art*, people love it. A horticultural art."

"Bah, humbug! To quote what's-his-name—Dickens." He was grinning. He liked having Nicca here in the Porsche with him, even only the few blocks to the university. He glanced at her. There was something different about her today. Definitely an excitement. Her color was so high, even hectic. The fingers of her left hand fretted restlessly at the edge of a magazine that showed beneath her books. An expensive magazine; he recognized it: *Architektur und Wohnen. Architecture and Living.* About houses and gardening. He could see the price in the upper right-hand corner. One hundred schillings. A lot for Nicca to spend on a magazine. "Planning on building?" he said.

"What?" She followed his glance down to the magazine. "Oh." She shook her head; her voice was low, but Jason detected a tremor. "No, not building. Just . . . planning."

The word *planning* thrummed through him, a small, rumbling thunder. Something in her voice: tremulous, expectant. He wondered for the first time if she had a lover. Or maybe there was a man in Rouen she wrote to, a fiancé? He frowned. He cast her a sidewise glance. But now she had absent-mindedly stretched out a hand and was circling, with one finger, the shiny silver lock on the glove compartment. He'd noticed she did that a lot, it was a habit she'd developed. She had some kind of fix on the glove compartment. Suddenly aware that he was watching her, she stopped. She withdrew her hand and turned to smile at him. It was a secretive smile, mocking yet somehow utterly lovely.

He felt like butter melting in sunlight. He looked away. "O.K.," he said, "the subject is topiary. I can stand a short discourse. Proceed."

By midafternoon, Josef Valasek had finished painting the white fence that formed the courtyard to the von Reitz's garage, with its chauffeur's quarters and guest apartment above. Before the von Reitz daughters had married and gone, there had been five cars in the garage. Now there were only three. Right now, of the three cars, only the Rolls was missing: Frau von Reitz had gone shopping. Gretl the cook had said something about Frau von Reitz picking up the gifts for the Volkering baby's christening on Sunday.

"Finished!" He surveyed the freshly painted fence with approval. It would dry quickly; the air was crisp, with a little breeze. He picked up the paint can and the brushes, and carried them down past the thick hedge to the workshop. The two dogs trotted after him. Max, as usual, was in the lead; Nicki, the younger one, followed, snapping at flies and butterflies like a foolish puppy. "Grow up!" Josef would sometimes say to Nicki, pulling at the golden retriever's silky ears. He was fonder of Nicki, perhaps because he had once saved Nicki's life.

The workshop was at the back of the von Reitz property. It was a low building, painted green. It held ladders, supplies, the latest, most expensive gardening equipment and the most modern electrical workshop tools. Josef kept it in meticulous order. He thought of it as *his* workshop. Beyond it were the woods; a back road through the woods led to the von Reitz property. Delivery people came through the back road, went past the workshop, and up to the back of the villa. Josef kept his station wagon parked beside the workshop. He arrived each morning at seven o'clock. Max and Nicki would be waiting, lying in the road, muzzles between their paws. On sunny days, the sun that filtered through the trees dappled their silky pelts and they looked as though they were covered with gold coins.

At the sink in the workshop, Josef cleaned his hands with a rag and turpentine. "You beauty!" he said aloud, looking at himself in the mirror and grinning. "You could be in the circus." He had flecks of white paint on his eyebrows and on his big, reddish-blond mustache. He had had to stretch up to look in the mirror that was hung too high for a short man like himself; he had deliberately hung it there, on the theory that stretching upward would make him a fraction taller. He saw that his balding head was sunburned—he should have worn a cap. But by nightfall the sunburn would have disappeared; he had the kind of white skin that reddened in the sun, but never tanned. In all his forty years, his skin had never toughened.

"A good day's work," he said into the mirror. He liked to talk to himself. He'd spread fresh gravel on the circular drive; he'd combed the pond free of weeds and scum, standing in the little boat . . . too bad that because of the dogs they couldn't have a white swan gliding around on the pond, or a pretty quail. Then he'd puttied in a new glass for a broken pantry window and finally he'd painted the fence. "Herr Do Anything," he said aloud. He wasn't like Werner, the chauffeur, with his useless hands, Werner who spent his free time looking at pornographic films on the expensive audio visual equipment in his apartment over the garage. "I'd rather be me."

Josef loved his daily life: healthy, sweaty, clean, busy. Eight years now with the von Reitzes. He was glad he was divorced, glad that his wife, who'd married again, was the one to keep the boy.

Cleaning the flecks of paint from his mustache, he found himself thinking of Sophie von Reitz. It was a terrible thing: her husband having been viciously murdered. Maybe when Frau von Reitz emerged from the sleepwalking fog, a fog that had enveloped her since her husband's horrifying death, she would sell one of the cars. She should sell at least one car. It was a waste. Werner these days just lounged around, yawning, polishing the cars. All he had to do lately was keep them in good working order and filled with gas. In fact, during the last couple of years, Herr von Reitz and his wife Sophie had gone out less and less frequently to dinner parties, to the opera or the philharmonic. Last year, to Josef's shock and amazement, they had not even attended the Opera Ball. Astonishing! When he had first come to work at the von Reitzes' and it came time for the Opera Ball, he would stay late at the villa and have supper in the kitchen with Gretl and Resi, the maid, just to glimpse the von Reitzes leaving in the Rolls, Werner snapping to in his smart uniform. Herr von Reitz would be in white tie and tails, with the Order of Merit on a ribbon round his neck. Sophie von Reitz would be breathtaking in a glittering formal gown, a quivering shower of diamonds in her sleek dark hair. The diamonds were part of the Bulheim heirlooms, reset in tiny platinum wires and secured to a curved comb; at the smallest vibration, the diamonds quivered and shot brilliant fire. Sophie von Reitz always wore the diamonds to the Opera Ball, whether she wore a cloth of gold gown or, once, a black taffeta gown that cast off a bluish iridescence like a raven's wing. Before the ball, the von Reitzes would dine with friends or at the Three Hussars, or the Sacher. Then they'd go to the Opera Ball itself, with its all-night dancing and casino, and the late buffet with champagne and the oyster bar with real pearls in the oysters. Afterward, the von Reitzes—ever since their marriage, so Gretl said—would then go on to the Kater Frühstück, the "hangover breakfast," at four o'clock in the morning at the Schwartzenberg Café or the Imperial. Gretl, who had been with the von Reitzes since their marriage, often talked about the earlier years, before Josef's time, when the two von Reitz daughters, debutantes in billowing white ballgowns, had accompanied their parents, wearing long white gloves, and had waltzed all night. "And look, now," Gretl would complain, "the young women spend a half-hour with the waltz! The rest of the time at the ball, they're in the discotheque!"

Josef's thoughts went back to Sophie von Reitz. She stirred something in him, something sexual. Strange how, every afternoon this whole past year or so, Sophie von Reitz had gone down to the garage, taken the Mercedes, and sped off alone. She never left word with Gretl or Resi as to where she was going or when she would return. Did she go for long drives alone? Perhaps she went to some secret meeting with a man. He pictured her entering a strange apartment, saw her going into a bedroom where a man was lying on the bed, flinging off her clothes as she walked toward him. He felt a stir of envy for someone who . . . who probably did not exist! Someone he imagined. Foolish! He knew it was all fantasy, Frau von

Reitz was a respectable woman; she would not do something like that . . . would she?

He finished cleaning the paint from his face, washed and dried his hands, and went outside. He stood on the dirt road, not thinking anything, just standing. The branches of a chestnut tree shaded the road, and a little wind rustled the leaves and sent glints of sunlight dancing on the ground. "No," he said aloud, thinking again of Sophie von Reitz: No, she would not . . . would she? He turned his head and looked toward the boxwood hedge, as though he could see beyond it, right through the newly painted fence and into the garage where, in the dimness, the answer might lay in the dark maroon, gleaming Mercedes.

"Now, stop it!" He gave his head a sidewise jerk. He must stop this foolishness, and he was getting hungry! It was three o'clock, time to go up to the villa for his afternoon *Jause,* his snack of afternoon tea and a big, warm hunk of Gugelhupf, shaped like a Turk's turban, and with a crusty top on which Gretl sprinkled slivered almonds because she loved them, and so full of raisins. Gretl had a generous hand with raisins. He and Gretl and Resi would eat the whole Gugelhupf while sharing a big pot of tea at the kitchen table. Sunlight danced through the leaves. "Come on," he said to the dogs. Gretl would give them a snack too.

He started up toward the villa, but he had taken hardly two steps when a sound reached him. It was the put-put of a motor scooter. He stopped. This back road was a private road; there was a sign at the turnoff at the boulevard—studded brass lettering on an oak post: VON REITZ: PRIVATE. This roadway was only for tradespeople. As far as he knew, no deliveries were due; Gretl or Frau von Reitz herself would have told him. The dogs were standing alertly. Nicki whined excitedly, but Max stood rigid, a low growl rumbling in his throat. Max was the better watchdog, the one with sharp teeth at the ready.

Josef waited. Birches grew along the sides of the road that curved left and right, but they had been thinned, Josef himself had done it. Now through the white-barked trees, he glimpsed flashes of yellow. A minute later, a girl on a yellow motor scooter put-putted into view. Max's growl deepened so Josef spoke sharply to him and Max uneasily settled back on his haunches.

The girl was sitting straight-backed on the saddle, but with her elbows amateurishly out too far. At sight of Josef and the dogs, she slowed and came to a stop a few feet away. As she stopped, she inexpertly put out a foot and almost toppled the machine.

Not a tradesman. The trespasser was a pretty, brown-haired young woman in tinted glasses. She wore a navy suit and had a heavy, dark-red, wool sweater tied around her neck and knotted under her chin. Balanced in the saddle of the scooter, she smiled at him. Well, smiling or not, pretty or not, she had better explain her trespassing. She could not have missed the studded brass PRIVATE on the oak post. Josef folded his arms and frowned, and waited.

"Herr Valasek? Josef Valasek?"

He was too startled even to nod.

"I recognized you right away—from the photos in the Sunday *Kurier*? That Wednesday . . . you were working in the gardens here when . . . when . . ." The girl's voice died.

He remembered the when so well—*when* those news photographers had swarmed out of nowhere, bursting into the villa, sending Sophie von Reitz into hysterics, snapping pictures of Gretl in the kitchen, stomping

through the flower beds on the grounds, startling him
where he was pruning, snapping pictures and pictures.

" . . . and in *Architektur und Wohnen*—I always get
Architektur und Wohnen, it is my favorite magazine—
the June issue, with the von Reitz gardens, four pages.
That was before . . . Anyway, in *Architektur und
Wohnen*, Frau von Reitz said the credit for the whole
garden plan should go to Josef Valasek."

He knew that. He had six copies of *Architekture und
Wohnen* piled up at home, one hundred schillings a copy.
But this girl, this interloper, what did that have to do
with—

" . . . and that the whole basic design of the topiary
near the pond had been Josef Valasek's."

That was the truth all right! His beloved topiary!
Besides that, the von Reitzes couldn't have managed
without him. The grounds would be a tangled forest.
Even the tennis court—it had been his idea to lay down
the hard surface. And the time of the snake when Nicki
was a puppy only three months old. *There* was a tale he
could tell this girl!

But he kept his arms folded and his face unsmiling.
"You have proved, Fräulein, that you can read. The
Kurier, Architektur und Wohnen. So how is it that you
were not able to read the sign on the road that says
private?"

Having asked the question, he found himself hoping
that the young woman would have a remarkable answer,
maybe even a magical answer, because he felt so good
here, in the dappled sunlight, the light breeze cooling his
face, his work done, Gugelhupf thick with raisins in the
offing . . . and this pretty girl, with windblown hair, on
the road a few feet away, a girl who recognized and
admired his abilities—no, more than admired, appreciated. That was deeper, thicker: *appreciated.* Looking at

the girl, who was smiling at him, he found himself wishing that, unknown to him, vandals had ripped the studded brass VON REITZ: PRIVATE from the oak post; or perhaps, in some gleeful crazy frenzy, some wild young pranksters had torn up the whole post itself and had carried it off to prop it—their idea of a joke—at night, outside the police precinct where Detective-Inspector Trumpf, who was charged with the responsibility of solving Herr von Reitz's murder, had his office.

"It was *because* of the sign," the girl said. "*von Reitz*. I was passing on the boulevard, I saw the sign, and I thought—Oh, not of that terrible murder, Herr Valasek! I suppose lots of people come snooping, curious, poking, asking questions—I thought of those beautiful von Reitz gardens! I wanted to see the real gardens, not just on shiny magazine paper. I hoped, if you were here, Herr Valasek, you'd allow—that is, I had the silly idea . . . I'd never dare ask Frau von Reitz. Besides, she must be in such a frightful state over the . . . the . . . her husband's . . ."

The girl was going on, apologizing, falling all over herself with excuses. It was making her warm. Her face was getting flushed and she loosened the dark red sweater from around her neck, so that it fell back like a broad collar with a V in front. She was a pretty sight on the yellow motor scooter, the color warming her face, the sun picking out golden glints on her short, soft-looking hair. Her name was Françoise Deplane, and she was from France, which explained her funny accent. She was a student at the university, a lover of gardens. In Vienna she had already visited the splendid gardens of the Belvedere, *"bel vedere,"* she said, "in Italian, beautiful to see." She was going on, talking so much that he hardly knew what to believe; so many people had come, bug-eyed, up the back road these past weeks. Yesterday a morbidly curious couple on bicycles had asked pointed sexual questions about the murder; he had turned them bluntly away, even tempted to set Max on them. Strange and ugly, those people, greedy, prying. And there were others: that radio man from "Liebe Leute," for instance, asking tricky questions that had gotten him nowhere, not with Josef Valasek. And now this girl.

Yet . . . yet . . . Nicki had gone tentatively to her, wagging his tail, that golden flag. She had put out a hand and was gently caressing his head, between his ears, as she talked. *Architektur und Wohnen.* Perhaps he was not so hungry after all; another half-hour would sharpen his appetite, food tasted better when you were hungry. Frau von Reitz was out shopping, Werner was driving the Rolls. It would bother nobody if he took this young woman on a little tour of the gardens. *Architektur und Wohnen* had left out a lot: for instance, his favorite path. Lined with dahlias now, it led to the fountain with the little stone nymph. "Well, then," he said, "I have a few minutes."

They left the Puch parked beside the workshop. It satisfied his soul wonderfully, strolling with this French girl on the pebbled paths lined with the perfectly cut hedges, cut very low, to give good views of the flower beds. During the next half-hour, Josef became expansive in response to Fräulein Deplane's exclamations of admiration. He showed her the topiary and explained how he'd shaped the crouching lion and the kneeling angels. He was surprised by her knowledge and enjoyed answering her questions. He realized how deeply he'd missed Herr Otto von Reitz's interest in the villa's gardens these last couple of years. He even mentioned it to Fräulein Deplane, how in the last two or three years Herr von Reitz had changed. "He used to be so fussy, interested down to the smallest detail; he would tap his nose and discuss and discuss whether a flower bed should be shaped like a diamond or a four-leaf clover." But then ... then he didn't anymore go trotting around the grounds after breakfast, his twinkling eyes sharply spotting bracken that needed cleaning up; or complimenting Josef on the chrysanthemums; or suggesting a bush be moved further from a path to create a better vista ... No, Herr von Reitz's mind was elsewhere. Corporation law, of course, was a complicated business; Herr von Reitz had become too busy for the domestic affairs of the villa in Klosterneuburg. And now ... a rich life cut down, the man gruesomely murdered! "What is it they say, Fräulein? Something about right in the middle of being most alive? ..."

"In the midst of life, death," the girl replied, "I think that's it. ... I suppose you also take care of the plants in the villa?"

Indeed he did, Josef told her. And the whole winter garden too. The winter garden was indoors; it was attached to the library. He also did the indoor work: carpentry, fixing a table leg, a balky door, cabinets. ... Yes, he was very much in charge here; and trusted. Of course Gretl, the cook, and Resi, the maid, had their duties; they, too, were trustworthy. They were responsible to Frau von Reitz. Werner, the chauffeur, of course took his orders from the von Reitzes ... rather, from Frau von Reitz, now that Herr von Reitz ... Ah, well.

Shortly after that, Josef became aware that the girl was flirting with him. It showed in the eager way she tipped her face up to him, smiled, made a gesture as though to touch his bare muscular arm below his rolled-up sleeves, then drew back as though recollecting herself. Could it be that her admiration for Josef Valasek's formal gardens extended to the physical body of Josef

Valasek? . . , Short, balding, broad-nosed, and dressed in dirt-stained pants and a blue workshirt, wet with sweat under the arms? He decided that was hardly possible.

But he gave no sign of his doubts: Instead, he smiled and clumsily flirted back. He was a little hurt. Had the girl been leading him around by the nose? Gradually, as they walked the paths and he pointed out the oval bed of asters, the miniature boxwood maze, he knew that there was something the girl wanted from him. Information? Unaware, he had already given her some. But there was something else she wanted . . . a specific something? Yes, that. She was laying down a trail of breadcrumbs, a trail to lead him to something else.

Back again at the workshop, Fräulein Deplane wheeled the Puch around to face the road. Then she held out a hand to Josef, thanking him.

"You are welcome, Fräulein." He was holding her hand. It was a soft-skinned hand, warm and a little nervously damp. Also, it clasped his hand firmly and held it, not letting go. The girl was looking at him through those lavender-tinted lenses, smiling, but there were tiny beads of perspiration above her upper lip and across the bridge of her nose. That soft, warm hand . . . He thought now that he had never had supper with anyone, never shared a companionable meal in the evening, and how pleasant it would be, say, under the chestnut trees at the Schweitzerhaus in the Prater, to look across the top of a mug of beer and see Fräulein Deplane laughing and flirting with him. Besides the beer, he'd settle down to all the wonderful dishes at the Schweitzerhaus, where he never went, because he was shy of going alone. Right then, he knew that if he did not ask this French girl to have supper with him, *she* would ask *him*, and he would say yes.

But he would be ashamed to make her ask. He would

do the inviting. Yes, he would ask her for . . . for tomorrow night. He held the girl's soft hand and he invited her to dine with him the following evening. As expected, Fräulein Deplane was so happy to say yes.

The dogs beside him, he watched her off, watched the yellow Puch disappear amid the birches. Tomorrow night, eating with her under the chestnut trees at the Schweitzerhaus in the Prater, he would find out what this pretty Mata Hari wanted from him.

Chapter 10

Nicca left the Puch in the walkway next to the garage in Hietzing. Karoline had gone out, so she handed Alma a scribbled note of thanks, saying that she had had a wonderful ride, that she had ridden all the way up to the Leopoldsberg peak to the ruins of the medieval stronghold over the Danube, and that she had also stopped at a garage on the way back and had had the tank of the Puch refilled.

On the U-Bahn on the way back to Frau Schratt's, she tried to keep her near-feverish elation in check. She had made contact with Josef Valasek! Her endless poring over magazines and newspapers was beginning to pay off. There had been a ninety percent probability that she'd find Josef Valasek on the von Reitz grounds. She had worried more about the dogs, imagining them springing at her with bared teeth. Gentle Nicki! And Max, who had half-closed his eyes with bliss and had stretched up his head as she'd run a caressing finger along his golden nose.

Yes, her persistence was paying off. *But only so far*, she warned herself. The Schweitzerhaus at the Prater. On the train, she unfolded her map of Vienna and found the Prater. It was across Vienna from Langegasse, the opposite side of the Ring, outside it and across the Danube. She studied the map's legend. Routes and transportation were marked in different colors. She saw that she could take the *A* or *B* trolley to reach the Prater. Six o'clock, Josef Valasek had said; he would meet her at the outdoor dining entrance to the Schweitzerhaus. The restaurant must have loomed so large in his mind that he had assumed she would know where in the Prater it was. She didn't. But she had nodded knowledgeably, her hand still in his. It didn't matter: Once she reached the Prater, she would ask someone. She would leave Frau Schratt's early, maybe even five o'clock. The Prater. She had glimpsed it from the air on the fateful evening of her arrival in Vienna, the plane flying low before it touched down at Schwechat. Her seatmate, a Viennese teenager, had pridefully enumerated the city's abundant pleasures. The Prater had over a thousand acres of meadow, woods, and lakes, much of it kept wild and wooded. Within it, were two race tracks, a golf course, bridle paths, athletic fields, and a stadium. It was also rich in leafy paths, taverns, outdoor cafés, and restaurants. There were picnic areas and snack bars . . . and of course the Volksprater: The People's Park. The Volksprater was the amusement park, its main attraction the giant Ferris wheel, well known because of *The Third Man* movie scenes.

So . . . she pictured herself already at the Prater, seated across from Josef Valasek in some hazily colorful restaurant called the Schweitzerhaus, drinking wine or beer, eating, flirting, leaning toward him across the table. How much would she have to wheedle and lie? . . . What would she promise to get what she was after? And this stocky little man, muscular, virile, with a reddish face and a broad nose, and small brown eyes that looked so appreciatively at her—what might he ask in return? But it was such a little thing she wanted! If only she could convince him that he was betraying no one . . . that he would have nothing to feel guilty about . . .

If only . . . At least she was taking a step. Even the tiniest step might carry her a little farther out of the nightmare. Who was it, in some fairytale, a girl who walked on a path of the sharpest broken glass, feet bleeding, but anyway forcing herself on? A girl? Or maybe it was a mermaid, a mermaid whose every step on land was agony because she had no feet at all. Yes, a mermaid.

A sexy blouse, or at least a romantic one, that was what she needed—red maybe. Did Josef Valasek find red appealing? Soft at the neck. And cheap. Maybe she could find one in Grengross' budget basement.

Church bells . . . Eight-thirty! Damn, she was still only half-dressed. No time now for breakfast, not if she wanted those precious minutes in the Porsche with Jason Foxe, on her way to her make-believe university classes. She pulled on jeans and a sweater and grabbed up her books. Going past the dining room, she wriggled her fingers at Herr Herbst alone in there reading the paper, but then she saw that Frau Schratt, who must be in the kitchen, had already put her roll and eggs on the table. She darted into the dining room, snatched up the eggs and roll and dropped them into her shoulder bag. *"Guten Morgen, Herr Herbst. . . . Auf Wiedersehen!"* Outside, she walked with ears pricked up for the sound of the Porsche behind her. Meanwhile she bit hungrily into the roll, wishing for butter.

"A walking sidewalk café." At Jason Foxe's baritone voice, that familiar pleasure swept over her. She got into the Porsche. "I'm late for my class. I didn't have time for breakfast." She took another bite of roll. *I'd rather see you.* A sword was hanging over her head, but she was alive and in some crazy way remarkably happy, even more so as Jason Foxe turned the wheel and the sleeve of his jacket brushed her sweatered arm.

"How are the castle plans going?" She really didn't care, she only wanted to hear his voice.

"Everything is in order, even the weather. Baron von Walenberg was on tiptoe with anxiety about it, but his astrologer has given him a favorable prognostication: Bright, sunny, warm." Also, an Austrian porcelain company was considering making a nature documentary about birds, "a fifteen-minute documentary, with Florian as consultant. They're sending a representative." A Tokyo bank in need of murals was also sending someone: Florian might be commissioned to do them. "A lot of money in it, Nicca." He called her Nicca without permission, ignoring the fact that she still called him Herr Foxe.

Listening, she wished that the weather were not so oppressively warm. She wished for a chill wind. She wanted to sneeze—she wanted a reason to snap open the glove compartment. She wanted to see if the sheaf of Xeroxed notebook pages in her handwriting was still there. It had looked well thumbed. She glanced at the round silver lock on the glove compartment; one touch of her fingertip, and it would snap open.

"I meant to mention," Jason Foxe said, "in case you didn't know, there's a secondhand bookstore on Renngasse. They buy current issues of magazines for half-price. *Architektur und Wohnen*, for instance, if you're through with it. That'll get you fifty schillings. I jotted down the address."

"Thanks." She took the slip of paper he handed her.
"Yes, I'm finished with *Architektur und Wohnen*." That
part was over; she was ready for the next step. She drew
an uneven breath. "Thanks," she repeated. Fifty schillings more toward the red blouse for tonight.

At five-thirty, the early evening crowd was coming in
at the main entrance to the Volksprater. To the right
loomed the Ferris wheel, the great wheel turning against
a sky streaked with long, salmon-pink clouds; the sun
reflected on the swaying, glass-enclosed cabins, turning
the glass to glittering gold. It shed a softer, rosy-golden
light on the amusement park. The air was faintly humid,
but constant little breezes flicked away at the humidity.
Nicca mingled with the people heading up the broad
main street, the Street of the First of May. She was
anxious not to be late. She wished she had a watch; twice
on the trolley she had asked strangers the time. Where
was the Schweitzerhaus? The street was lined with barkers, pinball machines and food stands. Music, canned and
live, came from all sides. A vendor was selling ears of
corn from an enormous, steaming iron pot; Italians with
ice cream carts painted in the Italian flag colors—red,
green, and white—were doing a brisk business; food
stands were selling *gabelbissen*—fork bits—that
appeared to be little cups of herring, pimento, cheese, and
peas. Popcorn, American soft drinks, beer, liquor—it was
all here. So was every kind of sausage: Polish klobasse,
Yugoslavian cevapcici with onions and mustard, German
bratwurst, Hungarian sausages, brilliant red with
paprika. *"Bitte,"* she stopped in front of a walrus-mus-
tached man in a T-shirt who was standing beside a barrel
munching an enormous pickle. *"Bitte,* the
Schweitzerhaus?" The man, chewing, gestured with his
thumb. "Ten minutes farther up. You will smell the

horses!" When she looked puzzled, he laughed. "The horses from the merry-go-round!"

"Thank you." Ten minutes. She had ten minutes more in which to wrack her brains for a clever lie to use on Josef Valasek. Her jaws ached with tension. She had spent half the night crouched on the edge of her bed, chewing a pencil, jotting down ideas, then discarding them. The rest of the night, she had lain in the dark, thinking desperately, ready to spring up at the slightest inspiration and write it down before she forgot it. But her mind had remained a wasteland, and she had stumbled around in a Sahara of ideas.

She walked on. Fewer barkers now, fewer amusement rides and snack bars; instead, there were open-air cafés and restaurants, and chestnut trees spread leafy branches along the street. How many minutes now? And still not a plausible reason to give Josef Valasek for wanting to get inside the von Reitz villa. Not one! Furthermore, she had no idea *how* Josef could sneak her in. Well . . . one tiny germ of an idea. Perhaps she could say: Tell them, tell the cook and maid, on an afternoon when Sophie von Reitz is out . . . say I am your cousin, that you want to show me this beautiful villa. But *why* should Josef Valasek agree at all? He owed her no favors, they were not even friends . . . or lovers. She flinched away from the thought.

Merry-go-round music; she was already there. Ahead, on the left, was the brightly-colored carousel. She smelled horses. In disbelief, she approached. The man with the walrus mustache had not been joking. The merry-go-round had real horses. Real mares and ponies were plodding around, pulling the merry-go-round to the music. Small children sat on the ponies; bigger children rode the horses, sitting tall, dreams in their eyes.

"Guten Abend, Fräulein Deplane."

Josef Valasek's voice. She turned. He was wearing a

plaid cotton jacket with brown pants. He had on a white shirt and brown tie. He looked so clean he might just have jumped out of a washing machine. His face had a shiny, scrubbed look; his reddish-blond mustache was combed and looked pomaded, and so did his remaining reddish hair.

"Guten Abend, Herr Valasek." She saw that his light brown eyes were taking her in appreciatively, even the red ruffled blouse she wore with the navy suit. She didn't really like the red nylon blouse from Gerngross'; but she had liked the cheap price, and she'd recognized that the ruffles, standing up from the collar of the navy suit, gave her chin an even more piquant look and quite beautifully set off her head with the short haircut.

"This way," Josef Valasek said. The Schweitzerhaus was opposite the merry-go-round. They crossed over. The vast, outdoor garden restaurant sprawled in several directions under chestnut trees, even around corners. Waiters in white shirts and black vests hurried, perspiring, among the tables, bearing trays of big glass mugs, bottles of beer, roast meats. Thick-leafed vines surrounded the dining area, living walls of deep green. People were eating at utilitarian tables, white rectangles or round green tables that could be cleaned with the swipe of a waiter's napkin. There were families with children; couples in cotton jerseys, pants, and sneakers; men without jackets, their wives or girl friends in shirts and skirts.

"Over here." Josef Valasek made for a table, letting Nicca trail behind him. It was a round table nestled in a green-leafed corner. "Sit here. You smell that? Roast pig shins!" His scrubbed, broad-nosed face looked blissfully happy. Seated, he looked around the restaurant as though it were a bright cloak he was drawing around him. "So!" He rubbed his hands, blunt workman's hands, with the fingernails tonight showing a rim of white under each nail, certainly due to effort with a scrub brush and pencil nail whitener. The waiter brought a menu, but Josef waved it away—he already knew what they both would have, Fräulein Deplane and himself. The Schweitzerhaus was famous for its specialty, roast pig shins that were huge, crackling-crisp roasts. "Look, you see, those people over there." He jerked his head toward a nearby table where three men in poplin windbreakers sat over beers. A waiter was setting down three plates, each with a roasted shin bone so big that the bones stuck up at least five inches. "We'll have the same," Josef Valasek told their waiter. He also ordered salad, bread, and beer.

For Josef Valasek, it was a feast and a party. As they ate, evening began to fall; colored lights came on, at first only weak pastel glimmerings against a still-rosy sky; then, as the sky darkened, the lights glowed bright. Josef Valasek did most of the talking. He described his costly plan to replant the entire winter garden—provided, of course, that Frau von Reitz was agreeable. She had plenty of money, she was a Bulheim. She had come rich to the marriage with Otto von Reitz, so they said. And Sophie von Reitz had always spent freely. Besides, he would catch her when she'd had a drink or two. "A drink or two?" Yes, he had noticed that lately she liked a brandy or so, big ones. And weren't people more likely to say yes after drink loosened them up a bit? Wasn't that so? Josef Valasek, waiting for Fräulein Deplane's response, tore a piece of crisp skin from the roast. Chewing, he cocked his head a little, giving her time, but she just poked at the roast with her fork, her chin tipped down in the red ruffle. So he talked on, describing an ingenious new gardening tool, the way a little carpentry could double closet space; how badly American movies shown on Viennese television were dubbed in German, the lips not synchronizing at all with the words—last

night, *Der Weg Nach Bali*, *The Road to Bali*, 1952, Bob
Hope, Bing Crosby . . .

She hardly heard. She smiled, a stiff smile. She was
frantic, her thoughts a caged bird, fluttering wildly, tearing its feathers against the cage in desperation for a way
out. Just the germ of an idea, only that, please God! She
had come this far. Now she was stuck. What had happened to her brain? Exhaustion? What? Think, *think!*
But she could not. In misery she stared blindly at the
three men in windbreakers gnawing meat off their roasts.

And then, out of the blue, an answer thrust itself upon
her.

Two men in black berets and uniforms, guns at their
belts, strode through the restaurant straight to the table
of the three men. Sudden silence struck the restaurant,
then a wave of whispers. *"Cobras!"* The whispers peaked
and died; everyone watched. The taller of the black-
bereted Cobras addressed one of the seated men; he was
asking for identification. The man made no move. The
Cobra patted his gun suggestively. The man took a
breath, then shrugged and handed over his papers. It
went more quickly with the other two men. In a couple of
minutes, the black-bereted Cobras were herding the trio
from the restaurant, but not before they had waited
patiently for the waiter to present his bill to their captives
and be paid. Then they were gone, moving so quickly that
a little breeze sent a crumpled paper napkin fluttering to
the ground. The restaurant broke into a storm of excited
talk.

Bewildered, Nicca looked at Josef Valasek. "What was
that? Cobras?" She had read something about the
Cobras, they were Vienna's . . . she couldn't remember
what. Some sort of police.

"That'll teach them!" Josef Valasek was tickled. He
smacked a work-hardened fist into his palm, "The

Cobras?" The black-bereted men were, he explained, Vienna's paramilitary airport-security and drug-raid police. "They can ask for your identification at gunpoint." At the airports, the Cobras watched out for bombs, terrorists, and equally nasty business. In Vienna itself, where the drug traffic was swelling to worrisome proportions, they could stop a suspicious-looking character on a dark street and at gunpoint make him account for himself. Reformed addicts and a dozen other sources created a network of police information that aided the Cobras in their activities. "Those three fish they just hooked—none of that was guesswork. They had come for those bastards."

"Oh?" Drugs. *A lethal injection in his thigh.* She felt a little breathless. A vestigial idea was coming to her, a wriggling, tiny tadpole. "Are there any women Cobras?"

"*Women* Cobras?" Josef Valasek looked surprised. He doubted it. "Maybe, I don't know."

The tiny, wriggling tadpole was trying to come to the surface; it gave a convulsive wriggle. Nicca leaned toward Josef Valasek; she said earnestly, "Several European countries, and even Russia, have women in paramilitary positions—even in high police positions. For instance, I could become, say, Detective-Inspector Deplane, Like a . . . a Detective-Inspector Trumpf."

Josef Valasek nodded; he was agreeable. He signaled the waiter for more beer. "If I had a daughter, I wouldn't be against it; a girl ought to have the same job opportunities as a boy."

"Yes." She nervously fingered the red ruffles. "I want to tell you something, Herr Valasek."

"Yes?" His light brown eyes looked very interested. He pushed his plate a little away and folded his hands on the table, regarding her.

She hesitated. "It was true yesterday, about *Architek-*

tur und Wohnen, how I admired your formal garden, I was really dying to see it. But, Herr Valasek, horticulture is not for me." She forced herself on, the wriggling tadpole growing froglike legs. "I plan to go into forensic science." Aware of his blank look, she struggled to find the right words. "Crime detection, Herr Valasek. I—"

"It is all right if you call me Josef."

"Josef. I want to help solve crimes. I'm taking a forensic science course at the university." The idea was a real frog now, jumping from lily pad to lily pad. "We search for clues, we find traces of the most minute things: fluff, hairs, grains of sand, we study them through microscopes. Of course I'm still an amateur, but—"

"Crime detection? At the university? You like that better?" Josef's voice was heavy with disappointment. "So, instead of flower beds, topiary—"

"Josef, remember yesterday when we were talking, what you said . . . about 'in the midst of life'? Herr von Reitz's rich, happy life cut off? *Viciously* cut off! By a murderous injection in his thigh! Someone who—" A shudder suddenly shook her shoulders uncontrollably, the red nylon blouse rippling visibly with the convulsion. "The cold deliberation of that murder! The cunning of a Claudius pouring poison into the ear of his brother the King while he slept in that orchard at Elsinore. Then creeping away . . ."

A string of colored lights hung along the top of the Schweitzerhaus wall of leaves behind Josef Valasek. The sky was blue-black; one of the colored lights—blue— shone down on Josef, shone blue on his balding head, gave his reddish-blond eyebrows a greenish cast, made dark hollows of his eyes. For an instant, it put her off; but need gave her courage. "Josef, I am pursuing that criminal. I want to help find Herr von Reitz's murderer." As she spoke, the realization of how convincing she sounded swept over her. It almost frightened her. So easy, they had become so easy, her fabrications! Then, with sudden enormous relief, she understood why this fabrication was so easy: It was easy *because it was not a fabrication*. It was not a lie. She was telling Josef the truth: She was pursuing the criminal, the killer, searching for clues, yet she could not tell Josef Valasek that her life depended on succeeding.

She could see that Josef was beginning to make peace with her defection from horticulture; she could see it in the slow way he was nodding his head and looking at her. He was tearing up one picture of her and replacing it with another. He was even approving; there was a shadow of admiration in his eyes for Fräulein Deplane's aspirations. "So then," he said ponderously, serious now, "you want to catch the murderess—that American girl."

She sat very still.

Josef Valasek, frowning, thinking, asked, "But how do *you* expect to find her, when the police are still looking . . . and even they . . ." He gestured, picked up his mug of beer, and took a long sip, regarding her over the rim.

She did her best to explain her inspiration that something within the von Reitz villa, some clue, might be a tip-off that could help her to find von Reitz's murderer. The police, brilliant as they were, were looking in a different direction. "You mean," pondered Josef, considering, "that Herr von Reitz could have known this American girl *before* that night? That something, a clue, in the villa, could, maybe, lead to her?"

Exhausted, she said limply, "Maybe could lead to . . . something."

There was a tiny sizzling sound from the wall of green leaves, and the blue light above Josef Valasek went out. He looked himself again, a stocky little man in a plaid

cotton jacket and white shirt. He wiped foam from his
red-blond mustache, then hunched forward and clasped
his hard, stubby hands on the table: "So, Fräulein
Deplane, that's it then: You want me to get you inside the
villa."

Long after they had eaten the dessert of cherry
palacinka and she had drunk hot tea and Josef had had
another beer, they sat talking. Josef confessed that when
Fräulein Deplane had appeared on the yellow Puch, he
had been suspicious that she was another of the visitors
who came greedily for gleanings, avid to take home the
self-inflating news that they had caught a glimpse of the
murdered man's widow, of what she wore, that they had
seen how she looked. Or they wanted to say that they had
chatted familiarly with the von Reitz's chauffeur, who
had told them for a fact . . . and so on.

But now he was wholly on her side. Exploring the villa,
was it? Yes, he had the keys. Yes, Sophie von Reitz was
out often in the Mercedes. The problem would be the
servants: Gretl and Resi. Either Gretl the cook, or Resi
the maid, was always there: they did not have the same
day off. Gretl's was Thursday, Resi's was Monday. And
then, there was Werner, the chauffeur. Luckily, of the
two apartments above the garage, Werner's did not face
the villa, his windows looked out over the woods. The
other apartment, the guest apartment, was, of course,
empty; in fact, no one had stayed there for years. So, no
problem there.

When Nicca suggested that Josef introduce her to
Gretl and Resi as his sister or cousin visiting from . . . oh,
France, and say that he was proudly showing her around,
Josef shook his head. Impossible! Gretl and Resi knew he
was an orphan who had never known his antecedents;
they'd discussed it often enough over tea and Gugelhupf

while exchanging tales of their childhoods. Besides, they might mention this "cousin's" visit to Sophie von Reitz, who also knew about his orphan background and his adoptive parents; it had been in his original application for the job. "A girl friend then? Suppose you introduced me to Gretl or Resi as your—" "No! No!" It appeared there was something Gretl and Resi knew about that too; Josef blushed and his eyelids momentarily came down over his eyes like shutters.

She cast about, suggesting, discarding. Josef was thinking hard too, she could see that; he had taken out a pencil stub and was doodling on the table, frowning, concentrating, as though trying to plan out this approach as he planned new designs for gardens, closets, a special kind of work table. Then— "Huh!" He dropped his pencil. *"Dummkopf!"* He struck the side of his head with the flat of his hand. "Stupid! The christening!"

That was it: the christening. The von Reitz older daughter, Frau Theresia Volkering, had given birth to her first baby. The christening was this coming Sunday. It would be at the Karlskirche, the famous baroque church near the Belvedere, not far from the Volkerings' house in Wieden, in the Fourth District. After the christening there would be an elaborate celebration at the Volkerings'. In honor of this event, Gretl and Resi had been given the day off. Werner would be occupied the whole day in the service of Frau von Reitz: that meant mostly chatting with the other chauffeurs outside the Karlskirche during the christening, then continuing to swap gossip and stories in front of the Volkerings' home in Wieden. Sophie von Reitz would, of course, have taken the Rolls.

Settled! The rest was easy to work out.

Josef Valasek paid the bill. Waiting for change, he looked around at the garden restaurant with its colored lights, at the people still eating under the thick-leafed chestnut trees. He heaved a great sigh of satisfaction. "Fräulein Deplane, if you should succeed at the villa and then lead the Vienna police to the killer, I don't ask to be mentioned in the papers. In fact, the opposite! But I would like it if we'd then celebrate over supper at this same table. Did I mention they also have a veal shank? And suckling pig?"

Chapter 11

A harpist sat plucking delicately on a gold-and-white harp near the French windows of the Volkering residence. The buffet was set out along the same wall. A hired butler and an extra maid circulated among the guests in the main rooms, carrying trays of champagne. Anton Volkering, the baby's father, had lost his head and ordered a nonsensically extravagant number of white flower arrangements, huge bouquets of them. Their expensive fragrance was now pervading the rooms. Ironically, Anton's uncle-in-law, Gustav Bulheim, had insisted on taking over the florist's bill as a christening gift. Not that that had been sufficient for the generous Herr Bulheim: the engraved little silver cup that had arrived in its gold box and tissue paper from Heugler's had been accompanied by Gustav Bulheim's card. The silver cup bore the baby's name, Viktor. The *o* in the name Viktor was a ruby. Sophie von Reitz's gifts had not been for the baby, but for her daughter Theresia and Anton: a brace-

let for her, cuff links for him. Heugler had crafted the
jewelry, faithfully copying the drawings Sophie von Reitz
had brought to his shop. Each piece of jewelry had the
baby's name and birth date cleverly worked into the
design.

Gustav Bulheim stood beside the piano in the main
living room, sipping champagne. He was ostensibly listening to Herr Flugler, chief accountant at Anton
Volkering's firm, but actually, he was watching for his
sister Sophie's arrival.

He wanted to warn her. He wanted to give her the gun
that was even now in his briefcase.

Late yesterday afternoon, he had tried to reach Inspector Trumpf. There were times when Gustav Bulheim
castigated himself for his single, dangerous weakness:
impatience. Still . . .

Yesterday, from breakfast on, when the soft-boiled egg
had been too hard and the toast cold, his whole day had
been a shambles. Herr Strobl had come down with a
children's disease that nobody over the age of eight
should be susceptible to, and he had spent an exasperating morning searching for mislaid documents. By midafternoon, a wretched lunch still burning in his chest, his
anger and frustration had begun to circle in on the police
investigation. For a whole week he had heard nothing. He
had known that his anger was due to a growing unease
over his sister Sophie's safety, and all at once, he had felt
it imperative to communicate his trepidation to Inspector
Trumpf. He had seized the telephone and called the
Rossauerkaserne, only to learn that the inspector was out
of town and not due back for two days. He had hung up, a
little relieved not to talk to the inspector in the heat of
anger, and had admonished himself to be more controlled. Yet, during the night, his smoldering unease had
burst into a raging conflagration. Never mind waiting for

Inspector Trumpf's return! He would act on his own. This morning, an official emergency meeting had kept him from the christening at the Karlskirche; he had arrived at the Volkerings' early, to find that his sister Sophie had not yet appeared.

" . . . create an international financial *débâcle*," Herr Flugler was saying impressively.

"Yes . . . yes . . . excuse me." Gustav Bulheim reached out and touched Anton's arm as his nephew-in-law passed: "Anton! Have you seen Sophie?" Sophie? No, she still hadn't arrived from Karlskirche so far as Anton knew; but he'd keep an eye out and let Gustav know the moment she appeared. Gustav Bulheim thanked him and submitted himself again to Herr Flugler who after two glasses of champagne was now talking nonstop. " . . . considering that South Africa's apartheid policy is enough to split . . ." Herr Flugler took a gulp of champagne—he no longer bothered to sip—and plunged into the depths of South Africa.

Gustav Bulheim's thoughts turned back to Sophie and his murdered brother-in-law. For his sister's sake, he had always tried to like von Reitz. Otto von Reitz and Sophie Bulheim had met at a weekend party in a country house in Carinthia. They had fallen in love and married within the year. Otto was then in his late twenties, a fledgling lawyer in his family's prestigious corporation law firm in Vienna. He was good-looking in a fair-haired, blue-eyed way and leaned toward fat. He was competent, shrewd, egotistical, and had developed a self-important manner that bordered on pomposity. Once Otto and Sophie were married, and Sophie was so deeply, romantically in love, Bulheim had made an honest effort to feel warmly toward Otto. He acknowledged that von Reitz had sincerely fallen in love with Sophie; it had been a marriage of love, nothing else. Also, when Otto looked at Sophie, something decent, kind, and loving animated his face.

But, on the other hand there was Otto von Reitz's peculiarly mid-Victorian overcontrol. Gustav Bulheim thought he was rather like a dieter who is afraid to go into the kitchen because he might gorge himself. Otto somehow made him think of Vienna's earlier Victorian attitude toward sex—Puritanical, yet simultaneously permissive and secretive. There was something in von Reitz's personality that Bulheim could not quite put his finger on, something he disliked.

He had managed, however, to form a kind of artificial friendship with von Reitz. It was a friendship passable enough on the tennis court, or hunting partridge and pheasant on weekends in Marchfeld, or amid the bustle of weddings, or at family parties where there were always children and dogs to distract attention. Then Bulheim's diplomatic career had begun to take him to Paris, Geneva, London, Washington, Rome; and he had had little opportunity to see much of the von Reitzes. When he was in Vienna, he'd occasionally dine with them in Klosterneuburg. Or he'd run into Otto at the Casino in the Esterházy Palace on Kärntnerstrasse. Neither he nor von Reitz was a gambler, but Bulheim found it pleasant to drop in at the little jewelbox of a casino with its green velvet chairs and mirrored bar. He would order an espresso and relax before deciding on roulette, baccarat, or black jack. He'd arrive at nine o'clock, the beginning of the expensive time; amateurs would be cashing in their chips and departing, it would be quieter. When Otto von Reitz stayed late at the law office, he would dine at Sirk's and he, too, occasionally dropped in at the Casino. When the two men met, they played at the same table, usually baccarat. After an hour, they would cash in their chips, those iridescent chips that gleamed like mother-of-pearl.

Outside, on Kärntnerstrasse, in front of the Grenadier, they would part, courteously shaking hands . . . strangers standing on different planets.

But was it months now—a year . . . longer?—since he had run into von Reitz at the Casino? Until this instant, gazing blankly at Herr Flugler, he hadn't realized it.

"Gustav?" It was Anton. Sophie had arrived. She had gone upstairs to see Theresia, who had taken the baby in its lacy white christening gown up to the nursery.

Upstairs, he found them in the baby's room, which looked as gorgeous as a Fabergé Easter egg, except for a few modern white plastic gadgets; one of which noiselessly sent a steady stream of mist into the air, and another that looked like a telephone transmitter, and was probably for monitoring the baby's slightest cry if you were elsewhere. Sophie was shaking out the lace christening dress, a family heirloom that in the distant past had been worn by both Sophie and Gustav. The nurse was slipping a soft blue flannel gown over the baby's head. Theresia sat collapsed in a white rocking chair, smiling beatifically at the scene. Gustav managed, with little more than a quirk of an eyebrow and a tip of his head, to draw his sister into the hall.

He led her into Anton's upstairs study. "What is it?" Sophie's eyes looked so hollow. They still had dark circles underneath that makeup had not quite covered.

He explained his apprehension. The American girl, Veronica Kent, could have had a vengeful reason to hate Otto von Reitz, "Revenge over a legal verdict, for instance," he explained. The girl was a psychopath, her rage might well extend to other members of the von Reitz family, to Sophie herself. "Only a hypothesis!" he emphasized, "But this young woman is a psychotic, who obviously has access to mind-altering drugs. God knows how crazy-dangerous she could be!" Therefore, at the von Reitz villa in Klosterneuburg, even with the protection of Josef Valasek and the dogs, and despite the presence of Gretl and Resi and Werner, Sophie must be vigilant. "For your own safety!"

And now, the gun: the gun downstairs in his briefcase. He had a permit. It was best if Sophia had the gun, he would give it to her. Later, he would clear it with Inspector Trumpf. Now, he would just—

"Absurd!" Sophie drew up her shoulders. "Craziness and rage? Oh, no doubt! Drug induced? Who knows! Anyway the girl must be thousands of miles away by now, dosing herself with drugs in Hong Kong or the Himalayas. Wouldn't that be more likely? Yet you think she'll turn up at Klosterneuburg!" Sophie laughed that hysterical little laugh she had lately developed. "Keep you gun, Gustav."

When he insisted, she shook her head obstinately. A strand of hair fell down; she had done up her dark hair for the christening, but carelessly, not with her usual eye for grooming. Altogether, despite her makeup and chic beige suit, she had a faintly unkempt look.

"Don't worry, Gustav." She kissed his cheek, stared into his eyes for a moment, then gave a sudden shake of her head and left. Troubled, he stood there in the den. He folded his arms, unconsciously falling into what his assistant Strobl called his "diplomat concentrating" pose. He could not understand it: How could Sophie refuse the gun? She had always been a timid girl; in their childhood on the family estate, he had rescued her from all kinds of Sophie-terrors, as he used to call them: harmless little snakes, toads, unidentifiable insects, imagined tramps and beggars near the stables. Admittedly she could be wildly furious when she lost her temper, but that happened rarely. So why was she now so brave . . . spurning the gun? She was, it seemed, even after her husband's murder, unable to face reality.

Ten minutes later, when Gustav Bulheim threaded his way among the guests downstairs in search of his sister, determined to prevail on her to take the gun, he learned from Anton that she had already left. Left? When she had only just arrived? Yes, not five minutes before, Werner had driven her home in the Rolls.

In Klosterneuburg there was a snap to the air and a smell of earth and forest. It had rained during the night; now the sun, falling on patches of wet bracken, fallen leaves, and damp moss, sent up a pungent smell so strong that you breathed a little shallowly, defensively.

It was close to noon as Nicca Montcalm, riding too fast on the yellow Puch, turned in past the VON REITZ: PRIVATE sign on the oak post, and sped up the road between the white birches. At the workshop, she stopped, breathing fast, balancing on the seat. "Josef! Hello!"

Max and Nicki loped to meet her, tails wagging, Nicki whining with pleasure. Josef, cutting wood with an electric saw, turned off the motor and glanced at his watch. She was chagrined, she was later than she had expected. But she couldn't help it. She had missed one U-Bahn to Heitzing. Then, when she had reached the Draxlers, she had found Karoline having a nervous crisis: the girl had awakened with a pimple on her cheek, just when she had a date with that boy from the Club! By the time Nicca had led Karoline from suicidal despair to skillful makeup, a half-hour was lost. Then she had found that the motor scooter was out of gas; Karoline had used the machine and had forgotten to fill it. Fritz had kindly siphoned gas from his own Puch to fill the tank. Another twenty minutes. She had told Josef Valasek eleven o'clock. Now, though she had ridden dangerously fast, it was certainly after twelve.

"I'm late, I'm sorry. . . . You weren't worried?"

Josef shook his head. "I figured, the Sunday traffic." He gave her an encouraging smile. He was wearing a cap and an old sweatshirt and khaki pants. In spite of the cap, his face was red again with transient sunburn. She saw that he had taken a bunch of keys from his pocket.

"You look different. Younger." He sounded surprised.

"Yes." She was wearing the cowl-necked sweater and corduroy jeans. Sunday was the day when half of Vienna went hiking, walking, climbing, mostly in the Green Belt, the Vienna Woods that were within the city limits. People took cars, buses, or trolleys to the woods; they hiked along some fifty miles of trails and went rock climbing on the Hohewand. They wore hiking shoes, pants, knickers, sweaters, open-throated shirts, even T-shirts and shorts with knee socks. They carried packs on their backs and picnic lunches. She would have been conspicuous, riding the motor scooter into the countryside in her proper-looking navy suit.

Josef led the way up through the garden walks, the dogs trotting along beside Nicca. The final path led through a grape arbor, thick with heavy-hanging bunches of red grapes almost ready for harvest; then they went through a kitchen garden.

"In here." Josef unlocked the back door. Inside, he closed the door against the dogs. He led the way through a hallway, then a pantry with tall, glassed-in cupboards. They came into the kitchen. It was big and modern, except for a fireplace with dark red, glazed tiles and an antique clock on the wall. Nicca glanced around, but the kitchen held no interest for her: It was not what she had come for. Whatever might help her would be elsewhere in the villa. At that moment the clock struck. It was an immense old clock with a yellowing face. It struck the half hour, with the muffled resonance of a gong struck with a padded drumstick. It made her think of scenes from a movie she had once seen: a Turkish prison yard, a guard striking an enormous metal disk; a prisoner, hands shackled, head hanging, led out into the dusty yard; a firing squad in turbans, waiting. Her hands were icy cold. She thrust them into the pockets of her jeans. "Come on, Josef."

But Josef did not move. Instead, he held up his stubby hands apologetically. "I'm sorry, I have a delivery coming. Hornbeams." They were young trees, he explained, due from the nursery: gray-barked birches. He had ordered them months ago. Now the nursery had telephoned, just an hour ago. He had to meet the truck—it would be coming up the back road in a few minutes—to sign the receipt, make sure they unloaded properly, and direct the planting. He didn't want the roots injured. "You will have to find your way around alone, Fräulein Deplane, but I am not worried. I trust you, and I wish you good luck, good . . . clues."

She followed him through the pantry to the back door. "The door locks automatically," he told her. "When I come back, I'll open it with the key."

"Yes." And at the last minute, "The Puch!"

Josef nodded. "I'll put it in the workshop, nobody will see it." He went out. Through the glass top of the door she could see the dogs following him through the kitchen garden. He went around a bend and disappeared. She turned and walked back. She felt very alone. In the kitchen, she looked at the yellowed face of the clock. An antique kitchen clock: that was all it was. But . . . time, time, *time!* Her hands were still icy cold.

A carpeted passageway brought her to the front hall. It was spacious and had a pink marble floor. Splashes of

rainbow-hued sunlight shone through a beveled fanlight
over the front door; to the left, a staircase curved up to a
landing. It was dead quiet.

She hesitated at the staircase. Where to look first? She
knew, from the Sunday features in *Die Presse*, that the
villa had originally belonged to an Austrian diplomat
who had served the Empire under Franz-Josef. And that
the house was known principally for its classical portico
and for the frescoes on its dining-room walls. She had no
idea where the study might be.

Start downstairs first, she decided, for who could tell
what tiny, betraying thing might spark some connection
in her mind? Suppose, for instance, a leather box lined
with cedar—a box of cigars, true Havanas now dried out,
yet with a particular aroma. If she opened that box and
drew in a deep breath, it might stir a fragmentary forgotten impression, hint at something. . . .

The room she entered first was a living room carpeted
in pale, costly colors, and with soft chairs and sofas.
There were tables with porcelain lamps, fresh flowers in
tall silver vases, crystal ashtrays, Indian sandalwood
boxes inlaid with ivory. She stood a moment, alert, waiting, looking carefully around. But the room gave her
nothing back: For her purpose, it was dead. She went on
through. The dining room. Sea green linen curtains at the
windows, cushioned chairs drawn up to a smoked-glass
table, a smoked-glass sideboard with a brass coffee service against one wall. Nothing, *nothing!* She did not even
pause to look at the frescoes.

Frowning, walking quickly, back she went, past the
staircase in the front hall. The room beside the passageway to the kitchen was a music room: there was a white
piano with the lid closed, a television screen, and an
expensive-looking hi-fi and audiovisual arrangement. The
Chinese red carpet was at least an inch thick. No music

at the piano—not even in the piano bench when she lifted the lid. Sterile here too, for her; she sensed it. She gnawed at her lower lip.

Back to the entrance hall. More doors: a bathroom and a sizable coat closet that automatically blazed with lights as she opened the door. Then, the last door. She opened it and came into the library. An inhabited room, she thought immediately.

The remains of a fire were in the fireplace, and a smoky, cold smell lingered in the room. Sophie von Reitz must have made the fire to take off the early morning chill. A soft chair had been turned from the fireplace to face directly onto a winter garden. The winter garden, a glass-enclosed extension of the library, was brilliant with flowers; just now they were particularly dazzling in the sunlight that shone down through the glass roof.

Beside the overstuffed chair was a table, upon it a pair of eyeglasses and a glass containing the dregs of a drink. Nicca glanced around; against one wall was a liquor cabinet holding bottles of liquor, glasses, and an ice bucket—all the accoutrements. A woman living alone now in this villa, was she lonely? Did she often sit in that chair facing the winter garden? There was a glass door beyond the profusion of flowers. How would it be later on—in winter, with a falling snow outside—to pull on boots and wrap yourself in a sable coat and walk through that summer blaze of chrysanthemums, dahlias, asters, and brilliant blood-red rhododendrons . . . to open the glass door and find yourself in the misty white of falling snow, a cold landscape?

Icy hands in her jeans pockets, Nicca abruptly turned away.

Upstairs, she found a study. But, disappointingly, it seemed more of a family den than von Reitz's personal study. Wood-paneled walls, bookcases. A black leather lounge chair, good for reading; a magazine rack beside it. The desk, near the window, was in current use: a pile of bills was held down by a glass paperweight, and on it there were pencils, a letter opener, a scattering of letters, a silver stamp box. It must be here, at this desk, that Sophie von Reitz herself now took care of the household bills. Nicca approached the bookcases. The books were outdated travel guides, almanacs, books on horseman-ship, skiing, Austrian history. Nothing of interest. Atop one of the bookcases were a few photographs in silver frames. She studied them. One showed a young man in a monocle. He wore a dashing black hat and had a flowing mustache. His stance was arrogant, somehow theatri-cal . . . in fact so theatrical that she picked up the photo-graph and studied it more closely. It not only looked theatrical, she realized, it *was* theatrical: The young man's face was made up; theater lighting shone dramati-cally up from below.

She was startled. She had seen enough early photo-graphs of Otto von Reitz within the past weeks—more than enough, in fact!—to recognize this man as the young Otto von Reitz. Odd that none of her concentrated reading had mentioned that von Reitz had had an early career in the theater.

One by one, she picked up the other framed photo-graphs and studied them. Here he was again, ragged, sitting at a table in a wretched hovel . . . but again thea-ter lighting was shining upward. And how conspicuously false, in the next photograph, were the mustache and beard! There were five photographs altogether, all with the same cardboard unreality. Someone had obviously prized them: they were the only photographs here.

Biting a thumbnail, she stood frowning, gazing at the photographs. Turn of the century? No, earlier. A time of Viennese baroque comedy, romantic poetry. It made her uneasy. Yet why should it disturb her? Something familiar here; but why? She bit her thumbnail, exasperated that what she was grasping at eluded her. But anyway, she thought, this is not it. *Let me think about this later.* An instinct seemed to tell her that these photographs were significant, but they were not enough. They were only tangential to . . . to something else.

The von Reitzes' bedroom, that must—*had to*—bear better fruit! With a sudden childish gesture, she crossed her fingers and shook them in the air. Besides her own anxious hope, she had a ridiculous feeling that she also owed it to Josef Valasek to come up with a clue that would help find Otto von Reitz's murderer . . . Josef, who was babying the young hornbeams out of the truck, or perhaps already guiding their bagged, loam-protected roots into the ground. He would be returning soon, coming in the back door; she would hear his footsteps on the stairs.

In the upstairs hall, glancing quickly into one room after another, she at last turned a handle and opened the door to a room larger than the others.

She saw at once that this was Sophie von Reitz's bedroom. It was wholly a woman's room. She had assumed the von Reitzes shared a bedroom. She had been wrong. Their rooms must connect, perhaps through a dressing room; there was a passageway on her left. She stood looking around. She had a faintly uncomfortable sense of being a *voyeuse,* yet she was too curious to cross immediately to the passageway. One of the casement windows had been left open, and a strong breeze had tangled the sheer coral curtain around the handle. A black, silk-knit sweater, thin as air, hung, drooping, over the back of the chair at the dressing table. A pair of white satin mules, not quite clean, had been kicked off and lay tumbled near the bed. A couple of dresses and a clothes

hanger lay on the bed. The bed itself, not even a double
one, had a copper-colored satin quilt and beige satin
pillows. The rug, too, was copper colored, the walls beige.
A big, square scarf, black and white, a *Jugendstil* design
showing a long-haired nude lying among circles and
stylized flowers, had been framed and hung over the bed.
It was the only decoration. It looked stunning and stylish.

She heard men's voices, Josef's voice giving orders. She
went to the casement window. Below, on the other side of
the tennis court, Josef stood over two men in earth-
stained pants. They were laying the long bundles of
trees—hornbeams, were they?—on the ground in a row.
She could already visualize the young trees grown tall, a
leafy windbreak at the back of the tennis court. Tennis.
She thought of the library downstairs, the chair turned to
face the winter garden, the dregs in the glass.

She turned back to the bedroom. It smelled too
strongly of perfume, as though a stopper had been left
off, or a perfume bottle overturned. She approached the
dressing table and saw a stain on the rug and a round
crystal bottle with a long teardrop stopper in the wastebasket. The hurried or nervous hand of the woman making up at that dressing table had knocked over the bottle.

A faint chime. On the dressing table, a square gold
clock announced the time: one-thirty. She turned and
went around the bed to the passageway.

On the left was a bathroom, on the right a dark,
doorless room. Nicca pressed a switch. A row of round,
frosted globes shed light on a long closet, surely ten feet
long. To the left hung men's clothes. Otto von Reitz's.
Nicca was taken aback: She would have supposed that
Herr von Reitz's widow would have had her husband's
clothes packed up, sent away, given to a charity. How
could the widow bear to see those clothes? . . . to smell
the cologne that clung about them . . . perhaps even to

brush against the beaver-collared coat, the hunting jacket, the country clothes, the business suits? Would it pain her to look down and see the rows of polished shoes and boots? How . . . how *terrible*.

To the right were Sophie Reitz's clothes. Nicca gave a soft sigh. A dozen boutiques' most elegant items on hangers, everything from a white loden coat to sparkling evening gowns in transparent shrouds. And yes, Sophie von Reitz did indeed own a sable; and next to that was a lynx, and next to that a black cashmere coat with stand-up collar of silver fox. Nicca wanted to reach out and caress the fur.

One-thirty. Get on with it.

She went into Otto von Reitz's bedroom. It was a square white room with walnut furniture, Prussian blue drapes at the windows. This was the kind of room that would belong to a corporation lawyer in his late fifties, a Viennese who, if he did not literally wear a gold chain across his vest as his father, grandfather, and great-grandfather had, at least did so figuratively.

Here she wasted no time. She went right to the dresser and began opening drawers. She searched among the layers of blue silk underdrawers and monogrammed handkerchiefs. She was looking for letters, notes, written words that might reveal a love affair; a blackmail note that Herr von Reitz might have contemptuously ignored—hatred or jealousy revealed in black and white, typed, handwritten, crudely printed. She searched for threats, insane rage, venomous words. She pulled out more drawers, drawers full of day and evening socks, of belts and suspenders; she felt between the layers of shirts: cotton, linen, silk. She stopped suddenly and went back to the closet in the passageway. Here she felt in the pockets of Herr von Reitz's suits and coats, even in the pockets of a padded tapestry bathrobe. Nothing but an occasional folded handkerchief.

Returning to the bedroom, she sat on the bed and went through the drawers of the night table. "Someone wanted to kill him!" she said aloud, in desperation. *"Who?"* She was almost sobbing with frustration. She yanked out the drawers completely and turned them over in the hope that a letter might have been taped to the bottom of one of them. No use. She slid the drawers back in.

She sat on the edge of the bed, drooping, hands empty. All this, her planning, her supposed cleverness, her flirting with Josef Valasek, the Prater, the yellow scooter— and nothing! *Nothing.* It had all been a waste. Slumped on the bed, she traced a finger absent-mindedly over one of the bronze bookends, a winged eagle that supported a few books on the bedside table. Books! She quickly pulled out one of the books, leafed through it and shook it upside down . . . then the others, eagerly, one after another. But not even a bookmark fluttered down. Again, defeat. She sighed. She glanced down at the book still in her hand. It was one of those limp, leather-covered volumes, maroon, gold-tooled. Baudelaire. *Les Fleurs du Mal. The Flowers of Evil.* She remembered a time when she had been fascinated by Baudelaire, his poems, his bitter and tortured views on love and corruption. She sat, holding the volume, the leather warm in her hand. Something was hovering at the edges of her mind, brushing at them teasingly like soft wings. Yes, *there!* Something recent . . . Baudelaire . . . Vienna, people dancing, a man waving a baton—he was like a wound-up toy—and over the music, a voice saying . . . saying—

The sound of a car motor outside the villa brought her to her feet. She dropped the book and rushed to the window. A gleaming brown Rolls was coming up the circular drive. Through the polished windshield she glimpsed a flash of sun on a chauffeur's visor. A moment later the car disappeared under the portico below. Sophie von Reitz had returned.

She rushed down the stairs. She had to get out before that front door opened. At the foot of the stairs, she darted for the nearest door, closed it behind her. The library. She ran across the room and through the winter garden to the glass door. Turning the handle, she stepped outside—and at that moment she saw a woman coming around the side of the villa heading her way. Sophie von Reitz! She had not gone in the front door at all. Quickly, quickly! Nicca closed the glass door behind her and turned immediately to face it, her back toward the woman approaching. She put her hands to her brow, shading her eyes against the sun, peering through the glass into the winter garden. Her heart was beating furiously. *Who are you?* the woman behind her would say angrily, furious. *What are you doing here, looking in my windows? Trespassing! Get out!*

She kept her back turned, peering . . . peering. Behind her, the footsteps stopped. The woman was standing there. Silence. Nicca could see the woman's reflection in the glass door. But still not a word. *Say something!*

In the distance there was the sound of a motor, a heavy, growling sound, the truck from the nursery leaving. Somewhere, far off, down the paths past the kitchen garden and the formal gardens, near the woods by the garage and workshop, were Josef Valasek and the dogs. Here at the villa there was only herself, and behind her the motionless figure of the woman reflected in the glass. And silence.

Her arms felt heavy. She could not stand here forever, peering through the glass, a statue in sweater and jeans. She gave up; she turned around.

A woman wearing an enormous plum-colored stole

over a beige suit stood there. Her clothing was expensive, her eyes dark and haggard in a white face. She looked angry.

"Well?" A husky contralto.

Well . . . she was Fräulein Deplane, a journalist, Sunday features for the *Kurier*. She had rung the front doorbell, there was no answer; she had assumed that the bell was out of order—surely there was a maid about, servants, someone—so she had come around to the side. . . .

"And your car?" Those dark eyes, haggard, stared at her.

Yes . . . her car. She had, in fact, come up the back roadway, the traffic on the Autobahn—

"And you wanted, Fräulein . . . Deplane?"

To find out who murdered your husband. To save my life. Feeling trapped, aloud, she said, "Possibly your opinion on how the police are handling . . ." Her voice faded. Sophie von Reitz was coming toward her, she was beside her, she was putting out a hand and turning the handle of the glass door. She went inside. There was the sound of a lock being turned.

The nursery truck gone, Josef Valasek washed the loam from his hands and came out of the workshop, feeling for the keys to the villa; yes, in his back pocket. He was starting up toward the house when Fräulein Deplane came running across the lawn, a fawn in jeans and sweater. She had ignored the curving path, and was speeding straight for the workshop. When she reached Josef, her face was so pale that he said loudly, "Here, here!" as though the words were a pair of crutches to prop her up. He grasped one of her arms and gave her a firm, gentle shake. "It's all right!" He had no idea what he meant, he knew only that Fräulein Deplane needed to hear such words.

"Frau von Reitz!" The girl tumbled out the news that Frau von Reitz had returned from the christening and had almost caught her in the house, but she had slipped out through the winter garden and then Frau von Reitz had seen her, spoken to her. She had told Frau von Reitz that she was a journalist. "I said I'd come up the back road. Josef, you can say you didn't see me because you were planting the hornbeams with the men from the nursery."

"Yes, yes!" he assured her, he would say that. "We're both safe, Fräulein Deplane. Don't worry, you did a smart thing. Journalists still pester Frau von Reitz, they come crawling around, they call on the telephone. Frau von Reitz certainly believed you! If you'd told the truth, she would have called the police! This way, by tomorrow she will have forgotten you entirely. Entirely! Just another snooping journalist." He felt alive, excited. It was an adventure. Even planting the hornbeams, he had imagined Fräulein Deplane inside the villa, stealthily lifting up a corner of a rug and finding a passionate love letter from Veronica Kent to Otto von Reitz, proof of the fiercely declared passion of the psychotic girl that the honorable Herr von Reitz had repulsed. He had envisioned Fräulein Deplane uncovering revealing information that would set the Vienna police back on their heels, mortify them. Fräulein Deplane's professor would give her the highest marks; her discovery would even make her famous. He said hopefully: "And clues? Did you have time? . . ."

"Yes. I found something."

"I'll get the Puch." Josef went inside the workshop.

When he wheeled out the motor scooter, he found Fräulein Deplane on her knees in the path; she had her arms around Nicki's neck and her face buried in his long, silky fur. Nicki sat on his haunches, patiently submitting. Max stood nearby, an elder stateman, surveying the scene.

"Here you are. I had some extra gas, so I filled the tank."

Fräulien Deplane released Nicki and stood up. "Thank you." Josef saw that she was a little shaky, not that she had much on her to shake. How could a girl with such a big appetite be so thin? She got on the saddle of the Puch. But then she just sat there, biting her lips and frowning, looking at him. She seemed worried and anxious, but her jaw was set determinedly. She sat for a minute, twisting her hands back and forth on the handlebars, thinking, frowning. Then she asked him how far it was to Mödling from Klosterneuburg, from Mödling to Hietzing. "What a trip!" he exclaimed, "Three hours at least, more likely four!" He described the route, shaking his head. If Fraulein Deplane was thinking of making such a trip on the motor scooter, she had better think again. That sweater wouldn't be warm enough in the wind; and by late afternoon the weather would turn colder, the wind would rise. It was already after two o'clock.

When he said that, she got such a stubborn look on her face that he yanked at his cap, told her to wait, and went in and got his leather windbreaker from the hook in the workshop. He forced it on her, almost pushing her sweatered arms through the sleeves. When he'd tugged up the zipper, jamming folds of her sweater inside, he had to laugh. The jacket made her look like a black sausage.

When she was gone, Josef oiled the lawnmower. Werner was back up in his apartment over the garage, and he had a window open. Josef could hear his TV: screeching brakes, revolver shots, and loud background music that Josef thought of as "car chase music."

He put the oilcan back in the workshop and was coming out of the door when something up toward the villa caught his eye. Sophie von Reitz. She was on her way down the azalea garden path, going toward his right. She wore black wool slacks and an old pink shirt and she carried a drink in her hand. She was heading toward the courtyard, the garage, where he had painted the fence. But if she had wanted Werner to bring the car around, she could have called him on the intercom from the villa—no need to go down and see him. And she wasn't going to the garage to get the Mercedes either, not with a drink in her hand.

But it wasn't his affair. She was his employer and she treated him well. Besides, he felt sorry for her, what with this terrible business about her husband. He got up on the lawnmower and tested the brake. He would do the north lawn first, around the pool, it needed it the most. As for Sophie von Reitz, he would never understand women anyway. Not Frau von Reitz or his ex-wife or even Fräulein Deplane.

Cars whizzed past, and the wind blew back her hair and made her eyes tear. But the black leather jacket kept her warm. She rode grimly, holding tightly to the handlebars, afraid that a sudden bump in the road would loosen her grip and cause her to lose control. Josef had been right, a strong wind was coming up. The clouds were wind-streaked, the sun was thinner and gave no warmth. She rode on. A carful of teenage boys passed, whistling and shouting at her. Another car came too close, then swerved away just in time, she glimpsed a woman's frightened, apologetic face looking back at her, saw children jumping up and down in the back seat.

She watched for road signs; she was trying to keep Josef Valasek's description of the route in her mind. An hour already, surely more than an hour now.

Mödling. How far ahead was it? She had to go there, had to go there *now*. She had had such extravagant hopes about a discovery at the von Reitz villa. Too extravagant! In the meantime, those overblown hopes had kept another worry battened down, but it was surfacing. *Mödling.* Daily, she had forced that fear from her mind: The dress and shoes buried in the Mödling woods. But at least once every day, perhaps while Herr Herbst was asking her at breakfast if she had yet found herself a favorite coffeehouse in Vienna, a *Stammcafé,* a home away from home, she would be thinking: Are they still hidden there by the tree, the shoes and green dress?

Worst of all were the times she was with Jason Foxe. Then it was unbearable to think of what lay buried in the Mödling woods. Jason Foxe . . . was it the wind on the Autobahn that brought tears to her eyes? She fiercely ordered herself not to think of Jason. Sometimes, when she sternly gave herself such an order about Jason Foxe, not five minutes later she would find herself smiling over a remembered conversation with him, or recalling Jason's touch on her shoulder, his baritone voice, or the way he had of looking at her lately.

Buried in the woods . . . were they still? Maybe they had been dug up, taken away: *She had to know.* Inspector Trumpf had the reputation of keeping his cards hidden from the media. Did *he* have them? Had he had the tiny flecks of blood analyzed? A bump on the road almost loosened her grip on the handlebars. *Pay attention.* She sped on, upright, cold wind on her forehead. She glanced down at the gas gauge, then remembered that Josef

Valasek had filled the tank. And if not Inspector Trumpf, then that would-be rapist, Rudi. In the daytime, Rudi pumped gas at Strohmayer's Service Garage off Langegasse; at night he did God knows what! But if Rudi had dug up the clothes, it would have been in the news ... unless Inspector Trumpf—what if this Rudi hadn't gone to the police but was searching for her himself, roaming the streets of Vienna, looking for her, hoarding his precious "evidence" for what it was worth? *Stop it!* Stop fantasizing. Enough of these imaginings! She must not, *must not*, torture herself further.

Another road sign. *Mödling!* Twelve kilometers. Of course the clothes would still be buried there, moldering away underground. She rode on, more slowly now, it was unwise to go fast when she was so tired. She longed for coffee, a thermos of hot, strong coffee, so she could stop by the roadside and warm up, but she didn't want to risk stopping at a roadside snack place. She would park the Puch, though, at the gas station near the subterranean grotto.

Five kilometers. What if, when she had assured herself that the clothes were still there—she was suddenly feeling more confident—what if she took the clothes away with her—left nothing that could ever be dug up? When she got to the woods, she could take off her sweater and tie it around her neck, wear only Josef's leather jacket. The jacket was roomy. The shoes would fit inside it, one shoe under each breast. The green dress she could crumple around her back and midriff. Later she would destroy them. Then she almost laughed: Destroy them how? She hadn't the faintest idea. She was so exhausted she was thinking nonsense, preposterous things. Once she had assured herself that the dress and shoes were still there, once she was relieved of her anxiety, she would leave them to rot.

Her hands felt cramped. She was riding so slowly now that she dared to lift a hand and flex her fingers. Only minutes now, minutes to Mödling. She sighed, a great sigh of relief, and arched her back, stretching. Then she put her hand back on the handlebars. She rode on toward the woods.

Karoline Draxler had been in love since three-thirty that afternoon. It was now almost six. She was too exhilarated to stay in one place. She went restlessly down to the pavilion, up to her bedroom, down to the kitchen, then back to the bedroom. She kept glancing impatiently out of the window, hoping to see Fräulien Montcalm approaching. She couldn't wait to tell her about Georg. Meantime, she tweezed her eyebrows, examined her complexion with the magnifying mirror, and made a note to buy perfume. Then she analyzed her sensuality, using a questionnaire in the magazine *Petra*. It was entitled: "Are You Sensual?" Your erotic radiation, your character, your soul were all revealed in your physiognomy. A woman psychologist from Hamburg said so. Sensuality was revealed in the middle of the cheekbone; it depended on the distance between eye, nose, mouth. Desire, the strength of desire, was above the upper lip. You could test yourself in the mirror. There were seven sketches of young women's faces, each labeled according to shape, and the shape of the eyes, nose, and mouth. Karoline studied the sketches. Which was she most like, which physiognomy? Not the Gentle. Not the Dreamy. The Hot-blooded, maybe.

Drone-and-hiccup—the motor scooter arriving at its slowest, down in the driveway. Karoline dropped *Petra* and flew downstairs. She found Fräulein Montcalm in the walkway, leaving the Puch in its usual place. Fräulein Montcalm was wearing a black leather windbreaker over her sweater. Her forehead and nose were wind-burned, her lips looked cracked. In fact, she looked terrible.

Karoline Draxler, no matter what her physiognomy, was a sensitive girl. She recognized at once Fräulein Montcalm's emotional state, one with which she was admittedly unfamiliar but one which aroused in her a protective sympathy, a sympathy so strong that she did not even mention Georg. Instead, she suggested that they have a cup of hot coffee at the kitchen table. One thing she knew: she must not let Fräulein Montcalm go back to Langegasse on the U-Bahn without having had some hot coffee. She might stumble and fall on the tracks. And pastry. Perhaps strudel or plum tarts. Alma must have something in the kitchen. But the pastry for Fräulein Montcalm only. For herself, just coffee without sugar.

On the way to the kitchen, Fräulein Montcalm said she would just stop off in the downstairs bathroom to wash. Fräulein Montcalm certainly did need a good wash—there was even a streak of dirt on one of her cheeks. And her hands! Dirty, earth-stained.

"My heavens, Fräulein Montcalm! Were you digging in the Wienerwald? Digging your way to China or digging for buried treasure, the way children do?"

"What?" Fräulein Montcalm looked down at her hands, at the dirt, the blackened rims of fingernails. Two fingernails were torn and bloodied. She held her hands palms up, fingers curled, staring down at their emptiness: "There was nothing *there,*" she said.

Karoline giggled. She was delighted that Fräulein Montcalm could joke back, even when exhausted. As for Fräulein Montcalm's dirty hands, "Stop sticking your nose into everybody's business," Fritz was always telling her, annoyed, "particularly mine." Fräulein Montcalm's dirty hands were her own business, Fritz would say, and he'd be right. Karoline quelled her curiosity.

"I'll have Alma start the coffee, You look chilled—the wind. It will warm you up. And I have so much to tell you!" Georg had invited her to the movies. She left Fräulein Montcalm to wash and went off to the kitchen. An Einspänner, she would have Alma fix an Einspänner for Fräulein Montcalm, that was best: a glass of hot black coffee with a nice big blob of whipped cream.

Chapter 12

It was a balmy afternoon. Jason Foxe, briefcase in hand, walked along the Kärntnerring. He had just finished taping a preliminary, informal round-table discussion with a dozen young Austrians. The material had been a bonanza. As far as he could see, it promised that the Texas Foundation for the Humanities hadn't wasted their money by investing in Jason Foxe, sociologist.

But his thoughts were on Nicca Montcalm. He was wondering if she had turned in the magazine, *Architektur und Wohnen*, to the secondhand bookstore. He seemed always to be worrying about her finances.

He reached the corner of Schwarzenberg Platz with its long vista of statues and baroque palaces, and suddenly there she was, Nicca, coming toward him. She had bought herself a beret. It was dark blue and she wore it slanted across her forehead and dipping down to one side; her soft, short hair curled out over the other side. She was also wearing gloves. That struck him as odd: The weather in Vienna was unseasonably warm, certainly too warm for gloves, even the cotton ones she wore. The warm wave had swept across Europe. The temperature was said to be in the 80s in Paris, and Zurich had registered a record high.

They met almost exactly in front of the Café Schwarzenberg. It was four o'clock, the hour of the *Jause*, time for pastries with tea or coffee.

Jason promptly said: "You're going to join me for some of the Schwarzenberg's hedonistic delights." He took her firmly by the arm. "The ravishment of ice cream and pastry. Don't struggle."

In the Schwarzenberg, he chose a table near the soaring oval windows. The Schwarzenberg Café was the most spectacular coffeehouse in Vienna. The high-ceilinged rooms glittered with mirrors, brass, crystal, chandeliers. Enormous porcelain vases of fresh flowers stood on pedestals and on silver-laden sideboards. The Viennese nostalgia for the old days was responsible for the Schwarzenberg's extravagantly expensive "Old Vienna" décor: It had been created in 1980 with the help of Vienna's Culture Department. Professor Schindler had even written a paper about it: "Der Weg in Die Vergangenheit"—"The Road into the Past"—for one of the sociological journals. The Schwarzenberg Café had even revived coffeehouse recipes popular in Maria Theresia's time.

Nicca Montcalm, in her beret, pored over the list of Vienna's old-time ice-cream dishes. She settled finally on the Du Barry: vanilla ice cream, strawberries, Grand Marnier, and whipped cream. Jason ordered cheese-toast and espresso. He was not hungry, but he found it amazingly satisfying to be at the Café Schwarzenberg at exactly four o'clock with Nicca Montcalm.

Over her ice cream, she told him that the Draxler

twins, as children, had gone on bird walks. "They're still interested in birds—Fritz can even imitate some bird calls." The twins had asked her what blowups of birds of Austria her friend Jason Foxe would be setting up at Castle Walenberg. "I told them I'd ask you." Jason gave her the names.

Half-smiling, he watched how blissfully she was enjoying the luscious-looking Du Barry concoction. She had taken off her gloves and was dipping out ice cream with the long silver spoon. There were small scratches on her hands; a bit of adhesive tape covered the tip of a finger. She saw that he had noticed. She flushed. "Sunday," she said "on one of the trails, the walking trails? I picked raspberries. The prickles were awful . . . like thorns."

"Yes?" He took a bite of cheese-toast and looked across at Nicca Montcalm. She had a French type of chic. Something—thorns, the beret—put him in mind of . . . of what? Whatever the elusive thought had been, it slipped away. Nicca Montcalm had begun to talk absorbingly about the twins, about the anguishes and joys of being sixteen.

In the arcaded courtyard of the university, built in the Italian Renaissance style, the sun sparkled on the Castalia Fountain. Jason Foxe stood nearby, waiting for Professor Schindler. It was three days after his afternoon *Jause* with Nicca Montcalm at at the Schwarzenberg Café.

Under the arcades, the statues of eminent professors gazed out of stone eyes at the fountain's graceful virgin guardian of the spring of purity. Students stood chatting in the sun-splashed courtyard or made their way to classes or midmorning snacks. It was so warm that they had taken off jackets or sweaters. The weather was dry, springlike; it created a sense of expectancy, the promise of burgeoning, new growth rather than the coming autumn.

"*Guten Tag, Herr Foxe!* Here I am, precise to the minute!"

Jason, poplin jacket slung over his shoulder, turned to see Professor Schindler beaming at him. Schindler had completed his project on Oscar Lewis and the Mexican sociological work and was feeling frisky as a week-old lamb. He could now turn his mind freely to his endless preoccupation—his fascination—with his true love: the sociological scene of Vienna at the time of Empress Maria Theresia. Professor Schindler was, in fact, one of a particular type of Viennese, those who hark back nostalgically to the romance and royalty of an earlier Vienna— a time of eye-winking, aristocratic love affairs, royal intrigues, and lavish amusements. They preserved the medals, ribbons, decorations, and photographs of any of their progenitors who had ever worn splendid uniforms or had the slightest relationship with the Habsburgs, even one so slight as having been bowed to at a masked ball. They were equally conversant with the marriages of Austrian nobility and their political significance. On Professor Schindler's desk, the best-thumbed volume was the *Almanach de Gotha*, which listed the antecedents of every aristocratic house of Europe, recording marriages, baptisms, deaths, and every familial relationship down to the last distant cousin innumerable times removed. If Professor Schindler were aroused from a sound sleep and asked to instantly name the progeny of any of the great houses of Europe, the professor, eyes still closed and half-asleep, could recite every name and relationship.

Jason handed over two worn pamphlets, the last of Professor Schindler's reference material. "Here they are, for your file."

"Thank you, thank you, Herr Foxe! . . . You'll come to Landtmann's for lunch with me, Herr Foxe? You'll be my guest?"

"Sorry, but I have an appointment with Königsmark, my ornithologist friend, the one I'm helping—"

"Königsmark! Baron Wilhelm von Walenberg's cousin? *That's* the one you've been—the one you'll be having the party for at Castle Walenberg? Ahhh! I didn't realize!" Professor Schindler rubbed his hands, he was delighted. "Königsmark, eh?"

Well, he knew a tale or two! Those Königsmarks at the time of Maria Theresia . . . "You know about Maria Theresia's Chastity Commission, Herr Foxe? No? Well, listen then, Herr Foxe. But first I must point out: You know the Viennese, a touch of past royalty, of aristocracy, attracts the Viennese—honey to bees. The Viennese revel in titles, scandals, royalty. They say that Americans are impressed by titles and royalty, but that's a flea to a giant compared to the Viennese! So perhaps a mention of that dashing Emmerich Königsmark, back in the romantic past: a touch of publicity, eh, Herr Foxe? It could have the Viennese running to the bookshops for your friend Königsmark's book on birds!"

Professor Schindler actually giggled. He was enjoying himself. "It was like this:

"Maria Theresia, such a delicious-looking beauty, an ample-breasted Empress with such white shoulders, and always masking and dancing and playing jokes—yet she was the great Empress. *She* ran the Empire. *She* decided every matter of war, of diplomacy, of state. She was too tactful to consult her husband, Franz of Lorraine, on such important matters. Franz was charming, but hardly a diplomatic or military genius. Maria Theresia did, though, have him crowned Holy Roman Emperor, but only because she, as a woman, could not wear that crown. Franz's true function, Herr Foxe, was fulfilled in bed.

"You have seen that voluptuous bedroom in the Hofburg, Herr Foxe? Yes? Astonishing, isn't it? Maria Theresia was fifteen when she fell in love with that handsome boy, Franz of Lorraine. She was eighteen when she married him. He adored her. Vienna, at that time, as you doubtless know, Herr Foxe, was most certainly even bawdier than England. Coarser, more vulgar. People in the streets of Vienna laughed and made ribald remarks about that royal marriage bed in the Hofburg Palace. And Maria Theresia was always pregnant. With Franz she conceived sixteen children on that royal bed.

"Incongruous, eh, Herr Foxe? The beautiful girl with the golden ringlets, there she was in those opulent rooms, always pregnant, always dashing off her famous, ungrammatical notes—such misspellings!—yet with shrewd, brilliant orders, ruling the Empire, handling everything from taxation to army supplies.

"But then what happened? There in the imperial palace, Maria Theresia, had become accustomed to having her imperial decisions instantly carried out. Surely this Empress, finally in her early thirties, still young, still beautiful, must have come to believe that whatever edict she proclaimed could be enforced.

"What happened, Herr Foxe, was this: Jealousy! The Emperor Franz became intrigued with a pretty girl, a dancer. Gossip brought Maria Theresia news of private little supper parties attended by Franz and invariably by the pretty dancer. Jealousy and anger! They say that the news made Maria Theresia flush so hotly that she flung open all the windows of that royal bedchamber and almost caught a chill. It was then, for the first time, she must have recognized, Herr Foxe, that in the Empire, flirting and gallantry had gotten out of hand. It had reached carnal proportions. Morals had gone to the devil. In her schoolgirl handwriting, Maria Theresia now issued a royal edict: Libertinism, adultery and shameless behavior *must no longer exist.* Impropriety would no longer be countenanced. Streetwalkers and other malefactors would be arrested and punished.

"In short, Herr Foxe, Empress Maria Theresia abolished vice."

"She abolished . . ."

"Vice, Herr Foxe! Vice! She set up a Chastity Commission. She put Kaunitz, her chief minister, in charge. That was . . . let's see . . . 1753. A body of secret agents fanned out through Vienna to ferret out hidden vice. Under Kaunitz, state police augmented the secret agents. They patrolled the streets, arresting girls found walking alone. Prostitutes who were caught were transported to southern Hungary. Streetwalkers became seemingly as virtuous as nuns, police agents hesitated to arrest girls who walked modestly with eyes cast down, fingering a rosary. The rosary business boomed.

"Chastity Police kept an eye out for pornographic pictures and books. Secret agents stood about unobtrusively in theaters and ballrooms, then pounced, making arrests. The Chastity Police were deluged with anonymous letters in which jealous wives accused their husbands of liaisons. Jealous husbands also sent the police missives accusing their wives.

"They say that half of Vienna doubled over in fits of laughter at Maria Theresia's royal edict. The rich, the aristocracy, the gallants, found all sorts of ways to circumvent the edict. Many of them established mistresses in the country villas of friends and secretly visited them there. As for Königsmark . . .

"Königsmark, a certain Emmerich Königsmark was one of a group of young, rich gallants. He made himself a

leader in establishing a glamorous secret society called
The Figleaf Brotherhood . . . Figleaf, presumably, to
audaciously and defiantly announce that only a figleaf
would cover their nakedness. All Vienna knew the
Figleaf Brotherhood's purpose was to annoy and thwart
the unhappy Chastity Commissioners. Königsmark, a
dashing charmer with a black, spiky mustache, was even
said to have had a hand in inspiring some adventurous
young ladies to establish a sister order to the Figleaf
Brotherhood: The Order of Free Ladies sprang up. The
young women went masked to riotous parties with the
Figleaf Brothers.

"Königsmark was arrested when police agents raided
one of those parties. The others escaped, except for a
handful. But the police had captured a prize: Emmerich
Königsmark. Young Königsmark and his friends were
sentenced to be shackled to the city gates, and to beg for
their food and drink from citizens who passed." Professor
Schindler was chuckling, rubbing his hands. "Can you
imagine what happened, Herr Foxe? I will tell you!
Viennese citizens, hearing the news, emptied the best
pastry shops, the best food shops. They brought the best
meats and wines and beer to the shackled gallants. Pretty
girls insisted on taking turns feeding them—chocolate
cakes with whipped cream from sympathetic, white little
hands."

The professor took Jason Foxe's arm. "Come into the
shade." They left the fountain with its virgin guardian
and moved to stand under the arcade. *"Zeitgeist,"* Professor Schindler said. *"Zeitgeist*: The spirit of the age.
The moral temperature of the times, Herr Foxe. What
you Americans call the *climate* of the times—an era's
ideas, its very mood, its potential for action. An awareness of these things, *that* is the essential awareness a
sociologist must have. So, I was speaking of the mid and

late 1700s, of Maria Theresia's time. There is a thread
going back from today's Vienna, with its computers and
its OPEC meetings, the romantic thread I spoke of earlier, in the minds of the Viennese, going back, *back*. They
cling. They waltz. They yearn. They have not yet let go.
So it might indeed be wise to drop in your press releases
your friend Florian Königsmark's connection with a certain Emmerich Königsmark of the black, spiky mustache: The Figleaf Brother."

The professor released Jason Foxe's arm, which he had
still absent-mindedly held. "You go to Castle Walenberg
when, Herr Foxe?"

"Saturday morning." Jason Foxe smiled down at
Schindler. The professor had papery-thin skin and blue-
veined eyelids. In his dusty-looking dark suit, he looked
exactly what he was: a professor who had taught at the
university for the past forty-five years. His children were
already gone, parents themselves. His vivacious young
wife had grown heavy and placid; she spent her after-
noons at Prückel's Café on the Stubenring, playing cards
with ladies and retired gentlemen of her own age and
weight. Since none of them would ever think of foregoing
their afternoon of bridge, rummy, or poker, the card
games continued uninterrupted, little square wooden
tables always being provided to hold the cardplayers'
coffee and snacks. Professor Schindler loved his life: Frau
Schindler made his supper, he had his journals, he read,
he wrote, he taught. He had never fallen in love with a
student, yet he was just vain enough to color his thick
gray hair with a brown rinse that sometimes came off on
his hands when he thoughtlessly ran them through his
hair. *Zeitgeist* was his favorite conversational subject. It
was clear to Jason Foxe that Schindler's advice about
publicity for Florian Königsmark was an attempt to

repay him, Jason, for his help with Schindler's Mexican project.

They parted in the arcade. Jason came out onto Dr. Karl Lueger Ring Strasse. He walked south, cutting through the Town Hall park. He had no intention of disinterring Emmerich Königsmark of the black, spiky mustache from his grave. Florian's new book was a masterpiece, it could stand on its own. As he walked, he read the botanical names on the labels of plants and bushes, then immediately forgot them.

He was thinking of Nicca Montcalm. That was natural, of course, for the park around him was full of students, lazing, chatting, laughing, taking the sun; some had cans of cokes and orange drinks. Could she be here after a class? . . . Nicca? He looked searchingly around.

That girl under the tree over there, eating an apple and reading . . . no, that wasn't Nicca. Neither was the girl with her arm around that tall boy. He wondered where she was. A pretty girl like Nicca, when she wasn't in class or with the Draxler twins, she undoubtedly had dates. With whom had she gone walking in the Wienerwald on Sunday, what young man? At night did she go to one of the dance bars, the Chatanooga or the Scotch? If he should drop in at the informal Trummelhof, would he find her there, eating, drinking, laughing, dancing in her jeans and white blouse, or maybe in that new blouse with the red ruffle? Nicca . . . Of course she had to study hard, too. Probably she was home at Frau Schratt's right now, studying. Political science was no cinch.

In the shabby Café Hawelka, she sat stubbornly turning over magazine pages, her back aching. Wearisome, endless. The hexagon-shaped clock ticked. An old lady sat knitting on the faded plush banquette, the knitting needles going click-click. At the stove behind the counter, Herr Hawelka was baking the morning's apricot cake.

A horror, it had been such a horror in the Mödling woods when she had dug ... and dug; and then, clenching dirty fists, had thought desperately: This is the wrong spot! The wrong tree! But she had known it was the right tree, that skinny elm. The shoes and green dress were gone. The distance between danger fashioned by fear, and *real* danger, was closing. A chill traveled up her arms, her back.

Click-click, the knitting needles. She picked up a magazine and riffled through the pages. It was the *Neue Illustrierte*, a weekly. The issue was a couple of weeks old, but somehow she had missed seeing it earlier. There were pages of ads: perfumes, headache pills, cigarettes, automobiles, hair driers. She riffled past articles on diet, politics, sex, personalities, crime. A phrase caught her eye: *"accomplices in love."* A shiver went down her back.

She sat very still. Her whole body was tense, yet she felt suddenly alive, alert. That expression: *"accomplices in love,"* it was all tangled up with roses and death. She riffled quickly back through the magazine, searching feverishly for the page. The phrase had been on the left side, just after the red Volkswagen ad—but now she couldn't find it. She riffled again, unsuccessfully, then again. She would find it, she had glimpsed it—it had to be there! Accomplices ... accomplices ... There it was!

It was halfway down the page. She saw now that she had misread it. Now she read it again, correctly, concentratedly—the full sentence of which the words *love* and *accomplice* were only fragments. *"Love is a crime that demands an accomplice."*

She flattened the *Neue Illustrierte* open with her palms. The phrase was in an article that covered both pages. She looked at the pictures on the two pages. There were only three. On the left-hand page was a snapshot of two teenagers, a boy and girl, on bicycles. They were laughing toward the camera. Next to it was a studio graduation photograph of a dark-haired young man with an earnest face. The third photograph was on the right-hand page. It was that of the naked body of a boy at the morgue.

She went back and read the single sentence: *"Love is a crime that demands an accomplice."* She sat there, gazing at it. She was trying to grasp a significance that was tantalizingly just outside her reach. She sat there for some minutes, just staring, thinking. Then she began to read the article.

Chapter 13

Inspector Leo Trumpf drove down Langegasse. It was a crisp, sunny day, dry and fresh. Pepi, beside him, was reading one of his cowboy paperbacks in Spanish.

The inspector was feeling remiss. He had promised himself to visit Jason Foxe, he owed him that. But here it was, three weeks later. At the Rossauerkaserne, he had been flooded with investigations. Under the snow-white luscious Schlagobers, the whipped cream and pastry surface of Vienna was a substratum of largely minor crimes that fell to him. As for the von Reitz murder, Herr Gustav Bulheim's offer of a reward regarding Veronica Kent had drawn a blizzard of anonymous letters chockful of false leads that had wasted police time and proved fruitless. Inspector Trumpf was worried. He labored under a black cloud: No thread, not a single thread dangled at the edge of his peripheral vision. This time, perhaps his luck had run out.

Jason Foxe was staying at Adalbert Brunner's pension.

The inspector knew the house. He'd always admired it, with its gleaming, black-painted shutters and six white marble steps. He had even visited the Brunners' pension a year or so ago—a little problem with one of the guests: a Swiss woman who had been caught shoplifting at Lobmeyr's and who had turned out to be wanted by the Swiss police for fraud.

There it was on the left, that elegant, yellow three-story with the faceted glass glitter atop, Herr Adalbert Brunner's expensive hobby.

A blue Porsche convertible was parked at the curb in front of the house, and Jason Foxe, in a handsome tweed jacket and dark pants, was piling an odd-looking assortment of material into the trunk. Aluminum spotlights, four-foot rolls of paper. Luggage rested on the street. As Trumpf's Volkswagen drew near, Jason Foxe straightened and glanced up. Trumpf stopped. *"Herr Foxe! Guten Morgen.* I was just coming to see you."

"Inspector Trumpf. *Guten Morgen* . . . to see me?" The American's baritone was not particularly friendly. But then, of course, Foxe had cause for resentment. Innocent though he had been, he had been hardpressed, by Trumpf, as The Foxe, a sharp-toothed invader of the vineyard—the luscious grapes a young woman.

"In fact, yes, Herr Foxe. Just to drop by." The inspector felt awkward. "I feel obliged—That is, the von Reitz investigation is progressing . . . though slowly, slowly. Detective Staral tells me you still call. I shall by all means keep you abreast of developments. I should also like to mention that, purely in the line of duty, regarding the word *ferociously*—the implication—and concerning the American girl's notebook, the possibility that perhaps you had removed significant pages . . . you understand of course that police work is police work. Police investiga-

tion, where kidnapping or murder is concerned, requires
standard procedures—"

"Never mind." The American's lips twitched suddenly, a suppressed smile. "Let's just consider it an inside
joke."

The inspector smiled back. This Foxe, a man worth
knowing, too few like him around. He watched Foxe toss
a suitcase into the back seat and pick up an armload of
spotlights. "So . . . a weekend in the country, eh?" He
knew perfectly well that Foxe was on his way to Baron
Wilhelm von Walenberg's Schloss in Styria, the press
party for Königsmark's *Birds of Austria* book; it had
been in the papers. Trumpf knew Florian Königsmark
was a friend of Foxe's, it was part of his job to know.
Though of course Foxe was now in the clear.

"Yes. In Styria." But Jason Foxe was looking past him.
The inspector heard the sound of running feet, and a
moment later a girl came panting up.

"Guten Morgen! I was afraid I'd miss you!" A light,
clear voice, breathless: "I'm on my way to catch the U-
Bahn. Here's something from the twins, it's for you to
take to Schloss Walenberg." She was holding an
envelope.

"Right . . . stick it in my pocket." Foxe juggled the
armload of spotlights and lifted an elbow: the girl slipped
the envelope into his pocket.

Trumpf, about to drive off, looked at the girl. She wore
a navy suit and under her arm was a pile of school books.
French, Trumpf noted. The girl was pretty, in what he
thought of as the "new" way: she had chicly shorn hair
and a brownish, made-up mouth, and wore big, lilac-
colored glasses. She spoke German with a French accent.
But it was an unusual French accent, one he'd heard
before, but he could not place. Elusively familiar . . . he
wanted to hear more. And besides, he could do her a

kindness. "Fräulein, I would be delighted—If you wouldn't mind squeezing in beside my son—this is my son, Pepi—I will drop you at the U-Bahn."

Jason Foxe introduced them. Fräulein Montcalm. She did not seem eager to accept the inspector's invitation, so he hastened to add that it would not take him out of his way. "Have a wonderful weekend," she said to Jason Foxe. She went around the Volkswagen, and Pepi opened the door. Fräulein Montcalm was about to get in, when she suddenly exclaimed. "The . . . the cassettes! I forgot them!" She slammed the car door shut. "I must go back, I forgot something. But thank you anyway, Inspector, I appreciate—Don't wait for me! I insist!" And she ran back up the street. True enough, he had an appointment with the chief, he didn't want to be late. In the rear-view mirror he saw Fräulein Montcalm disappear into an apartment building.

"They work so hard, they study so hard, those foreign students," he said to Jason Foxe. "I am correct, she is a student?" Yes, at the university. "Rooming down the street, yes? At Gabmayer's?" No, at Frau Schratt's. "Ah she comes from? . . ."

"France. Excuse me, Inspector, I am out of time." Jason Foxe's flat-cheeked face was impatient. He headed for Brunner's marble steps. "I must finish packing the car. *Auf wiedersehen,* Inspector. I appreciate your visit." He disappeared into the house.

Trumpf sat, reflectively pulling at his nose. A student from France. From where in France? He drove off.

It eluded him. All during his half-hour meeting with the chief, it nagged at him. He couldn't place the girl's accent. He prided himself on his knowledge of regional Austrian accents and his ability to distinguish the countries and areas people came from by their accents when speaking German. He was particularly good at Czech, Hungarian, Yugoslavian; but he was also good at distinguishing half a dozen accents of the twenty-four regions of France. This girl's accent was one he had heard before . . . but from which?

It kept tantalizing him. It was like trying to think of a familiar word that escaped him. He had once been so frustrated at trying to remember a book title that one midmorning he had jumped up from his desk and rushed to the Österreichische Nationalbibliothek to look up the title under the author's name. He recalled his almost physical relief when he had finally found the index card. Now he was ridden by the same frustration he had felt over that book title. The girl's accent . . . where had he heard the German words pronounced just that way?— how she had pronounced the word *Zwillinge,* for instance, the word for "twins." And then, rushing off, *Bitte, warten Sie nicht auf mich*—Don't wait for me.

But not five minutes after he had left the chief and was in his own office, he had a glimmering. He stood up. "What do you say we take a little trip to Claude's?" he asked Pepi.

Pepi looked at him, astonished. *"Hombre!"* Claude's was his favorite candy shop. He had half a dozen tricks for luring his father to Claude's, but never before had his father suggested going there. *"You* want to get chocolate?" he asked his father. *"You're* going to eat chocolate? *Hombre!* You want Mutti always to call you Knöderl?"

"Not for me—for you. It's Saturday, you got your Tachengeld this morning; you're going to spend it on candy anyway."

At Claude's, Pepi surveyed the glass cases with the eye of a professional shopper. He was a specialist. He was finicky, difficult to please. He began to argue price, qual-

ity. He used shame, resentment, anguish to get the most
for his schillings. Inspector Trumpf stood by listening to
the exchange between Pepi and Claude.

"Hombre!" Pepi was stricken. *"Hombre!* Twenty
schillings for six of the white chocolate! Even Demels
sells six of the whites for eighteen schillings!"

"Then get them at Demel's!"

"Demel's is all out of them."

"When I'm all out of them, I sell them for only sixteen
schillings!" Claude was triumphant.

Vanquished, Pepi made his purchase. Claude counted
out the chocolates.

Trumpf, listening, found what he wanted. He felt the
same relief as he had in the Nationalbibliothek when he'd
sagged against the wall, the index card with the title in
his hand. He had always been friendly with Claude; he
regularly bought Klara's birthday box of chocolates from
him and he and Claude often chatted. He even knew that
where Claude was from, it was colder in winter than in
Vienna. The St. Lawrence froze and had to be cleared
with icebreakers. Claude was from Quebec.

Trumpf drove slowly back to headquarters. It was
absurd to make a connection, of course, far-fetched. Why
waste time on it? Still . . . he drew up to the curb a block
from the Rossauerkaserne and sat thinking. Pepi, beside
him, was eating one of the white chocolates and reading
his book.

Suppose, just suppose . . . Trumpf reflectively ran his
hands along the sides of the steering wheel. His peripheral vision was at work. Age six when her parents were
killed . . . Yes, a little girl growing up in Quebec in
French-speaking relatives' home, attending a French-
speaking convent school. Teachers, friends, playmates—
all French-speaking. Not strange, not strange at all, that

elusive accent when she spoke German. If he were right, that is.

He pondered. Of course, any number of students from Quebec could be studying at the university. Still . . . hadn't Jason Foxe said the girl was from France? Might Foxe have *assumed* she was? On the other hand, *perhaps the girl had told him so.*

Inspector Trumpf's blood coursed faster. He was beginning to feel happy. The possibility he toyed with existed.

He started the Volkswagen, turned around, and headed back toward Langegasse.

Frau Schratt answered the door. She reminded the inspector of someone, he couldn't think whom until he realized it was his mother: the same broad brow under the pinned-back gray hair, the kind eyes, the sturdy body; even the serviceable black, laced shoes in which his mother had gone about the kitchen, brought in wood from the cold yard, lighted the stove. And the apron, almost the same apron. She was dead three years now. She had died in their village near Gmünd on the Czech border, died in the same house where she had brought up her two orphaned children. So much he might have done! Visited her more often, sent more money, written letters. But the roads to the village from Gmünd were mud tracks in summer and blocked by snow in winter. His job had demanded more of his time, and there were Pepi's childhood sicknesses, Klara's miscarriage . . . on and on. It was too late now. A twist in his heart.

"Bitte?"

Inspector Trumpf pulled himself together. He introduced himself and asked for Fräulein Montcalm. "I hope I am not disturbing her studies?" Frau Schratt, in a deep-toned, pleasant voice, informed him that unfortunately Fräulein Montcalm was not at home.

"Ah! *Schrecklich!* Too bad!" Fräulein Montcalm was one of eighteen interested young woman who had been recommended by the university for part-time secretarial positions offered by the department. Four young women had qualified, Fräulein Montcalm among them. One of the four would be working for Inspector Trumpf's assistant, Staral, there was just the final—"I wanted to—But perhaps I can leave a message for her?" He slapped his pockets. "Ach! Not even my pen! And a bit of paper if you have it?"

"*Natürlich.*" She led the way to the dining room and seated him at the table. From a drawer in the sideboard she gave him paper and pen. He picked up the pen, feeling like a schoolboy assigned an essay. He hadn't the least idea what to write. But then, of course, it didn't matter; he could scribble anything. "And an envelope, Frau Schratt?" Frau Schratt looked surprised; but she obliged, again resorting to the sideboard. Yes, he would write something, then at the last minute he would exclaim that he had changed his mind about a message, he would have his assistant telephone Fräulein Montcalm later. He would crumple the paper and put it in his pocket. He would apologize for wasting Frau Schratt's time.

He lifted his head from the paper and looked approvingly around the dining room. "Ach! What wonderful rooms in these old apartments! Turn of the century, *nicht wahr?*"

Frau Schratt smiled, a shy smile. "Yes, that molding, the walnut . . ." She took a step toward the kitchen.

"Just what I was thinking!" *Delay her, delay her.* "And the patterned wallpaper, those fleurs-de-lis . . . do you know, that's the same wallpaper that is in the

Sacher's dining room? It was there in Franz Josef's time. The very same!"

"The same?" Frau Schratt was surprised. "The very same?" She approached and rested a hand on the back of a chair. She looked around, wistful. "It has faded so, this wallpaper was·here when my parents . . ."

It was so easy, Trumpf thought. The naïve and innocent were always so gullible. Like his mother, Frau Schratt could be turned into warm strudel, you had only to touch the right chords.

He managed to touch several. From wallpaper they moved on to the new rage for Biedermeier and he was told that a dealer in antiques had offered a tempting price for the Biedermeier couch in the parlor. But the couch was not for sale, it had been her father's favorite. But so tempting, the offer, such a lot of money! And what with the expense of keeping such an apartment . . . But of course, pointed out Inspector Trumpf, taking in roomers helped pay the rent, *nicht wahr?*

"Indeed!" Frau Schratt last year had had a Czech graduate student of philosophy in the *Kinderzimmer* and an Italian science·student in the maid's room. There was also a permanent guest, Herr Herbst, an accountant at Gerngross', in the *Herrenzimmer*. Now she had a woman visiting from Prague, in the *Kinderzimmer*, and Fräulein Montcalm in the maid's room. Yes, yes, exclaimed the inspector, Fräulein Montcalm, he had been forgetting. "Let's see, she is new at the pension, correct?" Frau Schratt wrinkled her brow. "Yes, of course! For the fall semester. Three weeks . . . yes, exactly three weeks, she came the day after Herr Herbst's birthday."

The inspector nodded. He felt again in his pockets, without success. "My list, I must have left it . . . She's twenty years old, I believe it said, and from Paris."

"No, no!" Frau Schratt shook her head. "Not from Paris! Mademoiselle Montcalm is from Rouen."

"Yes, that's it, Rouen! I must have given the list to my assistant, it is his job. But this warm weather, everyone running around in shirt sleeves, he's down with the flu. So is half the department. The chief himself is probably answering my telephone as well as his own! I felt compelled, in the emergency . . . Well . . ." He stood up. He would be at the Volkskundemuseum later in the day, two minutes away from Langegasse, at Florienigasse. "Perhaps if I have a minute or two, I'll stop by later. When does Fräulein Montcalm return?"

"At one o'clock, she is always here by one." Frau Schratt hesitated, then blushed. "I— She has lunch here on Saturdays, I give her a little something . . . and tea." She added apologetically, "Nothing special, there is always something left from supper." Trumpf's heart twinged again. So like his mother! He knew that in Vienna, landladies of pensions gave only breakfast, if anything. Moreover, they were martinets with iron-clad rules: They did not tell their roomers what they *could* do, they posted notices listing what they could *not* do. But Martha Schratt was not of that ilk. He would bet she had let the Czech student smell up his room with *Salzgurken,* the big, garlic-smelling pickles from a barrel. As for the Italian, the *Kinderzimmer* had probably reeked of Gorgonzola cheese and Genoa salami. Inspector Trumpf's mouth watered. He tried not to think about the salami.

He crumpled the note and stuck it in his pocket. He assured Frau Schratt that he would stop by around one-thirty, if he had a minute. Otherwise he would telephone. He hoped he had not taken too much of Frau Schratt's time, he had enjoyed . . . *Auf wiedersehen.*

At headquarters, he immediately made a telephone call. "Yes, September tenth, name of Nicca Montcalm.

Proprietress, Martha Krieger Schratt, Langegasse."
Within moments, the passport department was back on
the line. No, no record of a passport with the name of
Montcalm registered by Martha Krieger Schratt of that
address. He hung up, made another call, and learned that
no Nicca Montcalm of Rouen, France, or Quebec,
Canada, was registered at the university. Shrewd, clever
Trumpf! He sat back, pleased with himself. Yet . . . he
sighed. His heart twinged for Martha Krieger Schratt,
proprietress.

He looked at his watch. Already ten-thirty. When he
returned to the Schratt apartment at one o'clock, not
one-thirty—he had purposely lied to Frau Schratt—he
would be waiting there for her. He would bring Detective
Staral with him in an official car. They would have
Fräulein Montcalm accompany them to the Rossauerkaserne for questioning. By Austrian law, no warrant was necessary: They could hold her for forty-eight
hours. If longer, they would need a formal warrant from
the magistrate. But well before that time, they would
have checked her fingerprints against those found in
Veronica Kent's room at the Hilton.

But Inspector Trumpf knew that checking would be
superfluous. He had already trapped his quarry. Peripheral vision. Strange, how a psychopathic personality
could on the surface be so winning, have such charm . . .
while behind that pretty façade lurked a monster.
Enough to make one shudder.

Well . . . ten-thirty. Two-and-a-half hours to go.

Jason Foxe turned off the Autobahn onto a highway.
The highway would bring him to a turnoff on the right.
He'd have to watch carefully for the dirt road, not to miss
it. It would take him to Karlsdorf, a little village where
he and Florian, who'd been photographing birds near

Anspang, had once stopped. They'd had a memorable dish of veal gulyas at a Gasthaus in the village.

It was now midmorning. The rolling meadows smelled sweetly of hay, the sun shone, a breeze tenderly caressed his face. Perfect . . . except that he was hungry. Ordinarily, at around ten-thirty in Vienna he would drop into Sperl's where, seated at one of the round marble tables with rococo iron bases that surely hadn't been dusted since around 1870, he would have a satisfying portion of gulyas, or dumpling with minced lung.

But today he had left Vienna early. He had only taken time to fill up on gas at Strohmayer's. It was a relief that a different overalled gas station attendant was on duty. The fellow with the rust-brown, dirty hair must be off. He had begun to be irritated at the unblinking way the fellow stared at him as though he, Jason Foxe, were a specimen under glass. The mean-looking eyes held both envy and admiration for whatever this specimen, the Foxe of the Foxe affair, possessed. And whenever the fellow polished the Porsche's windshield, he stared through the glass at Foxe and moved the chamois with slow-motion strokes, gliding over the glass as though the glass itself were an extension of Jason Foxe's body. Foxe endured it with a mixture of stoic irritation and, surprisingly, compassion; but compassion for what, he couldn't say. In any case, Strohmayer's was convenient to Langegasse. And what right did he have to object to the way the bastard looked at him? The hell with it.

Karlsdorf's main street was narrow and cobbled. It was so short that when he drove down it he could see ahead the fields and woods of open country at its far end. A couple of hundred yards down, on the right, was the Gasthaus, the Goldener Hirsch. He parked and went in.

The gulyas was made Hungarian style, simmered into a delicious stew of veal, onions, tomatoes and paprika. It

was as good as it had been the time before, with Königsmark, maybe better. With it he drank a light beer. He
was halfway through the gulyas, when he remembered
the envelope Nicca Montcalm had slipped into his
pocket.

He put down his fork and took out the envelope. Nicca
Montcalm, a puzzling girl. Over her ice-cream at the
Schwarzenberg Café, at one moment she was bright and
funny, telling ridiculous anecdotes about Karoline and
Fritz Draxler, then the next instant, the long silver spoon
would pause over the Du Barry and Nicca's jaw would go
rigid as she looked down at the adhesive on the tip of her
finger. He had sensed that suddenly she had not been
there; she was alone somewhere. He had seen it happen to
her before. Once in Frau Schratt's dining room. A couple
of times in the Porsche. Each time, it made him visualize
her running through a nightmare of dark streets. He had
a feeling that if he could see her eyes through those tinted
lenses at such times, they would have a look of concentrated horror. *Why* he felt that, he did not understand.
He wished he could see her eyes, the lack of eye contact
blocked her away; it kept her apart, inaccessible.

And he had begun to want Nicca Montcalm more
accessible, he couldn't deny that. But something inexplicable stood in the way. With Nicca, he was still in the
dark. Yet, sadly, she was the one who saw darkly. Had
the congenital weakness she suffered from damaged the
appearance of her eyes? Had it reddened them, made
them shrunken and small? Was she a victim of trachoma,
the conjunctivitis inflaming the inner surface of the
eyelid?

He tore open the envelope. There was a sheaf of one-
hundred-schilling bills clipped together with a paper clip
and a folded note. He unfolded the note and read: *Here
are two thousand schillings for a copy of* Birds of Aus-

tria. *The money is from Karoline and Fritz. They beg
that Florian Königsmark will please autograph the book
to both their names. They have only enough money for
one book because the book is expensive and Fritz is on
short allowance due to circumstances beyond anybody's
control (especially his parents'!).* The note was signed,
Nicca.

He reread the note, taking in the words: *Karoline and
Fritz . . . autograph . . . short allowance.* But his mind
was discarding the sense. He was staring at the handwriting, unable to comprehend what he saw: Those crossed *t*s
with the dash that leaped ahead, betraying impatience;
the rounded *o*s, the heavy pressure at the end of strokes,
signifying courage.

He was looking at Veronica Kent's handwriting.

Elbows on the table, he held the note with both hands,
staring at it. The same handwriting as in the Xeroxed
notebook. The same strong upward strokes, the round *d*s
and *b*s of the notebook. He had only an amateur's knowledge of handwriting—his teenage fascination with gra-
phology had given him that—but he didn't need even any
special skill to tell him what he was looking at. A bank
clerk behind his grill would recognize the similarity of
the handwriting. The handwriting of two different people
could not be this similar. Impossible! He knew that. Still,
he could not—Nicca Montcalm. Veronica Kent. His
mind went tracking this way and that, crossing and
recrossing paths, detouring, circling, coming again to
that margin, that border, beyond which lay belief.

"Herr Ober!" He beckoned the waiter. "The public
telephone, *bitte?"* It was down the hall, next to the
Toilette. Frau Schratt's phone number was in his little
address book; Adalbert Brunner had given it to him in
regard to the shirts. He put in his schillings and dialed.
When he heard Frau Schratt's voice, he pressed the red

button to complete the connection. "Frau Schratt?" He did not want to alarm her. He said with false ease, "This is Herr Foxe, Jason Foxe, I—"

"Herr Foxe! You didn't go to *Schloss* Walenberg, then? What has happened?"

"Nothing. Nothing at all." He was on his way to Castle Walenberg, he told her. He had stopped on the road for a little snack. "While I was eating, I remembered a bet I made with Fräulein Montcalm: I bet I could guess her age. I want to play a trick on her. So will you take a look at the register and tell me her age? It is just a joke."

A pause. Then Frau Schratt's solid, deep voice: "Herr Foxe, impossible. I cannot—"

"Only for a joke! In the end, I'll pay her the bet—fifty schillings." Another pause. Frau Schratt's voice was troubled now. "Two things, Herr Foxe: In the first place, the register does not give the visitor's age. In the second place, it is something else, Herr Foxe, isn't it? I would be obliged if you would tell me." There was a little catch in Frau Schratt's voice, a throb of emotion that betrayed such strong feeling Jason Foxe, after a moment, said simply: "Yes. Something else. Fräulein Montcalm may be in trouble. I want to help her. But I must know, Frau Schratt: Fräulein Montcalm had no passport?"

A silence, then Frau Schratt's voice, thinned by the telephone connection: "Yes, Herr Foxe. She had no passport. I took her in anyway."

So there it was. Not that he didn't know. Frau Schratt was talking on, worriedly, something about student politics: Fräulein Montcalm had gotten herself involved . . . fracases with the police, broken heads, arrests. "Riots! Tear gas. The students wanted only a *peaceful* demonstration!" Fräulein Montcalm had been arrested for kicking a policeman. . . .

Jason Foxe listened, holding a handful of schillings. Fräulein Montcalm had borrowed a friend's passport, then mailed it back to Rouen, unfortunately her own passport had not yet arrived. Frau Schratt sounded as though she were wringing her hands, but of course that was not possible because she was holding the telephone. "Student politics! Herr Foxe, I should have guessed trouble, the way the inspector, Inspector Trumpf—"

"Trumpf?"

"Yes, he came this morning looking for her. Something about a part-time job in the department, assistant to his assistant; she had qualified. What nonsense! Where was my foolish head? A detective inspector does not run around Vienna like an underling to— No, not if *all* the police in Vienna are down with the flu! And what's more . . ." Again the throb of emotion in Frau Schratt's voice.

"What's more, *what?*"

"What's more, neither does a detective inspector pursue such a small matter as a passport. Unless . . . unless . . . Herr Foxe, is it possible that someone was seriously hurt in that riot in Rouen, that Fräulein Montcalm—"

"No! Absolutely not, Frau Schratt." It was a relief to tell that small truth. So. The shrewd Inspector Trumpf! He had tracked his quarry through Vienna to Langegasse, where, holed up in the maid's room—

"Herr Foxe?" Frau Schratt's voice was apprehensive. "Yes?"

"Inspector Trumpf knows Fräulein Montcalm will return here at one o'clock. Is there anything I can do—to help Fräulein Montcalm?"

He had an irrational impulse to laugh. To help poor, beset Nicca Montcalm, involved in student politics! "Yes, there's one thing: Don't let Inspector Trumpf know that I telephoned you ... or that I know anything about Nicca Montcalm and the passport."

He hung up and stood at the phone. Nicca Montcalm, Veronica Kent—a psychopath who dealt a double death? Hell, no! He would have to hear it from Nicca herself, hear her say *I killed him.* He thought of her pretty mouth with the brownish-pink lipstick, her lovely brow framed by tendrils of hair; he felt again the softness of that hair when he had cut her bangs ... and standing there at the phone, he cursed and groaned. He loved two girls, Nicca of the tinted eyeglasses—what were her eyes *really* like?—and Veronica Kent of the notebook, his mad infatuation which was asexual. *Who has ever wanted to sleep with the Venus de Milo?* He loved Veronica of the notebooks, but he wanted to sleep with Nicca Montcalm.

With sudden feverish haste, he dug into his pockets. Plenty of schillings. He put them on the little platform under the phone and began to dial. Two telephone calls later, he had the train information he needed. He dialed information. Waiting for the operator to give him the Draxlers' number in Hietzing, he was in a clammy sweat. What if the Draxlers had a *Geheimnummer*—an unlisted number? But luck was with him, the operator furnished the number. The Draxlers' maid answered the phone. Yes, Fräulein Montcalm was with the twins. One moment, please.

"Nicca?" He hardly waited for her surprised, "Herr Foxe?" but said urgently, "Look, you're in trouble. I'm in a village called Karlsdorf on the way to Schloss Walenberg. Now, listen: You must leave the Draxlers' immediately and meet me here."

"Trouble?" Her voice was wary: "What trouble?"

"The trouble is that Inspector Trumpf will be waiting for you at Langegasse when you return. Take the U-Bahn back to Vienna, then take a taxi to the South Station. Get on the eleven o'clock train to Wiener Neustadt. At Wiener Neustadt, switch to the eleven-thirty-nine local to Aspang. You'll reach Aspang at twelve thirty-three. I won't meet you—too risky. At Aspang, take the post autobus that goes to nearby villages, including Karlsdorf. Tell the driver to let you off at Karlsdorf. *Karlsdorf.* Have you got that? Karlsdorf. I'll be waiting on the road. *Be there.*"

A silence.

"Be there," he repeated; then said fiercely: "Be there . . . Veronica."

He pressed the phone to his ear. He heard something like a deep, indrawn breath. Silence again. Her voice, when it came, was flat.

"Karlsdorf. I'll be there."

He hung up. He was now an accessory to murder.

Chapter 14

In the kitchen Martha Schratt took the leftover liver-and-dumpling soup from the refrigerator and poured it into a pot. Six dumplings, so three each. She put the pot on the stove. Then she went into the dining room and set two places for lunch.

The table set, she stood there, kneading first one big wrist bone, then the other. It was a habit that betrayed anxiety, she had done it since childhood. "What is it, Kinderl?" her mother would say, smiling down at her; and it would turn out to be a mislaid doll, a school friend who had abandoned her for another child, or fear of going on a Sunday trip to the Prater because she was afraid to ride the Ferris wheel and afraid to say so. Later, married, when the Nazis had taken over Vienna, Stefan Schratt had come to know his wife's wrist-kneading well. He used to take her two wrists in his strong, talented hands. "Liebling, don't worry!" and he would swing her hands back and forth. "Come now! *Genug!*" And he would hug her to his chest.

She left the dining room and walked down the hall past the master bedroom that had been her parents', and later hers and Stefan's. Past the water closet and bathroom, was the *Kinderzimmer,* where she had had a crib, then a real bed, and even a little red table with two child-sized red chairs. The *Kinderzimmer* had the best light for an artist, so later when she and Stefan had married and come to live with her parents, it had doubled, at first, as Stefan's studio.

At the door of the *Kinderzimmer*, Martha Schratt paused. She kneaded her big wrists. Stefan, Stefan! In the autumn of 1940, the Nazis had drafted him into the army; six months later, when civil documents showed he was married to a Jewish woman, he was discharged. The Nazi party had then pressured him to divorce his Jewish wife or face being shipped to Theresienstadt, the labor camp; from there, it would be Auschwitz.

But Stefan was a fighter, and clever. He did not refuse, he temporized, while desperately trying to work out a plan to smuggle Martha to safety. He finally found an underground contact, but the arranged escape was weeks away when the blow fell. Stefan was notified to report as "husband of a Jewish wife." They both knew what that meant: Stefan's last chance. And she, she would be left with no chance at all. Despair! *She* had despaired; Stefan had not. Reporting, he told the officials that his Jewish wife had disappeared. Disappeared? Gone where? *"Herrgott,* who knows? Run away! I told her I was going to divorce her, better to get rid of her than go to Theresienstadt! Next morning, she was gone."

The officials had eyed him and made notations. Two days later, the doorbell had rung. The Gestapo. A search warrant for Martha Krieger Schratt, fugitive Jew. But

Stefan had a friend or two: an hour before the Gestapo arrived, he'd received a whispered alert over the telephone.

What a masterly actor Stefan had been! The Gestapo had found him drunk and bleeding, face slashed, blood running in rivulets. Cursing, bleeding, weeping, he had lurched back to the *Kinderzimmer*, the Gestapo in his wake. "Look! Look!" His precious paintings slashed, torn, ruined, his paints scattered, his easel overturned. "The Jewish bitch!" he had sobbed; she had returned, demanding money, snatching up his watch, even his cuff links. When he had shouted at her to get out, she had seized a knife and slashed his paintings. "My best work! A fortune in paintings! Destroyed!" He had struggled with her, she had gone at him with the knife and slashed his face—he could no more control her than a frenzied clawing cat. Ah, Stefan, Stefan, how cruelly he had cut his face. He had poured schnapps over himself and slashed his paintings. "I attacked her, finally!" he had gloated, reeling into a Gestapo agent and clinging to his lapels, breathing schnapps into his face, "I think I broke her arm! But she got away . . . and what a foul mouth she had!" The agent, in a convulsion of disgust, had shoved him off. Martha Schratt, hidden behind the still-wet oil, *Landscape Number Four,* that leaned against the wall, had seen it all through a slash in the ruined canvas. The Gestapo had searched the apartment anyway. They had been thorough. But they had not looked behind *Landscape Number Four*. Later, in Merano as a kitchen maid, and then hidden in the mountains, all she could think of was when she would see Stefan again. But she never did.

Genug! Enough! Stefan had said it. She stopped kneading her wrists. She continued down the hall to Fräulein Montcalm's room. In her childhood and youth, this had been Dora's room, Dora the maid, bustling and roly-poly, a *mischlinge*, offspring of a mixed marriage of Jew and gentile. Since then . . . Ah, well. Now, Nicca Montcalm.

The door was locked. She opened it with her passkey.

The room was neat, and pervaded by the smell of apples. Apples were cheap in autumn. You could plant a whole apple orchard from the number of seeds in the apples Fräulein Nicca ate in her room. She probably dined nightly on the apples she smuggled in that capacious shoulder bag; apples and bread. Martha Schratt sniffed experimentally. Ach! Probably not even a bit of cheese! If she looked in the girl's bottom drawer, she knew she would find a little one-cup electric gadget for heating a cupful of water and making tea.

So . . . Why was she standing in Fräulein Nicca's room at noon today, hearing the bells chiming the hour? Why? It was connected to being the hunted young Martha in 1941; yes, there was a *Verbindung*, a tie, between herself and the French girl. Moreover, Herr Foxe's telephone call . . . He wanted Martha Schratt to help protect the girl against the inspector, although he had not said so. Not outright. Herr Foxe . . . whom she liked . . . and whom she instinctively trusted, as had Adalbert Brunner, from the first.

She looked toward the bowlegged bureau with its fat, curved drawers. She had set the dining room table, surely Inspector Trumpf would believe she expected Fräulein Nicca at one-thirty. She was not sure herself whether Fräulein Nicca would come or whether Jason Foxe, somehow . . . She kneaded a wrist, then stopped herself. She had come to Nicca Montcalm's room looking for something to hide from Detective Inspector Trumpf, should he insist on poking his nose—But hide what? Student-inciting posters? Probably that.

Reluctantly, she approached the bureau. She began to

open the drawers, half-turning away her face. Her search was designed to protect Nicca Montcalm. Still, it was an invasion of the girl's privacy.

The upper and middle drawers yielded pathetically little. Nicca Montcalm's luggage had never arrived from Rouen; it had been misdirected, then lost; it was being traced. "Sent not to Vienna, but to Venice! ... What a mix-up!" the girl had told Frau Schratt, her tone exasperated. Neither had the passport arrived from Rouen. Martha Schratt had finally pretended to herself that she had forgotten about it.

The bottom drawer. She pulled it open. Ah, the electric gadget for making tea. Martha Schratt smiled and shook her head. The drawer also held a tan sweater and skirt that Martha Schratt looked at in surprise. They were of good quality, a fine wool, yet she had never seen Nicca wear them. Underneath the sweater and skirt was a sizable pile of clippings. Ah, the student politics! Martha Schratt drew out the bundle, straightened up, put it on the dresser, and looked at it with a sigh of satisfaction. She would take it away.

She glanced at a clipping ... then another—then quickly at others. The material had nothing to do with student politics. Nothing! The clippings concerned the von Reitz murder. Pages torn from magazines, items clipped from the most obscure publications, whole pages of a Sunday supplement series on the von Reitz family. The supplement series had sections underlined: genealogy, political life, business career, family life.

Frau Schratt looked from the bundle on the bureau to the tan sweater and skirt. She stood there, dazed. Then she walked to the window, and from there to the door and back to the window as though to escape the bundle on the bureau and evade its certain, terrible knowledge. Ah, no! No! But she knew it was true. Fräulein Montcalm was the girl the police sought in the murder of Herr Otto von Reitz.

What was she to do? She knew a dreadful secret. She should run to the police, to Detective-Inspector—She caught herself up. Inspector Trumpf! But of course he suspected! He would be returning to the apartment to apprehend Fräulein Montcalm. He knew she would be back at one o'clock. *But Fräulein Montcalm would not be here.* Martha Schratt knew that positively now, and she knew exactly where Nicca Montcalm would be. She would be with the person helping her escape: Jason Foxe.

Martha Schratt realized that she had stopped walking. She was standing in front of the bureau, staring into the bureau mirror; she saw the face of an elderly woman with gray hair and anguished eyes. *Herrgott!* Was she to set Inspector Trumpf on Nicca Montcalm's trail? Nicca Montcalm, Jason Foxe . . . two people she had come to feel close to her heart, where before there had been room only for Adalbert Brunner—Adalbert, bearded and clear-sighted, who yesterday had brought her a cyclamen plant that now stood on the kitchen window sill . . . Adalbert, who as a fifteen-year-old in the winter of 1940 had brought her not flowers, but bread, defiantly climbing the stairs under the noses of the Nazis. Adalbert, who weeks ago, despite Kraus and his "Liebe Leute" broadcasts, had believed instinctively in "The Foxe's" innocence, and had been proved right.

What was she to believe? She longed to believe in Nicca Montcalm, Fräulein Montcalm, with whom she felt a *Verbindung*, almost as though they were one. But . . . *Herrgott*, what was she to do?

From down the hall came the peal of the doorbell. Inspector Trumpf had arrived. Martha Schratt stood at the bureau, kneading her wrists.

* * *

He was sitting on a rock by the side of the road when the post autobus stopped and Nicca got out. Her hair was ruffled, her face dead-white. Her jaw had that rigid look.

The bus lumbered off. Jason said in English, "Lunch time. How about something to fill that cavity called the stomach? There's a swell Gasthaus here, the Goldener Hirsch."

The rigid jaw softened; Nicca shifted an armload of books. She said in English, "How did you find out?"

"Come on."

Walking on the dirt road into Karlsdorf, he explained it all, including his phone call to Martha Schratt. Then he said, "Now you tell me. The works."

She did, partly on the road and partly in the Goldener Hirsch over lunch. She barely touched the food. Jason, listening, ate heartily. It was quiet, only a handful of people lunching. In a cafélike alcove off the dining room a few people read newspapers and drank beer. Her voice yearned after the Schreyvogel correspondence, the Nestroy she had coveted. It trembled when she spoke of her cowardice in not giving Herr von Reitz the insulin he so desperately needed.

"I pitied him, I wanted to help him, I— His bald head was sweating, he was appealing for help, begging me for help, but"—she shuddered—"my . . . my fantasy."

"Fantasy?" "Yes." Her inexplicable terror of the syringe. "Yes . . . that he—that he meant it for me—the injection." It was that, the crazy fantasy, that had caused her to lose control. "I struck it out of his hand! Then he grabbed me, somehow I got hold of that bronze parrot. . . . "

He had stopped eating. He sat regarding her. She leaned forward. "I swung it, he fell. *That was all.*"

He waited.

"Except that when I started to phone for help, I

thought I saw him move. I dropped the phone and rushed to him; I thought I could save him with an injection. But he hadn't moved at all! It was only, I suppose, that I was wishing so hard that he was alive." She looked at Jason.

He said nothing.

"I panicked. I thought I had killed him, and I didn't want to die!

"First, I just ran. Then I saw that gold-toothed waiter! After that, I was desperate for a place to hide, where I would have time to think, a hole to crawl into until—"

"Right," Jason said; he felt almost happy. "Listen, will you do me a favor?"

"Yes . . . what?"

"Take off those damned glasses."

She took them off and put them on the table. He looked at her. "Finally." Very light blue eyes, a violet blue; dark, short, curly lashes—almost like black rims, those lashes, they were so curly, thick, and black. The effect was so lovely that it stunned him.

"Someone else killed him."

"I know." He had known it all along. Well, almost known.

"The . . . the person must have come in right after I left, whoever it was, and killed him while he lay helpless." She looked away. "Helpless because of *me*, helpless because *I* had struck him. That's what tortures me." *My fault.* The words were almost tangible.

He could not comfort her there. He thought: Some guilts are fancied, some are real. Hers was real: she *was* guilty.

But not of murder.

"Then, when the medical examiner's report finally— When I realized *I* hadn't killed him, but someone had killed him with a lethal— Then I began to figure it out." She leaned forward, face flushed, her incredible eyes wide: "Whoever killed Herr von Reitz cleaned up afterward; nothing was found in that private office—no syringes, nothing except the bronze parrot."

"Nothing to—"

"To complicate the situation. It was simplicity itself: *I* was to be the murderer, the . . . the patsy. If the police thought I killed him with the bronze parrot, fine. But if the autopsy revealed the lethal injection, that was fine too—that only made me a psychopath who had done everything but slash some crazy slogan on the dead man."

Her voice was low, excited: "You see why I can't give myself up? It is my *life*. I have only one! Whoever said 'The truth will out'—Shakespeare?—could have been wrong. Because life *isn't* like that! I could end up paying someone else's penalty. People do, it happens!" Her eyes were desperate, begging understanding. "I refuse that possibility. *I will not be that murderer's victim!*"

He sat frowning, thinking. Into his silence, she pursued: "Time! Every day I gather scraps of information, I search for the smallest news item, I *work* at it—I *try*! And I *do* find things, little things. *Sooner or later . . .*" Her blue eyes stared stubbornly, unconquerably into his.

Time; she wanted time for a miracle to happen. She got up each morning and ate the two boiled eggs and the Kaisersemmel and went forth into Vienna, searching for her miracle, her murderer. Meanwhile she lived on a razor's edge. He gazed back into the blue, unflagging eyes and didn't know whether to laugh or weep. But he could not begrudge her the only card she held: hope. He could also make a quantum leap: he could believe that between the two of them they could, given time, find something to save her, clear her. Meantime, he would have to get her over the border. The dogs panted too hotly after her; so, Yugoslavia, Italy, maybe Hungary . . . but without a passport?

"Jason?"

Come fire or fury, the wrath of Jehovah or the Austrian police, he'd somehow—

"Jason?"

He gave her a smile. "Tell me what information you've dug up." It was his neck, he had a right to stick it out.

The Goldener Hirsch was emptying; two waiters already sat at a table near the kitchen, eating; another was refilling salt shakers and resetting tables. Jason spoke rapidly, in a low voice. "You can't stay anywhere, not without a passport, that's the law. But Castle Walenberg— I can't show up at Baron von Walenberg's party with an unknown girl, that would be stupid. Trumpf is as intuitive as a psychic. When you don't show up at Langegasse, and he realizes you've been warned off, he just might intuit a connection with me. So I'll have to *smuggle* you into the castle.

"We'll move fast. The brilliant Trumpf must already be having a heart attack because his bird-in-the-hand has flown. He's damned well broadcasting your description this minute. We'll get you other clothes, change your looks."

"How?" She sent an alarmed glance around the dining room.

"Damned fast. Go into the alcove, sit in the darkest corner, order a G'spritzen, and begin reading a newspaper, holding it up to hide your face. Stay there until I come back."

When she had picked up her books and glasses and left, he headed for the telephone near the *Toilette*. He'd make a quick call to Florian at Schloss Walenberg to excuse his lateness—a flat tire, say, to forestall any curiosity about what was delaying Jason Foxe and the precious blowups. Then he'd raid what shops he could find in Karlsdorf, get clothes for Nicca. He'd tie her hair in a bandana, dump the lilac-tinted glasses. But her eyes, those incredible, unforgettable eyes, she'd need dark glasses. Then, the head-cracking problem: How could he smuggle her into the castle? Never mind, once he'd disguised her and they were on the road, he'd figure out something.

He felt for schillings for the phone call.

But another customer was using the phone, he stood with his back to Jason, a man in a cap and sweater, hunched over deep in conversation; he looked immovable as a rock. As Jason approached, the man dropped more coins into the phone, he was in for a long conversation. Christ! A hell of a time— He wheeled and left quickly, there would be a phone in the *Konditorei* across the road. Passing the table where he and Nicca had lunched, he dropped schilling notes on it and called to the waiter that he would be right back, and *"Bitte, meine Rechnung."*

At the *Konditorei,* the phone was free; he called information, got the number, put in his schillings, and dialed. Waiting, hearing the phone ringing, knowing the hugeness of the castle, the butler, the staff, the confusion of guests who must already be arriving, he knew he could hardly hope to reach Florian himself. But at least he could leave the message ... with, he hoped, a servant trustworthy enough to deliver it. Ah! Someone had picked up the phone; there was a confusion of voices in the background, like the cackling of a barnyard of chickens; then a single, polite voice: *"Bitte?"*

Inspector Trumpf had no *Schadenfreude.* He could not gloat over the misfortunes of others. He even recoiled from the German word signifying the malicious joy people took in others' misfortunes. Now, at one o'clock, introducing Detective Staral to Frau Martha Schratt in the square hall of the Langegasse apartment, he felt an undercurrent of resentment against his profession: It was unfair that this big-boned Frau Schratt, so gullible, so naïve, would have to pay for being duped by Veronica Kent. The pity of it was that in any police crackdown, it was almost inevitable that innocents, "fringe innocents," as Trumpf thought of them, were bound to get hurt.

The inspector and Detective Staral followed Frau Schratt into the parlor to wait for the French girl. The inspector still thought of her as "the French girl," even knowing she was not. He had left Pepi at the office, he didn't want the boy there when they took the girl in. They had come in an official car, Staral driving.

Still standing, Trumpf wasted no time: It appeared that Fräulein Montcalm was in trouble, he would have to question her. "That is why Detective Staral is with me. We will have to ask her to come with us." At least, he thought, he would have the kindness not to demand to see Frau Schratt's register.

Frau Schratt was gazing back at him with such an expression of anguish that he felt his stomach muscles contract. "Trouble?"

"Ach! It is our job to investigate, Frau Schratt. Don't worry yourself." The inspector became aware that Detective Staral was looking at him in astonishment; he favored his assistant with a glance filled with animosity.

"Bitte, setzen Sie sich." Frau Schratt's voice was composed. Trumpf was thankful for that. They sat down, Detective Staral on the Biedermeier sofa, Trumpf in a worn leather armchair. "It is so chilly, *nicht wahr?"* Frau Schratt chafed her hands. "These stone buildings." At the ceramic stove in the corner, she shook briquettes from a bag and lighted the fire. When it had a good start she

excused herself. *"Entschuldigen Sie, bitte,* I must attend to things in the kitchen." With firm steps, she left them. In a few minutes, a delicious smell of soup drifted into the parlor.

They waited. Quarter past one. Half-past. They could hear Frau Schratt bustling in the kitchen, a clatter of dishes, spoons against china. Quarter to two. Where was the girl? Inspector Trumpf got up and went into the dining room; there were two places set at the table. He came back to the parlor and sat down again. It was so quiet. A clock was ticking somewhere; Trumpf realized in surprise that it was his wristwatch. Detective Staral was leafing through a magazine, wetting his finger to turn the pages.

At two o'clock, Trumpf guessed. "Frau Schratt!"

She appeared in the doorway; a fresh apron, worried eyes. *"Bitte, Herr Inspector?"*

"Fräulein Montcalm would have telephoned if she was not coming home to lunch ... *nicht wahr?"* Frau Schratt hesitated, then nodded. "So ... she will not be coming, *nicht wahr?"* Frau Schratt, after a heartbeat of time, nodded again, slowly, looking back at him. "Then, Frau Schratt, *where can she be?"* He was being cruel now. He felt sad and angry; he felt that his mother had betrayed him.

Frau Schratt was silent. She stood there in her sturdy black shoes and the apron with its bib. She was gazing at him with that anguished look and kneading first one big wrist and then the other.

"Well?"

She shook her head. She spread her hands, a gesture of emptiness. "I don't know."

Did she know? Could she have warned the girl? He sighed. "Which is the girl's room?"

Frau Schratt led the way down the hall. In Nicca

Montcalm's room, Detective Staral, using tweezers, took from the bureau top a bottle of nail polish and a celluloid comb and dropped them into separate plastic bags; the bird had flown, but not her fingerprints. Frau Schratt stood by, watching while they went through the bureau drawers and the closet, and came up with nothing interesting.

When, ten minutes later, Trumpf departed he left behind him Detective Staral to monitor phone calls; there was also the absurd, impossible chance that Fräulein Montcalm might return. He left Staral seated in the dining room before the place setting presumably intended for Fräulein Montcalm. Seated opposite him was Frau Schratt. From a tureen of steaming broth, she was ladling liver dumplings into soup plates: three for Detective Staral, three for herself.

In the *Konditorei*, Jason Foxe hung up the phone and went quickly across the road to the Goldener Hirsch where he paid the lunch bill, then plunged into the alcove and plucked the newspaper from Nicca's startled hands. "Come on!" He threw money on the table and, with an arm around Nicca's shoulders, propelled her toward the door. Outside, he shoved her into the Porsche and leaped over the back into the driver's seat. The car shot forward, the village street was eclipsed, fields and meadows rushed by.

"Have you lost your buttons?" Nicca looked at the speedometer. "And where are the clothes?"

"We have a new scenario. . . . How does this grab you?" He had reached Florian, he told her. Schloss Walenberg was in a turmoil, Baron Willy's delicate emotions were throwing him into a near-hysterical state. It was all because of his mother, the old Baronin. The Baronin's faithful Josephine, her nurse-attendant for six-

teen years, had slipped on the stairs and broken an ankle.
Not ten minutes before! Guests were arriving, and Willy
was distractedly edging toward a nervous collapse. "Tell
the Baron that the troops are arriving," Jason had said
jubilantly. He was a few minutes from Hartberg, he
would stop at the Hartberg hospital and arrive in an hour
or so with a fill-in attendant. He would deliver her to the
Baronin's own quarters, the south wing, with its peaceful
courtyard—he would drop her off there. Florian had put
a grateful Baron Willy on the phone . . . so grateful that
the Baron would have a Piper-Heidsieck, 1966, chilled
and waiting, just for Jason Foxe, Jason concluded. He
glanced at Nicca, wishing he could see her eyes along
with her profile, the pretty earlobe, the line of her jaw—
like in a Picasso painting, simultaneously profile and eye.
He also wanted to touch her, fit her snugly into his arms.
"At the hospital, we'll chivvy them out of a nurse's
uniform."

"I'm not a nurse! What if the Baronin should have an
attack of . . . of whatever ails her? She could die! I
wouldn't—"

"Nothing ails her. The old lady is hooked on having a
practical nurse, she can't admit she wants a companion to
push her around in her wheelchair and play gin rummy
and pray with her in her little chapel. An honest-to-God
companion would be self-indulgent. The Baronin is
ultrapuritanical. She attends chapel three times a day,
and her hobby is to embroider bookmarks with religious
sayings. She gives them to Baron Willy's friends." He
wondered momentarily what religious quotation the
Baronin had given to Danilo, her son's lover.

The Porsche sped on. Blue sky, billowing clouds, innocent fields. "Well?" He risked a glance. Breezes were
making tendrils dance on the girl's brow.

"Well . . . glasses, then. I'll need dark glasses."

On the Autobahn again, the traffic was heavy; weekend traffic. Beside him, Nicca was silent, he could sense her tension.

"Trumpf is off the trail," he said cheerfully, "I can hear the gnashing of his teeth from here." Then, gently, "You'll be safe with the Baronin. Don't worry."

She didn't reply. Minutes later, he was aware that she was stealing glances at him; then she began rummaging in her shoulder bag. "Damn!" she said under her breath, "I've lost it."

"Lost what?"

"Oh, nothing . . . my lipstick."

A tutor! Inspector Trumpf put his elbows on the desk and his face in his hands and swore explosively into his palms. A clever devil, that Veronica Kent. Tutoring was the only job you could get in Vienna without showing a passport. He could still hear Frau Draxler's high-pitched voice on the phone a moment ago, apprehensively inquiring as to the inspector's call concerning Mademoiselle Montcalm, the children's tutor. A driving accident? But no, the girl did not have a car! She always came to Hietzing on the U-Bahn. Yes, Inspector, a boy and a girl, twins, French lessons, the twins were getting on magnificently. Inspector Trumpf had had an almost uncontrollable urge to blurt out, *"Gnädiges Frau,* your children have been closeted Wednesdays, Fridays, and Saturdays with a murderess." He could picture a horrified Frau Draxler in the Hietzing villa holding a real linen handkerchief to frightened, quivering nostrils.

Instead, he had said, "You say, Frau Draxler, that Mademoiselle Montcalm does not have a car? . . . So, then it must be a mistaken identity. The young woman who had the accident is heavyset, she was wearing a . . . a pantsuit, you call it? Reddish hair, a—"

"No, no!" came Frau Draxler's relieved voice. "Our Mademoiselle Montcalm is slender. She wears always a blue suit with a skirt and a white shirt; and the lilac-tinted glasses. . . . " Frau Draxler's relief gushed over the phone, a veritable torrent.

"Vielen Dank! Vielen Dank!" And Trumpf had hung up.

He dropped his hands from his face. He had had her almost in his grasp. Gone, vanished, with no trace. He felt old, tired; his back ached. He looked at Pepi, curled up near the window with his paperback. He felt more like Pepi's grandfather than his father. Maybe it was time he resigned. Maybe Staral could do better, even with his asthma. Staral's psychology-oriented doctor called it "smother love" because Staral lived with his mother and when Frau Staral had made her annual pilgrimage to visit her sister, Staral was miraculously able to breathe again.

Trumpf had learned about the Draxlers from Staral. A youngster who identified herself as Karoline Draxler had called Frau Schratt's apartment to say that Mademoiselle Montcalm had left her lipstick on the bathroom sink—she had not lost it. So Mademoiselle Montcalm was not to spend money on a new lipstick. End of message.

Well. He would proceed with his tiny fragment: the description of the girl as he had seen her in front of Adalbert Brunner's on Langegasse only hours before. But by this time Veronica Kent would have discarded the identifying clothes and those lilac-colored eyeglasses. He sighed. His cupboard was bare. Staral, still at the apartment on Langegasse, had been able to pry nothing more out of Frau Schratt except some nonsense about student politics.

Trumpf shook his head in sadness and despair. Frau

Schratt. Hadn't those Jews learned anything from the
Nazis? Krieger, Martha Schratt's father, had been
Albert Krieger, curator at the Kunstistoriches Museum
of Burgring. When Trumpf was a school kid, his whole
class had visited the Greek, Etruscan, and Roman anti-
quities. Herr Krieger had shaken hands with their
teacher and smiled down at the children; he was short
and round, with smiling eyes and a little goatee. *Athlete
from Ephesus*, that was the statue Trumpf remembered
best. Auschwitz, that's where Herr Krieger had ended
up.

   "Hombre!" Pepi said, "am I thirsty! Can I get a
coke?" Trumpf nodded. "I already owe Sergeant Popp
twenty schillings," Pepi said; he was eying his father.
Trumpf felt in his pocket and handed over schillings; he
didn't have the heart to reprimand Pepi for borrowing.
He smiled after the boy, shaking his head.

   And oranges. Trumpf couldn't eat oranges. 1941. He
had been about ten years old and visiting his cousin in
Vienna. The pair of them were strolling in the Nachs-
markt among the vendors of grapes and cabbages, melons
and potatoes, eating oranges, when a truckload of uniformed Nazis had screeched to a halt and the soldiers
had leaped out and begun to round up Jews. Housewives,
other shoppers, children tried to flee. A girl in her twenties, the age Martha Schratt would have been then, had
tried to crawl under a vegetable stall, but a soldier—No,
Trumpf had never been able to eat another orange. He
took Vitamin C capsules, sustained release, five hundred
milligrams; Klara insisted on it lately, because of his diet.

   "We are the victims of our culture," he said aloud to
the empty room. Hippie kids in jeans on the Kärtner-
strasse asking well-dressed people for money, openly
smoking pot; the craze for Video games, and most incom-
prehensibly an American artist wrapping Texas in mus-

lin, or maybe it was Florida. And the constantly shifting
religious games, cutthroat: this week the Moslems and
Christians killing each other in Lebanon. Pretty soon the
Buddhists would join in—why not? A religious free-for-
all. What else was new?

"Victims of our culture," Trumpf repeated hopefully.
He knew that when he waxed philosophical he would
soon feel better. It was a sign that he was again on the
upswing. He and Martha Schratt were products of the
same culture, the Austrian culture. Loose as it might
seem, they had a mysterious relationship; their destinies
intertwined, fatefully intertwined. Inspector Trumpf
thought a moment. He liked that: fatefully intertwined.
He smiled.

He stood up and stretched, loosening cramped muscles.
His mind was working again. Hands in pockets, he tee-
tered back and forth. Premise: The girl was totally on her
own—the clothes on her back, a few schillings in her
purse, no passport—again on the run. She couldn't get
far. He sat down and reached for the phone. An alert.
First, the girl's description, for—

He was lifting the receiver when his interoffice phone
buzzed; light number three blinked; a steady light on four
indicated someone on hold. He pressed the button.
"Bitte?" It was Sergeant Felder on the switchboard,
edgy, indignant. A man on the phone, refusing to talk to
anybody but Trumpf, claiming to have important information about the von Reitz murder, probably another
crackpot: "He gave me his name and address *three times*,
the suspicious bastard! He sounds like he's afraid we'll
steal his wallet." Trumpf smiled to himself; last week's
embarrassing news was that three policemen had been
found guilty of being paid off by traffic violators. Kraus,
on the radio, had played it up big. Honest police like
Felder were aggravated; their virtue was besmirched.

Indignation stood out on them like quills on a porcupine. "I'll take it," Trumpf said. He pressed button four.

The voice was rough, a lower-class voice with a country accent, not the Viennese dialect. Almost immediately Trumpf heard central's warning whistle, the disconnect tone. Sergeant Felder must have had the man on the phone several minutes, just to get even, frustrate him. The coarse voice was excited, but cagy: "The American girl, the one who killed that lawyer, von . . . von? . . . "

"Von Reitz."

"*Ja,* von Reitz! A reward of fifty thousand schillings, *ja?*"

"*Genau* . . . exactly."

"Then it's mine! I found her, I recognized her!" Coarse voice shaking with excitement, the caller poured out information: The girl was in Karlsdorf, a village southwest of Anspang, north of Hartberg, she was in a Gasthaus, the Goldener Hirsch, she was traveling south with a man in a car. "I am following them, I—"

"What make of car? And the license number," interrupted Trumpf. A pause; then the voice full of peasant cunning that was so familiar to Trumpf as a police investigator: "I didn't get that yet, but I am following . . ." So the man was afraid they'd cheat him of the reward, was he? Too suspicious even to call the Gendarmerie in charge of the rural district, they might claim credit. He had to call Trumpf in Vienna, make an arrangement, seal his part in it. And he didn't even trust the inspector! But was the woman really Veronica Kent?

The inspector mouthed a silent thanks to the police officer who had come in and was placing a slip with the caller's name and address on his desk. Into the phone, he said, "Excellent! . . . What is the young woman wearing?"

The man told him: white shirt, blue suit. "A pretty girl,

I recognized her. I—Only, you know, from television, that passport picture."

Trumpf's blood raced, he grabbed a pencil and scrabbled around the desk for a sheet of paper. "And the man she is with?"

The coarse voice reluctantly replied, "All right, I got the guy's license number. The car's a Porsche. But I get credit for the girl *and* him, don't I? I found them both, didn't I? I'm the one who's doing the following, so if there's a reward for him, that's mine, right? And I know who the guy is, too."

"Trust us," Trumpf said. "We're not a den of thieves. . . . Who is it?"

"The guy from the roses," came the voice. "Foxe."

Trumpf, making notes, broke the point off his pencil.

Jason Foxe. The inspector held onto the phone as though a high wind were about to blow it away. Nicca Montcalm and Jason Foxe. He looked at the slip of paper with the caller's name. "Herr Polzer, you have a car?"

"A motorcycle."

"Good. Better than a car, less conspicuous. Stick close to them! They may aim for a hikers' hut; they may stop for food supplies. At the first opportunity, call the nearest Gendarmerie immediately. Don't worry! The moment I hang up this phone I will inform the various Gendarmerie Headquarters, and they will alert the districts. The Gendarmerie will have your name, Herr Polzer, and they will close in immediately on the pair."

He hung up, dizzied by the windfall of—he glanced down at the name—Rudi Polzer. He massaged the back of his neck with both hands, bending his head forward and back, loosening the muscles. If Jason Foxe and the girl headed for a mountain hut, this cunning Rudi Polzer would be on their trail, a human leech. The trap would

snap closed. Or if Foxe was fool enough to take the girl to
Schloss Walenberg, Polzer would also be on their heels.

But Polzer up against the cleverness of the Foxe?
Hardly a match! Therefore . . .

Pepi was coming in, a can of Coke in one hand, his
paperback in the other. "Pepi, how would like to visit a
beautiful castle in the country?"

"Sure." Pepi buckled the can and let it pop back.
"When?"

"Now," said Inspector Trumpf.

In the Goldener Hirsch, Rudi Polzer hung up the
phone, gloating. The reward! *Rudi's Service Station,* red
overalls with black name on the back—and getting even
with the blue-eyed bitch from the Mödling woods. He'd
be in the papers and on television. Magazines would
interview him.

And look how God was on his side—even though he
never went to confession. What he did was nobody's
business, not even a priest's. Take today. He'd been
sitting on the Honda saddle, indecisively twisting the
handlebars, gabbing with Hans Strohmayer and with
nothing to do on his Saturday off, when Jason Foxe had
driven up for gas.

There was no way to explain to a priest why he, Rudi,
had decided to follow Jason Foxe. The priest would
insinuate that he was *ein Wärmer*—a homosexual. But
that wasn't it, he was a stud with girls, even forcing them
sometimes. Besides, he hated *die Wärmen*. Just seeing a
couple of them walking together would make his skin itch
with nervousness; and he would clench his fists and jut
out his chin in fierce denial of their existence.

So this, with Jason Foxe, was different. He could not
have said why he followed him. But there was that
mystifying thing about Foxe. That very first time he'd

seen the Foxe drive into Strohmayer's in the open Porsche, it was as though instantly he had wanted some special thing from Foxe . . . as though he'd wanted something of this Foxe to rub off on him. It was queer, it was the way Foxe moved, the lean, flat-cheeked face that was not handsome, the way Foxe turned his dark head . . . it was hard to understand. It was more like, in some peculiar way, he, Rudi, wanted to *be* Jason Foxe.

Rudi Polzer would have spit on the word *romantic*. He equated it with poetry. Poetry made him snicker. But this Foxe, it set up a longing . . . One hot summer evening when he was a kid, a traveling circus had stopped in his village. There had been a trapeze, a band had played, and a long-haired girl in spangled tights had swung slowly back and forth on the trapeze, swinging against the darkening sky. The sight had made something swell in his chest, a pleasure mixed with heart-twisting pain. In some peculiar way, Jason Foxe reminded him of that magical evening, he could almost hear the band playing.

So, following the Porsche on the Autobahn and turning down the rutted road to Karlsdorf, he had seen Foxe go into the Goldener Hirsch. He himself was not hungry so he had strolled around Karlsdorf. Down a side street, he had happened on a motorcycle service shop. He'd chatted with the owner, a young Hungarian who it turned out, knew one of Rudi's motorcycle friends. The Hungarian had treated him to a couple of bottles of beer and they had talked motorcycles.

The encounter had left him somehow satisfied, the time well spent. When he parted from the Hungarian, he was ready to climb back onto his Honda and return to Vienna. But first, something to eat. *Bauernschmaus*—pork with sauerkraut—a big plateful. He walked down the road back to the Goldener Hirsch. Foxe's Porsche was still there. So what of it? He stuck out his jaw: Foxe didn't own the world. He went inside.

And then, and then—

Inside, among the customers lunching, Rudi saw the Foxe. He sat at a table with his back turned, and across from him was a pretty girl. As Rudi passed, the girl looked straight across the table at Foxe, speaking urgently, eyes wide. Blue eyes with black fringes. Eyes he had unmistakably seen up close in the woods at Mödling.

In the alcove, he sank down at a table, wild with excitement, heart pounding. It was she, the American! The murderess. The eyes were unforgettable. They had stared into his, only an inch away, at Mödling. The image of those eyes was frozen solid in his mind; he had seen them plenty of times behind his closed eyelids, dreaming of a reward, those light blue, black-fringed eyes. The reward! . . . He felt for schillings for the phone. Plenty.

On the phone in the Goldener Hirsch, he sweated and cursed the sergeant on the switchboard at the Rossauerkaserne, the sergeant who was torturing him, dangling him, while he agonized with impatience. But he hung on, stubbornly, sweat under his armpits, tenacious; he would speak to nobody but Inspector Trumpf. He had seen Trumpf's name often enough in the newspapers about the von Reitz murder. So, sweating, pouring schillings into the phone, he hung on until he got through to the inspector.

Now, hanging up in a fever of excitement, he gathered up his change from the platform under the phone, hands trembling so that a few coins fell on the floor; he did not even bother to pick them up. The tension had stirred his kidneys, his bladder, as though he'd drunk a couple of quarts of beer with the Hungarian, not just a couple of pints. He couldn't wait, not another instant. He went into the *Toilette* and relieved himself.

When he came out and entered the dining room of the Gasthaus, his heart almost stopped. A waiter was clearing the empty table where Foxe and the girl had been sitting.

He tore outside. And stood there, cursing. The little Porsche was gone.

Chapter 15

Schloss von Walenberg lay in Styrian country, across the Wechsel mountain range, west of the Lafnitz river between Styria and Burgenland. Seventy kilometers to the south lay Yugoslavia; the Italian border, southwest through Carinthia, was perhaps two hundred kilometers away. It was in prime hunting country, its forested mountain slopes and deep green meadows full of game. The abundance of roe deer, red deer, mouflon, hare, pheasant, and partridge had been the chief reason Baron Willy's ancestor, Baron August von Walenberg, had built the castle in the thirteenth century.

Baron Wilhelm von Walenberg stood waiting in the courtyard in front of the Baronin's apartments. He was abnormally sensitive. The disaster with his mother's attendant had left him shaken. Josephine, middle-aged, dependable, had been with the Baronin sixteen years, now her farmer brother had taken her home to their

village, rattling away in his dented truck. The Baronin
had wept like a child.

So now, waiting for Jason Foxe and the new attendant,
Baron Willy took agitated little steps, pacing the flagged
courtyard outside his mother's private apartments. He
was chain-smoking thin, brown cigarettes.

Willy von Walenberg was an only child. His mother,
the Frau Baronin, had given birth to him, but after that it
was as though she had no further control . . . not that she
had had any even in the conception of her offspring. A
certain careless brutality had characterized the late
Baron Heinrich. But then, she had had no say in the
marriage either. She had been married to Baron
Heinrich at eighteen, right out of the convent. Her two
years of marriage to the middle-aged Baron, who had
been killed in a hunting accident, had frightened her
back into the refuge of her religion. In the little chapel
connected to her private courtyard, she found solace.

Portraits of Baron Willy von Walenberg, growing up in
the Schloss, showed an exquisite little boy with wide
brown eyes and delicate hands and a perky, elfin smile,
like Puck in *A Midsummer Night's Dream*. Baron Willy
was now fifty-five. He was small, with delicate bones, and
as fragile as an Augarten teacup. He had fair hair like a
dandelion puffball, downy and on end. He worked at a
token job in the Austrian Department of Finance in
Vienna, and he kept a tiny apartment, decorated in Art
Nouveau, on Annagasse. It had hi-fi, and a good stock of
vintage wines, his sole comforts in this uncertain world.

Ears alert for Jason Foxe's car, the baron now paced,
his steps on the flagstone making an odd, clunky sound.
Baron Willy was five feet six inches tall, but gained an
extra two inches courtesy of handmade shoes with built-
up heels. The clunky-sounding heels were hollow, but
nevertheless weighty and often tiring. He wore a fawn-

colored suede suit, with knickers. He had anxious brown eyes in a finely wrinkled face. He wore tan pancake makeup.

At the sound of the Porsche, he made a squeaky sound of relief. For all he knew on the way from Hartberg it could have gone off a cliff, not that there were any cliffs, but still—

"Ach, Jason! Grüss Gott!" He approached the Porsche. "My mother has been awaiting you and"—he bowed to the young woman at Jason Foxe's side—"the *gnädiges Fräulein."*

The new attendant murmured an acknowledgment. She had short, chestnut-colored hair pinned unbecomingly flat to her head and behind her ears. Her face was narrow and she might even have been reasonably attractive if she had taken the trouble to make up. But of course she was not at Schloss Walenberg to win a beauty contest. She wore dark glasses, a wise move in Baron Willy's estimation, for the Styrian sun in autumn was brilliant, white, rather than yellow. The young woman was also efficient; she already wore a white uniform, so fresh it was still creased. Baron Willy, who was inclined to make instant judgments, liked her at once. He gave her a welcoming smile, happy to show the small white teeth that were really his own, uncapped and even as a row of soldiers on parade.

Her name was Hilde Hoffmann. Out of the car, she proved to be a slim young woman. She held a small valise.

"My mother sends you her most grateful thanks!" the Baron said to Jason who had kept the car motor running and remained in the driver's seat, one hand on the wheel. "You know where the main courtyard is, the servants will unload your car and park it."

Jason nodded. *"Auf Wiedersehen!"* he said. He gave a cheery wave of his hand and the car moved off.

"Don't forget!" Baron Willy called after him, "The Piper-Heidsieck! Nineteen-sixty-six, one of the best years! Just for you, Jason! And perhaps one little glass for me. And Florian! A glass for Florian!" The Porsche was already at the archway. Foxe raised an acknowledging hand and waved, without looking back.

Baron Willy took Fräulein Hoffmann's little valise from her—how light it was!—and bowed her toward the entrance. *"Bitte, Fräulein Hoffmann."* Following with the featherweight valise, he felt a tremulous upsurge of love toward the world: His mother, bereft of Josephine, would nevertheless have Fräulein Hoffmann. She would peacefully read her Bible, embroider, and play gin rummy with Fräulein Hoffmann. All this thanks to Jason Foxe.

"Madness," Florian said. "This is madness. You're not only playing the fool in love, you're playing a dangerous game. God *damn* love! Shakespeare was right: 'Love is merely a madness; and, I tell you, deserves a dark house and a whip as madmen do. . . .' "

Jason pulled the trigger of the staple gun and drove the final staple into the three-paneled screen. They were in the immense, shadowy library. The blowups of the drawings and reviews were now stapled, the aluminum spotlights were set up just inside the terrace doors. The heavily balustraded west terrace had broad steps going down to the lawn. On lawn and terrace, guests moved about, chatting and drinking chilled Styrian wines. Jason had told Florian everything.

"You could end up in prison."

"I could. But she didn't kill him."

"And you think, given time, you'll find out who did?"

"Possibly. In the meantime, we may need your help."

"Mad," Florian said. "You're mad. On the other hand"—he shrugged—"I am a dedicated outsider. Consider me with you in your madness."

"Thanks." They stood looking at each other, neither one quite smiling. Florian, intrinsically elegant, was leaning on his cane. He had taken pills to alleviate his pain, but a spasmodic little tensing and retensing of his jaw betrayed twinges of it; a nerve had been unalterably damaged. The watercolors on the screen showed brilliantly-hued birds on the wing. For an instant, Jason saw the young Florian ski-jumping in the Tyrol, body sailing above the crowd, arms outspread. He had worn a white woolen cap with a red pompom.

"Herr Königsmark?" Florian's editor, a round-faced little man with white mustache and white eyebrows, stood apologetically in the terrace doorway. "The centerpiece is missing from the table! Are you almost through?"

"I'm coming." Florian put a hand on Jason's shoulder. *"Gehen Wir."*

On the lawn, Königsmark was immediately surrounded by bird fanciers, entomologists, members of ornithological societies, and a gaggle of journalists. Jason stood apart, gnawing his lips, figuring. Around him, servants jacketed in the famous deep Styrian green moved among the guests, offering trays of tiny grilled sausages, cold smoked trout, and cold asparagus with mayonnaise. At a snow-white buffet table, cold roast partridge and other Styrian delicacies were being served. The press party would last until six o'clock.

Baron Willy's handful of weekend guests, personal friends, would dine at eight-thirty. Most of them had come to hunt. The Schloss was huge, the servants plentiful. In the morning, bent-over, old servant women in black would scurry around, taking care of the awakening guests. "It is the old way," Florian had explained. "They come into your room when you are naked, to take care of your bath, the towels, your hot water. As though they are not human. It is their function." Once, said Florian, on the occasion of the Baron's fiftieth birthday, the big Packard of a guest who was bringing Florian with him from Vienna had gone into a ditch near the Schloss. Baron Willy had sent out strapping servants who, with their bare hands, had picked the big car from the ditch.

"Jason! Grüss Gott!" Bruno Königsmark, Florian's young brother, was at Jason's elbow; he had driven from Vienna with Florian. "Look at them! They're wearing him out!" He jerked his head angrily at the crowd around his brother. *"Es gefällt mir nicht!* They'll exhaust him!"

Bruno was eighteen, but he protected his older brother like a mastiff growling away intruders from a sleeping child. He was wiry and slender, with gray eyes and fair hair that he wore very short; he having several times, to his discomfort, been mistaken for a girl. He was constantly in love, currently with the Madonna-faced daughter of a first violinist. When he was not eating, studying, sleeping, or protecting Florian, he was on the telephone with Marcia, the violinist's daughter.

"The only comfort I can give you," Jason said, "is that Florian will live to *not* regret it. The weekly news magazines will compare him to Audubon. And fame, Bruno! Fame! Someone once said, 'The final test of fame is to have a crazy person imagine he is you.' This book will make Florian's reputation. Just think of all the people who will then claim they're Königsmark!" At that, Bruno gave him a mollified smile and seemed less likely to wade into the crowd and rescue his brother.

"Jason Foxe!"

A flutelike voice, an American accent. A young blond

woman in a cherry red jacket and taupe pants came breathlessly up, a man in tow. Instead of holding out a hand, she jammed her hands into her pants pockets, thrust out a hip and rested her weight on one foot: a high-fashion magazine pose.

"Jason *Foxe!*" Raised eyebrows in a not-quite-pretty face. Hortense Wicks. "What are *you* doing here?" She sounded as though she had found a pig's snout in a bucket of diamonds.

"Friend of the author," he said. But because Hortense Wicks's insecurity touched him, he smiled at her. She was a social snob. Even in the few hours they had been in bed together, her conversation had revealed wistful social longings. He also knew that she gave the impression of haughtiness simply because, conscious of having a short neck, she held her head high to keep her back straight and her neck long. "The Modigliani neck," she had described it to Jason as they lay in bed; she had been talking enviously of one of the Austrian models. Hortense Wicks's childhood must have been filled with longings to be not Alice but the Duchess. Not a princess, but the queen.

"Kurt von Baer," she introduced her companion, sounding pleased with herself. Von Baer was a well-packed man in worn tweeds and a red tie. He looked as though he might own a castle or two himself. Another Austrian blue blood; there was that *von.* Jason presented Bruno who murmured *"Sehr angenehm,"* then excused himself and moved off, scowling, toward the crowd around his brother.

Hortense Wicks looked surprisingly attractive. Her eyes were bright and happy, her face prettily flushed from the sun. She abandoned the outthrust hip pose to rest a hand familiarly on von Baer's arm and bring Jason Foxe up to date in a surprisingly relaxed, friendly fashion: the fashion crew had left . . . she was taking a month's vacation in Vienna, "An entire month! If you have clout on the magazine, you can get it."

Jason, listened, nodding. He was aware of sexual emanations flowing like electric sparks between Kurt von Baer and Hortense Wicks. He was also wondering if Miss Hortense Wicks had her passport with her. He was wondering if she slept with it under her pillow. He was wondering if, were Nicca to bleach her hair blonde, she could pass for—No, forget it. Their faces were too unlike. And though Hortense Wicks might be sleeping with her passport under her pillow, that pillow was undoubtedly guarded by Herr von Baer.

"We're staying the weekend, we're hunting in the morning," Hortense Wicks was saying. She looked happily up at von Baer who responded by tucking a wayward blond wisp of hair behind her ear. There was unmistakable love and tenderness in the gesture.

"Well . . . *Auf Wiedersehen!*" Hortense said. She wiggled her fingers at Jason and moved off, a bright, fashionable shaft in the sunlight, one hand in the crook of von Baer's arm. In love, that pair was in love, as in love as . . . as Willy von Walenberg who was approaching, smiling, signaling to a green-jacketed servant with a tray of wines and glasses. *"Bitte, Johann! Kommen Sie hier her!"* And to Jason:

"The wines are chilled to perfection . . . try a Styrian white." The servant offered the tray. "Leutschach," the Baron said, "on the left. Then Ehrenhausen, then Gamlitz." He indicated each of the wines. "My own preference is Ehrenhausen." Jason chose the Ehrenhausen. He sipped and make complimentary noises.

Strategy, maps, plans, the border. Danilo Lovchen, the Yugoslavian, was the Baron's estate manager; as such he'd be knowledgeable of the countryside, the byways, paths, roads, "Your Sohn, Baron—we've never met."

"Indeed? *Indeed?* You've never met Danilo? Come, then!"

Danilo Lovchen was at the buffet table, stuffing cold roast pork and bread into his mouth. Baron Willy waited, anxiously giving his beloved Danilo time to swallow without choking; then he performed the introductions. Danilo Lovchen was a Serb. He had a physique like Apollo, brilliant red cheeks, and dark hair and eyes. Even in repose, his body suggested elasticity of movement. Instead of a jacket, he wore a white shirt with wide, flowing sleeves, and a red vest with black braid. Apparently the roast pork had not been salty enough. Danilo licked his palm, poured salt into it from a shaker, then licked the salt from his hand. He bowed, acknowledging Jason. *"Ich freue mich."* He had a deep, masculine voice. He wiped the corners of his mouth with his knuckles, then patted his pockets and frowned. Baron Willy hastily offered his pale alligator cigarette case. "You smoke too much, mein Sohn." Danilo responded with a contemptuous shrug.

Danilo Lovchen knew this Styrian countryside, not only the von Walenberg estate of forests, meadows and streams, but farther afield. He had also lived two years in Maribor, just over the Austrian border, in Yugoslavia, a tantalizingly short distance away, perhaps eighty miles from Schloss Walenberg. Jason was eager to hunt, he told Lovchen. He understood the hunting hereabouts was exceptional . . . *nicht wahr?*

"Ja! Ja!" Damilo laughed with pleasure. "The black cock almost leaps into your hand! The partridge waddles up and nudges your rifle! The hare embraces your wrist! A paradise for huntsmen. And fishing? In the Lafnitz near Furstenfeld, the pike begs for your bait. But *our*

pike, in the von Walenberg streams, gives you a game. You have to trick it, there's more excitement. Then—smack!—you've got it!"

Lanes, roads, passes, mountain trails often used for tracking roe deer, fords, footbridges, little villages—Danilo knew them all. Talking, laughing, he smoked cigarette after cigarette, imperiously holding up two fingers to the Baron each time he wanted another, and the Baron hastened to oblige. While Danilo talked, Baron Willy stood aside, nodding and smiling like a proud mother whose prodigy was giving a brilliant performance. Occasionally he cast a wistful glance around the lawn, as though to gather in a wider audience.

Six cigarettes later, when Jason Foxe parted from Danilo Lovchen and the Baron, the surrounding countryside was indelibly impressed in his mind. It was imprinted down to the smallest village and most obscure road. He stood alone near the buffet table, flicking a thumb, gnawing a lip. Yugoslavia was the best bet. A dangerous game, Florian had said. And yes, it was: with prison for life to the loser. Never mind that. What he searched for was the valuable missing piece he needed as soon as possible: a passport. The rest would fall into place.

He looked across the lawn. Among the towers and turrets and eaves and roofs of Castle Walenberg he glimpsed the round turret on the south wing, the wing that housed the Frau Baronin's apartments. Somewhere in that wing, the old woman and the young one were as remote, as isolated from the castle activities as if on another planet. Wrapped in safety.

At least for now.

"Hombre!" Pepi said. "We forgot the carrots!" He sneezed. The tapestry on the stone wall of this dank,

unused tower in the jumble of towers and turrets in the
south wing of Schloss Walenberg, featured a downcast
maiden astride a white unicorn. The unicorn's horn was a
color between orange and coral, and it certainly did
resemble a carrot. Inspector Trumpf acknowledged
Pepi's reminder with a grunt, and an unchanged face of
gloom.

The inspector was troubled. He had no appetite anyway, not even for tafelspitz, and forget carrots altogether.
He had a bitter taste in his mouth. This must be the
twentieth unicorn he had seen prancing on tapestries in
his unauthorized exploration of Schloss Walenberg. He
was in no mood to appreciate the handiwork of noble
ladies cloistered in nunneries in the Middle Ages. Centuries past did not interest him. What troubled him was the
present.

Everything had gone wrong. He had arrived at the
Schloss, he had mingled with the guests, he had spotted
Jason Foxe. Tickled by his windfall of luck, he had
searched confidently for Veronica Kent. But she was not
on the lawn, she was not in the drawing rooms, the
library, or on the populated terraces. *Zum Teufel!* Pepi
at his heels, he had hastened out to the main courtyard
where servants had taken his car from him. *"Nein,"* the
swarthier of the two servants had insisted, *"Niemand!
Herr Foxe ist allein gekommen! Allein!"* The man had
even remembered summoning helpers from indoors to
carry Herr Foxe's awkward paraphernalia of aluminum
lamps and rolls of paper. Herr Foxe had carried in his
own luggage, which was merely one of those nylon overnight bags, "Blue, with a black stripe," the fellow had
added helpfully.

Hastening indoors, he had phoned headquarters. If
Foxe had dropped the girl off somewhere, then Rudi
Polzer, tenaciously sticking to the Porsche, would know

where; he would have called headquarters with the information. But on the phone, Trumpf had learned from Detective Staral that there had been no word from Rudi Polzer.

That was when he had lost his appetite.

But he was stubborn, his mind played constantly with deductions, and he had a streak of the romantic that played like background music to his musing. He reasoned simply that when Jason Foxe had sent red roses to the wrong room at the Hilton, he had not even known Nicca Montcalm because "Nicca Montcalm" had not yet existed. He had met her later. And he had fallen in love, *passionately* in love—why else would he dive again into a whirlpool that might suck him down? And now, having rescued his maiden, his beloved, he certainly wouldn't hide her in the nearby forest and bring her food in a knapsack or a picnic basket, and he wouldn't count on the birds to feed her, as in some fairy tale like Hansel and Gretel. Foxe would want her warm and seductive body close to his, undoubtedly on the finest linen sheets Castle Walenberg could provide. More practically, thought Trumpf, his mind relinquishing romance, the Foxe had had no time, without a plan, to hide the girl elsewhere.

Ergo; Veronica Kent was here in castle Walenberg. Foxe had somehow spirited her into the *Schloss.* How? The *how* no longer mattered: The girl was here.

So Inspector Trumpf had begun to explore the castle. He had investigated with a light tread and light fingers, and even the twitching of his nostrils, the suite allotted to Jason Foxe and that allotted to Florian Königsmark, also the rooms or suites of the other guests staying the weekend. A fruitless search. Not so much as a whiff of perfume. He had then essayed the formidable task of searching the myriad rooms of the *Schloss.* It was a remarkable revelation, but not the one he was after. It took him hardly an hour to recognize the hopelessness of the task. There were rooms and apartments that doubtless Baron Willy von Walenberg himself had never seen.

The inspector realized this unhappy fact at the exact instant of seeing that twentieth unicorn. "*Komm,*" he said despondently to Pepi. "*Lass uns 'rausgehen.*" And he turned his back on the unicorn with the carrot horn.

They emerged after countless turnings in passageways and descending winding stone stairways, into a small, sunlit courtyard. It was so still that the stillness itself had a vibrating intensity. A chapel in the baroque style formed one side of the courtyard. "Ahhh! ... " The inspector breathed a sigh of pleasure. The glories of nature left him indifferent, the visions of man delighted him. Since childhood he had responded to the baroque, it seem to him playful, enchanting, a world created by masterful pastry chefs.

"*Komm.*" He made for the chapel.

Inside, in the dim coolness, frescos and paintings lined the walls; sunlight filtered through stained glass depicting haloed virgins, bearded saints. Votive candles in glowing ruby glass flickered at the high altar. "*Schön ... Schön!*" Trumpf said aloud, only to hear a violent "Shhh!" from Pepi, who tugged at his sleeve. "*Leute!*" Pepi whispered, pointing.

The inspector saw them then: two people near the altar; they were approaching, coming up the aisle toward the back of the chapel—an elderly woman in a wheelchair propelled by a white-clad attendant.

"*Grüss Gott,*" the old woman said, when they reached the inspector and Pepi. She held up a hand, signaling the attendant to halt. "You enjoy my chapel? It is thirteenth century, rebuilt last in the sixteenth century, though the *Schloss* itself was rebuilt in the seventeenth." She wore a black dress with heavy folds. A knitted gray shawl was around her shoulders and her white hair was covered by a cap of jet beads. Her head trembled slightly with palsy so that the beads made little clicking sounds. She had a doll-like face with rouged cheeks. "You wish, mein Herr, that the boy become a good Catholic? Yes, yes!—so you bring him here. *Gut!* I have something here for him," and she fumbled in a pocket of her voluminous skirt. "No, not here! But wait . . . wait." More fumbling in the other pocket. "One moment . . . something precious for the boy! And for you as well, mein Herr."

Inspector Trumpf hoped it would not be candy. When he was a child, his elderly aunts always gave him hard candy, or else marzipan in the shape of turtles, eggs, rabbits, or hens. He hated marzipan. Waiting, he looked at the white-clad attendant. The sun had moved, dulling the stained-glass windows, the remaining colored light cast a grotesquerie of crimson, blue, and smoky green, turning the attendant's white uniform into motley. She was a young woman with hair hidden by a stiff white cap, and she wore dark glasses, not that she needed them here in this dimness. He wondered how she could see at all.

"Ach! Here they are! They were hiding." The old lady shuffled through some mysterious-looking strips of stiff, embroidered cloth. "Only three left. Well . . ." She peered at one of the strips, then handed it to Pepi. "It is never too early for the boy to profit by the Bible." She handed another to the inspector. "One for you, mein Herr." She turned abruptly, craning her head around and peering at her attendant. "I have not yet given you one, *nicht wahr, Fräulein . . . Fräulein? . . .*"

"Hoffmann."

"*Ach, ja. Fräulein Hoffmann.*" The old lady handed the third strip to her attendant.

"*Danke schön, Frau Baronin.*" The attendant's white cap had slipped a little to one side, revealing an earlobe.

Inspector Trumpf caught a glimpse of green, the attendant was wearing little green earrings in pierced ears. Or rather, Trumpf was quick to amend, she wore a green earring in at least *one* ear; he must not, according to police training, record in his mind that the attendant wore *two* green earrings, one in each ear. There was no firm evidence of that. According to police training, it was legitimate to make the assumption that the young woman had two ears. That was as far as he could factually go. It was the kind of thing he impressed constantly on Detective Staral.

"Be a good boy." The old lady, jet beads clicking, gently touched Pepi's cheek, and said to Trumpf, "I too have a son. A good boy, my son, a *good* boy." She signaled the attendant, and the young woman released some gadget at the back of the wheelchair and propelled it forward.

Inspector Trumpf stood in the chapel doorway watching the progress of the Frau Baronin and her attendant across the flagged courtyard. A woman servant opened an arched door and closed it after them. The inspector looked down at the embroidered strip in his hand. It was a bookmark, embroidered with some words. He read it aloud: "The wicked flee when no man pursueth; but the righteous are bold as a lion." Proverbs. And true. A lion, Leo, he was the lion, bold and righteous. In pursuit of the wicked.

He was also using his peripheral vision. He was thinking that the Baronin was not so senile as to forget a familiar attendant's name, particularly one as simple as Hoffmann. He stood a moment, beetling his brows; then he crossed the courtyard to the arched door; it had no bell, no knocker. There was no sense banging with a fist; that would be like a flea trying to attract the attention of an armadillo. He pushed open the door. *"Bitte?"* he called.

"Who is it?" A tall, bespectacled woman servant in black confronted him; she had a square jaw and the stance of a guard dog. The inspector said smoothly that he wished to ask the Frau Baronin if he might have one of her remarkable bookmarks for his wife. "I am grateful for the one she has just given me and"—he patted Pepi's head—"my *Sohn*." However, not to disturb the Baronin herself, perhaps the Frau Baronin's new attendant, Fräulein Hoffmann—

"Nein!" the bespectacled guard dog said sharply. The Baronin and her attendant were already at tea. However, she added, "The Baronin attends chapel at five o'clock in the morning. Perhaps if the *gnädige Herr . . . Guten Tag."* And the massive door swung closed in Inspector Trumpf's face.

He contemplated the heavy oak. Perhaps his imagination was overworked. He was in a forest in which every tree took on the shape of the elusive girl, every rippling brook murmured in her voice, every falling shadow was her shadow. *Nevertheless.* Nevertheless, the dark of five A.M. would find him at the chapel. He raised his head. He could swear he smelled chicken roasting on a spit, it would be that flavorsome Styrian roast chicken, *Steirisches Brathuhn.* His mouth watered. The delicious smell would be coming from the party on the lawn, where there were chilled wines, a buffet. *"Komm."*

"Hombre!" Pepi said, crossing the courtyard at his father's side; he was studying his bookmark.

"What does it say?"

Pepi read it aloud: "Thou shalt not commit adultery."

Chapter 16

"Fine," Jason Foxe said. He was in shock, but he didn't bat an eye. There was grease on the inspector's chin, a blissful look on his moonlike face, and a delicious-looking chicken leg in his right hand. He stood on the lawn, smiling at Jason. Jason gazed back, sick at heart. Trumpf was at Castle Walenberg because he was either a bird fancier or an extraordinary detective. Foxe reflected grimly that the second supposition was the correct one.

He pulled himself together. The inspector would leave the castle outguessed, outfoxed. Nicca was safe; no need to tense up.

"So ornithology interests you, Inspector?" A tinge of mockery in his voice.

"Yes. I am a specialist in birds, Herr Foxe. Pheasant, partridge, even chickens . . . roasted, of course. There is no match for Steirisches Brathuhn."

"Hunting them, too? . . . Perhaps you hunt?"

The inspector fumbled in his pocket for a handkerchief

and wiped his greasy mouth. "Not birds, Herr Foxe. Never birds."

The Devil's boots don't creak. Nicca read the embroidered bookmark and broke out in quickly muffled laughter. She sat across from the dozing Baronin at the card table in the Baronin's sitting room. The fire was lit against the autumn chill, the room was cozy. After tea, the Baronin had gotten out the cards and Nicca had taught her how to play Spite and Malice. The old lady had loved it "even better than rummy," but that hadn't prevented her from slipping into a doze. She sat in a down-cushioned armchair, propped up by pillows. Her head lolled to one side; her mouth, a little open, was a faded rosebud. She looked like a peasant grandmother in a child's collection of folk dolls.

Nicca fingered the bookmark. The Devil's boots don't creak. The Baronin was certainly confused. The quotation wasn't from the Bible, neither the Old Testament nor the New. It was one of those dark old Scottish proverbs, served up warningly to boy sentries of warring clans, boys who ate cold gruel then went into the dark to stand guard. And here the warning had surfaced in what Nicca thought of as the Baronin's Biblical Fortune Cookies. She wondered what Inspector Trumpf's bookmark had said.

Inspector Trumpf. She saw again his rumpled figure outlined in the chapel doorway, the boy at his side, and herself approaching closer, closer, coming up the aisle behind the wheelchair; the melancholy-eyed face materialized before her in the dim chapel. She felt the icicle of fear along her spine.

But the inspector hadn't even noticed her. When the Baronin had hesitated over the name and she had supplied it, the inspector's face had remained blank as a calf's.

Morosely, she bit a fingernail. This bookmark. Who, in this case, was the Devil? Was she, Nicca, an instrument of the Devil, striking Herr von Reitz, paving the way for the assassin to kill the helpless man, or had the killer programmed the lawyer's death? Was his death already in the cards, and had she, Nicca, been the unlucky provider of the occasion?

Perhaps Inspector Trumpf himself now wore the Devil's boots. At least, he wore them if she, Nicca, was destined to pay for someone else's crime. Mornings, teaching the French subjunctive to Karoline and Franz, irresistibly and silently she would conjugate, *Had I killed him, had you killed him, had he, she, it, killed him.* And the gerund! Almost, she had given Franz the example: *Having thought she killed him with the bronze parrot, she fled.*

Now, ironically, since life was forever handing you a prize and then tripping you as you bore it out the door, she had fallen in love with Jason Foxe. It was bitter, exciting, frustrating. She thought of the lovers with whom she had shared a bed; she thought of the husband who had been a boy and who would probably always be a boy. She had envisioned love as a crystal goblet, round and full, brimming with a rich wine that spread fire and laughter and love at every sip. She had never drunk from that goblet, it had always eluded her.

Even before she had felt Jason Foxe's hands on her hair, combing, cutting, before she had felt his breath blowing on her forehead, blowing away the cut hairs . . . before he had driven her determinedly to Hietzing— "They will not burn you at the stake"—she had glimpsed the brimming goblet but it was forbidden her, the hunted. It was no relief to sense that, besides, Jason Foxe's heart was engaged elsewhere. It was a locked box—he already loved. And then, the irony! Seeing in the glove compart-

ment of the car her Xeroxed notebook! There were times
when, at night in bed in the maid's room, she had wept
and giggled and wept again at the absurdity of the
situation. She was pursued as a murderess; how could she
have involved him? She could not.

But he had involved himself.

The rich wine. She felt a stirring in her breasts.

"Fräulein Hoffmann?" It was the square-jawed Frau
Schall, protector of the Baronin, a shushing finger to her
lips. "*Still! Ruhig* . . . quiet!" She carried a little pink
pillow with ruffled edges. She eased it gently between the
Baronin's lolling head and her shoulder. She turned and
said in a whisper: "The Frau Baronin will sleep now until
six o'clock. She dines at six-thirty. You will dine with her.
At seven-thirty, she has her bath. *I* bathe her, I have
always bathed the Baronin. Then I will help you put her
to bed. You will read aloud to her. Deuteronomy; I have
marked the page. Two pages and she will be drowsing.
She sleeps like an infant, the Baronin! She will be asleep
by eight o'clock. She rises at four to pray alone. She
awakens by herself, as though she had swallowed an
alarm clock. At five o'clock exactly, you accompany her
in the wheelchair to the chapel. *Verstehen Sie, Fräulein
Hoffmann?*" Frau Schall was becoming hoarse with her
forceful whispering. She leaned toward the Baronin and
gently pulled down a rucked-up sleeve. Her square-jawed
face was fleetingly that of a mother bending over a child.

She turned to leave, then turned back. "If in the chapel
the Baronin does not wish to speak to the gentleman, she
will pat her left shoulder. Sometimes she wishes not to be
bothered. In that case, Fräulein Hoffmann, you go right
past, with only a *Guten Morgen* . . . *Verstehen Sie?*"

"The . . . gentleman?"

"With the little boy. He wishes a religious bookmark
for his wife, he even asked to accept it at your hands—

'the new attendant, Fräulein Hoffmann,' he said—
though how he knew you were newly engaged, I cannot
guess. However, the Baronin likes to personally give her
bookmarks. From her own hands. Understandable, *nicht
wahr?* Also, such an honor! A bookmark bestowed by the
gnädige Frau Baronin von Walenberg herself!"

"*Natürlich.*"

When Frau Schrall had disappeared, Nicca sat
motionless. On the table beside her lay the big Bible,
tooled leather with a gold clasp. Next to it a rococo
porcelain clock, all pink cherubs and dancing nymphs,
ticked and ticked, each tick a minute *ping*. The Devil's
boots don't creak. Yet with each tiny *ping*, he approached
closer.

She had to do something. But what?

The wizened little woman servant, almost a midget,
kept ducking her head, smiling and ducking her head,
backing away from Herr Foxe. She had found him easily
enough among the strange people on the west lawn. She
was from the Baronin's staff, but she knew Herr Foxe,
the American friend of Florian Königsmark, all the
Schloss Walenberg servants knew him from the days
when the handsome Herr Königsmark, a seventeen-year-
old, had walked around on two good legs and had brought
the American boy to the Schloss. Besides, Herr Foxe was
a tall man, and with his black curly cap of hair he stood
out among the guests, guests dipping *Grazer Zweiback*
into their wineglasses, then sticking their necks out like
pecking chickens to keep from getting the powdered
sugar on their clothes. A whole barnyard of beautifully
clothed pecking chickens, all strangers—except of course
for Herr Königsmark, the darling. She could just glimpse
the top of his fair head, he was so surrounded by people,
like a queen bee working bees have clustered around.

Bobbing, ducking her head, she turned and scurried back; she had done her job, she had delivered the note from Fräulein Hoffmann to Herr Jason Foxe.

Baron Willy von Walenberg had given his favorite apartment in the east wing to Florian Königsmark and his brother Bruno. The sitting room, once oppressive with heavy, dark furnishings, was now pale and modern. The paneled walls had been bleached to gold and honey-colored drapes framed the windows. There were down-soft white chairs and a modern sofa with plump cushions. The lamps had pale, sand-colored shades. A fat silver bowl of fresh-picked flowers stood on an English kidney desk.

Prominently displayed on that desk was a framed photograph of Marcia, the first violinist's daughter with whom Bruno Königsmark was in love. The photograph was the first thing Bruno had unpacked, though he would be away from Vienna for only a short weekend.

"Ach! Ach!" Bruno, on the sofa, was listening in fascination and consternation to Jason Foxe who was pacing back and forth. The two were alone in the room. *"Verdammt!"* Along with consternation now, outrage. "Parents!" he exclaimed ... and then: "Romeo and Juliet!" His face was flushed, he never took his eyes from Foxe.

"So you see," Jason finished, halting before Bruno, "her parents are wooden-headed! Marriage? Out of the question! The mother has hysterics, fainting fits. Impossible! They suspect Vera might elope with Wolfgang, the mother is frightened, the father so suspicious that he has locked up Vera's passport, taken away her allowance."

"Ach! Ach!"

Jason eyed Bruno's flushed face. He recapitulated: "So

if Vera had a passport and could get across to Yugoslavia, Wolfgang would meet her there, they would marry."

"Is she the one in pink . . . who stood near the buffet table all afternoon? The one with curly hair?"

"No, no! Vera wasn't on the lawn. She's a bird fancier. Her parents permitted her to come only because the family chauffeur drove her; he's been with them twenty years. He's more her jailer than chauffeur. They can trust him to keep an eye out, and he'll drive her home Sunday night.

"But poor Vera! She wept all the way from Vienna to Schloss Walenberg. Her eyes are so swollen with weeping that she stays, ashamed, in her room."

"*Armes Kind!* Poor child!" Bruno turned to look at the photograph of Marcia. "So!" He banged a clenched fist on his knee, his eyes were brilliant with excitement, his voice shook: "So! You are for Vera and Wolfgang. Well, so am I! I'm as much for them as you are! Just as much! I don't have to know them, to feel for them." He gave a vexed exclamation: "Ach! If my passport were only here! . . . Never mind . . . we need the other things, anyway. Tonight after dinner—"

"Use Florian's car. You'll—"

"Yes, I'll bring my bike back in the car. And a knapsack and the passport. You'll give Vera enough money? Without her allowance—"

"I have plenty."

They went over it carefully, exhaustively: Early tomorrow morning, Bruno would arrive back from Vienna with the bike, the knapsack, and his passport. But he would not return to the castle. No, it would be safest if he would telephone from the nearby village of Altdorf when he was back and ready to meet Vera at the assigned spot on the road. It would be around eight o'clock in the morning; people would already be breakfasting at the

Schloss. The telephone call received, Vera, disguised as a boy in Bruno's clothes, was to stroll casually across the field on the southeast side of the castle; she would follow the stone wall until she reached the dirt road.

Jason sat down beside Bruno on the sofa, his crudely penciled map on his knee. "She'll get to the road three miles from Altdorf. You'll be waiting in the car, you'll pick her up and—

"Drive her a mile from the Yugoslavian border! She will bicycle across the border with the knapsack and the passport!" Bruno laughed with excitement. His face glowed. "An Austrian boy on a bicycling holiday! And at the inn in Maribor, Wolfgang will be waiting for her! And they will marry and live happily ever after!"

And there she will be safe. Jason folded the crude map. All this lying to Bruno Königsmark was turning his stomach. But he was desperate, and there was no other way. One thing he was learning, he thought wryly: A man in love has no conscience.

"And for dinner tonight," Bruno recapitulated, "I'm to tell Willy that my best friend, Eugen Tierstein—" He hesitated. "Does that name sound real to you?" And at Jason's nod: "—that my friend Eugen is arriving late this afternoon and will be here tonight for dinner."

"Exactly . . . because it would look odd if your friend 'Eugen' appeared tomorrow morning at breakfast out of the blue! A new face would attract everybody's attention." Particularly that of the indefatigable and prescient Detective-Inspector Leo Trumpf who seemed to have a row of eyes around his head. Trumpf would be sure to obtain an invitation for overnight; he probably already had.

"And when people breakfasting see 'Eugen' stroll off across the meadow, they'll never think it is Vera!" Bruno laughed, delighted. "He'll never suspect!"

"Who?" For a moment Jason had lost the thread.

"The chauffeur, that damned jailer. 'Keeping an eye on her.' He could be hanging about anywhere."

"Right . . . that's why we have to—"

"The disguise."

"Right." He felt exhausted.

Bruno jumped up. "I'll get my clothes."

"Right." He sat morosely on the sofa when Bruno had left. He could hear him in the next room whistling the Bach Concerto in D minor for two violins. He looked over at the photograph of Marcia. This ridiculous scenario! Only a man in love would think it up, and only a boy in love would believe it.

And there was another hurdle: Florian Königsmark. Florian might well blow the whole thing out of the water when he discovered Jason had involved Bruno in the Veronica Kent affair. Florian was bound to find out, no help for it. But he'd had to act immediately, he'd had no choice. A Catch-22 situation. It could still be a débâcle in which he lost both Nicca and Florian.

"These are for dinner tonight." Bruno was back, flinging an armful of clothes onto the sofa: trousers the color of doeskin, a shirt, a dark jacket. "My shoes are too big, but here are some extra socks, she can stuff them further with paper if she has to, though my feet are small." Bruno reddened, as embarrassed at his small feet as he was overly conscious of his narrow, girlish face. "What about her hair?"

"I'll take care of that."

"Boys have a darker skin than girls . . . I'll sneak some of Willy's pancake makeup."

"Fine."

Somewhere in the room, a clock chimed. Jason became aware that under his jacket his shirt was soaked with nervous perspiration. He had to hurry, get Nicca out of

the Baronin's apartments fast, any minute Trumpf
might—

"And these, for tomorrow." Bruno threw down gray
knickers, woolen knee socks, country shoes, a sport shirt
and sweater.

"Fine. Perfect."

Bruno crossed his arms and stood smiling, thrilled with
himself, a vein pulsating at his throat, his face glowing,
blazing with color. "Can I meet her now? So we can all
go over it? What room has Willy put her in? Her eyes are
probably still swollen like eggs, poor thing!"

A sound at the door. They both turned. Florian looking
cheerful, but leaning tiredly on his cane. "Whose eyes are
swollen like eggs, 'poor thing'? About what?" He hitched
his way into the room and collapsed into a chair. "I could
use a schnapps, a Kirschwasser. . . . Whose eyes are
swollen?"

"Vera's of course! But when she hears how I'm going to
help her give her parents the slip—I can't wait to see her
face! She'll light up like the sun." His own girlish face
was bright. He laughed, he was his own blazing sun.
"Jason says you'll phone Wolfgang so he'll know where to
meet her in Maribor . . . *richtig*? Ach! I'll never meet
Wolfgang. But I don't care. As long as they're together.
Look, these are the clothes," and he gestured with satisfaction toward the sofa. "They'll fit well enough."

Florian put aside his cane. "The Kirschwasser, the
decanter on the left, if you don't mind, Bruno." He did
not look at Jason, but a muscle in the side of his face
twitched and his eyes had grown cold, colder than Jason
had ever seen, cold to freeze the heart.

"And another favor, *bitte*," Florian said when his
brother brought him the cherry schnapps. "Can you find
Herr Steigman, the photographer from the *Kurier*, a
short man, bearded, hung with a hundred cameras or

so—he must already be waiting for me in the library. Tell him we'll have to do the photographs some other time. Today has been too . . . I'm a little—"

"I knew it! *Verdammt!* I knew they'd exhaust you!" From a blazing sun, Bruno's face turned to a thundercloud. "Steigman had better not give me an argument!" He was already at the door. "He can take the photographs in Vienna! At the gallery!" The door crashed closed behind him.

Snow. It seemed to Jason that the room had become as silent as though it were buried under ten feet of snow. Florian took a sip of schnapps and put down the glass. He looked at Jason, his eyes cold, cold as the snow. He said, "Now. Tell me about Vera and Wolfgang."

It was after six, the press guests had departed, the staff had removed the buffet tables, and the west lawn had been raked so efficiently that the last rays of sun caught not a single flicker of white cigarette paper or glint of crushed aluminum from a discarded film package. Most of the weekend guests were having their before-dinner nap.

In the library, Baron Willy was feeling fragile and unhappy, and was yearning for his bath. He searched forlornly for an opening to excuse himself to Kurt von Baer and his American woman friend. He found their presence unbearable because they were in love. His heart twinged with envy, knife twists of envy. He too was in love, but his love was a lonely business, he wanted to deliver loving things to his beloved, to Danilo, but Danilo was constantly impatient with him and treated him rudely.

He was jealous of Kurt von Baer anyway—that von Baer stood almost six feet, that he was handsome, robust, and had charm. True, von Baer had no money. He was a car salesman—he sold Mercedes Benzes on a showroom floor in Vienna—with only two good city suits and a bare handful of worn-out country clothes. His inexpensive and rather small apartment was in the unfashionable fifth district. When he hunted at Schloss Walenberg, he used a borrowed gun. Von Baer had met Miss Wicks when she had rented a Mercedes for a photographic shooting in the Wienerwald. Kurt had driven the car to the location. Miss Wicks had been impressed; von Baer had style, though the family fortune had dwindled away a hundred years ago. She had asked him to pose with the models. Later, he had taken her to dinner.

So . . . unbearable, their presence, this pair in love. His smile was strained. These heavy shoes! He was suddenly so exhausted he felt as though his vertebrae were crumbling and he would collapse into a heap of bones and tweed. He had to get to the jacuzzi in his apartments above. Twenty minutes in the hot tub would revive him. Bowing, blushing—why, he wondered in despair, did he always blush at parting from someone? Would he ever know?—he excused himself.

But in the hall, another hurdle awaited him: a fat man in a shabby brown suit accosted him.

"Baron von Walenberg?" The fat man fumbled in various pockets. He had a round face, eyebrows like a thicket, and a grease spot on his tie. He located his identification and presented it. "Detective-Inspector Leo Trumpf, Criminal Investigation Corps, Vienna." He had a deep, rumbling voice. It seemed that a criminal wanted by the Vienna police had been seen in the vicinity of Schloss Walenberg. Inspector Trumpf, whose case it was, had been in Klagenfurt with his son. Headquarters had contacted him, he had driven north through Graz, and here he was. The District Gendarmerie had already been informed, they were ready to assist, in the eventuality—

the inspector would be indebted if he and his son could impose on the Baron's hospitality for the night.

"Natürlich." Baron Willy shivered with alarm. "A dangerous man?"

The Detective Inspector's thickets of eyebrows rose. "Certainly a dangerous person, Herr Baron."

The Festenburg suite, the Baron would have it prepared; he would also be happy to have the inspector and his son join his guests at dinner. The inspector bowed: he himself would be delighted, but his son was only nine; would it be possible for the boy to have a light dinner in the suite? Baron Willy bowed. Nothing easier. *"Danke schon, Herr Baron."* The inspector rubbed fingers across his chin, it made a bristly sound. "And perhaps a razor, if one should be available? *"Gewiss! Gewiss!* Everything!" The housekeeper would receive instructions.

Baron Willy watched the Detective Inspector shamble off. He walked like an aged bear. But there was a protective solidity about him. Willy thought of his mother, the Baronin, he thought of Buckingham Palace and the intruder who had invaded the Queen's bedroom. He was glad of the aged bear.

In his dressing room, he stripped, first taking off the heavy shoes. The water was churning in the hot tub. He slipped in and closed his eyes, he let his arms float away from his body. Another reason he was glad of the inspector's presence: He had planned on twelve for dinner. But then it had become thirteen, what with some young friend of Bruno's arriving . . . a late request, but he could never refuse Bruno or Florian Königsmark anything. Thirteen, a dangerous number. Not that he was superstitious—certainly not! But with Inspector Trumpf, everything was fine again. Fourteen.

"Indeed?" The voice as coldly penetrating as the touch

of ice. Jason Foxe had never heard Florian speak so coldly. He had never seen such a flat glacier in Florian's eyes. He himself burned with a white-hot heat:

"As an *innocent!* I enlisted Bruno as an innocent! He knows nothing about Nicca, he is therefore not an 'accomplice.' So how could the law hold him responsible if something went wrong? They couldn't!"

"Tell me more. Reassure me." Cold, arctic cold . . .

"No physical danger either! Not to Bruno. And . . . Can't you think about Nicca?"

"No."

"Damn it, Florian, don't you see? I couldn't wait for you. Trumpf was on the lawn, watching, stuffing his face with Grazer Zweiback and watching me. I had to take a—"

"—chance on hoaxing my brother by not telling him the truth: that you're in love with a girl who may be a murderess."

Like slogging through quicksand. "Hoax him, sure. But, look, suppose I had been able to get you? I was going to ask you to go along with the nonsense about Vera and Wolfgang, I was going to ask you to let Bruno help Nicca without him knowing the truth and without him running the danger of being an 'accomplice.'" He stood before Florian, hands on hips, leaning forward, vehement. "You know something? I damn well think that if I had told Bruno the truth, told him about Nicca, left him to make a choice *for or against it,* he would have chosen *for* it. Jumping in with both feet! Taking the risk! Making himself vulnerable to the law. Bruno knows about love."

"And I don't?" An unevenness in Florian's voice.

Another tack; quickly another tack.

"Passionate! Bruno was passionate about Vera and Wolfgang, it was high adventure. You should have seen his face! It glowed, he was on fire." And it was true; the boy's face had blazed. "When I told him about the lovers, he rose to the occasion, he loved it. How much fairytale romance does one ever find in life? How much high adventure?"

Florian was staring at him. "*Herrgott!* Are you telling me you're *doing Bruno a favor?* Letting him help your girl escape?"

Their eyes locked. Florian absent-mindedly felt for his cane. He put it between his knees, clasped his hands over the gold knob, and rested his chin on his hands, still looking at Jason. But gradually the contact dwindled; he had gone somewhere else. Jason held his breath. Something on the sofa slid to the floor. Socks. Jason bent down and picked them up and tossed them back on the sofa. For him, an eternity passed.

Florian said: "So. There is a woman in Villach. She was my nurse when I broke my leg. She is thirty-nine to my twenty-nine, ten years' difference. We write, we . . . see each other. But I have not wanted her 'tied to a cripple,' so we do not marry." Chin still on his clasped hands, he turned his head toward the window. The evening was already blue, a breeze fought with the honey-colored draperies and won, an autumn freshness blew into the room. "Perhaps I will write to her tonight. We could have a house in Vienna, in Sievering. I know just the one, stone, with broad windows. For me, that could be my 'high adventure.' " He looked back at Jason. "Let it stay as it is, with Bruno."

The socks were again on the floor. Jason picked them up and wound them into a ball.

"I suppose," Florian said, "you have also solved the problem of finding another attendant for the Baronin—when your Nicca metamorphosizes into a young man?"

He hadn't. "Not yet, I've been cracking my brains, it's a job for Houdini. And it's already six o'clock!" He took out Nicca's note, unfolded it: "At six-thirty Nicca dines with the Baronin, at seven-thirty Frau Schall bathes the Baronin, at eight o'clock Nicca reads to the Baronin who will probably fall asleep at around eight-thirty. Where, before six-thirty, do I find another attendant? 'Fräulein Hoffmann' can't just disappear, what would I tell Willy and the Baronin . . . that Fräulein Hoffmann, like Josephine, also broke an ankle? Two broken ankles in one day? That she was called to her dying father's bedside? That she turned into an angel and flew to heaven?"

Florian rose to leave. "None of the above." At the door, he turned. "I'll have Nicca in your room in fifteen minutes. At six-thirty, the Baronin's favorite cousin, Florian Köningsmark, will dine with her and make her laugh at his jokes. At eight o'clock, that same Florian will read her to sleep. As for tomorrow . . . well, I have an idea."

"Florian?"

"Yes?"

"Thanks."

Florian poked his cane at the carpet. "Thank *you*."

His breath caressed her forehead, blowing away the cut hairs. "Now you look like a boy." Wearing only a white slip, she sat soldier-straight, holding a towel close around her neck. Her bare legs were twisted around the rungs of the chair. Her earrings lay in a crystal ashtray. The boys' clothes were on another chair, the shoes beneath.

Downstairs, they were already having cocktails. Up here in Jason Foxe's room, the stereo played softly. She could see the open windows, the curtains stirring gently against the drapes.

"But you'll still sound like a woman. So don't speak, just bow and nod."

"Yes." She could feel his thigh against hers. She concentrated on the open window, the blowing curtains. She felt marvelous.

"A shy boy. Just mumble, if you have to. I'll run interference. So will Bruno."

"Yes." Loving the smell of him, so close; loving his hands touching her head.

"I am destined always to cut your hair." His voice sounded strained. He blew again on her forehead although he knew, and she suspected, that there was not a single hair left to blow away. She turned up her face to meet his, she put up a bare arm and encircled his neck. His mouth came down on hers. The goblet, she thought, the goblet, brimming with wine.

They did not even think to turn down the brocade coverlet on the bed, so that afterward the bare skin of her buttocks and back bore tiny scratches from the gold threads woven into the brocade. And he, afterward, lying on his side as they murmured, whispering, half-laughing, embracing, later found scratches along his thigh and on his upper arm, the arm that lay beneath her shorn head and her shoulders in his embrace.

Chapter 17

"Young people lend enchantment to an evening," Baron Willy said to Inspector Trumpf, *"nicht wahr, Inspector?"*

They stood in the great hall. It was eight-fifteen. Cocktail glasses tinkled, people talked and laughed. Baron Willy wore an informal raw silk suit, the trousers a shade darker than the jacket, the jacket faintly striped with the deep rose color of his shirt, the darker rose of his tie. Inspector Trumpf wore his brown suit. But a manservant in a black-and-gray striped apron had borne away his shirt, suit, and shoes while he showered. By the time he had toweled himself dry, his clothes had been returned: shoes polished, suit pressed, grease spot gone from his tie.

Baron Willy's friends were thrilled at having Detective Inspector Leo Trumpf in their midst. But Trumpf had insisted that the Baron explain that he was at Schloss Walenberg simply as an invited guest.

"Young people ... yes, true." Strange, he had been

reflecting on exactly the same thing. He had been thinking that youth was lyric, beautiful. He, too, had been
gazing across at the three young people standing
together: Danilo Lovchen with his brilliant cheeks,
tonight wearing a velvet jacket of Styrian green, and the
two young men with him, to whom Danilo was holding
forth volubly, arms gesturing. At the moment he was
holding up his hands, one out, one alongside his face, as
though sighting along a rifle barrel. The two young men
looked hardly out of their teens. They were dressed a
little foppishly, in the "new wave" look currently popular
with Viennese youth. Their hair was close cropped in the
new, low-key style, and one of them wore pale amber
aviator's glasses, the "in" glasses that cost a fortune.

Both boys were lightly tanned. One was fair haired, the
other dark. The fair one was Königsmark's brother,
Bruno. Trumpf had met him that afternoon. But the
dark-haired one, the one in the amber glasses, Eugen
Tierstein, he had met only five minutes before. Tierstein
was a friend of young Königsmark's, just arrived. Baron
Willy had barely introduced him when Jason Foxe had
appeared, rudely shouldering young Tierstein aside, and
before the boy had hardly murmured *"Sehr angenehm,"*
Foxe had loudly engaged the Inspector in a conversation
about forensic science. Tierstein had bowed and drifted
away.

"My *dear* Baron!" Hortense Wicks appeared, cocktail
glass in hand, wearing a short, beaded dress straight out
of a 1920s movie, with ropes of pearls. Her blond hair
was artfully tousled and bound with a fuchsia-colored
headache band. "And"—recognizing the Inspector, Miss
Wicks's glow dimmed—"and Inspector Trumpf." She
turned immediately back to the Baron. "My dear Baron,
you *will* be hunting with us tomorrow, won't you?"

Baron Willy bowed and managed a smile, though the thought of hunting made him ill.

"I do hope so!" Miss Wicks fluttered mascaraed eyelashes.

"I seldom hunt, Fräulein Wicks." Baron Willy sighed, and perspired wretchedly into his rose-colored shirt.

"Baron, that man with the little mustache, isn't that the reviewer for *Die Woche* over there . . . Kindermann? I'd just love to meet him." Delighted, Baron Willy assured Miss Wicks, delighted to introduce her.

Inspector Trumpf watched his host bear off Miss Wicks . . . or was it the other way around?

Dinner was served in a small gallery. Baron Willy's thirteen guests sat at a modern glass-and-brass table that seemed to float on a thick island of carpet on the stone floor. Inspector Trumpf ate the delicious Styrian specialties and drank the wines with a mixture of guilt and ecstasy. The Baron sat at the head of the table; Danilo Lovchen presided at the foot. Trumpf was at the Baron's end, between two women. Directly across from him, also between two women, was Kurt von Baer. Miss Wicks sat farther down, across the table. Opposite her, flanked on one side by Bruno Königsmark, and on the other by Jason Foxe, was young Tierstein.

A manic-depressive. For the first time, it struck Trumpf that Jason Foxe might well be a manic-depressive. Foxe was certainly in a manic state tonight, face hectically flushed, dark eyes brilliantly intense, and talking nonstop. Trumpf thought of drugs, then discarded the notion. But Foxe was curiously overstimulated. He was monopolizing the conversation at that other end of the table so loudly, so demandingly, so overridingly, that neither poor Bruno Königsmark nor young Tierstein had a chance to get a word in.

At his own end of the table, the inspector found him-

self beseiged by guests demanding stories of his capture
of extortionists, kidnappers, murderers. He obliged, with
as much attention as he could spare from the gastronomi-
cal delights of Baron von Walenberg's table.

After dinner, they had coffee, liqueurs, and chocolates
in the west drawing room. It was a vast, shadowy room,
but before the fireplace was a luxurious oasis of soft
couches and chairs set on a richly colored oval rug.
Jewels flashed as women moved about in the rosy light
from the lamps, and the air was warm and perfumed. To
one side, the well-trained Johann presided at the great
silver coffee urn. He wore a short, claret-colored jacket
with ivory buttons on which the von Walenberg crest had
been carved. Johann was a nephew of the Baronin's
Josephine, and Baron Willy had used his influence to
have him trained for three months at the Imperial. Baron
Willy often congratulated himself on the result; it was
one of his few and cherished successes.

For the Baron, this after-dinner hour was precious. It
was his favorite time. This softly lighted circle of friends
was the civilized world, just as the vast, shadowy gloom
outside this oasis was a primitive world—raw, bone-
chilling, fearsome. . . . Thinking of it provoked the touch
of a cold finger down his spine.

Tonight was exceptionally pleasurable—there was the
added celebration for dear Florian's book. Florian just
now was sitting alone at the bridge table beside the
fireplace, smiling to himself and pushing around the ivory
mah-jongg tiles.

And Danilo, his Danilo. Danilo had flung several silk
cushions down before the fire and had settled himself
there, smoking cigarette after cigarette and snapping the
butts over his shoulder into the flames. His cheeks were
even more brilliant in the firelight. He had taken off his

green jacket. He wore his Montenegrin red waistcoat embroidered with gold, a white shirt with flowing sleeves, and loose, dark blue breeches and white stockings.

At the Baron's left, Valerya Protassov, the Russian interior designer, in her hoarse voice was admiring Trude Gabmayer's stunning platinum belt buckle. Trude Gabmayer, the wife of Dr. Gabmayer, giggled with pleasure. She was a peculiar kind of neurotic, so preoccupied with clothes that, despite the efforts of three expensive psychoanalysts, she still changed outfits four and five times a day. Dr. Gabmayer often complained that his wife's wardrobe was pushing them out of the house. "My daughters go shopping in my wife's closets," he had confided to his friend, Baron von Walenberg. "I'm at least thankful for that!" Dr. Gabmayer was a prominent internist and heart specialist. Baron Willy had met him when a terrifying heart attack had brought the doctor to Willy's apartment on Annagasse ten years ago. The heart attack had turned out to be indigestion. But out of that scare had developed a lasting friendship: Baron Willy had discovered in Dr. Gabmayer a distaste for killing animals. "Do you know," the Herr Doktor had told him indignantly, pacing the floor that night of the "heart attack," "that the 'kindly' old Emperor Franz Josef recorded that between December 2nd, 1848 and July of 1861, he had killed 28,876 pieces of game? That is a *fact*. The Emperor bragged of it. Outrageous! The record exists, it is in the Archives." Since that meeting on Annagasse, Dr. Gabmayer and his neurotic Trude had been constant guests at Schloss Walenberg. This evening, the Baron was tickled, thinking about how, while his other guests hunted tomorrow, he would have Dr. Gabmayer to talk to; Johann would bring them little sandwiches and tea and coffee in the library. The library contained some remarkable old medical books that would

surely fascinate Dr. Gabmayer. Thinking of that cozy
library scene, Baron Willy smiled spontaneously at
Trude Gabmayer. This evening she wore a flowing sapphire silk dress, clasped at the waist with the magnificent
gold belt buckle that had attracted Valerya Protassov's
admiration.

"You like it, Valerya?" Trude Gabmayer asked
eagerly. "Karl Karma designed it." Karma was Vienna's
current sensation, a painter and sculptor who dressed
only in gold and black.

"Karma? I've heard that now he also gilds the Rolls
Royces of rich Arabs. Fantastic, the way those Arabs
fling money around!" Valerya Protassov raised her voice
and projected it like a bullet at Jason Foxe, standing a
few feet away. "Herr Foxe! You're an American, and
you've got something to do with—what is it? A Texas
Foundation?—so you should know. Besides, you're a
sociologist. Is it true that those millionaire Texas women
wash their pearls in soapy water and scrub them with a
toothbrush?"

Jason Foxe turned to answer Valerya Protassov. He
had been chatting with Bruno Königsmark, while
Bruno's dark-haired friend, Eugen Tierstein, stood
politely by, listening. Baron Willy noticed that young
Königsmark and his friend Eugen, that charming, fop-
pish pair, were not drinking cognac. Instead, they were
sipping the mineral water from Bad Gleichenberg, the
Styrian mineral water that in the Baron's estimation put
Perrier to shame. The castle pantries always held towering cases of the Bad Gleichenberg.

"A sociological inaccuracy." Jason Foxe smiled at the
skinny, elegant Russian woman. "The truth is that Texas
women never wash their pearls: When they get dirty,
they throw them away."

Valerya Protassov gave her crackling laugh. She

moved closer to Jason Foxe, glancing without interest at his two young friends. She was thin as a greyhound, with narrow, assessing eyes, sleeked-back black hair, and a dark red slash of a mouth. She wore a cinnamon-colored satin dress, bias-cut and clinging. The girandoles in her ears were clusters of sapphire and topaz brilliants that dangled almost to her shoulders. She spoke with an exaggerated Russian accent, despite the fact that her branch of the Protassov family had fled Russia for Italy before she was born. She was in her forties and unmarried. She was said to be a descendant of the Russian Countess Protassov, the *éprouveuse* who tested the lovers of her intimate friend, Catherine the Great, to be sure they were free of disease. Baron Willy thought the late Countess Protassov's chore more shudderingly dangerous than being a king's taster. Two or three years before, turning over old documents in the castle library, Willy had come across a hundred-and-fifty-year-old letter in which a von Walenberg ancestor mentioned seeing Countess Protassov in 1814, when she had visited Vienna. By then she was in her seventies and had grown enormously fat. "She was holding court like a bejeweled leviathan, a whale beached on an Empire sofa. Her bosom was a tidal wave on which rode a treasure in jewels—portrait pins encircled with tiny diamonds, jeweled brooches, necklaces! Yet I must imagine, my dear Dieter, that once she had been a fair enough young Countess. . . . It was enough to make me determine to ride more and avoid stuffed goose."

Valerya Protassov was making Baron Willy uneasy, the way she was standing so close to Jason Foxe with that familiar, daring look in her eyes. Willy prized Valerya's talents: She had decorated his apartment on Annagasse, and she had redesigned and decorated two suites in the east wing of the Castle Walenberg. He spent happy,

absorbed hours with Valerya, discussing further redeco-
rating projects for Schloss Walenberg. But . . .

But Valerya Protassov's evening was never complete
unless she indulged in a bit of arrogance, created a scene.
And the Russian woman was not shy. She had gazed
several times with open interest at Jason Foxe, at his flat-
cheeked, lean face, his dark head. Now, standing close to
Foxe, she reached out and ran a red-tipped finger along
the rim of his brandy glass; it was just enough pressure to
make the glass dip in Foxe's hand, enough to make a
contact between them; it was a typical "Valerya" erotic
advance. "So, you are joking about your Texas million-
airesses. Well, Herr Foxe, a *true* story is this. . . . "
Valerya Protassov smiled and withdrew her finger:

"When Czar Alexander of Russia and the Czarina
Elizabeth visited Vienna in the early 1800s, one night
they attended a theatrical performance at the palace.
The Czarina wore her famous pearls and diamonds. Just
as the curtain was about to rise—crack!—her collar of
pearls broke. Pearls flew in all directions, rolling under
chairs and against the velvet curtains. Down went the
gentlemen around her to collect the fortune—only to
hear the Czarina command them with a laugh: 'Gentlemen! Do not bother! It is not worth the trouble of dirtying
your knees!' "

Laughter rippled through the room, amusement mixed
with incredulity. Valerya Protassov looked challengingly
at Jason Foxe, her arched black eyebrows raised even
higher, as though to say: Your turn, Herr Foxe. Exceed
that. Go me one better. Baron Willy had a faint intui-
tion—or was there something guarded in Jason Foxe's
stance?—that the American, standing there with Bruno
Königsmark and young Tierstein, did not want to be
spotlighted. But it was too late; people had already
turned, their attention attracted. They stood expectantly,

listening, smiling, waiting. In a verbal tournament with Valerya Protassov, the other person was always bloodied. Baron Willy put a worried hand to his dark rose tie.

"I'll go in the opposite direction, Frau Protassov. I'll plead the other side." Jason Foxe's voice was ironic, but there were lines of humor around his mouth. "The Czar Alexander and the Czarina visited Vienna during the Congress of Vienna. That would be when the Czarina treated her pearls like kopeks. It would have been during Vienna's nine-month-long extravaganza of fireworks, royal balls, all-night waltzing, parties—all to entertain the monarchs of Europe and the Czar of Russia. Everything lavish as cakes piled on top of cakes, truffles on truffles. *More* was thought to be *better*. The royal guests choked on a surfeit of pleasures: a palace ball almost every night, each time with eight thousand candles burning in the crystal chandeliers. Or consider the Emperor's sleighing party, the guests riding in thirty-two gilded sleighs lined with velvet and drawn by horses wearing tiger skins. A boy archduke naïvely complained that with all that magnificence, no one noticed the snow!"

Jason Foxe smiled into Valerya Protassov's narrowed eyes. "But the most overdone exhibition during that royal extravaganza, to my mind, was Salieri, the composer, conducting a concert of one hundred pianos all playing at once. One hundred strawberry tarts . . . they all taste the same. What would you say, Frau Protassov, to instead of one hundred pianos, *one* piano?"

A pause; an expectant hush . . . then Valerya Protassov gave Jason Foxe an acknowledging little bow of her sleek head. "One strawberry tart will do, Herr Foxe." Laughter again on all sides; on its heels, people turned away; general conversation broke out again. Baron Willy discovered he had pulled his tie out of shape. Dr. Gabmayer came up to Valerya Protassov and engaged her in a

discussion about the health merits of tofu as opposed to
red meat; Jason Foxe turned back to Bruno and young
Tierstein.

Baron Willy, altogether relieved, felt the warm fire of
the brandy spreading through his limbs. Everything was
again harmonious: the murmur of conversations broken
by laughter . . . Danilo lounging on the silk cushions,
smoking cigarettes and whistling to himself . . . Johann at
the silver coffee urn and liqueur bottles, pouring a brandy
for Detective Inspector Trumpf.

And how charming Hortense Wicks looked! Kurt von
Baer's American friend looked, in fact, rather like a
flapper in a delightful old black-and-white movie in her
short, beaded dress and headache band. She stood with
Kurt von Baer who was enthusiastically discussing hunting with two women. One was Margarete Auer, Willy's
"best" friend, despite the fact that Margarete adored
hunting. The other woman was Margarete's married
sister, Linda Carroll, visiting from London. Both women
were in their early fifties. Margarete, the older, was
stocky and robust and had a laugh that could shatter
wineglasses. Her sister was an almost identical younger
version of Margarete—the same reddish hair, the
doughy, peasant-looking face, and the small brown eyes.
Margarete was the widow of a distant relative of Baron
Willy's. To Willy, Margarete had always seemed sub-
stantial, like his childhood nurse, who had held his small
hand firmly while he stared at the enormous horses in the
stable, frightened and fascinated. That was the way he
thought of Margarete Auer: his hand safely in hers.
Margarete was wise, too. There had been that time last
year when Willy had thought to have Danilo marry so the
young man would have a wife and children living on the
von Walenberg estate—a family. It would tie Danilo to
Schloss Walenberg. But Margarete had forcefully dis-

couraged him from suggesting it to Danilo. "He is a Montenegrin!" Margarete had pressed home to Willy. "Vain, yes—they all are. And a little cruel; revengeful too. But those Montenegrins are also proud. You cannot provide Danilo with a 'little family.' If you don't want your peacock to fly away, don't attempt to pull his feathers!"

Baron Willy paused for a moment at Margarete's side. How fond he was of her! And he had come to realize how right she had been; he was glad she had dissuaded him. Margarete Auer, tonight wearing her usual brick-colored dress that wrinkled in the seat, her small eyes snapping with anticipation of tomorrow's hunt, Margarete Auer was his true friend.

Baron Willy glanced about—and winced: That devil's advocate, Valerya Protassov, had loosed herself from Doctor Gabmayer, and with a predatory step was creeping up on Detective Inspector Trumpf. The inspector, unaware of the menace, was sipping brandy and talking with Florian Königsmark. Florian, his cane resting against his chair, still sat at the card table; he had built a little house out of the mah-jongg tiles.

"Inspector Trumpf!" Valerya Protassov's loud, hoarse voice pierced the inspector like an arrow. "The criminal mind, Inspector . . . Great criminologists are great, I believe, Inspector, because they have the same quirks in their minds as criminals, but they just happened to fall on the side of justice." She added, in her challenging way, "Wouldn't you agree, Inspector?"

Inspector Trumpf swirled his brandy. His melancholy eyes under the thick brows looked gravely at Valerya Protassov. "That is not a foolish concept, Frau Protassov. I cannot tell you how many times, surely hundreds, I have wished to have a criminal mind. Not forever, mind you, but only for a few minutes: just long enough to slip down those devious, cunning paths." The inspector looked more than ever like a brown bear. He even gave the impression of being clothed in shaggy fur rather than the brown suit . . . perhaps it was those thicketlike eyebrows. "Who knows?" the inspector went on, "one day I may find myself with the facility of seeing into the criminal mind, and therefore, *presto,* Fraulein Protassov, I'll become a great criminologist . . . or, on the other hand"—he smiled at the Russian woman—"I'll become a criminal."

Valerya Protassov laughed; she was having no luck tonight, but she didn't care for easy prey. "A temptation," she began. . . .

But a single note of music plucked from a string thrummed through the room. Conversation halted; people turned. Danilo again plucked the *gûsla,* the one-stringed Montenegrin instrument, his brilliantly colored face bent over it. Several guests who were standing, sank into soft chairs. Then Danilo began to sing. The words, in the strange tongue, sounded sometimes harsh, sometimes liquidly lyrical. Baron Willy knew Danilo was singing a song of valor, relating warriors' deeds, bloody battles well fought, victories hard won. Danilo's singing always made the Baron think of Homeric bards, tales recited to music. Now, listening, Baron Willy moved back until he stood on the edge of the lighted oasis. He wanted to take it all in: His guests in the rosy light and luxurious warmth, listening to Danilo—his Danilo. Behind him was the vast darkness, the cavernous, cold stone.

Inspector Trumpf understood only a handful of words in Serbo-Croatian, but he was absorbed by the thrumming of music. It was only when Danilo Lovchen put aside the *gûsla* and stood up, stretching and lighting a cigarette, that Trumpf noticed that the party had been reduced by two: Bruno Königsmark and his friend Eugen were missing. "Billiards, probably," Baron von Walenberg remarked, when Trumpf mentioned the fact. "Having a game or two."

So the castle had billiards, had it? And undoubtedly table tennis and weights and exercise machines. Inspector Trumpf patted his stomach and thought of exercise machines, the electric kind where you pressed a button and the machine exercised you and you became slender without effort. Good. Just the thing. It wouldn't interfere with the boys' billiards. He went over and spoke to Johann.

When he reached the room, a veritable gymnasium, he found he was right about the exercise machines. One was a rowing machine, the other an electrically run bicycle. And the billiard table was a beauty, mahogany and green felt, brightly lighted with green, cone-shaped lights.

But the room was empty.

Well, just as well; he didn't want spectators anyway. The boys had gone somewhere else. They were young, they had other pleasures in mind, maybe they'd gone to the village.

The inspector eased himself onto the saddle of the bicycle and pressed the button.

Pepi had been down in the great kitchens. First, he had eaten his dinner upstairs: trout, which he didn't like, then dessert of Griess Schmarren. He had picked the raisins out of the farina and left them. He had then read his paperback. But by nine-thirty he had finished the book. He was also hungry again. He bet himself that down in the kitchens they had freezers full of chocolate ice cream.

He turned out to be right. *"Ein Kind!"* A jolly, round woman had cried out when he appeared in the busy kitchen. He was a novelty, a child guest. He was also

Detective Inspector Leo Trumpf's son. The woman seated him at a wooden table, filled a soup plate with ice cream and poured chocolate sauce over it. Men and women bustled around him, bearing platters in and out of the kitchen, calling him "Liebling" and jokingly asking how many crooks he had caught.

But when he left the kitchen, he got lost. He could not find his way back. Left? No, right. He wandered down a hallway . . . stone floor, arches, lights on iron things that looked like hat-stands. He heard voices, then footsteps on stone, approaching. The voices were low, the footsteps quick. Two people appeared, coming toward him. Two young men. Viennese, he saw at once. He knew the type, he had seen them on the Kärntnerstrasse. He bet they even went to the Casino. He had envied them for a long time. Some day he would be one of them, and dressed like that besides. The two young men stopped and looked at him.

"Guten Abend," the fair one said. "The procedure after eating is to get rid of the remains left on one's face."

Pepi ran his tongue quickly around his mouth, making the widest circle possible. He tasted chocolate. He wiped his mouth with the back of his hand. He blushed. "Which way to the Festenburg suite, *bitte?"*

"I happen to know, so you're in luck."

Listening, nodding while the young man directed him, Pepi kept looking at the young man's friend, the dark-haired one. Those were the kind of glasses he wanted, aviator glasses, amber. But his father had said he was too young. Now, in the hall, Pepi studied the young man minutely, taking note of all the enviable points, from shoes to pants, preciously storing it all up in his mind.

Five minutes later, when he reached the Festenburg suite, he was still basking in the fantasy of being at least eighteen and the image of that dark-haired young man.

The very image. Except . . . well, except for one thing. But never mind about that.

The brocade coverlet lay on the floor at the foot of the bed. They had made love, then dozed; then, awakening, made love again. It was past midnight. They sat propped up against pillows. Nicca was peeling an orange. "How long can I be Bruno? In Yugoslavia."

"A week, two weeks. Then a false passport, you'll become someone else. There are ways. My connections are surface, but I'll deepen them." He took the orange section she handed him.

"Meantime," he went on, "in Vienna I'll hire a couple of sharp professionals to delve into Otto von Reitz's relationships with friends—and enemies—and to ferret out everything in Sophie von Reitz's personal life. Even Gustav Bulheim's. We'll find the worms under the rocks. If you're thinking why Trumpf and the criminology department haven't done that, you have to remember the rock they're obsessed with is Veronica Kent. My sharpies will be unobsessed."

She chewed an orange peel. "It will cost money."

"For sure. Plenty. I'll find it." Confidence in his voice, he talked on. She handed him orange sections, concentrating on his plans, nodding. But then, at a rustle in the wardrobe, the insignificant depredation of a mouse, she worried.

"I feel Trumpf's hot breath. If he catches me now, we'll have no time for the unobsessed . . . I'll be done for!"

He gathered her to his bare chest. "He won't catch you. Think about tomorrow. Think about tomorrow morning when Bruno's phone call comes, and you walk down the steps of the terrace and across the meadow and through the forest into safety."

But she did not think of tomorrow morning, because they had eaten the entire orange and they might not see each other for weeks or months or maybe never, and the only luxury was to make love here, now, in this magnificent, soft bed. She raised her head and licked his bare shoulder, little licks with the tip of her tongue, turning her shorn head slowly from side to side. She felt his arms tighten around her.

Dr. Erich Gabmayer, in his bathroom in the north wing of Castle Walenberg, swallowed the entire handful of vitamin pills all at once—no point in taking them one by one—and washed them down with a few gulps of water. He'd rejoin the others downstairs for just a thimbleful of cognac and a cup of the decaffeinated coffee that Baron Willy's man, Johann, brewed so deliciously. He had a good half-dozen theories about nutrition that he wanted to discuss with Valerya Protassov.

Dr. Gabmayer rinsed out the glass. He had returned to his suite right after Danilo Lovchen had finished his minstrel-like performance, and he now thought of the young man's pleasing voice. Baron Willy should speak to Danilo about his smoking.

As he crossed the bedroom to go downstairs, Dr. Gabmayer noticed that Trude had laid out two nightgowns on the bed, "creations" she called them; one was a strawberry-colored filmy thing, the other a slithery silver. Dr. Gabmayer gave a snort of helpless laughter. It was not unusual for him to retire with a wife wearing one nightgown and to wake in the morning to find her wearing another. He was about to leave the room, when he noticed that it was a little stuffy; the place needed airing. He went to the casement windows and pushed them open. The breeze that swept into the room was warm; the early autumn was astonishingly mild. In Vienna, according to

Die Presse, the rose gardens at the Hofburg were actually putting forth new buds.

Dr. Gabmayer leaned out, taking a breath of the fresh country air. Below, moonlight shone on the empty stone courtyard. A few centuries ago, the von Walenbergs had had their own castle guards. There would have been armed men down there, watching. Now there was no one. . . . No, not quite. Someone was crossing the courtyard, walking swiftly, quietly, heading in the direction of the garages. It was the chauffeur of one of the guests, no doubt; or perhaps one of the castle servants. For a moment, though, he had mistaken the figure for that of young Bruno Königsmark, Florian's brother. He must see to his eyes.

Kurt von Baer knew himself fairly well and had never been particularly proud of that acquaintanceship. Now, in the castle, he lay on his side in the massive bed beside Hortense Wicks, who was asleep. He was absent-mindedly curling one of Hortense's blond ringlets around his finger. He felt stripped of all his pretensions. He was troubled. He had fallen in love. Moreover, he wanted to marry, actually to *marry* Hortense Wicks. He had always assumed that when he was ready, he would choose a European heiress, one to whom a name like von Baer or Auersperg was a priceless asset, enough to bring to a marriage.

Kurt von Baer was descended from a noble but profligate family that had wasted a considerable fortune. A property of twenty thousand *jochs*—about one million acres in Hungary—and a fortune besides, had been squandered. One of his ancestors, Konrad von Baer, friend of Count Ilya Tolstoy, the grandfather of Leo Tolstoy, had admired the large-handed and eventually ruinous ways of his aristocratic Russian friend. Imitating

him, he had indulged in such extravagances as sending
his laundry to Holland to be washed. The pleasures of
Konrad's descendants had leaned toward women, horses,
and politically involved friends who fed on the von Baer
riches, voracious rats in the family granary. An ancestor,
Nicholas, had had the added eccentricity of scenting his
horses' stalls with perfumes from Paris. Through care-
lessness and waste, the remains of the von Baer family
fortune had dribbled away. By the time Kurt von Baer's
father, Georg, was in his twenties, he and his brother had
managed between them to lose whatever remained. Both
brothers were dead now, so was Kurt's mother. Frau von
Baer had been a vaguely intellectual young woman, the
daughter of an immensely rich stock speculator, in
Prague, who was also a well-known collector of famous
first editions. Georg von Baer, on the strength of his
aristocratic name, had married into the Czech riches,
only to see his father-in-law's business suddenly wiped
out. The poor man, crazed by his ruin, had set fire to his
collection of first editions, including an illustrated Gothic
Bible worth enough to buy, at the least, a small palace.
By the time Kurt von Baer's younger sister was born, the
marriage was overdue for the dustbin. But a divorce had
not been necessary . . . Georg von Baer had been killed in
a car crash before the baby had been weaned.

Kurt von Baer's older sister, Paula, had married well;
her husband, von Kübeck, a successful manufacturer of
precision instruments, had factories in upper Austria and
Switzerland. She was rich, pretentious—a snob. The von
Kübecks had a neoclassical house near the Belvedere;
their children were at school in Gstaad. Kurt von Baer
always brought his current lady friend to Paula's for
afternoon tea or coffee. Paula's drawing room was hung
with portraits of Konrad, Nicholas, and other assorted
von Baers, all qualifying for rococo gilt frames. If Kurt's

current female companion had not previously been sufficiently impressed with Kurt's glorious antecedents, she
was thoroughly impressed by the time tea with Paula was
over.

Kurt von Baer was not so stupidly blind that he did not
realize impressing these women had been his intention. A
self-inflating intention. At the same time, he disliked
Paula, hated her pretensions, and felt uncomfortable,
even shamed, by her foolish snobberies. Yet he suffered it
all—deliberately, truculently—and persistently tried to
close his eyes to his own snobbery.

He had already taken Hortense Wicks to visit Paula.
The effect on Hortense should have pleased him
immensely. But instead, he had found himself angry,
hurt, and offended that she had been impressed.

As for his younger sister, Julianna, who had a three-
room apartment in one of the tenements in Ottakring
along the Gürtel, he never took any of his women friends
to visit her. It would have mortified him. Yet it was at
Julianna's that he felt comfortable. It was in Julianna's
living room that he relaxed; it was Julianna who was dear
to him . . . Julianna who laughed at his tales about his
fellow car salesmen and then told him jokes and stories
about her customers at the Österreichische Werkstatten,
where upstairs she sold little felt dolls for children, toys,
and even fancy kitchen equipment like rolltop wooden
breadboxes. Julianna was twenty-six and skinny. When
Kurt visited her, he always brought her the most fatten-
ing pastries. The last time, since Julianna was a serious
but amateur sculptress, he had brought her a whole box
of Demels' little marzipan busts of astronauts, movie
stars, and pop singers.

Yet . . . it was Julianna he kept hidden.

Now in the massive bed in Castle Walenberg, perhaps
because of the Russian woman's story of Czarina Eliza-

beth's indifference to her priceless pearls, and Jason
Foxe's recounting of the imperial extravagances at
Vienna's Congress, he felt as if a veil had been ripped
away, exposing his own superficial values, his little
greeds, his overblown social snobbery. He recognized in
Hortense Wicks similar values. Hortense loved him, he
was positive . . . almost positive. But, did she love *him,* or
did she love "von Baer"? He felt as insecure as a boat-
man who has lost his oars. Yet how could *he,* a von Baer,
feel so insecure in relation to Hortense Wicks, who'd
been born in Ohio?

The blond ringlet was around his finger. He slid it off,
rolled over onto his back, and gazed up into the darkness.
He did not want to think about it anymore. In the
morning, early, he would take Hortense to the gun room
to choose their guns. He would, of course, choose for both
of them and then show her how to use the gun properly.
Before they went into the woods, he would have her
practice for a good half-hour. He smiled in the dark,
thinking fondly of how he had taken Hortense shopping
for a proper hunting outfit, of her happily laying out the
clothes before they went to bed. He hoped that tomorrow,
when they went hunting, she would at least get a rabbit.

The Baronin von Walenberg rose early, not only for
love of God, but because she also loved the dewy freshness of dawn. Sunday mornings were especially holy. At
five o'clock this Sunday morning, the air was an elixir,
promising a perfect day. The glorious dry weather also
sharpened the Baronin's appetite. However, she never let
a morsel of food pass her lips before attending chapel.

This morning, she had prayed in the chapel, as usual.
Now, as her attendant pushed the wheelchair toward the
open chapel door, knowing that across the courtyard her
breakfast would be waiting, her empty stomach rumbled.

She longed for breakfast. They emerged into the rose-and-gray dawn.

"Guten Morgen, Gnädige Frau Baronin." A man stepped authoritatively in front of the wheelchair, blocking the way. It was that fat man in the brown suit, the man from yesterday, this morning without the little boy.

The Baronin was a gentle woman, and kind, but today her hunger was sharp. She glared at the visitor. Yet it made no difference to him. He was not looking at her. He was staring at her attendant. Then he made a sound in his throat. The Baronin had heard a sound like that before. In her youth she had had a dog, a little white schnauzer, and one terrible day a carriage wheel had rolled over his paw. All the time the paw was being bathed and bandaged, he had made that same sound, interspersed with whimpering. She had not had a dog since. Their hurts were too painful to her.

No matter. This would be the man that Frau Schall had mentioned; yes, a bookmark for his wife. *"Grüss Gott!"* She thrust the bookmark into his hand and patted her left shoulder, signaling the attendant to move on. The man stepped aside. He did not even thank her.

The Baronin breakfasted at the table in the window niche overlooking the courtyard. Boiled eggs, crisp Styrian bacon, toast with plum jam from good Styrian plums, coffee. The man in the brown suit was gone; the courtyard was empty. *"Bitte,* more jam on the toast," the Baronin told the attendant.

"Gewiss." Josephine's niece smilingly lathered more jam onto the toast. She was a pretty young woman with brown eyes, and she wore her long brown hair in a great, shining braid coiled into a bun atop her head. When the Baronin had been a girl at the convent, she had had hair as thick and luxuriant as that of Josephine's niece; but, sadly, the rules of St. Ursulinen had obliged her to keep it

hidden under a *haube,* a bonnet. Irma, Josephine's niece, proud of her beautiful hair, always went bareheaded.

Irma had been a surprise, dear Florian's surprise, because he loved her. When the Baronin had awakened at four in the morning to pray, there was Irma, smiling down at her. Not the strange new Fräulein Hoffmann, but Irma! Irma Trost! . . . Irma, from Josephine's village, not ten miles away, Irma to whom the Baronin had sent a birthday present every year since the child's fifth birthday, the year Josephine had come to work at Schloss Walenberg.

It was Josephine's brother who had delivered Irma to the castle the previous evening; she would stay until Josephine was able to return. "It was Florian," Willy had told the Baronin, laughing, "all Florian!" Florian, it appeared, had planned it all the time and Fraulein Hoffmann knew of it. "She left last night, but she sends you her good wishes."

"You see, Kinderl," the Baronin had replied instructively to her son, "you did a kindness for Florian with that party. Now Florian returns the favor."

Willy had nodded, but he seemed uncertain, even a little puzzled. "Florian did not even tell me until late last night." *"Natürlich!"* the Baronin had responded. "One does not give away surprises!"

But now . . .

"And toast more bread, too, Irma, Liebling." So filled with good works, the world. This morning, this Sunday morning, God was surely smiling on Schloss Walenberg.

Leaving the Baronin's courtyard, Trumpf was furious at himself. His peripheral vision had been right. He should have acted immediately—immediately!—pushed open that oak door, forced his way past the guard dog, insisted on interrogating Fräulein Hoffmann! But instead, he had imagined he was overly suspicious. It was his *business* to be suspicious, not to think that he was becoming psychotic and seeing the girl in every guise . . . tree, brook, white-clothed attendant! But instead he had gone and eaten Steirisches Brathuhn, making a pig of himself. Now "they" had switched attendants. Veronica Kent was in the Schloss certainly, masquerading as someone else. She could be a laundress, the wife of a stablehand, a milkmaid—God knows what!

And who were "they"? Foxe surely needed Florian Königsmark's connivance . . . or did he? Certainly not Baron von Walenberg's. The Baron would swoon like a maiden if he knew that Detective Inspector Leo Trumpf's "dangerous criminal" had been within a hundred feet of his mother. So what could he, Trumpf, do now? Arrest whom? On what charges? That someone named Rudi Polzer had claimed he had seen Jason Foxe in the village of Karlsdorf with a girl resembling—*Verdammt!*

There was only one hope: that Florian Königsmark was involved. He, Trumpf, would get hold of Baron von Walenberg, and he would frighten the little Baron to death by revealing his suspicions that "Fräulein Hoffmann" was the murderess he stalked. He would demand to know by what means she had come to be the Baronin's attendant, exactly when, placed there by whom. He would face Königsmark with his cousin the Baron, and count on familial pressure, the flow of blue blood and red between them, to break down Königsmark, make him reveal what he knew.

Of course there was another way: He could persist. He could find the girl himself . . . again. He made a wry face.

Meanwhile, it was five-thirty, the morning wet with dew. The castle slept. In an hour or two, the kitchens of the castle would be bustling, servants would be churning cream into fresh butter, baking fresh rolls. And in this countryside, too, they made Sterz, the bread made with corn, then cut into squares and served hot. In the henhouse youngsters would be gathering the freshest of eggs, for the guests who were going hunting would soon be stirring, getting up for breakfast. The Baron, too.

Back in his room, he found Pepi sleeping soundly. He undressed slowly, painfully, groaning. After the electric bicycle, he had exercised on a rowing machine for fifteen minutes until the timer pinged. That *verdammte* rowing machine! His arm and leg muscles ached, his back was on fire, he could hardly bend over. A long, hot bath.

In the bathroom, he ran water for the bath. Looking at himself in the mirror, waiting for the tub to fill, he groaned. In his haste to get to the chapel, he had not shaved. The thought of lifting his aching arms, even to shave, plunged him into gloom. For just a moment, he felt he was on an escalator moving backward in the case of the murder of Otto von Reitz. But only for a moment.

Chapter 18

She stood in the embrasure behind the draperies in the library. She watched steadily, hardly blinking. The French windows overlooked the terrace where servants were serving breakfast. She wore the gray knickers, woolen knee socks, and a V-necked sweater over an open-throated sport shirt . . . and of course Bruno's amber aviator glasses.

Earlier, Jason had brought her a buttered roll and coffee in his suite; she could not breakfast on the terrace with the other guests—too risky. Her feminine voice had best not dare even a *Guten Morgen*. Now, when Jason got the telephone call from Bruno, she would simply stroll out and across the terrace, nodding greetings as she passed.

It was so pretty there, on the east terrace. The glass, wind-protection screen shielded it, and the morning sun baked the flagged terrace although the crisp, dry air smacked of belated autumn. Ah, the benefits of riches.

Two white-jacketed servants stood behind chafing dishes suspended over blue gas flames. Only three people were breakfasting at the round glass tables with curliqued iron legs. Some guests must already have gone hunting; others would be sleeping. It was seven forty-five.

Jason was there, breakfasting with Florian Königsmark. She felt she was seeing him through a magnifying glass that revealed each hair of his dark eyebrows, the texture of his flat cheeks, and the small lines in the jutting, sensuous lips. Under his shirt was a tiny mole just beneath his left shoulder blade, on his hip a livid scar from a hockey injury he'd suffered at nineteen. On his groin—

She tensed. A servant was at Jason's elbow, speaking to him . . . now Jason was throwing down his napkin, getting up, excusing himself . . . he was following the servant indoors. *The telephone call.* When he came out again onto the terrace, he would turn toward the embrasure and run a finger thoughtfully over his chin. The signal.

Waiting was agony. Her eyes seemed frozen open. She saw Florian Königsmark beckon a servant for more coffee . . . saw two women come out, pause to greet him, and move on to the chafing dishes. Then came Inspector Trumpf, trailed by a small boy; that would be his son, Pepi. Even from here, the inspector looked tired. His face sagged, his chin was white with talcum. She almost felt sorry for him. In minutes she would be free of him. Safe.

"Papa," Pepi said; he fidgeted in the chair. He looked at his father who was devouring a beautiful, golden omelet. There were just the two of them at the table.

"Ummm?" His father's mouth was full.

"Papa. Two boys from Vienna. You met them last night?"

The inspector nodded. Bruno Königsmark and his friend, Eugen Tierstein. But he hardly listened to Pepi. He was keeping an eye out for Baron von Walenberg. Not ten minutes ago, he had knocked on the Baron's door and had been informed by a polite servant that the Baron was dressing and would see him at breakfast in a few minutes.

"For my birthday, could I have a pair of aviator glasses like that? Like that boy's?"

The inspector chewed and swallowed. He sipped coffee. "Those are for older boys. So not this birthday. Maybe when you're older." He felt on safe ground. By the time Pepi was older, amber aviator glasses would be out, a new fad would be in. A black eye patch. A monocle. A Ubangi plate in the lower lip.

Pepi said, craftily, "But I'm planning to be a pilot. The glasses would help me practice."

"I thought you wanted to be a gaucho—a cowboy. Besides, pilots don't wear glasses like that. Only boys in Vienna do . . . eat something. You've had only a roll. We'll get you some of the little sausages. And you should have some eggs." Trumpf took a sip of coffee.

"Is he a tutti-frutti?"

The inspector choked on the coffee. He didn't know Pepi knew about homosexuals, much less Vienna's slang word for them.

"A tutti-frutti? Why?"

"He wears earrings."

The inspector stared at his son. "I didn't see earrings."

"Well, *sometimes* he does. He has holes in his ears."

The inspector sat back. He forgot about omelets and sausages. He felt things rolling around in his head like the balls in one of those click-click games, all the little quicksilver bits rolling into their proper holes. *Pierced ears.* A *Wärmer*, a *Bächener*, a tutti-frutti—such a one, whatever the term, might have *one* ear pierced, it was the style. He leaned toward his son:

"*Both* ears?"

"Both."

All the quicksilver bits rolled into place. The inspector wiped his mouth with his napkin and put it down. He picked up his plate and put it in front of Pepi. "Here, eat my eggs." He moved his elbow against his hip, feeling the hardness of the automatic pistol at his belt. Regulation, but he had not fired it since his promotion ten years ago; and before that, less than a dozen times, always under extreme conditions. The pistol fired six bullets. Each bullet had to be strictly accounted for, to the Department. He had hoped never to use the pistol again. He still hoped he would not.

He looked around. Florian Königsmark, alone over there, breakfasting so unconcernedly. He . . . and his brother Bruno too. Definitely involved.

And there, stepping out onto the terrace, was the master planner himself: Jason Foxe. He was turning and facing the Schloss, running a finger thoughtfully over his chin.

And now . . .

Now, coming out onto the terrace was the young Eugen Tierstein. The boy wore knickers and hiking clothes. He bowed toward the few breakfasting guests, even toward Trumpf himself, mouthing an inaudible *Guten Morgen*. Then he lifted his arms high in a great, embracing gesture, turning his face up to the sun. What a glorious morning! Then he walked leisurely across the terrace and down the stone steps onto the meadow that stretched toward the forest. He began to stroll across the meadow.

For an instant the inspector sat open-mouthed. Then he knew. He knew that if Eugen Tierstein crossed that meadow, he would not return. The murderer of Otto von Reitz would escape.

Elephantine as he was, he could move with surprising swiftness. He was down the terrace in a flash and lumbering swiftly after the boy.

From the terrace a warning shout. Jason Foxe. The stroller glanced back and started to run. Trumpf pounded after his quarry, smashing down damp grass, gaining, gaining, silently cursing the rowing machine and the agony shooting through his legs and back. But he was covering ground, lurching forward against the wind, a graceless greyhound. He imagined himself a cannonball flying, a wasp speeding across the meadow with the velocity of light. He was moving faster than the killer, he would have her, he would be on her before she reached the forest. He crashed on, aware all along of a pounding behind him, someone pursuing, a rasping breath. It could only be the Foxe. The girl was nearing the forest. This *verdammte* pain, his legs, a stitch in his side; now, speeding on, he tore open his jacket. As a last resort he would have to use his pistol, *verdammt*, there was no other—

An arm from behind caught him violently around the throat, a stone building fell on him, he went down. His cheekbone grazed stones, grass and dirt filled his mouth, he was choking on dirt. The world disappeared into a vortex that swirled around, then spewed him up again. Someone was trying to strangle him, no, had grasped the back of his jacket and was pulling his face out of the dirt.

He sat up, spitting out dirt and grass, and turned his head to look across the meadow. The boy was nearing the forest, it was a concealing wall of sunlight-dappled green; in a few seconds the boy would be swallowed by green. "Halt!" He staggered heavily to his feet. "Halt!" His voice did not even carry, he spat out dirt ... and as he drew his gun Foxe forced down his arm, and the girl disappeared into the forest.

Gone. He whirled on Foxe, wrathful, hand still tight on his pistol. "You're under arrest. Back to the Schloss. *Move!*" He'd get the District Gendarmerie on the phone, pinpoint the area, they'd close in. The quarry was trapped. As for Foxe . . . He glared at the American, who for the last time had blocked his pursuit, and Foxe, rumpled, dirt-stained, gazed expressionlessly back at him. He gestured with his pistol. *"Move."*

At that instant, from the forest, came a shot. Then, a scream. Not an animal scream, but a scream from a human throat—a woman's throat.

The world hung still. Then Foxe took a precipitous step toward the forest. "Jesus!"

"Stay there!" At the fierceness in Trumpf's voice, Foxe stopped short, jerking his head around to the inspector who leveled the pistol at him. But seeing the anguish in Foxe's eyes, Trumpf could not forbear pity. "Hunters," he said. "They've wounded an animal, a poor shot. . . . " He knew he sounded unconvincing.

In the forest, someone was shouting. Trumpf could not take his eyes from Foxe's face. It seemed to him that nothing was more naked and vulnerable than the face of love.

"Not an animal!" Foxe made an inarticulate sound deep in his throat, then threw a white-hot look of defiance at the inspector and launched himself toward the forest.

Suddenly he halted. The green curtain of leaves was parting. Someone was coming from the forest. No, not someone—people. Two people bearing a body. A man in hunting clothes followed.

"All right," Trumpf said. "All right." He put away his pistol. With Jason Foxe at his side, he walked across the sunlit meadow to meet the approaching group.

The two people carrying the body were slight. Hortense Wicks, in hunting clothes, was the one in front, trudging along, her arms under the body's knees, supporting the lower extremities. In back, supporting the upper torso and staggering under its weight, was Nicca. Kurt von Baer limped along behind.

As Inspector Trumpf and Foxe reached them, Hortense Wicks whimpered and let go of the body. The feet slipped to the ground. Hortense, her face greenish, turned away, retching, and began to vomit. Nicca lowered her burden's shoulders to the grass. Her sweater was stained with blood. She sank down on the ground, crosslegged, plucked a blade of grass, and began to chew it. She did not look at anybody, not even Jason Foxe.

The inspector knelt over the recumbent figure. A young man. He wore boots and jeans and a square-shouldered brown leather jacket open over his shirt. He had not shaven recently. His beard was rust-brown. He was no one Trumpf had ever seen before. Unconscious, but not dead. His shirt was soaked with blood.

"Only a shoulder wound." Von Baer, standing above Trumpf, went on: "Not dangerous. But that kind of flesh wound bleeds like the devil."

The inspector lifted a hand without looking up. "Your scarf, please." Von Baer hesitated a fraction of an instant, then as Trumpf glanced up, he reluctantly pulled the ascot-tied scarf from his neck. "Gucci," he murmured.

The inspector expertly bandaged the shoulder. Meanwhile, he ordered von Baer back to the castle to telephone for a doctor and to have a makeshift stretcher brought. Von Baer limped off. Trumpf took off his jacket and covered the wounded man. It would help prevent shock. Never mind that he'd get blood on his jacket, never mind that he was embarrassed by his sleeve bands and his vest with the raveling buttonhole, not to mention the pistol at his belt. A cop was a cop, detective inspector or no. Business was business. If he'd wanted to go into the bakery business, he'd be rolling dough, not bandaging wounds, *nicht wahr?*

Miss Wicks had stopped throwing up. Her face was red, her eyes bloodshot. Blond hairs stuck to her damp forehead. She blew her nose into a handkerchief that was coordinated with her hunting outfit. "He won't die?" Her flutelike voice quavered. She poured out the story . . . how she and Kurt had been kneeling in cover, hoping to spot a deer, when they'd heard a shot, then a scream followed by someone shouting for help. They had found Eugen Tierstein kneeling over the deer, only it wasn't a deer, it was this wounded man. "He was still conscious. He was lying there, cursing, *cursing*, the *filthiest*—He was cursing Herr Tierstein." In the midst of the foulest cursing, the man had fainted. He had been bleeding badly. Kurt, in his rush to help, had twisted an ankle, he had been useless. It had been up to Hortense herself and young Tierstein . . .

The inspector kept nodding. He was holding the wounded man's wrist. The pulse was strong and good. The fellow was regaining consciousness, his eyes were opening. They opened on the inspector bending over him. He stared at Trumpf; then his eyes slid around to Hortense Wicks and to Jason Foxe, and finally to the boy sitting crosslegged, chewing the blade of grass.

"Bastard!" he screamed suddenly, and he spat upward into Trumpf's face. "Crooked bastard cop! Greedy bastard!" He was screaming, snarling, his neck cords straining, his face contorted. He glared at the inspector who was wiping spittle from his face. "Thief! Cheating me out of the reward! You knew where he was taking her!"

He rose on an elbow, pouring out invectives and bitterness. He had roved the roads, asked clever questions; he had picked up the trail through luck, hearing in a tavern about Schloss Walenberg. Spying from the woods with binoculars this morning, he had spotted first Jason Foxe and then Trumpf breakfasting on the terrace, and he had known for sure that the girl was there, that Trumpf— "You bastard!"—was cheating him. "But I have proof, I have her green dress, I've got her shoes too! They prove it!" He had dug them up in the Mödling woods. He carried them with him always, in the pouch of his motor-cycle. "They have blood on them."

"Jessas!" He lay back suddenly, white and sweating, gasping. He stared bitterly at the sky, saying he had not known the boy in knickers strolling across the meadow was that crazy murderess. "But when you started running after him, and the boy began to run and Foxe tackled you—then I knew! The reward rushing into my arms! Like a miracle! I stood up to grab her. . . . "

And got shot.

"But it is my money. Mine! See? She is here! *There.*" He jerked his head at Nicca, crosslegged on the grass. Jason Foxe had moved to stand close beside the knickered girl. The wounded man looked at the pair of them: at Nicca and at Jason Foxe who stood so close beside her that if she were to lean her head an inch to one side it would find a resting place against Jason Foxe's thigh. The wounded man's face quivered suddenly. He let his head fall back again and closed his eyes. Tears squeezed out from beneath his eyelids.

Chapter 19

"Sophie?" said Gustav Bulheim, when he heard his sister's voice on the phone. "Good news! I wouldn't have called so early on a Sunday—Did I wake you? But good news!"

"Truly?"

"Truly!" Ach, poor Sophie, she had not been herself lately, all nerves, sometimes laughing, sometimes crying. This wonderful news, it would help her become her old self again. "Veronica Kent—they have caught her! Inspector Trumpf, the Gendarmerie in Styria. They are bringing her back to Vienna. She was trying to escape to Yugoslavia." He pressed the phone to his ear, smiling, waiting.

"Truly?"

"I have it from the Rossauerkaserne. Detective Staral called me, on instructions from Inspector Trumpf." He tried to tell her the rest: in the excitement, someone shot . . . Jason Foxe involved . . . Foxe in custody along with the girl.

But Sophie kept interrupting and breaking into that new laughing and crying habit of hers. She sounded so odd that if it were not ten o'clock in the morning, Gustav would have sworn she had been drinking. Since Otto's murder, she had been acting strange, sometimes brooding, sometimes hysterical. And she'd been drinking Scotch by the liter. She was taking the grisly affair hard, like an endless Greek tragedy. That had surprised Gustav. In fact, these last years, he had even fancied—But no, Sophie was not the kind to divorce. To Sophie, divorce was a stigma; she was ridiculously old-fashioned in that way. Besides, Sophie was adamantly romantic. She believed in undying love. At eighteen she had married Otto von Reitz for love . . . how could it ever end?

Right now, though, she had abruptly become silent. Bulheim heard only the hum of the telephone lines. He summoned his most cheerful self. "So, Sophie, we must have dinner, a cheerful, pleasant dinner . . . *nicht wahr?"*

No answer.

"Sophie?"

But Sophie was no longer there. Gustav Bulheim heard the clatter of the phone being dropped. The connection was broken. Ach! This whole *verdammte* business. Even the good news was too much for poor Sophie. *Schrecklich* that because of his own affairs, he had neglected Sophie. Sophie, his own family! And she, alone now, in that villa. He should take her to Italy, a vacation—the lakes, perhaps Maggiore. Gustav Bulheim sighed and put down the phone. He would try to be a better brother.

At eleven o'clock that same Sunday morning, Leon Kraus sat on his living room couch with his feet on the coffee table and his arms folded on his chest. He gazed

despondently at his shoes. So: Veronica Kent and Jason
Foxe in custody. *Trumpf's Triumph.* Kraus could taste
envy, a metallic taste. He had tasted it immediately upon
hearing the news. Now, abruptly, he felt overcome by an
aversion to his "Liebe Leute" program. He hated to think
of talking to his *Liebe Leute* about Detective Inspector
Leo Trumpf's *coup.* But he could not avoid it.

He was also sick of the word *amateur* being teamed
with *criminologist* in the radio introduction of "Liebe
Leute." But his producer insisted.

Kraus twitched his feet. He hated the entire radio
station, he thought in disgust. They paid him shamefully
little; he should quit. But "Liebe Leute" was good publicity, so good that the name Leon Kraus commanded high
prices for magazine articles, articles on sensational subjects—the only kind he enjoyed writing. He knew the
seductive subjects—sex, drugs, murder, money, adultery—in their endless combinations. He knew how to
whet the public's appetite. And what a response he
evoked!

The thought comforted him. His feet, on the coffee
table, rested on a pile of letters from readers of his last
week's *Neue Illustrierte* magazine piece based on inter-
views with a half-dozen teenagers trying to combat their
drug habit. Heartstrings stories, with enough lurid material, ranging from prostitution to thievery, to entice the
reader. Some of the teenagers had seen the light via
religion; two had become frightened after bad trips, hor-
rifyingly described. One girl had fled drugs in shock after
witnessing her boyfriend's death from an overdose.

Kraus had received a crazy letter about that last one,
the sixteen-year-old—one of those unsigned letters that
showered down on him like confetti after a particularly
sensational article. The letter had said something about
Otto von Reitz. He had tossed it aside . . . the world was

full of *Verrücktes,* crazies. And they all wrote to him,
Leon Kraus. That letter. About three lines long. Usually
readers rambled on for pages.

He took his feet off the coffee table. He riffled through
the letters, stopping occasionally to savor, smiling, a
particularly flattering one. Ah! Here. Written in pencil
on cheap paper. The anonymous reader had torn out
pages of the magazine article and clipped them to the
letter. The reader had also circled the sixteen-year-old's
name with a red pencil. Kraus read the three lines: *Would
you like to find the real murderer of Herr von Reitz?
Ask Rosa about the fat man with the birthmark on his
neck.*

Kraus sat back. He had interviewed Rosa Fischer
weeks ago. A heartbroken youngster with swollen eyelids.
A back-page item in the *Neue Kronen Zeitung* had led
him to her. It had been the usual item about still another
teenager's drug death. His girlfriend, Rosa Fischer, had
seen him die.

But what could Rosa Fischer have to do with the von
Reitz case? Nothing.

He tossed the letter back onto the coffee table and sat,
drumming his fingers on the arm of the couch, smiling
cynically at his thoughts, at his most alluring fantasy. He
saw himself electrifying his *Liebe Leute* as he brilliantly
demolished Detective Inspector Trumpf and, in fact,
Vienna's entire Criminal Investigation Department by
revealing the *real* murderer of Otto von Reitz. Except
that . . .

Veronica Kent was the real murderer.

Leon Kraus sat for some minutes longer. Then he got
up, took a light coat, checked to make sure he had his car
keys, and headed for the door. It would be an hour's drive
to the drug rehabilitation center west of Vienna.

* * *

The nurse in charge recognized him from his former visits to Rosa Fischer, and this time she tore a sheet from a blank prescription pad and asked for his autograph. He scribbled his name with a flourish. The nurse then directed him to the playing field. "You will find Rosa Fischer there."

It was an all-girls game of volleyball. He sat alone on a bench in chilly autumn sunlight, waiting. Finally a whistle blew. Rosa's side had won. She came off the field with two other girls, jubilant, smiling, chatting. She was a rounded, short-haired blond girl with small wrists and ankles. She wore shorts and sneakers and a long-sleeved dark jersey.

"Herr Kraus!" She waved her friends on.

Kraus stood and they shook hands. Rosa looked healthy and happy. Remarkable, the change since a few weeks ago. Gone were the sallowness, the staring look, the nervous tic at the corner of her mouth. Her parents must be weeping with joy.

They sat down on the bench.

"I *loved* the article!" Rosa said enthusiastically. "Are you here to do a sequel on how well I'm getting along? Splendidly! I've gained three pounds. I'll be entering the university at midterm. Biology is a bore, I'm thinking seriously of studying journalism, I—"

"Not a sequel. I want to ask you something else. . . . Go back a bit."

"Go *back?* But I've already told you everything! It's all in the magazine!"

"All?"

She stared at him; her smile was gone. "Yes . . . all."

"Tell me," Kraus said, "tell me about the fat man with the birthmark on his neck."

She sat hunched over on the bench, her arms wrapped around her body as though she had stomach cramps.

Kraus shifted back a little and placed the tape recorder on the bench between them. Occasionally the girl faltered in the telling, and at such times he asked a question, pushing her on.

The whole sex thing, the disgusting ugliness, what they were doing—"I could not tell it! My parents! . . ." She broke down and cried.

But there in the thin, chilly autumn sunlight, the tape unwinding, Rosa Fischer told it. Tears stained her face and ran down into the corners of her childish mouth. At an early point in the telling about the fat man—"He slapped my face and called me a whore"—she tortured out the castigation as though she merited it. And when she came to Ernst Braun's death, she spoke with a controlled disbelief, as though still clinging to the possibility that it had not happened. All. She told it all. It did not take long to tell, perhaps half an hour. It was short, it was sad, it was ugly. And its end was death.

When Kraus snapped off the tape and left Rosa Fischer alone on the bench with unacknowledged words of comfort, he felt like a diamond prospector who had turned up a pebble in his gravel pan, brushed it off, and found himself with what looked like an egg-sized diamond . . . but one that might be just a pebble after all. Veronica Kent still could have killed Otto von Reitz. But now there was this other strange possibility; strange and exciting, it played tag through his mind.

He thought about it driving back to Vienna, the tape safely stowed in the glove compartment. He was on to something, it winked at him like a diamond, that something. But it was not enough. He replayed the tape in his mind. He imagined scenarios. Twice, absorbed, he almost crashed into another car.

By the time he reached the outskirts of Vienna he knew he had only one possibility of verifying his find as a

true diamond. He would have to commit a crime himself—go outside the law. It was the only way. He had had
enough experience with Vienna's criminal investigation
people to know they discounted him as half-clown, half-
sensationalist. They snickered at him: *They* were professionals; *he* was an amateur.

"Sophie?" It was Monday morning. Again Gustav
Bulheim was on the phone, calling his sister. When he
heard her voice, he launched into pleasantries, beginning
with a comment about the crisp autumn weather, so
invigorating, so—

"What is it, Gustav?"

Gustav Bulheim cleared his throat. The fact was, he
explained, he was concerned about her—her hysteria, her
jumpiness. He had taken the liberty— That is, he had
spoken to their old family physician, Dr. Schumann. Dr.
Schumann had agreed that perhaps tranquilizers . . . Of
course, he, Gustav, knew what an anathema drugs were
to Sophie, but tranquilizers were hardly drugs. "And,
under the abnormal—"

"No, Gustav."

Gustav Bulheim knew that tone of voice since childhood: Sophie's *No.* The stubborn, unmovable final *No.*
He sighed. He feared to upset his sister further, but
perhaps he had better mention a bit of news. He had
learned it this morning by phone from Inspector Trumpf.
It had not been officially released, but the alert media . . .
At any minute Sophie might hear a newsbreak, a *Sondernachrichten*, and tailspin into another crying-laughing
fit.

So Gustav Bulheim cleared his throat and told Sophie
the news.

Leon Kraus, the amateur criminologist who did the
radio program, "Liebe Leute," had been arrested. A

policeman patrolling on the Opernring had seen a flash of light, like a wandering flashlight beam, in an upper window of an office building. The officer knew the window to be that of the murdered Otto von Reitz's office—as who, in Vienna, did not? The policeman had called for assistance. The police had burst into the von Reitz office. The intruder was Leon Kraus.

"Sophie?"

"Yes, Gustav?"

"You're all right?"

"Yes, Gustav. I'm fine."

Jason Foxe jumped up when Nicca was brought into Chief Fuhrmann's office. She was still in knickers and shirt, but her bloodstained sweater was gone. Also gone were the lilac-tinted eyeglasses. He had not seen her since yesterday morning when they had been arraigned before the *Untersuchungsrichter*—the Investigative Magistrate. The Magistrate had taken approximately two minutes to order Veronica Kent held on suspicion of murder and Jason Foxe held as accessory.

Two hours from now, at five P.M. Tuesday, they would be transferred from the holding pen at the Rossauerkaserne to prison cells at Landegericht, across the city.

So why were they here in Chief Fuhrmann's office?

It was three o'clock and pouring rain. Thunderclouds darkened the city. On the rain-lashed streets, cars drove slowly, headlights on. In the chief's office, fluorescent tubings on the ceiling made the room bright and shadowless. On the chief's desk, a goose-necked lamp shed extra light.

"Guten Tag." Inspector Trumpf entered, accompanied by a thickly built man, well-tailored, and with a crushed-looking bulldog face. Herr Gustav Bulheim. Introduced,

he stared with controlled rage at Veronica Kent, alias Nicca Montcalm.

Chief Fuhrmann surveyed the quartet, now seated. "And where, Inspector, is our linchpin? Ah! ... There! Herr Kraus!"

The man entering wore a belted, olive-green suit, a maroon turtleneck, and saddle shoes—the casual style of someone not under the conventional dress restrictions of office employees. He was in his thirties, of medium height, his fair hair corrugated like a blond washboard. He had green eyes in an alert-looking face that was just going pudgy. He acknowledged the introductions with an air of total self-confidence. He carried a tape recorder.

So this was Kraus. Jason Foxe watched him set the tape recorder on a corner of Chief Fuhrmann's desk and draw up a chair. Kraus had been arrested—breaking and entering. He, too, must be in custody. In Austria there was no such thing as bail. So, a fellow prisoner. A nice irony!

"Inspector?" Chief Fuhrmann's pale eyes were on Inspector Trumpf.

The inspector stood up. An unorthodox meeting, admittedly. But they were to hear a tape. Transcripts of the tape would later be made available. The meeting had been urged by—here the inspector cleared his throat—by Herr Kraus. He sat down.

Leon Kraus reached over to the tape recorder and depressed a key. A scratchy sound, first. Then girls' voices, laughing, talking, fading; then a bird twittering— cut sharply off ... only to come scratchily on again— birds twittering this time, then a girl's voice: "I lied. We didn't buy the stuff on the street, Ernst and I. But what does it matter anymore? Ernst is dead. I guess it was an accumulation, we'd had other stuff the night before, something Ernst got from a friend in his class ..." A pause, the twittering of birds; Kraus's voice: "The fat man ... what about him?" Another pause.

"The fat man ... My parents would have died of shame! And what would it have helped? It started ... Ernst and I went one night to dance at the Kursalon. He picked us up, he was rich, we drank champagne—two whole bottles!" Another pause. "At first it was only pills, and him taking us to dinner at different places, expensive places. The pills turned colors so bright, and everything became so funny ... we would laugh and laugh. Then he suggested this other, just a little scratch under the skin. The first time was at night in his office, just a scratch for Ernst and me. Then he watched us make love. It was a torment, but such a desire ... I thought I would explode with it! Ernst too. We couldn't stop. He kept watching and laughing. When we were through, he slapped my face and called me a whore. That made him reach a— You know. Only it was more like a convulsion.

"After that, we went only twice to his office. The other times we were at Ernst's apartment. Only it was all three of us, the sex ... and just little injections with a syringe. Ernst and I got wild for the stuff. We used to talk about it together—how we'd get hold of some of the capsules and inject each other alone, without him, just for us. Only we didn't know what it was! And he wouldn't tell us. He'd only let us have it to do it with him—the sex." A pause, the tape sibilating.

"He had these crazy sexual fantasies.... Sometimes he would tie up Ernst, and then it would be him attacking me while Ernst begged him not to, and then him over-powering me and beating me in some crazy ecstasy. Then—*Herrgott!*—it was like an infection, I *wanted* him to do it. I didn't care finally that it was him, not Ernst! I just wanted it, *wanted* it! Without stopping ..." A sigh. A silence.

"I guess we were getting used to the stuff. It sort of wore off. He brought something stronger. He wouldn't tell us where he got it. He said we couldn't afford it anyway. Besides, he said he wasn't giving away any free trips. 'I'm not so rich I can afford to give away free trips.' Only of course we knew he was rich. By then we knew he was Herr von Reitz and that he was terribly rich. Ernst told him so, told him he knew about his money, and he just laughed and said, 'But not so rich in little playmates!'

"But then . . . the awful part." The voice quavered and stopped. Twittering birds; then Herr Kraus: "You mean Ernst's death?"

Presumably the girl nodded, then spoke again: "It was Ernst's birthday. Herr von Reitz said we'd all have something special for it, something new he'd just gotten. Then, unexpectedly, he had to go to Hamburg. But he said that because it was Ernst's birthday, just this once he would relent and leave us a free trip. 'One free trip for my little playmates,' he said. And he gave us a capsule. He—"

Leon Kraus turned off the tape. "Let me interrupt to tell you that what then happened in Ernst Braun's apartment occurred the day after Herr von Reitz had presumably left for Hamburg . . . although in actuality von Reitz's dead body was already lying in his private office." He pressed the recorder key; the girl's voice continued:

"It was true, the part I told you for the magazine—about being in Ernst's apartment . . . except that I didn't mention we were naked when the doorbell rang. And then we heard a key in the lock, so it had to be Ernst's mother—she was the only one with a key to his apartment. Ernst had just given himself the injection. So I yanked on my shorts and shirt and told Ernst I'd get rid of her.

"She was in the kitchen with a bag of groceries. I told her Ernst and I were studying. She *knew* he couldn't stand anyone around when we were studying! But she took her stupid time putting the groceries away anyway. She even smoked a cigarette. By the time she left and I got back to Ernst, he was dead."

Leon Kraus again clicked off the machine. He looked around at his audience. "In case anyone here missed my article in the October eighth issue of *Die Neue Illustrierte*, Rosa Fischer was herself hospitalized for shock. Then her parents sent her to a rehabilitation institution near Krems. Ernst Braun's body went to the morgue— another teenage victim of drug overdose. The diagnosis was respiratory failure."

Kraus's voice hummed with satisfaction. Clearly, he was experiencing his finest hour. His corrugated hair gleamed gold under the flourescent light. He tapped the tape recorder. "Now. Let us return for a moment to the sexual . . . ah, *pas de trois* that so intoxicated Otto von Reitz. What exactly was the procedure?"

He depressed the recorder key. A bird twitter; then Kraus's voice: " . . . was the procedure?" And Rosa Fischer:

"Procedure? What difference does that make? I've told you everything! . . . Well, he once said that hypodermic means under the skin and so does subcutaneous. Both from the Latin . . . or did he say Greek? And syringe meant— I forget. Anyway, he said it was simple; you could do it anywhere on your body as long as it wasn't intravenous: your thigh, an arm, behind your knee—it didn't matter. That's what we did. Herr von Reitz would inject himself, then sterilize the syringe with rubbing alcohol on a bit of cotton, then do Ernst and me the same way. Is that what you—"

Kraus clicked off the tape. He looked around at the attentive faces. "With that information, and postulating certain things I will explain in a moment, I made an illegal entry into the private office of Otto von Reitz."

In Kraus's alert face, his green eyes flashed with anticipation. He glanced, smiling, toward Inspector Trumpf who sat staring down at his hands clasped in his lap, then . . .

"There," announced Kraus, and he turned his green gaze to something on Chief Furhmann's desk. All except Inspector Trumpf leaned forward. It lay on a sheet of white paper. A syringe.

"I will explain in a moment where I found it."

At that, Chief Fuhrmann's long pale hand caressed his chin. He glanced at Trumpf, as Leon Kraus continued.

"The syringe has on it what I suspected it would have: Herr von Reitz's fingerprints."

They were all staring at the syringe.

"The syringe is empty now. Its contents are in the Rossauerkaserne's forensic laboratory. The contents? A lethal drug combination, enough to kill three men."

A torrent of rain rattled the windows, thunder crashed. On Chief Fuhrmann's desk, the light flickered.

"Lethal? Impossible!" Nicca's voice was incredulous. "If they were his fingerprints, it had to be insulin! His diabetes! I lost my head, I had some crazy— I knocked the syringe out of his hand! I struck him with the bronze parrot. I left him lying there! Vulnerable! To be murdered!"

Leon Kraus smiled at her incredulous face, a patronizing smile, the specialist dealing indulgently with the novice. He almost chortled: "Guilt and naïveté! Such a dangerous combination! It inclines one to fantasies—and to putting one's head in a noose." He almost rubbed his hands. "But of course, *mein liebes Fräulein,* you are unaware of another fact: Herr von Reitz did not have diabetes."

The desk light flickered and went out. No one paid any attention. No one spoke. They were all looking at the girl in knickers.

"Then if he had ... with the syringe ... if I hadn't ..." She put a hand to her throat. The color left her face.

Kraus inclined his head, smiling. "In that case, *mein liebes Fräulein*—alas!"

Jason Foxe heard a sharply indrawn breath from Gustav Bulheim on his left. No doubt it wasn't easy to be faced with such peculiar revelations about one's relatives. And as for Nicca ... Jason Foxe looked over at Nicca Montcalm who was Veronica Kent, his lover and his one-armed Venus. The whole works.

Gustav Bulheim said, "Herr Kraus, you are telling us that ... that my brother-in-law ... that Otto von Reitz? ..."

"Herr von Reitz was killed by a lethal dose he himself injected into his thigh. The procedure, Herr Bulheim! The procedure! We have just learned from Rosa Fischer the procedure preceding sexual activities. Himself first ... then a tiny injection into the unsuspecting Fräulein Kent's arm.

"How Otto von Reitz obtained these sensually stimulating drugs, we don't yet know. But he obtained them. And he was rich. ... Apparently he demanded, and was able to obtain, stronger and stronger drug combinations, drugs that produced more and greater erotic results. A risky business. *Entschuldigen Sie*—a *deadly* business. In his case resulting in respiratory failure and death."

Gustav Bulheim spoke again, voice shaken: "Then, the teenager? ..."

"For Ernst Braun and Rosa Fischer," said Kraus, "a 'free trip' for Ernst's birthday. Sad and ironic! Otto von Reitz thought he was giving those youngsters a wildly

erotic weekend, sexual ecstasy, an orgy. A generous gift!
Ernst injected himself and died. On the basis of new
knowledge, thanks to this tape, a search of Ernst Braun's
effects, packed away in his mother's apartment, was
made. The empty capsule was found in an aspirin tin,
Ernst had dropped it into a mug of pens and pencils on
his desk—perhaps when he heard his mother at the door.
The capsule bore Ernst Braun's fingerprints. But the
aspirin tin? Otto von Reitz's fingerprints. Need I tell you
that the residue in the capsule, analyzed by the forensic
laboratory, was identical with the contents of the syringe
I found in Herr von Reitz's office?"

Sibilant sighs in the room; the rain beat, the chief
examined his pale hands; the world dripped with tragedy
and revelation.

"Herrgott!" Gustav Bulheim was enraged. Veins stood
out on his forehead, he smashed a fist on the arm of his
chair. "What kind of incompetence! The police searched
Otto's private office weeks ago!" He glared at Trumpf,
then in fury at Chief Fuhrmann. "Why wasn't that
verdammte syringe found then? My sister Sophie is half
out of her mind! I too have suffered! This young
woman"—Bulheim violently flung out an arm toward
Veronica Kent—"has been tortured with guilt, fleeing!
Now a man has been shot in the woods! *Herrgott! Why
was the syringe not found?* Is this the sort of detective
work with which the Criminal Investigation Department
provides Vienna? *Sagen Sie mir!* Half the population of
Vienna could be drowning in the Danube, and the police
department would be running back and forth on the
banks looking at the sky! Half!" He sat pounding his fists,
bulldog jaw outthrust, his powerful body demanding an
answer.

Chief Fuhrmann examined his pale hands, then looked
at Trumpf. "Inspector?"

But surprisingly, Leon Kraus answered. Washboard hair gleaming, alert face alight with positive joy, he seemed barely able to contain himself. And what was he saying? Jaxon Foxe found himself suppressing astonished laughter. By God, Kraus was apologizing to Herr Gustav Bulheim for the Federal Criminal Investigation Department! But the radio criminologist was astute, no denying it. For an amateur, Kraus was hell on wheels.

"The criminal department, Herr Bulheim, made a thorough investigation of that private office. Thorough! As soon as Herr von Reitz's body was found! They vacuumed for fibers, they dusted for fingerprints, they explored every surface, they took all the necessary samplings for analysis. Exhaustively, Herr Bulheim." Leon Kraus looked happily at Inspector Trumpf. *"Richtig,* Inspector?"

"Richtig." A gloomy voice.

"But we all must realize, Herr Bulheim: *at that time* it was thought Otto von Reitz had been killed by a blow on the head with the bronze parrot. In such a case, they had no reason to explore *upward*—toward the ceiling, for example. Anyway, absurd to explore upward—except, of course, in the case of ballistics, for bullet holes.

"But after visiting Rosa Fischer, I began to think. A bronze parrot! Yet Otto von Reitz had died of a lethal injection. And hearing Rosa describe the 'procedure,' I realized the injection could have been self-inflicted. If so, Veronica Kent was not a psychotic murderer who had fled, taking the syringe with her, as"—here Leon Kraus, amateur criminologist, could not refrain from a smug glance at Inspector Trumpf—"as the police hypothesized.

"After all, that syringe was the only proof of her innocence." Kraus looked with satisfaction at the syringe on the desk. "Unless a *third* person had made away with the syringe, it had to be still be in Otto von Reitz's private office. The answer could only be: If not *down*—the area the police had logically covered—then *up*." Leon Kraus raised his arms, palms upward, as though lifting his attentive spectators to heaven. "Up! Up! Up on the walls! And there I found the syringe. Lodged on the ledge of a frame, behind one of the portraits."

They were turning from Kraus and looking at her. . . . She was spiraling back into that office of paneled walls and gilt-framed portraits . . . she was seeing the loose, wet look to the man's prim mouth as though an inner elastic holding it tight had broken . . . she was back with the macabre, the insane idea . . . back with him taking her arm, holding the syringe—*"No!"*

In Chief Fuhrmann's office, she said, dazed, "I flung up my arm, it struck his, the syringe went flying up over the desk. . . . "

" . . . and lodged behind the portrait." Someone else in the room said it. Leon Kraus? Herr Bulheim? She didn't know.

But now their attention had left her; they were listening again to the amateur criminologist. She listened too. Kraus's voice rang with hard facts, true knowledge; they rang like genuine coins flung down on a counter. Hard currency.

"Rosa Fischer said she once went with Herr von Reitz to his office, just the two of them, a Sunday night, Ernst had to study for exams. The 'procedure' was the same as with the three of them, only simpler: Von Reitz filled the syringe from the capsule and gave himself an injection, and then used a bit of cotton with rubbing alcohol to sterilize the needle for Rosa. He flushed the cotton and the empty capsule down the toilet. And was ready for"— Leon Kraus shrugged—"for whatever."

Whatever. She had escaped the whatever: the

whatever that had killed Otto von Reitz, and that would have killed her too. She clasped her hands tightly together to steady herself.

She looked around for Jason Foxe.

Chapter 20

Inspector Trumpf still sat, chin in hand. The voices around him were bees buzzing. People were standing, talking. Leon Kraus was fitting the tape recorder into its leather case. A police guard was approaching Jason Foxe. Foxe would go back to prison—God only knew for how long!—on the charge of collusion with a suspected murderer. Regardless of the girl's innocence, Foxe was now a criminal, he had been an accessory, he had interfered with the law. The inspector looked over at Veronica Kent. There she was in knickers, her hand on Jason Foxe's arm. Five minutes ago, she had been stunned by Kraus's revelation. Three minutes ago, she had looked wildly happy. Now with her hand on Jason Foxe's arm, and looking into his eyes, she was miserably biting her lips. Trumpf could see that Foxe was trying to reassure her, probably telling her he'd be out of prison in twenty-four hours. A comforting lie. Buzzing, buzzing, the voices in the room.

But still the inspector sat, musing. Something here disturbed him.

The real murderer.

The real murderer was whoever had put those capsules into the avid hands of Otto von Reitz. Somewhere out there, peripherally, was the real murderer . . . a murderer who felt safe, a cunning murderer. Was that murderer himself a taker of drugs? A mind affected by drugs could wander down any strange horrifying bypaths . . . fantasizing, forgiving, condemning, senselessly but demonically turning a glaring eye on whatever characters had inadvertently wandered onto the stage and become part of his drama. A drug-crazed mind could— Trumpf glanced again at Veronica Kent. With Jason Foxe in prison, the American girl would be alone, unprotected, vulnerable . . . and unsuspecting. Or was he, Trumpf, inventing dangers that didn't exist . . . sniffing around in an empty lion's den?

He pondered. The anonymous note . . . *Would you like to find the real murderer? . . . Ask Rosa Fischer about* . . . But Rosa Fischer's knowledge went only so far. Far enough to clear Veronica Kent. Then, a dead end. No, not quite: *The anonymous writer of the letter.* That unknown person who had knowledge of Rosa Fischer's connection to Otto von Reitz . . . that person might lead to the murderer.

But who was the writer? A faceless, hooded figure stood just outside the inspector's peripheral vision. The penciled note, on cheap paper, now in the folder marked Otto von Reitz, had yielded no clue.

"Inspector?"

At his elbow, Gustav Bulheim. Haggard, suddenly lined face, eyes already cleared of shock . . . but sad, sad. He thanked the inspector for his intensive work on the case, and added: *"Traurig!* Tragic! The dark and light

forces that war in a man's heart! Otto, in the eyes of
society a respectable lawyer, intelligent, kind, sophisticated, an appreciater of music—and he was all that. But
his darker temptations, that side, the corruption of such
as Rosa Fischer and Ernst Braun . . . for that, poor Otto
paid terribly! As though he had been *made to pay,* almost
as though someone . . ." Herr Bulheim broke off, he
looked confused; he blinked his protruding eyes as though
the concentrated blinking would return to him his lost
train of thought.

"Someone, indeed!" Leon Kraus had joined them.
Cock of the walk. Trumpf tasted metal. Kraus was
almost on tiptoe so eager was he to answer with authority
any question on criminology, humanity, the fate of the
universe, infinity, God—and perhaps flying saucers.

"Someone, indeed!" Kraus repeated. "A shrewd criminologist never ignores the 'someone' who, one in a thousand times, might provide a lead. In the von Reitz case,
an anonymous letter led me to Rosa Fischer. By the way,
my radio program, 'Liebe—' "

"A letter?" Gustav Bulheim. It seemed to Trumpf that
across Herr Bulheim's face alarm flickered like firelight;
there was even a flutter of the man's nostrils, quickly
controlled. "A letter?"

"My dear Herr Bulheim!" The Deity that was Leon
Kraus sounded almost merry. "The public mistakenly
assumes that a criminologist makes mysteriously brilliant
deductions, and—*voilà!* But I assure you, Herr Bulheim,
it is only by an astute criminologist recognizing the value
of a seemingly trivial clue out of a morass, that . . ."

Trumpf had ceased to listen. He excused himself. He
was suddenly in a hurry.

It was an hour's drive to Klosterneuburg. The rain had
stopped but the roads were still wet, so he drove slowly.

He missed Pepi, but Klara had returned from her mother's and Pepi was, anyway, back in school; the special school project had started. At the von Reitz villa, he parked in the circular driveway under the portico and then walked past thick green bushes to the front door.

Sophie von Reitz herself opened the door. She had on black woolen slacks and one of those loose, sand-colored overblouses that looked like coarse potato sacking but were fashionable and expensive. She had heavy, dark hair, long and carelessly tied back with a ribbon. She wore no makeup. Her face was pale and there were dark circles under her eyes.

"Inspector Trumpf?" Her voice was calm. "I was expecting you. My brother Gustav just telephoned. He has great respect for you. He guessed you might be coming here. He said I would know why."

She stepped outside and closed the door behind her. "Come with me."

He followed her around the side of the house. The grass was wet, the air chilly. A yardman in a warm jacket was raking wet leaves from around bushes. They skirted an enormous oval swimming pool covered with canvas; to the left, leaves blew across a wet tennis court. They reached the garage, certainly a five-car garage. There were quarters above, an outside stairway on each side; obviously two apartments. Sophie von Reitz headed for the one on the left.

"We'll go up."

She went first. Inspector Trumpf puffed up the stairs behind her. It took her a long time to unlock the door. There were three keys and they had gotten wet; so were her hands wet with rain. She fumbled. "I am not used ..." Strands of her dark hair had got loose and fallen across her eyes, getting in the way. But finally the last key turned.

They came into the room.

"One thing," Sophie von Reitz said, and she broke into a helpless, hysterical-sounding giggle. "He was very *neat.*"

The room was indeed neat. Weighty-looking books were neatly ranged on shelves—books on chemistry, books on drugs. It was a model laboratory, everything shiny, efficient, expensive—on a plastic-topped table, transparent plastic bins of tuberculin syringes, empty gelatine capsules in two sizes, stoppered glass bottles of powders. A leather-bound loose-leaf notebook, legal-sized, when Trumpf opened it, revealed formulas written in an exquisite, tiny handwriting. Formula upon formula; note upon note. The last formula to appear was dated the day before Otto von Reitz's death.

Trumpf went through it all. The leather-bound book went back three years. When he had seen all he needed to see, he turned to Sophie von Reitz. She was standing, leaning against the wall near the book shelves, tears running down her face.

Trumpf said, "He made them himself, the capsules."

She nodded. "He knew I suspected. He sickened me . . . I wouldn't let him near me. I began to hate him. But did he care? Oh, no! He was obsessed. *Obsessed!* Do you understand that? I don't know what sexual partners he found . . . or where—in brothels, on the street, in nightclubs. He was out of control . . . I think now he was no longer sane! Nothing was enough of an aphrodisiac; he was after a stronger and stronger drug." Her arms hung at her sides. Trumpf wondered when Sophie von Reitz had given up battling shadows in a war long since lost. "Then," she went on, "that girl from the Hilton, the American—"

From the outer stairway, a sound; footsteps. Someone was mounting the stairs; a heavy tread.

Gustav Bulheim stood in the doorway. He looked from Trumpf to his sister. "The yardman said I'd find you—" But the room itself stopped him short. He looked around, bewildered. *"Herrgott!"*

"Gustav! I thought you guessed!" His sister was equally bewildered. "I thought that's why you telephoned! *There."* She gestured toward the table. "They're Otto's notes, Gustav. He made the capsules."

"Herrgott!"

Incredulous, Herr Bulheim approached the table with its paraphernalia; then he turned and looked at the books. *"Herrgott!* He was a lawyer, not a chemist! What did he know of pharmacology? Nothing. *Nothing!* He must have had an illicit drug source, been buying who-knows-what hard drugs, then himself mixing—*Herrgott!* Russian roulette would be safer."

"Two years ago," his sister said, "I found the keys. Sometimes I would come up here and read his notes. I could see it was getting . . . I was so frightened! But . . ."—she turned out her palms, a helpless gesture—"I was not able to stop him. He would look at me and smile; it was my husband Otto smiling at me from behind his glasses, only it was not Otto, no longer Otto von Reitz. Gustav, it was not Otto! *He had become someone else.*

"Then that girl from the Hilton, Veronica Kent . . . Otto murdered, the girl vanished . . ." Sophie von Reitz, with a weary gesture, combed strands of dark hair back with her fingers; her eyes, within their dark circles, were stained. "Is it true, Gustav, what you just told me on the telephone? That it wasn't the girl, but Otto *himself*, with the syringe? . . . The dreadful irony of Otto himself . . ."

"It is true, Sophie."

That queer, half-hysterical giggle from Sophie von Reitz. "I thought *she* had killed him! But through some crazy accident—a stupid orgy. I felt sorry for her; I was hoping she'd escape! I used to wake up at night and think: If she were to come and bang on my door and beg me to hide her, I would hide her! I would save her! And, Gustav, I would have thanked her! *Because I could not have stood any more!*" Tears were again sliding down Sophie von Reitz's haggard face. "At the christening, I did not want your gun, Gustav. I had Werner drive me home. I was hoping, thinking, maybe she *would* come— oh, not to kill me, I was positive of that—but to beg for help. I *wanted* her to come, Gustav!

"And, Gustav, she *did* come! There she was, at the door of the winter garden. And I could do nothing, offer nothing! It was as though I were frozen—trapped between the girl and Otto."

"Ach, Sophie, you torture yourself. It was probably not even the girl, but someone else, snooping, you know how—"

"No, Gustav!" Sophie shook her head. "It was Veronica Kent. I know, because I spoke to her in English and she answered in the same language. She was so panicked she didn't even realize we were speaking English." Sophie von Reitz looked around the room with its plastic-topped table and plastic bins of tuberculin syringes. Her lips trembled. "When she was gone, I poured myself a glassful of whiskey and came down here and got drunk. Dead drunk. Do you know why, Gustav? Because I had not saved her!"

Gustav Bulheim crossed quickly to his sister's side. "Ach, Sophie!" He put an arm around her shoulders and rocked her, soothing her. "But you *did* save her, Sophie. Be happy for that! You saved her with your letter to Herr Kraus! That's what I meant on the telephone—that the letter gave him the lead. Poor Sophie, I have worried so about you! All through this, you acted so . . . Just now, at the Rossauerkaserne, when I learned about your letter to

Herr Kraus, I guessed your agony, your— But, Sophie, how did you find out about Otto's connection with Rosa Fischer?"

Inspector Trumpf, too, awaited the answer. At the Rossauerkaserne, in the chief's office, witnessing Gustav Bulheim's reaction when Leon Kraus mentioned the anonymous letter, he had guessed that the letter had come from Sophie von Reitz. That suspicion had brought him to Klosterneuburg in the hope that the letter writer could lead him to the supplier of the lethal capsule. Well, so she had: Sophie von Bulheim had exposed the "real" murderer—Otto von Reitz himself, with his laboratory in the garage.

Still . . . how *had* she known of the connection between her husband and Rosa Fischer? He waited.

"Sophie?" her brother was repeating. "How?"

Sophie von Reitz looked from her brother to Inspector Trumpf, then back. Her face was puzzled. "Letter?" she said. "What letter?"

Twenty-four hours later, Inspector Trumpf sat in the chief's office. The police had already completed their work in the laboratory over the garage in Klosterneuburg. Gustav Bulheim had moved his sister Sophie into his bachelor apartment on the Schottenring, and what with the Portier and Bulheim's own battery of servants, the apartment was as impregnable as a fortress. The media could gain no foothold.

Meanwhile, Veronica Kent's deposition, given at the Rossauerkaserne, had led to the gold-toothed waiter at the Kursalon. Under questioning at headquarters, the waiter had revealed a glimpse of Otto von Reitz's subterranean life. Trumpf recounted it to the chief.

"Like a bloated toad! He would sit at the Kursalon like a *verdammte* toad waiting to snap up flies: a boy or girl alone, a woman, sometimes a couple—like Ernst and Rosa."

Squirming, the waiter had admitted that, yes, he would lead such people to Herr von Reitz's table, Herr von Reitz tipped him generously. "A generous, lonely man! At least, I assumed . . ." The waiter shrugged. "How could I suspect? . . ." "And precisely why, Herr Senyi, did you not come immediately to the police when Herr von Reitz was found murdered? You recognized the girl entering the Hilton later that evening—*nicht wahr?*—the girl you had led to Herr von Reitz's table that very evening. . . . *Ja oder nein?*" "*Aber, Herr Inspector!*" Married with two children! What if he were to lose his job at the Kursalon for being mixed up in a murder? His employers were so strict! "No, no! The police know their job! I knew they would catch her without my help! And they did . . . *nicht wahr?*"

Alone with Trumpf, the chief caressed his chin with his pale hand. "The waiter suspected, or *he knew,* his generous customer wished to assuage more than loneliness. A tacit collusion. A whiff of the sewer here."

"I'd swear to it. A pity we can't hold him!" Trumpf beetled his brows in frustration. This slimy waiter would pay no penalty. But Martha Krieger Schratt, of the kind heart, would pay; her license would be suspended, or at the least she would pay a fine.

The public ate it up—a mélange, satisfying to the taste. After all, not only was the blue-blooded millionaire lawyer Otto von Reitz *his own murderer,* but aristocracy was also involved—Baron Wilhelm von Walenberg, not to mention Austria's famous bird artist, Florian Königsmark. Erotic drugs, teenagers, death. Veronica Kent and the Foxe.

Photographers jostled each other to take pictures of

Veronica Kent in knickers and short haircut coming down the steps of the Rossauerkaserne into freedom. A handful of teenagers flung roses at her, shouting "The Foxe! The Foxe!" All Vienna knew that the Foxe of the Affair of the Roses was Veronica Kent's lover.

One after another, little firecrackers mixed with skyrockets: The seventeen-year-old Bruno Königsmark was found asleep in his car on a country road near Schloss Walenberg; a real Eugen Tierstein, aged eighty-seven, turned up, demanding "satisfaction," but satisfaction for what, nobody could determine. Veronica Kent was glimpsed having supper at the Schweitzerhaus outdoor restaurant with the von Reitz's gardener, Josef Valasek, clinking beer glasses and eating roast veal shank.

Then, there was the matter of Rudi Polzer, the garage mechanic who had been shot in the shoulder in the forest at Schloss Walenberg. Herr Polzer's motorcycle pouch had yielded up Veronica Kent's green-gold dress and the blood-flecked shoes and stockings, along with Rudi Polzer's cap and sweater and a considerable amount of neo-Nazi literature. Polzer had talked threateningly of suing Baron von Walenberg for his injury, but it turned out that he had no case. He had been a trespasser, and it had been impossible to determine whose stray bullet had struck him. A half-dozen guests had borrowed guns from the Baron's gun room, but no one knew which gun each had chosen. At any rate, the guns had been cleaned, polished, and put away. Consequently, ballistics tests would be meaningless.

Rudi Polzer's rage was considerably lessened, however, when he received Gustav Bulheim's reward for apprehending Veronica Kent. "I saw immediately that she was not a boy!" Polzer told the press. It did not matter to him that Fräulein Kent had stopped in her flight, shouted for help, and carried him from the forest. He insisted furiously that Herr Gustav Bulheim had offered the reward for the girl's *apprehension*—"And I apprehended her!" The offer had mentioned nothing about whether she was innocent or guilty; "So the money is mine!" Rudi declared. Herr Bulheim conceded the point.

Leon Kraus, amateur criminologist, was in the limelight. His radio audience swelled; he was given a raise. The producers of "Liebe Leute" dropped the word "amateur" from his introduction. After all, their own Leon Kraus had been responsible for proving Veronica Kent's innocence. Kraus alone had saved the innocent American girl from a lifetime prison sentence . . . though of course it had been Detective Inspector Leo Trumpf who had subsequently tracked down the identify of the supplier of the murderous capsules.

Only one mystery remained: the identity of the writer of the anonymous letter to Leon Kraus, the person who knew of the connection between Rosa Fischer and Herr Otto von Reitz? *How?*

Doubtless, though, that too would be revealed in time. In any event, it all made for fascinating coffeehouse conversation.

Chapter 21

Veronica Kent had moved back to the Hilton. Her stay at the hotel had been paid for in advance by that best-selling American author, Sarah Hamilton, and Fräulein Kent was taking advantage of that circumstance. However, she had requested a different room from 865.

Frau Bertha Tröger, arriving for an appointment with Fräulein Kent, had ploughed through the press like a battleship. Frau Tröger, in her tweed suit, a new fedora with a feather on her head, was proud of herself. She believed implicitly that by originally raising the alarm over Veronica Kent's disappearance, she was responsible for "saving" Veronica Kent for the important research of the remarkable and revered Sarah Hamilton—she, Bertha Tröger!

However, one thing bothered her. She was uneasy because Veronica Kent and The Foxe were lovers. Love, with a man of the Foxe's looks—the dark eyebrows, the flat cheeks, and the strong jaw with the jutting mouth—

love with a man like that could involve Fräulein Kent in such a passionate affair that her work might suffer. But, *Gott sei Dank,* the Foxe was still in prison!

Frau Tröger was ashamed of her relief at Jason Foxe's detention.

But nevertheless, thankful.

And on Tuesday of that week, in the afternoon Detective Inspector Trumpf found time to drive out to Pepi's school, pick him up, and take him to Kleemann's on Mariahelfer where, when a clerk became available, Pepi announced exactly what he wanted—"Those"—and pointed at the pair in the glass case. The clerk took them out. They were expensive, the amber airline pilot's glasses—and too big. "I'll grow into them," Pepi told the clerk encouragingly.

It took some time to heat and bend the side pieces to fit over Pepi's ears. Pepi, seated before the little mirror, turned his head critically from side to side, then shook it violently to make sure the glasses sat firmly. The inspector waited patiently. When everything was done to Pepi's satisfaction, the inspector ungrudgingly paid the bill.

Later that same afternoon at the Rossauerkaserne, Inspector Trumpf, after brooding at the wall for a half-hour, reached a sensible solution. He therefore picked up the phone and had himself put through to the Passport Department. He had never used his influence to obtain any favor or clemency for a person who had committed a crime, and he would not do so now. He would not ask that Frau Schratt be forgiven the fine for her illegal act of taking in "Fräulein Montcalm" without a passport. Instead, he would pay the fine himself. Frau Schratt would never receive a demand for payment. He had the fleeting, irrational thought that his mother had suffered enough. When he reached Passport, he stated his wish and was asked to hold the line. A moment later he was connected with Payments. Again he was asked to wait. Holding the phone, he heard the cushioned click of fingers on a computer. A moment later he was informed that the fine for Martha Krieger Schratt had already been paid. Payment had been made, in person, by Miss Veronica Kent.

Across Vienna, in the tenement-crowded district of Ottakring, along the Gürtel, Kurt von Baer stood in the living room of his sister's little apartment and introduced Hortense Wicks to Julianna. Somehow or other, this seemed to him the most momentous act of his life. Julianna shook hands with Hortense, who looked stunned: She had been expecting another Paula, another luxurious home. Kurt held out a cardboard box of pastry to his sister. "And I brought you this."

"Oh, you'll make me so fat!" Julianna reproved her brother, but she looked delighted. To Hortense Wicks she said, "He's impossible, isn't he!"

Hortense Wicks, in a tailored suit with a frothy white chiffon blouse, looked at skinny Julianna who was wearing a coverall and sandals. She looked around at the walls that had no gilt portraits at all, not one—just posters. In one corner near the window was a table on which sculpting tools rested, as well as the half-sculpted clay head on which Julianna had been working when they'd rung the doorbell. Hortense looked at the worn books on a shelf, at the comfortable old couch, the hifi equipment. A basket filled with a half-dozen little felt dolls lay on a table right at Hortense's elbow. She picked up one of the soft little dolls, looked at it blindly, then just held it; she held it very tightly. "Yes . . . impossible," she echoed. Something was falling away from her, something tight and constricting and lonely-making. "Impossible," she repeated, determined not to cry. She had never been so happy.

The premature baby was doing nicely in the incubator at the hospital. According to the birth announcement in *Die Presse,* it was a girl and weighed five pounds, one ounce. The parents, Marianne and Franz Mahler, had named the baby Liselotte. Two days after the birth announcement, a package was delivered to the Mahlers' pretty little villa in the Thirteenth District. The package was from Braun's, on Graben. Marianne Mahler, still languid and heavy after the birth, exclaimed with delight when she had untied the ribbons and found four little pink nightgowns embroidered with storybook animals: squirrels, bunnies, kittens. The card in the little envelope was signed simply: Miss Gaylord.

When Marianne Mahler read the name, she was tempted to telephone Franz at the jewelry shop and tell him about the gift, but she decided against it. She would wait until he came home; he was so busy at the shop, getting things in order. They had returned to Vienna four days ago from their three-week stay with Marianne's elderly parents in Switzerland, and they had barely unlocked the front door when Marianne had felt the pains. Four hours later the baby had been born. In bed, in the hospital after the birth, Marianne had read all about the astonishing von Reitz affair. She had seen the photographs of those involved, including those of Miss Veronica Kent who, even with her short, boyish haircut, Marianne recognized as the girl Franz had saved from that brute in the Mödling woods.

Marianne Mahler, feeling luxuriously lazy, placed the card back in the box, right on top, for Franz to see. Meantime, she could not stay awake another minute. She lay down on the chaise, dragged the light wool blanket up to her shoulders, and, smiling, slipped deliciously into sleep.

At approximately the time Inspector Trumpf was calling the Passport Department, Veronica Kent took a taxi from the Hilton to Herr Gustav Bulheim's fashionable address. She had an appointment with Herr Bulheim and Sophie von Reitz. Over tea, attended also by Gustav Bulheim's assistant, she asked about the precious research documents in the family's possession ... only to learn that Otto von Reitz's bewhiskered ancestors had never corresponded with Johann Nestroy, playwright and actor.

"Schreyvogel ... of the Burgtheater?" she asked with unhappy foreknowledge.

"Es tut mir leid ... I am sorry, Fräulein Kent, but my brother-in-law's progenitors had no connection with famous artists of the Vienna theater. The von Reitz family dealt strictly in international law. Herr von Reitz, in his school days, acted in amateur theatricals. One winter, in a retrospective of Vienna theater, he acted in several plays of the Schreyvogel period. I believe he also once told me that he wrote a short piece about that era. It appeared in the school paper." Up came the porcelain teacup, down dipped Gustav Bulheim's bulldog face to sip the brew.

"Yes," she said. "I see." Of course. Those silver-framed photographs in the study in Klosterneuburg ... for instance the young man with the monocle, the dashing black hat, the flowing mustache. Perfect for Raimund's *The Spendthrift.*

"I also am sorry," Sophie von Reitz said softly. She had a low, husky voice. Her face was pale and wan, but composed. Her dark eyes, beautifully made up, looked

large and luminous. Her hair, perfectly groomed, was
coiled up with casual elegance, and held by a long,
lacquered red Japanese pin. She wore a skirt and a
handsome, saffron silk shirt with pleated sleeves snugged
at the wrists. She was a stunning woman. A moment
later, when the telephone rang in the next room, Herr
Strobl answered it and almost immediately returned to
summon Herr Bulheim. The two women were left alone.
Sohpie von Reitz leaned forward and put down her teacup. "That day in the winter garden, I did not mean to
frighten you! I was so confused! I think, by that time, I
was half-mad."

Frightened? Yes, so terribly frightened. It was easy to
acknowledge that now ... and the other curious thing.
"At first, Frau von Reitz, yes, frightened. And then when
I left the villa, even *more* frightened: Terrified! Terrified
that later you might realize the intruder was Veronica
Kent, that you'd telephone your brother and Inspector
Trumpf. The police would grill poor Josef Valasek. . . .
But then, afterward, when I kept calling Josef and
nobody came to question him, I knew. . . . " She was
smiling at Sophie von Reitz.

"Knew?" Sophie von Reitz sat back, regarding her.

"Knew that when you came up behind me at the winter
garden, you had known *at once* that I was not a journalist
from the *Kurier*—that you knew I was Veronica Kent.
And I knew that you would never tell the police."

Sophie von Reitz's luminous dark eyes showed her
surprise. She said soberly, curiously: "That's true, Fräulein Kent ... but how did you guess that?"

How had she guessed? She thought back over the
agonizing hours before she had known: "It took me two
frightened days, Frau von Reitz, days of not knowing
whether I'd have to run away and hide again. I kept
going over and over—minutely, in anguish—our meet-

ing. Your reflection in the glass when you stood behind me . . . your silence . . . our conversation. Going over and over it. Until finally . . ." She was smiling again at Sophie von Reitz, looking straight into the sober, dark eyes, smiling, waiting. An answering smile began to tug at Sophie von Reitz's mouth.

"Finally, Fräulein Kent?"

"Finally I realized you had spoken to me, deliberately, in English."

It was only a breath of an instant before they both began to laugh; it was laughter of wonder and relief and sympathy.

When a minute later Gustav Bulheim returned from his telephone call, he found his sister Sophie and Fräulein Kent deep in a discussion about the fascinating intricacies of researching material for the famous Sarah Hamilton. He was pleased to see that Sophie had become so much like her former self. As for Fräulein Kent, so pretty and almost ridiculously chic with that boyishly cropped head that doubtless would set a new style in Vienna, he had to admire her for something else: Despite her disappointment over the nonexistent historical documents in the von Reitz safes, she had taken that news philosophically. *De mortuis nil nisi bonum,* that poor, wretched brother-in-law of his.

"You weather difficulties well, Fräulein," he complimented her, when she rose and they shook hands in parting. He was thinking also about Fräulein Kent's other dismaying situation. Her lover, Jason Foxe, was in prison.

"Thank you. . . . Goodbye."

Back at the Hilton, she found that there was still no answer from the Examining Judge's office to her inquiries about Jason Foxe's detention. She felt as though her lifeline had been cut off. In her bedroom, hands to her cheeks, she sat on the bed, staring at the telephone which obstinately refused to ring.

About five o'clock that afternoon, shortly after Veronica Kent had returned to the Hilton, Jason Foxe, in a prison cell at Landegericht, received an official message: The *Untersuchungsrichter* had determined that Jason Foxe's interference with the law warranted a sizable fine, but that Herr Foxe would not be held in custody. He was to be released immediately.

The first thing Jason Foxe did, before leaving the Landegericht, was telephone the Hilton.

Any minute.

She stood in front of the bathroom mirror, combing her boyish-looking haircut.

He had been released an hour ago. His voice on the phone had sent her flying into the shower, and from there into fresh clothes. By this time, while her heart was still thumping wildly with excitement, he would have showered at the Brunners' and put on fresh clothes, including a shirt hand-ironed by Martha Krieger Schratt.

She combed the hair at the sides forward against her cheeks. Too short . . . but there was just enough length on the right side to make a Spanish-looking spit curl. On the left, she combed the hair sleekly back behind her ear. Then she outlined her mouth with the pink-brown lipstick and filled it in. Finally she fitted green earrings into her pierced ears. They would set off the coral dress that seemed to flirt with her knees when she walked.

Nervous with anticipation, she roamed the bedroom, straightening the already straight window blinds, filing a fingernail that didn't need filing, picking up an infinitesimal piece of lint from the rug. Finally she stopped at the writing desk and looked down at some scribbled research notes. Researching was like being a detective, an Inspector Trumpf. It was full of false trails, hidden traps, backtracking, devious motives encountered. Moreover, you needed double vision to see the face value of information while skeptically probing for the story behind it; there always was one. No. More than that. Each tale had various levels, depending on who was doing the telling, and with what motives.

Harrowing weeks, lost time! "Never mind!" Sarah Hamilton had shouted into the phone, from Vermont. "For Schreyvogel correspondence, I would have done the same!" And as an afterthought: "We're breeding Millicent!" Millicent was Ellery Hamilton's favorite goat.

Perfume! She went quickly into the bathroom and dabbed perfume in the hollow of her throat.

The phone rang. She flew to answer it.

"Nicca? I'm just leaving Langegasse, I'll be there in twenty minutes.... I'll call from the lobby."

"Yes."

"Nicca?" Something queer in his voice made her hold the phone closer to her ear. "Yes?"

"Leon Kraus, that full-fledged professional criminologist, has written a bang-up article on the von Reitz case. Teeming with sex, sensuality, and death. But extra big on Kraus himself—Kraus the sleuth, solver of the case with his brilliant deductions and criminal expertise. Kraus, emerging as the Sherlock Holmes of Vienna."

She laughed. But Kraus, Kraus had saved her. He was anything but a joke. "I'd love to see it."

"It will be in next week's *Neue Illustrierte*, but Kraus is so proud of it that he sent me an advance copy." So oddly intent, his voice! What was he getting at?

"Lots of photographs and ..." What *was* it in his voice?

" . . . and a photocopy of the anonymous letter."

Now she guessed. She waited.

"I recognized the handwriting."

"Everything," she said. "I told you I was trying everything. I even managed to sneak into the von Reitz's villa. In Otto von Reitz's bedroom I found a volume of Baudelaire's *Flowers of Evil*. It reminded me of something . . . I didn't recall what. I couldn't make a connection anyway, not *then*. There wasn't anything to connect *with*, not yet . . . so I almost forgot it.

"Anyway, I kept on looking, I'd sit in Hawelka's and read every news item, every magazine about the von Reitz case. Searching! *And I found something*. My writing to Kraus, that note . . . That was my most desperate hope."

"Found what? What made you suspect a tie between them—Rosa Fischer and Otto von Reitz? How in God's name? . . ."

She sank into an overstuffed chair, one leg folded under her; phone at her ear, she gazed at the blue evening on the Kursalon terrace, champagne glasses on the table, she herself following Herr von Reitz's bespectacled gaze as he watched the two women he took to be lesbians, dancing together. She told him, then. "And he said with such . . . such *unutterable* contempt: 'That pair! I have seen them dancing together before, the dark one caressing the other woman. . . . With people like that, love is a crime that demands an accomplice! . . . Disgusting, *nicht wahr?*' "

Blue darkening to purple evening, Strauss music, chocolate cake; *"Love is a crime. . . ."* Into the vibrating silence on the phone: "Then one day . . . one day at Hawelka's I picked up the *Neue Illustrierte*. 'Teenagers: Drugs and Death,' a roundup by Leon Kraus, Kraus quoting a sixteen-year-old, Rosa Fischer. . . . The girl said something so strange. She said that taking sensuous drugs turned her on to sexual activities even with a man she despised, a man who physically revolted her . . . but that the erotic need was so intolerable, so overpowering, that it forced her—and I am quoting her—that '*It turned love into a crime that demanded an accomplice.*' "

She cupped a hand under the phone. What she saw now was herself in Hawelka's lifting her head from the *Neue Illustrierte*, staring in a trance . . . then looking down again at the magazine article.

"And it came back to me, the Baudelaire at Otto von Reitz's bedside table. *That's* what had echoed in my mind, what he had said at the Kursalon about the two women he thought were lesbians: *Love is a crime that demands an accomplice.* That's a phrase from Baudelaire.

"You see? It was too much of a coincidence! The girl Rosa in the magazine—and Herr von Reitz. The same expression! Almost. The two deaths from drugs! There just *might* be a connection. Rosa Fischer . . . it seemed to me she might have heard that Baudelaire phrase from Otto von Reitz. It is too sophisticated for a teenager. But von Reitz, that reader of Baudelaire, oh how it suited *him!*"

She paused, then pondered aloud into the phone.

"I think now that von Reitz must have taunted Rosa and Ernst with their erotic indulgences, all the while whipping them on, sharing the sexual activities, then chastising them and castigating them with disgust and rejection—his final sexual ecstasy. Or perhaps he taunted Rosa with her 'crime' that time Ernst was studying for exams and he got her to turn on with just him."

"So, you—"

"That phrase! That coincidence. It was a possibility. So I wrote to Kraus. It was a . . . a . . ."

"Long shot. And a hit."

"I thought someone else had murdered Otto von Reitz. Kraus had Rosa Fischer's confidence, at least partly. I thought she might give him a lead as to whoever it was."

"Whomever."

"Whomever. But he was his own victim."

"Twenty minutes," Jason Foxe said. "I'll call you from the lobby."

When, twenty minutes later, he called, she went down. She saw him across the softly lighted, luxurious lobby. He was standing near the entrance to the Klimt bar. They were, finally, to have a drink together.

She stopped at the desk and put down her key, then turned—

And collided with someone.

"*Vorsicht!*" The man grasped her arm to steady her. She looked up. Tanned face, silver gray hair. The romantic stranger of her first day in Vienna. But today he wore no white scarf. She stared. She stared at the smooth, clerical collar.

A priest.

"I'm sorry," she managed to say. "I'm sorry, Father. Really, I should be more careful!"

The priest smiled, acknowledging her apology.

When he had gone, she stood there, stunned. Then suddenly she laughed. It was a laugh so open and spontaneous that a pair of middle-aged guests, passing by, smiled involuntarily at her. She didn't notice. She was laughing because the world was ridiculous and amazing, and sometimes you walked through life and it was an innocent field, all little flowers and firm ground, and you were safe; but at other times there were snares and hidden holes, and before you knew it you could be in deep trouble. You had to be wary.

So, yes, careful, she should be more careful. And she would be.

Walking across the lobby toward Jason Foxe, unsure of him—how could you ever be sure?—*Careful,* she warned herself. *Be careful!*

"There you are!" He was smiling at her, holding out both hands. She took his hands, so warm, so engulfing . . . and taking them, she knew how passionately she loved him and that careful was the last thing she was going to be.

By the year 2000, 2 out of 3 Americans could be illiterate.

It's true.

Today, 75 million adults… about one American in three, can't read adequately. And by the year 2000, U.S. News & World Report envisions an America with a literacy rate of only 30%.

Before that America comes to be, you can stop it… by joining the fight against illiteracy today.

Call the Coalition for Literacy at toll-free **1-800-228-8813** and volunteer.

Volunteer Against Illiteracy. The only degree you need is a degree of caring.

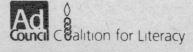

Ad Council Coalition for Literacy

Warner Books is proud to be an active supporter of the Coalition for Literacy.